KICK ON

KICK ON

a novel

KELLY JENNINGS

Deeds Publishing | Atlanta

Published by Deeds Publishing
Marietta, GA
www.deedspublishing.com

Library of Congress Cataloging-in-Publications Data is available upon request.

ISBN 978-1-937565-67-1

Books are available in quantity for promotional or premium use. For information, write Deeds Publishing, PO Box 682212, Marietta, GA 30068 or info@deedspublishing.com.

Second Edition

First Edition, 2012

10 9 8 7 6 5 4 3 2 1

CONTENTS

This book is dedicated to my mother, Virginia R. Jeffries
(August 19, 1938 - October 2, 2012)

who taught me at an early age that

I can be or do anything I wish

as long as I put my mind to it.

You were right.

INTRODUCTION

I was lucky enough to have been raised in Panama. I am the third generation of my family to live and work in that beautiful country. Many of the places in this book either existed in the Panama Canal Zone of my youth, or still exist today in what is now the Republic of Panama.

Of special note is the Bush pony. Much like their northern counterparts, the American Mustang, Florida Cracker, and the Chincoteague pony, the Bush pony played a vital role in the telling of history. They are descendants of the Spanish horses brought to the New World by explorers hungry for adventure and wealth. They were used to transport heavy loads of gold and precious gems across the isthmus of Panama to the fleets of Spanish galleons waiting along the Caribbean or Atlantic coastline. They played an unwitting role in the plunder of local Indian tribes, the growth of the Spanish Empire, and the building of a country. They have carried cowboys, plowed fields, pulled fire engines, jumped fences, competed in gymkhanas, and accomplished just about any other task set before them with great aplomb. Today, within the interior regions of Panama you can still see their heads peeking over the cabs of the trucks in which they are transported. Hardy, strong, and resilient, they stole my heart as a child, as well as taught me the bare basics of riding, like staying on.

ARRIVAL

The pilot came over the speakers with the usual updates on local weather and time. I was reluctantly getting used to the procedure by now. *"…tray tables in the upright and locked position…"* The pixie-like flight attendant, who had kindly found a blanket for Haley earlier in the flight, picked up where the pilot left off in her sing song voice. I tuned out the remainder of the announcements and tried in vain once again to stretch out my long legs under the seat in front of me. No luck. Exasperated, I pulled them back underneath my seat.

We were here, finally. The overhead lights of the cabin dimmed as we prepared for landing. Shifting again, I laid my tired head back against the headrest, which was profoundly uncomfortable in the upright position required for landing. Glancing to the right, I looked past where Haley sat at the window and out into the dark night, nothing. The green and red lights on the wing of the plane blinked in a reassuring rhythm as they illuminated the silver edge of the wing. The jungles of Panama rolled below us like a dark and ominous ribbon. Slowly, as the plane made its descent, lights sparkled out of the darkness. A few at a time, then larger clusters, until the full lights of the city lit the earth below. Overhead, the speakers made a pinging noise—once, twice, speaking in a language only the flight personnel knew.

A bump beneath us, followed by screeching tires and then the nose of the plane dropped as my ears popped. "Is Dad here? He promised he would be here to meet us," Haley asked excitedly, her eyes alight.

"I'm sure he is Kaboose." Kaboose was Uncle Joe's idea of a joke. My younger sister, Haley, was an unexpected pregnancy, the result of an anniversary vacation for Mom and Dad on a train through the Banff National Forest in Canada, hence the nickname.

Oh Lord, I hoped he was here. I had just flown to a foreign country with a twelve year old and neither of us spoke the language or knew a soul other than our father. Not to mention, I was bleary with exhaustion. Exhaling audibly, I steeled myself for what lay ahead.

As we gathered our carry on luggage, the plane taxied to the gate. Ten minutes later we were headed down the narrow gangway to the terminal. The tropical humidity assaulted us as we disembarked from the plane; it permeated through the thin metal walls of the metal gangway as we crossed it. Then, as the door to the terminal opened we left the stagnant air behind and stepped into the cool air-conditioned terminal.

Haley dropped her backpack and ran ahead. "Dad!" A tall, blonde haired man stooped down and enveloped Haley in his big arms. "Hi, baby girl. How was your trip?" Mike Todd was a big man, almost borderline lumberjack in size and breadth. His size though was deceiving, as he had a gentle side to him. A panda bear more than a grizzly.

"I got three wings, Dad." She proudly showed him the plastic wings pinned to the front of her blue shirt. Her gaze quickly turned serious and she looked back up, "the pilot said I can fly now, but that's silly." She frowned again, glancing back down at her plastic wings.

"Hi, Dad." Extricating himself from Haley, he stood up and wrapped a strong arm around me. The familiar scent of his cologne settled around me and I couldn't help but smile. His green eyes met mine with blunt appraisal.

"Lauren, you look exhausted," he said gently as he clasped Haley's small hand in his.

"You got that right," I mumbled. My ears still felt thick, blocked from the change in air pressure and I wasn't sure how loud I was talking. "Let's go pick up your luggage. The company car is waiting out front." He turned around and slipped through the mass of passengers that were heading down the stairs towards the baggage claim, towing Haley in his wake. I fell in step, bringing up the rear and grateful to no longer be in charge.

Small terminals mean small distances and few carousels. This translated to a very big blessing for someone as exhausted as I was. Before long we had our bags loaded and we piled into the back of the company car. It was a limo no less. I laid my head back on the seat. My eyelids, feeling thick and heavy slid shut and I shut out the world around me. There would be time to see my new home later, besides there wasn't much to see in the dark anyway.

**

I awoke to silence, not fully aware of when or where I was. One by one, slowly, methodically, I stretched my limbs between the soft sheets. The crisp smell of the freshly laundered sheets met my nose—lavender, no wonder I had slept like the dead. The tropical sun knifed its way through the narrow slits of the white plantation shutters in my room. Closing my eyes again, I let my ears savor the silence. Fighting to stay awake, I lost track of time in the silent room, drifting gently in and out of sleep. *Ahh, silence and stillness.*

No wait—there was a sound. Pulling myself towards consciousness, I listened closely. There it was again. A bird was chirping and from what I could tell it had settled right outside my window. Giving up, with a deep sigh I reluctantly opened my eyes to face the day. Out of habit I rolled to the right and searched for my alarm clock. A small glass vase with fresh gardenia blossoms sat alone on the bedside table, no alarm clock in site.

Right, I was in a different land. I rolled onto my back, staring at the white washed ceiling above me. A ceiling fan with large wicker paddles spun slowly in the center of the room,

Well, at least you won't have to stare at the backside of an airline seat again for a long while. The question was, how long?

It was the same time zone, but after yesterday my internal clock was spinning. Welcome home, Lauren. I took a deep breath inhaling the sweet scent of the gardenia, then sat up resignedly and swung my feet over the edge of the bed. My bright, freshly painted red toes landed on the rug next to my bed and I wiggled them. Winking back at me, they looked odd. Callista, or Calli as I called my best friend, had dragged me to a spa before I left Asheville for some "girl time," as she called it. She insisted that my toes would be seeing much more daylight in the tropics. She even made me leave the spa in those silly cardboard flip flops they provided, then promise not to put my riding boots on before I left. I frowned at the memory. No problem there. My boots were one of the first things I packed. Another deep breath and I stood up. *What time was it?* I was lost without a clock. I fumbled my way to the bathroom where I had left my watch; 1:36 pm, it read. I had been asleep for nearly fourteen hours.

After a steaming hot shower I grabbed for the only towel I could find and wrapped it around me. It came up short, the ends barely coming together. Clutching it around me with one hand I padded back into my room, leaving a trail of water droplets behind me on the wooden floor. I was beginning to feel alive again. The numerous flights we had taken yesterday had taken their toll.

My bags were on the floor just inside the door where I had dropped them last night. The largest suitcase already lay open. Clothes spilled haphazardly from within. I had a vague recollection of trying to find something to sleep in last night. Dropping to one knee, I began to dig through the mess. Quickly giving up my one handed search for clothes, I dropped the tiny towel on the wooden floor behind me.

After digging through the neatly folded piles toward the bottom, I managed to fish out a pair of denim cut offs and a white, cotton eyelet top. I dug deeper for a bra and underwear and pulled out a handful of lavender colored lace. The silken feel of Aubade lingerie brought back a flood of memories. Aubade was made with the finest French lace. Jacob had taste—that was for sure. My heart squeezed in my chest like a vise, like it had so often since that day in February. Bringing the delicate lace bra to my face I held it gently against my cheek, remembering when he had given it to me. A frown crossed my face and I blinked back the tears. Not practical for my new life, I told myself. I dropped the bra back on the pile of clothes, blinking harder as I fought back the tears that threatened to spill over. Digging deeper, I came up with something more practical with fewer memories attached. Plain. Cotton. Perfect. I stood up.

In front of me, on the back of the bedroom door was a full-length mirror. Pausing, I studied myself with a critical eye. I had always been on the thin side, but the stress of the last few months had left their mark. I was lean. The ten pounds or so I had lost only served to accentuate the muscles on my light frame.

My skin was porcelain white, well all but my arms and face. Those were spattered boldly with freckles. The rest of me rarely saw the sun. A mass of thick red hair hung past my shoulders in big damp curls, a few of which clung damply to the sides of my face. Following my reflection down past my hips and back up to my face, I was met by my mother's amber colored eyes. Lately, the deep gold and ambers had lost their sparkle. With a sigh, I closed my eyes. After a moment I hesitantly lifted my lids, hoping by some miracle to see something other than the hollow shell that I saw staring back at me. No luck. At five feet ten inches I rarely needed to wear heels, most assuredly not lately—and not with Jacob. Another frown floated across my face, fighting back a fresh wave of tears, I turned away to get dressed. *Not now Jake,* I pleaded. *Not now.*

I dressed quickly, skipped the makeup, and left my hair to dry naturally. Slipping out of my room, I pulled the door shut behind me and set off in search of the kitchen. The house felt empty. I took some time to explore the house after finding a note from Dad on the kitchen table that read:

L-

Took Haley to lunch, then running by the office for a minute. We will bring dinner home.

Love, Dad

The house was a single story with a very, airy, tropical feel about it. Actually the interior looked like the centerfold in an expensive architectural magazine. You know, the coffee table type, spotless and pristine. The walls were white washed and quite tall. Colorful native art in bright primary colors hung from the walls. In nearly every room, ceiling fans spun lazily from tall wooden ceilings on long brass rods. The dark wood floors were laid with brightly colored, woven, rugs that gave the interior a welcoming feel. The main living area had a large flat screen TV, and leather furniture with wood accents. A wall with several large picture windows ran down one side of the room with a set of French doors nestled at about the mid point. Just on the other side, a large covered veranda ran the entire length of one side of the house. Crossing the living room, I headed towards the French doors, which opened with a soft click. Stepping out onto the shaded porch I could smell a deep earthy smell mingled with the fresh air that comes after it rains.

All along the veranda, lush green vines wound their way up white porch columns towards the grey tile roof above. Barefoot, I padded my way across the cool tile floor. A well, manicured lawn sloped away from the veranda down towards a pile of dark grey rocks that marked the beginning of a cliff. I recognized the rocks from pictures I had seen and knew that a small sand beach could be found just below, and beyond that, the Bay of

Panama. Dad had emailed me pictures right after he arrived, but they simply didn't do the place justice. It was gorgeous. Walking out from under the shade of the wide veranda, I made my way towards the small cliff. It had rained while I slept and the grass felt cool and damp on the soles of my bare feet. Stopping to savor the moment, I closed my eyes and inhaled the earthy undertones of the tropical air along with the scent of warm salt air from the bay.

With a sigh, I opened my eyes and for the first time in a very long while, I allowed myself to slow down enough to really feel the fresh grass beneath my feet. Wiggling my brightly colored toes I luxuriated in the feel of each blade as it found its way between my toes and tickled my feet. I closed my eyes again, searching for peace. How long had it been since I had walked barefoot across grass, much less, slowed down enough to breathe, I wondered. I couldn't remember to save my soul. *Sigh.* "Too long, too damn long," I murmured.

I could feel the tropical sun beating down on me and I opened my eyes again. One glance to my left told me that the sun was well past its zenith and starting its slow descent towards the horizon. Beginning to feel the heat, a bead of perspiration fell down the front of my neck and rolled between my breasts. Turning, I headed back towards the cool comfort of the house. *This humidity would take some getting used to.* As I reached the porch doors, my stomach started to speak to me in mumbles and grumbles. *Yeah, yeah, I know.* Reaching for the cool metal of the door handle, I slipped back inside where it was cool.

**

The next few days in my new home flew by. I had few chances to leave the house what with all the unpacking there was to do. We had sold most of our household goods before leaving North Carolina. The few precious family mementos and antiques we had kept were placed in Uncle Joe's garage in Virginia for safekeeping. The rest we sold, that left mostly clothes and small personal items, which had arrived by freight thanks to Dad's company. With Dad at work I took my time unpacking, and filling my days with the comfort that comes with setting up a house. With all the recent changes in my life, the need to nest and feel secure was strong.

Those first few mornings in the new house were a bit of a blur. A part of me felt very much in limbo, trapped between two worlds—that which I knew well, but didn't necessarily want to continue with, and that which I knew nothing about and was apprehensive of what was to come. Each day dawned like the last, but again and again I found myself waking up feeling as if everything around me was surreal. What I would have given to be able to push the pause button on my life. This thought crossed my mind almost daily. I just needed time, a momentary reprieve so I could catch my breath. I just needed time, I kept telling myself. With time the world would right itself again. Then the sights and sounds of my new surroundings would find me again and I would make myself return to work unpacking. These everyday chores kept my mind occupied and thoughts of the past at bay.

Tired as I was at the end of each day, unfortunately, once in bed, the nightmares I had endured nearly every night for the past three months seemed to find me again. Even though I was a world away and tried daily to work myself into an exhausted stupor, they found me. Running away didn't seem to be helping one bit.

A spark of joy, which lit up my life, came with watching Haley in her new surroundings. At times though, I found myself envious of her young, innocent age and free spirit. She was adjusting to her new life with ease, absorbing everything new and exciting around her and she helped to buoy my spirits. Me, I was hoping for a fresh start here among people I didn't know.

Trying to ground myself with mundane house chores I stayed busy. My first goal, other than unpacking and of course remembering to breathe in and out, was to get Haley settled. After that I could take the time I needed to find a job, or sign up for some online courses, or something. Honestly I really wasn't quite sure what I was going to do, at this point, I was in a career shift. Actually, truth be told, I was lost. I had left my old job as a nurse rather abruptly in order to help Dad with Haley. Now, adrift, and not working in recent months, I had to face the facts. The time had come for me to get my life in order again. At least that was the plan. Ah, but plans never seem to bend to the will of the person who sets them in motion. Do they? Oft times in life they have a mind of their own, or so I had found out.

Before Mom fell ill, my plans had included going back to school. Since I had already received my nursing degree and had a job I enjoyed at a local hospital, my original thought had been to take my nursing to the next step and get my Bachelor's degree. Eventually I wanted to get my Masters as well. Jake had pushed me to choose nursing, in fact Jake had steered my life in many ways.

We had met in our senior year of high school. Originally from Oklahoma, his family had moved to North Carolina when the company his dad worked for transferred him. His parents had bought a farm on the edge of town, just down the road from us, and decided to try their hand at organic farming.

Actually his mom dreamed of the organic farm. His dad, bless him, went along with it because he had wanted room for their daughter's new pony, Wonder. Well, that and he worshiped the ground his wife walked on, that much was evident. Jake and I became fast friends, spending time together when I came over to give Elena lessons on "Wonder Bread" as we liked to call him. He was an overfed white Shetland/Welsh cross that always seemed to have a light brown tinge to his mane and tail from the soil on the farm, no matter how many times Elena soaped and scrubbed his hide. As fate would have it, he ended up being one of the most dependable and safe ponies I had ever known. He was a true gem and worth his weight in carrots.

Now and again, when I did let my mind wander back, I found that I couldn't recall when we started dating. It just sort of happened one day. And the rest, as they say, was history. Boy meets girl, they fall in love—yadda, yadda—the typical all American love story. At least it started that way. The ending, well that was another story altogether.

And so, my first few days in Panama ticked by without much fanfare. I enrolled Haley in school, and happily took charge of driving her there and picking her up. It gave me something to focus my energy on, another mundane chore I could do successfully every day, one that required very little thought or emotion. My life had been so busy, so full and now…now I was living a zillion miles away from anyone I knew, trying to pick up the shattered pieces of my once perfect life, shattered pieces that could never be completely put back together. Hell, at this point I would have been happy to just be able to sweep them up into a dustpan.

**

Before I knew it Saturday had arrived. Haley had thoroughly and completely fallen in love with her new school over the past week, and I was already trying to keep up with the names of her new friends.

I had managed to complete the task of enrolling in a few online business courses, which would have to do for now since I had no clue what sort of career I wanted. I just knew that I couldn't go back to nursing. I also had figured out how to survive the local traffic hazards (sort of) and the house was finally in order.

Apparently it was customary to hire the locals for everything from gardening to housekeeping. A bit too archaic for me, this was one idea I would have to get used to. At least I didn't have to hire them; Dad's company had found both a maid and a gardener for us shortly after we arrived. That was one less thing for me to worry about, especially since I was still having trouble picking up the pieces of my own life and getting Haley to school and back. The day they arrived I had spent the better part of an hour worrying about how in the hell I would communicate with them. My Spanish consisted of a Taco Bell menu and the few words I remembered from the Taco Bell Chihuahua commercials. God was indeed with me, for they both spoke English quite well.

I did worry about how we were going to afford our new hired help, but Dad assured me that with his raise and the much lower cost of living (a definite advantage), he had it covered. Which really meant, I had it covered, since he rarely remembered to pay the bills. So Carmen and her husband Roberto moved into the bungalow on our new property two days after we arrived.

Today I had promised Haley a trip the local zoo. Roberto, the new gardener, was a short rather round man with a weather worn face. This morning, he was kind enough to draw me a map. Getting lost while driving was an art form for me. After making sure I understood the directions, twice, he headed back out into the yard, shaking his salt and pepper head from side to side, to trim some bushes. Seeing as how I didn't have much more confidence in my ability to find the zoo than he did I chuckled to myself and watched him go. Since arriving, Roberto had spent the majority of his time hunched over the manicured landscape with all shapes and sizes of pruning shears. I was learning fast that here in the tropics everything seemed to grow bigger, faster, and thicker.

Just then, Haley came bounding into the white washed kitchen wearing a brightly colored, striped, tank top, denim shorts, and flip flops, her blonde curls bounced around her tiny face. Haley, while petite for her size had a big personality. Beaming back at her, my heart lurched in my chest as it always did when I saw Mom in Haley's smile.

"Ready, Kaboose?"

"Ready, Freddy!" She was grinning from ear to ear, eager for our outing. She had the rare ability and childhood enthusiasm to turn a trip to the grocery store into a grand adventure.

Dad had acquired an older model Toyota Land Cruiser shortly after we arrived. It was white, sort of, 4-wheel drive, and had a steel grill that had been added to the front. It was more battering ram than vehicle, but by all appearances it was safe. The engine roared to life as we settled in on the faded green vinyl seats.

Thirty minutes and a few wrong turns later and we turned into the entrance to the zoo. The Summit Zoo was tiny by American zoo standards; even so, Haley was out of the passenger side door before I had the ignition turned off. She was infectious in her excitement. "Wait for me," I laughed, hurrying to catch up.

Two hours later we both had a crash course on the native wildlife. Jaguars, oscelots, kuatamundis, spider monkeys, and vampire bats made the time fly by. The zoo even had a charming stone bridge that crossed a small creek teeming with native waterfowl. Haley chattered non-stop as we made our way from one enclosure to the next. She wanted to make sure I knew everything there was to know about each animal. I listened intently as she read each plaque set in front of the enclosures. Thank goodness they were in English and Spanish. Eventually Haley's stomach reminded us it was lunchtime.

We grabbed lunch from a vendor and ate it in the cool shade of a pre-historic looking tree just across from the sloths. Not much excitement here, I mused. The hot, meaty empanadas were mouth watering, I remembered to get the bottled water, and scored a bonus point for me. God only knew what was in the local water, I thought dryly.

Loaded back in the Land Cruiser, the tropical heat, excitement of the day, and a full belly took their toll on Haley.

"I think I'll take a nap. Can you get us home OK?" I had enlisted her as my copilot on the drive to the zoo.

"Yes, Copilot. Roger that!" I said with more certainty than I felt. "Just close your eyes. I'll wake you when we get home." Dark afternoon rain clouds were starting to build overhead as I turned the key in the ignition.

Haley was out before I had the old Land Cruiser backed out of the parking lot. At the entrance to the zoo, I stopped, glanced left, then right. My map, where was my map? I glanced around the cab in a panic, flipping open the center console and digging through my purse. Not here.

H O N K!

Several cars had materialized behind me. *Oh crap.* I glanced at Haley and she was still out. Taking a deep breath I pointed the Land Cruiser to the left. The four lane divided main road was filling up with late afternoon traffic. Worried I might get lost, I tried to look for familiar landmarks while avoiding a collision with the local drivers. The roads were full of rickety buses covered in bright, gaudy paintings, old, rusty economy cars that looked held together by a wing and a prayer, and the occasional sleek European sedan. I was quickly discovering that third world driving was a mix of Russian roulette, poker, and just plain chance. I clearly took a chance every time I got behind the wheel, as did those around me, I thought wryly. Most local drivers drove like madmen, swerving in and out of traffic so abruptly and randomly that I was often left white knuckled. Apparently no one here knew what a turn signal was. At times I had to remember to breathe. It didn't help that they waved their hands, shook their heads, and yelled things I couldn't understand, although Roberto had informed me that they usually involved expletives about other people's mothers; charming.

Thankfully, the road began to look more familiar. It was then that I saw it. The metal sign flashed by so quickly I wasn't sure I had really seen it. White with green lettering, it read

Albrook Riding Club. Horses. An actual stable—that was a good sign. One look was all it took, and my mind was already spinning with possibilities. The Land Cruiser began to drift into the neighboring lane and a car honked loudly. Recovering quickly, I turned my focus back to the chaotic road. A rust bucket on wheels pulled alongside and I managed to escape with only a dirty look.

I had kept the essentials that every true rider never gets rid of, my saddles, boots, helmet, and breeches. When I sold my horse, Pogo, I gave most of my minor accessory tack to his new owner. I had grown weary of selling off bits and pieces of my life so I just passed my stuff along to her knowing how much she appreciated it. Like me, she struggled to balance a job, her love for eventing, and life in general, all things that I could relate to. Besides, I just couldn't stomach selling anything else. It had left a bad taste in my mouth. At least he had a good home. Of that I was sure. He was the perfect horse to take his new rider up the levels.

I looked for a place to turn around so I could go back to investigate, but decided not to chance it. The jungle, here as nearly everywhere that wasn't developed, lapped right up against the side of the road. Occasionally there was a thin gravel shoulder, but the bright orange clay was often molded into a deep ditch filled with water from the afternoon rains. I decided to ask Roberto about the stable and try to come back later.

ALBROOK

Another week flew by. Haley had settled in to a familiar pattern with her schoolwork and was already learning Spanish. Even though she was too old for Sesame Street back home, she spent her afternoons watching the Spanish version of Plaza Sesamo and soaked up the language like a sponge. In the morning before school and when she got home I would often catch her practicing her new language on Carmen and Roberto who seemed to enjoy the attention.

I attempted to run errands; when I felt bold enough, to familiarize myself some more with my new surroundings. Well that, and to improve my third world driving skills, such as they were. Other than Haley's school and the zoo, I hadn't explored much of Panama at all. We were living in a small subdivision adjacent to a small town. Just across the Canal from us sat Panama City, the capital. It was world renown as both a banking center and as a hub for foreign ship registries.

It was the following weekend before I managed to find the time to drive back to the stable. I found the green and white sign easily enough. Turning off the main road, the asphalt came to a ragged end and a mix of gravel and clay crunched under the tires. A thick expanse of trees separated the stable from the hustle and bustle of the road. Well maintained, white, three board pastures ran along both sides of the narrow road as I left the main road behind. The barn itself appeared quite a bit the worse for wear. It was a shed row style barn with two rows of stalls facing outward onto covered walkways. Originally painted white and red, the colors had faded and the paint could be seen flaking off. The low-slung roof of the barn was constructed of mostly corrugated metal. Glancing up, I noticed concrete cinder blocks, which appeared randomly down the length of the roof, probably I thought, to hold down errant sections of the metal roof on windy days.

Like most barns on a Saturday morning, there were people of all ages scattered about. A couple of kids were taking a jump lesson in the arena in front of the barn. The occasional parent wandered out from under the nearest shade tree to follow their kid back to the barn, while still others sat in their cars with the A/C running. I found a parking space facing one of the pastures full of horses. Well actually, they were mostly ponies. Short, sturdy and very workmanlike ponies were everywhere. They reminded me of Mustangs or Florida Cracker Horses. The few horses I did see looked like Thoroughbreds.

I'd had serious reservations about coming this morning and now I hesitated to get out of the Land Cruiser. Selling my event horse, Pogo, was one of the hardest things I had ever done and I wasn't sure if I wanted to get attached to another horse. For me, horses had always been an all or nothing endeavor. It wasn't something I could dabble in. Not only that, but I didn't know how long I would even be in Panama. Leasing a horse had never really appealed to me. Besides, by the looks of what was in front of me there wouldn't have been much choice anyway. This was a crazy idea. *What was I doing here?* I fiddled nervously with the car keys, spinning them around one finger. "Come on, Todd, what's the worst that could happen," I scolded myself aloud trying to build up the courage to climb out from behind the steering wheel.

Well, I was here so what could it hurt. Resigned, I stepped out into the sunlight and my tennis shoes crunched on the gravel parking lot. Shoving the car keys into the front pocket of my denim shorts I wandered toward the barn. Maybe I could walk around, love on a few horses, get my fix, and then get out of Dodge, I thought. No harm, no foul, just in and out. Most of the horses with their heads hanging out of the stalls had expectant looks on their faces as I approached the shade of the barn aisle. Feeling guilty for not bringing carrots with me I tried to make it up with well-placed scratches and pats. Occasionally I stopped to murmur softly to a few of the horses. In no time at all I'd made my way around the barn. Most of the horses were either being ridden or were out to pasture. No one questioned me, and most people I passed smiled, gave me a friendly nod, or said hello. It felt good to be around horses. They were a tonic for my soul.

Eventually I found myself leaning against a fence on the side of the arena watching a lesson. A brunette with medium length hair, wearing a tan colored visor on her head, stood in the middle of the arena. She was built to be athletic and seemed at ease with the four little girls she was working with.

"Sarah, sit up, you are leaning forward again. That's right… remember that imaginary line I showed you. Keep your shoulders over your hips and feet."

"Theresa, you better ask for more from Whiskey before you get near the arena gate, you know he's going to stop! Put your leg on him. Keep him going, kick him again."

Whiskey looked like trouble. Ten strides out from the gate the look on his face went from sheer boredom to Cheshire cat.

"Now, Theresa, make his feet move," hollered the brunette. A well-timed kick changed the look on Whiskey's face back to one of boredom as he trotted past the gate.

I couldn't help but smile. I honestly couldn't remember how many "Whiskey's" I had encountered in my life. Glancing up, I noticed the sun was almost directly overhead and I was beginning to wish I had brought my baseball cap. Turning my attention back to the arena I watched as the brunette pulled off her visor and shoved the opening around her leg just above the knee. Pulling a brightly colored rubber hair band from around her tan wrist she haphazardly pulled her hair back in a ponytail while never taking her eyes off of her charges. The visor went back on her head.

"I enjoy watching the younger kids take lessons," a voice next to me said. So engrossed was I, that I never heard anyone come up. "Oh, sorry, did I startle you?"

The voice next to me was attached to a drop dead gorgeous statuesque blonde. Her hair was also pulled up in a ponytail, but hung much longer down her back. She was immaculately dressed from head to toe in what were clearly expensive riding clothes. She wore a pair of light buff full seat breeches without a single smudge on them and a baby blue sleeveless polo shirt. They were easily three hundred dollar breeches if I had to guess, and very out of place for her surroundings. Her black leather dress boots were polished to a shine. Her pixie-like face was tastefully made up and her hazel eyes met mine.

"No, I was just watching the lesson." I replied, thankful I had made an effort to look presentable today. Not that it mattered standing next to a Barbie doll, I thought to myself.

"That's Elaine." She pointed to the brunette.

I nodded and turned back to watch. "She has her hands full with the little dun."

"Oh, Whiskey, yeah he can be a real turd sometimes. But he also is point and shoot over the jumps. The kids just love him because he builds confidence and makes them think they can jump the moon. They practically fight over him."

"I'm sorry, I'm Lauren Todd." I turned towards her.

"Deanne," she thrust her hand towards me, "Connell."

We shook hands. Her grip surprised me. I had expected a wimpy, girlish handshake from her appearance. Okay, I thought, maybe Barbie is tougher than she looks.

Releasing my hand she said, "Do you ride?"

My heart squeezed in my chest. "I did, I had to sell my horse when we moved." I cleared my throat, buying a moment to collect myself.

"I thought you looked new," she smiled.

"How could you tell? Do I have that new car smell?" I said sarcastically.

She laughed, "You are funny. No you are wearing white tennis shoes."

I glanced down at my feet and back with a quizzical look on my face. Meeting her eye I could tell she was serious.

"The clay, it's the clay. Anyone who has lived here a while learns real fast that white shoes never stay white. It's no use even trying."

"Oh, right," I acknowledged, not quite sure how her gorgeous buff breeches fit into the logic of that scenario and still managed to stay clean. But then again I had no doubt that Barbie never worried about such things.

The lesson was wrapping up and the kids steered their ponies toward the arena gate. Whiskey, of course, made it to the gate first. I watched as a few parents ambled over to collect their charges. The brunette turned and started walking in our direction as if she expected to see us waiting there, her ponytail swinging behind her. From across the arena, her gaze met Deanne's and she gave a thumb's up sign.

"We're a go for the trail ride," she smiled at Deanne as she reached the fence.

"Elaine, this is Lauren," Deanne tilted her head in my direction.

Elaine propped her foot up on the lowest rail of the fence, her smile was warm and inviting and her dark brown eyes met mine. She was just a tad shorter than I, but more muscular. She wore a pair of plain, tan breeches, a tank top, well-worn brown leather paddock boots and matching brown half chaps. She clearly looked to be the polar opposite of Deanne. *Must be Skipper*, I thought to myself. "Hey," I offered my hand. Elaine's grasp was firm and self-assured. With her left hand she reached behind her back and pulled a pair of gloves from her waistband.

"Do you ride, Lauren?" she inquired, smoothing her gloves out.

"Sold her horse before she got here," Deanne interjected with a wave of a well-manicured hand. "See, white tennis shoes."

Either not bothering to acknowledge the shoe comment, or seeming to take her word for it, Elaine continued. "Nice to meet you. Hey, if you're around next Saturday you should come ride with us. We treat ourselves to a low-key trail ride once a week. It gives us a chance to relax and ride for fun." She threw Deanne a conspiratorial wink. "Besides, it gives me the chance to straighten out some of the lesson ponies at the same time. They can get rank after a week of going in circles." She rolled her eyes for dramatic effect in the direction of the kids in the barn.

I hesitated, chewing on the inside of my lip. I had closed a lot of doors lately and I wasn't at all sure which, if any of them I wanted to open back up. Life was so much easier for me lately when it was all boxed, taped, labeled and stored safely away. Before I could rationalize my way out of my self-contained box, I nodded. Steeling myself I managed a friendly smile. "I evented some back in the States," I said at last. There, it was out. The inside of my lip was tender.

Deanne's hand flew to her heart, "Good God almighty, are you crazy? In case you hadn't noticed, those jumps are fixed obstacles!" she exclaimed in an exaggerated southern drawl. Her long eyelashes fluttered daintily. The corner of Elaine's mouth turned up in a grin as she tried to keep from chuckling.

With the grace of a ballerina, Deanne turned smoothly on her boot heel and headed for the barn, still talking over her shoulder. "Why anyone would gallop 'cross a field and jump something that ain't gonna come down is beyond me," her voice trailed off.

"Don't mind her. It took me years to get her to trail ride with me. Thought she'd never go," said Elaine, her eyes still on the departing Deanne. "Deanne likes flat land with no obstacles whatsoever." Playing with her gloves she added, "You know, I don't think she has ever jumped a horse. Oh, and don't mind the accent," her eyes were laughing, "she slips into it when she gets dramatic. Deanne is all about overall effect and appearances." Turning back to me her face changed, "Don't let the look of her throw you though, that girl can ride. Anyway, will you come on Saturday? We could use a new face."

"Yeah, sure," I hesitated, "what time?"

"Ten sharp, we have to go before it gets too hot and the afternoon rain kicks in."

"Okay. Thanks."

"Good, see you then." With that she turned and headed towards the barn. With one last look around I pulled the keys from my pocket and headed for the parking lot.

I made my way back home, making one quick stop for gas along the way. I was beginning to recognize landmarks, which was good since I hardly remembered how I got home. The wheels in my brain turned round and round while I weighed the pros and cons of getting back into riding again. The fact was, I was drawn to horses, barns, and everything that was associated with them. Quite frankly, I needed a push to get out of my rut, and new friends were a part of making a fresh start. *Right?* Pulling into the driveway I turned off the ignition and sat for a moment. Thumbing through the keys absentmindedly, I mulled over my situation. The fact was, other than Calli, I had shut out most of the world when I lost Jake and it was time to pick up the pieces and live again. It was time to get back in the game. Climbing out of the Land Cruiser I headed into the kitchen to make myself a drink.

**

Dad and Haley headed for bed early. After cleaning up the kitchen I reached into the freezer for the pitcher of margaritas I had made earlier and set it on the tile counter. Several slices of lime sat in a puddle of lime juice on the cutting board next to the sink. Picking one up, I ran it along the rim of my glass, squeezing as I went. Flipping it over, I dunked the glass into a plastic container full of coarse margarita salt, and then filled it with the frozen margarita mix. Pulling a half empty bottle of Patron from the cabinet under the sink, I poured what amounted to a shot and a half of the tequila over the top. Using my finger to stir, I headed out onto the veranda to enjoy the tropical night.

Settled into a wicker chair with a view of the lawn I stuck my finger in my mouth. Wrapping my lips around it, I pulled it out slowly, making sure I didn't leave any salt behind. If there was one drink I had mastered over the years, it was a seriously good margarita. Unconsciously I wiped my finger on my denim shorts. Suddenly I could hear my mother's voice from deep in my consciousness admonishing me not to wipe my hands on my jeans. Frowning, I stared at my guilty finger. I had to admit, this was one habit I would probably never lose. At the barn, I was incessantly wiping my hands on my breeches. In fact, I couldn't remember a time when I hadn't. The frown became a smile as I thought of all the dark colored breeches I had bought over the years in an effort to at least appear clean. With a sigh, I pulled one knee up to my chest and settled back to nurse my drink. Before long the alcohol allowed me to travel safely down memory lane.

I was there when Mom died. I watched helplessly as cancer slowly kidnapped the mother I had known and left a shell behind. We made sure Haley never saw her wasting away. It was not a memory I had wanted and definitely not how Mom had wanted Haley to remember her. After the funeral, I dove into my riding headfirst. I set goals I thought I could never achieve and spent every hour I had between the barn, Jake, and taking care of Dad and Haley. Exhaustion was my friend and Jake had stood quietly beside while I worked things out in my head.

I glanced down into my margarita glass. There was a bug in my margarita and by the looks of it jerking around I had to wonder who was more drunk—me or the bug?

Hey wait, wasn't that a song? *Hmph.* I fished it out and took another sip, the cold Patron and Cointreau slid down my throat. Absently, I licked the salt from my lips, wondering just what I was doing in a third world country. I headed back to the kitchen for another margarita.

What else could I have done? I couldn't leave Dad to look after Haley on his own. Dad was just too smart for his own good. Well, too cerebral anyway. He had made a career working for government think tanks, but ask him if he locked the front door of the house and he would just look confused. His brain was his biggest asset, just not when it came to raising a twelve-year old girl. No, I had to come. I loved Dad and Haley too much and besides, I owed it to Mom. "So, Todd, you sold your horse, put the brakes on your dreams and here you sit, drunk. Well, at least you are moving forward," I muttered into the muggy night air. *Hmph.* I had to admit, things could be worse. Most people truly would consider this to be paradise.

The house Dad's company provided us with sat on a rocky ledge overlooking the Bay of Panama. Over the last week I had found it rather soothing to watch the ships come and go in the moonlight, gliding past our little piece of paradise. To my left, I could see the ghostly lights of ships as they entered the bay to transit the Panama Canal, or as they emerged from under the Bridge of the Americas on their way out to sea. To my right lay the blackness of the Pacific Ocean. If my mind didn't wander, which tonight it did, I could follow the lights of the ships until they faded into nothing. Tonight, after two margaritas, with an extra special splash of tequila on top, the lights faded too quickly for me to follow.

The well-manicured lawn, with its beds of tropical flowers and foliage, tonight was a landscape of muted grey and black shapes, which rose like islands in a dark sea. Everything here in my new home was green; in fact I had never imagined there were so many shades of green in the world. Tonight though, like my mood, even the foliage was flat and colorless. A set of steep, shallow, stone steps led from the end of the yard down to the beach below. In the daylight they were tricky enough to navigate, tonight after several margaritas, they were off limits. Paradise had its limits tonight. The glass found its way back to my lips.

Crap, there was another bug in my drink. I gave up and set it down on the wicker table where it promptly fell over. Frowning at the empty glass, I turned it upside down by the stem and watched the last drops hit the stone floor beneath me. Maybe tomorrow would show more promise, I pushed my way out of the chair and staggered back into the dark house and to bed.

I could feel the frosty air around me—on my skin and as it burned my lungs when I inhaled, cold as ice. My lungs ached with each breath. Smooth, shiny metal was everywhere around me. It ran half way up the walls, draped every cabinet, and supported the bed and light fixtures. Intense bright, white lights hung from above in the shape of fat globes and long, sleek cylinders. The strong acrid smell of antiseptic clung to everything around me.

Voices, muffled voices moved in and out around me, buffeting me like a gentle breeze, words without form, shapeless and soft. Steadily they grew louder, reaching a crescendo, pushed along by a rolling tension. They became more intense, hurried, strained and eventually peaked. No longer did I find myself buffeted, but rather tossed around like a rag doll. Every fiber of my being wanted to escape, run, but I couldn't. I opened my mouth to scream but nothing came out. Transfixed, I knew I must stay rooted to this spot. I had been trained to stay. Suddenly the white lights grew harsh then were gone in an instant. In their place was a red glow. Red was everywhere a rich, deep crimson. Blood red.

I awoke with a start to loud music blaring from my new alarm clock. Sweat trickled down my neck, hitting the pillow beneath my head. Slowly, I forced air into my aching lungs, tense muscles released as I freed myself from the nightmare that held me. Lying still, I patiently waited for my breathing to return to normal, then sat up and silenced the alarm clock. Returning to reality after the nightmares was becoming all too normal for me, I thought wryly; becoming a part of my life. Shrugging off the last remnants of the ties that sought to bind me when I slept, I scooped up my riding clothes from the chair where I had laid them out the night before and headed to the bathroom. Thank goodness, earlier this week I had found the box they were in.

Today was Saturday and I was finally going to get the chance to ride again. I was glad I had taken Elaine and Deanne up on their offer of a trail ride. Showered and dressed in my riding clothes I padded down the hall past the living room in my socks.

Reaching the end of the hallway, I could hear Carmen shuffling around in the kitchen and the smell of bacon wafted past me. I followed my nose to the kitchen. Carmen had taken over the kitchen shortly after arriving, smoothly assuming her role as cook and housekeeper with a firm 'take charge' attitude. In fact, she reminded me of a ship's captain. The kitchen was her wheelhouse and as long as it was in order and running smoothly I could approach her. So, I left the crew quarters behind me and headed for the wheelhouse, to test the waters of her mood.

As I rounded the corner I glanced in to gauge her mood. She had her broad back to me and was humming. Assured of calm seas ahead I ventured forth. Carmen, as always, seemed to know I was there. As was customary for her, she wore a floral print, cotton dress and a pair of leather sandals. Her thick, inky black hair had strands of silver creeping in along her temples, and she had pulled it back tightly into a chignon at her neck. She was plump, but not soft, and her skin was the color of dark chocolate. She turned on her heel, handed me a plate full of bacon, scrambled eggs, and toast. *No grits*, I thought wryly. I had yet to find grits anywhere in this country and even if I did I wasn't sure I would be able to get Carmen to fix them. The yellow cornmeal I had proudly brought home from the store last week was much too coarse for this southern girl, and my attempts at explaining what I wanted to Carmen were met with looks of disgust mingled with disbelief. What I would have given for a bag of plain, white hominy grits with warm butter and cheese melted throughout. Grateful for my breakfast, I kept my mouth shut. Maybe I could have Calli mail me some grits, I thought to myself.

"Thank you, Carmen," I said as I accepted the plate and headed for the kitchen table. Carmen had decorated the kitchen herself shortly after arriving, and the bright colored yellow tablecloth was decorated with white poppies. Matching lemon yellow curtains and hand towels gave the room a homey feel and looked crisp against the white washed walls and wood floor. They also set off the bright Mediterranean blue tile countertops. Moving off to do some housework, Carmen left me alone to eat. It was already after nine o'clock when Dad wandered in.

"Mornin'." Making a beeline for the coffee pot, cup in hand, he stopped short and took in my riding clothes. Deciding to avoid the obvious, he poured a cup of hot coffee into his favorite mug, kissed me on the forehead and headed back out the way he came. Stopping in the doorway, he put one hand on the doorframe and turned slowly, smiled, and said, "I'm glad you're back in your breeches." And then he was gone, whistling as he walked away. My heart squeezed in my chest. It had been forever since the last time I had heard him whistle. *He just needed time, just like you do.* I chided myself.

Finishing my breakfast quickly, I rinsed my plate and dumped it into the dishwasher. I had left my paddock boots and half chaps just inside the front door last night. As I picked them up I noticed they had been freshly oiled and I smiled while putting them on. *Thanks, Roberto.*

I found the stable easily, parked the Land Cruiser, reached in the back seat for my helmet and gloves, and made my way to the barn. The parking lot was nearly empty as most of the kids were done with their lessons.

I could pick Deanne out from a mile away. Her golden hair and sparkling clean riding clothes made her stand out amongst the everyday grime of the barn. She and Elaine were standing in the aisle closest to the arena. Standing next to them was a dapple-grey thoroughbred and a large brown and white paint pony in crossties tacked up and ready to go.

Elaine saw me coming and waved, "I am so glad you came, this will be fun."

Out of the corner of my eye I saw Deanne roll her eyes. "I'm still not sure why I let you talk me into this every week. I mean look at this day, not a cloud in the sky and I could be lyin' on the beach right now."

"Ignore her. She just likes to hear herself sometimes," Elaine responded. "Deanne, lying on the beach everyday gets boring, even for you. Besides, it's the rainy season and that means it rains here every day!" Rolling her eyes in Deanne's direction, Elaine continued, "Lauren, this is Fletch," she slapped the pony on the neck. Startled, he shifted and suddenly raised his head. "Oops, guess you were napping little guy, and this is Manny," she waved a hand toward the grey. I'm going to put you on Othello, he is the chestnut right there," she motioned towards the stall on the right. "All of the tack is just outside the stall. He is already groomed and ready to go. If you need anything just shout, I have to run to the bathroom before we get going." With that she turned and headed towards the far end of the barn. Deanne, perched on a tack trunk, was busy talking intently on her cell and waving her hand around dramatically.

Not at all sure what I had gotten myself into, I set my helmet down on an old plastic chair and stuffed my gloves into it. Sliding open the stall door I eyed my charge. He eyed me back. "Othello is it? Well, let's see you closer." I walked up to him with my hand outstretched and he promptly pinned his ears. "Oh, like that is it?" A second later he seemed to think better of it and simply turned his head away from me instead. Clucking to him softly I waited. After a moment, I did it again. The third time he sighed, turned so I could see the wide blaze running down his face, then walked up to me and nuzzled my palm. Chuckling, I patted his neck, "You're all show aren't you?" His ears flicked forward with interest. I tacked Othello up, then after checking the length of the stirrups, I led him out of the stall. Shoving my fingers into my well worn leather riding gloves, I slipped my helmet on and buckled the strap.

We mounted up and Elaine led the way out of the stable to a gate behind the pastures. Beyond the gate were rolling green hills of saw grass standing tall and still. Not a single breath of wind moved and the sun was almost directly overhead. Through the middle of the saw grass, a dark orange path wound its way up the hill and Elaine turned her pony towards the trail. We rode single file in amiable silence up the first several hills with Elaine on point and Deanne behind me. Riding single file, there wasn't much of a chance to talk, for which I was grateful. I had a good feeling about Elaine, she was easy going. But Deanne, I was having trouble reading her. It wasn't that she wasn't nice, just maybe a bit aloof.

As we crested the top of the last hill, Elaine reined up on Fletch and pointed. At the base of the hill, just off to the right was a beautiful green field that was freshly mowed. Cross country jumps rose out of the sea of green, their weathered wooden shapes like the backs of big brown whales breaching the surface. Cross country jumps. Oh, how I had missed eventing. Until now, I hadn't realized just how much I had been suppressing my urge to gallop and jump. Othello danced beneath me with anticipation and a big grin split my goofy face. I felt my heart swell in my chest, pressing hard against my ribs as the adrenaline kicked in. Shifting in the saddle, I took it all in, my eyes missing nothing.

Eventing was for me an adrenaline high—the ultimate escape from the world around me.

Cross country jumps are solid, fixed obstacles that show no mercy to riders that navigate them poorly. A good eventing team is one that is composed of a horse and rider that can read each other, constantly adjusting speed, balance, and rhythm until the two become one. Gifted riders can squeeze the last ounce of courage or ability out of a horse in order to execute a course safely and on time. By the same token, a truly talented horse can fill in the mistakes of their rider and finish the course in much the same way. For me, the rush of jumping cross country was like a drug. My palms started to itch then sweat in anticipation as we made our way down the hill. Splitting up, we each found a clear spot in the sea of grass to ride our horses.

Getting down to work, I took my time warming up Othello. He was very responsive and sensitive to my aids and I found myself getting lost in the feel of him beneath me. He listened intently as I stretched his muscular frame, bending first left then right, making a large figure eight in the soft grass. Every few strides, he would flick his inside ear back towards me as if to say, "Is this right?"

As we approached the first warm up fence, a two foot tall simple, log fence, I could feel him bunch beneath me and coil like a spring a full three strides out from the fence. He was so eager. I made him wait patiently until we reached our take off spot before the jump, but it took all I had to keep him steady until then. When I did let him go, he leapt like a deer and cleared the fence with a least two feet to spare. Adrenaline started to course through my veins and the shear joy of jumping overtook me as I rode him to the base of another small fence, which he jumped beautifully. Circling, we cantered back to the first fence and I quietly asked him to take off a little sooner and he responded by giving me a perfect, but longer distance. We were in the zone.

Landing from the fence, I settled him nicely between my seat and legs by merely sitting more upright. "Good boy," I crooned. I started to pick off bigger fences one by one as we cantered around the field. Turning left or right at my leisure, then taking the next fence we came to. With each jump behind us, I grew bolder, and so did Othello. He felt as though he was smiling in the bridle. Poor guy, I thought, he was probably so weary of being ridden in circles or over small stadium jumps. After about the ninth or tenth fence I pulled him up out of breath and grinning from ear to ear. Reluctantly he slowed, then trotted and finally came to a walk. Letting the reins slide through my fingers, I gave him his head and let him stretch, reaching down to pat his sweaty neck. So preoccupied had I been with my adrenaline high that I never even noticed that I had been the only one jumping. The girls were sitting quietly on their mounts at the base of the hill smiling at me so I rode up alongside Elaine. Fletch promptly pinned his ears to let Othello know that he was in charge.

"I am so sorry. I should have asked if I could jump him. Er, I mean, I just assumed. But he really seemed to handle it well— the height, I mean." I shrugged apologetically searching their faces to see if I had royally messed up by jumping their lesson horse. Some people could be really funny about such things.

"Yeah, um……so how much eventing did you do back home?" Elaine asked, studying me.

"We competed at Intermediate for one year, Pogo and I. He was my project horse that I picked up cheap. I referred to him as my Wal-Mart warmblood. He looked more warmblood than thoroughbred and so I figured he probably would be the only warmblood I ever came close to owning!" I chuckled at my own wit. Deanne and Elaine exchanged glances.

Suddenly I felt as though I was being interviewed. As usual when I was nervous, I kept talking, "I found him through an ad in the local paper. The story was that the lady I bought him from got him as a gift from her husband. She used to ride years ago and he bought Pogo straight off the track. I am guessing that someone unloaded Pogo on this poor guy." Glancing down, I fiddled with the buckle on the reins, pushing the end out of the leather keeper and back with my thumb. "Anyway, she couldn't ride him so I gave him a shot. We started at Novice level and made our way to Intermediate, just the two of us. I had to sell him when we moved." When I looked up, both Elaine and Deanne were trying their best to suppress smiles. "What?"

"Oh, nothing," Elaine's voice rose a notch. "So, the question is, do you want to ride again?"

"Do politicians lie?" I grinned back at her, the adrenaline still fresh in my veins. "I gave up on my riding because I had to sell Pogo, and I guess I really never imagined that I would get much of a chance to ride here. I mean, who ever heard the words Panama and eventing in the same sentence." I shrugged my shoulders again and turned to take in the dark green jungle that skirted the edge of the jump field. "I mean come on—this is a real jungle, like Mogli, Tarzan, Indiana Jones, and all that crap. You don't see many horses in movies that include jungles, now do you?" I turned back towards them expectantly.

Deanne burst out laughing, "Oh Lord girl, no you sure don't. But then again we don't wear grass skirts, beat drums, or live in thatched huts either!"

Elaine jumped in, "So, do you want to ride? Not trail ride, but seriously and competitively?"

I was quickly catching on to the no-nonsense side of Elaine. "Sure," I asked cautiously, "what are you getting at?"

Out of nowhere, a huge clap of thunder interrupted us and a wall of grey rain appeared over a nearby hill. "Crap, we better boogey it back to the barn." Fletch had already started for the path through the saw grass and Elaine pushed him into a trot. Deanne and I slipped in behind them just as another clap of thunder shook the air around us.

We slipped under the low roof of the barn with the horses in tow just as the rain reached the closest pasture. The grey wall of rain came down hard on the metal roof. The sound was deafening.

After removing the tack and settling the horses in their stalls we gathered to wait the storm out in the barn aisle. Deanne, perched on a tack trunk outside Manny's stall, sat staring petulantly at her cell phone. The fat, raindrops hammered the metal roof with such fervor that conversation was a moot point, especially on a cell phone. Balancing on an overturned bucket, Elaine went to work stripping off her spurs and half chaps, laying them in a neat pile on one end of the tack trunk. They had left an old plastic chair for me. Boasting only one remaining arm and a split where one of the legs met the seat, I made every effort to sit down gingerly.

Rainy days to most riders are like an unwelcome guest who often arrives unannounced, stays longer than you would like, and messes up your schedule. For me, the opposite was true. They have always offered a respite to otherwise busy barns. Rainy days usually keep the fair weathered riders at home and this nearly always meant that the barn would be empty save for the horses. As a little girl I had spent many such days hiding out in the barn where I took riding lessons. Located down a dirt road a half a mile from our home, the barn became a second home for me. Nearly every day after school I would pedal my bike as fast as my little legs would go, to the barn. Dad had always worried about me riding back and forth on my bicycle, but Mom knew I had found my passion.

On rainy days, parents would rush to pick up their kids from the barn, but I would stay behind, with my bike propped up against the outside of the barn, and ride out the storm content in my own little world. Listening now I could hear the hypnotizing sound of horses munching hay. The soft shuffling noises created as they moved about in the stall, the occasional sigh or sneeze, and fat, raindrops pelting the roof above were like a symphony to me, always changing in tempo and rhythm, but the music stayed the same, a familiar tune.

As I grew up, rainy days meant cleaning tack and quiet alone time, time to think, to reflect. That was where I had gone when I found out about Jake. I had plunged out of the trauma room, where I worked as a nurse, incoherent and dazed. Apparently I had driven to the barn in a pouring sleet, or so they told me later. That was where Calli had found me. She had known where to look when Dad called her in a panic. Funny, after all those years spent in a barn, Dad still didn't realize there had been just one place for me to go, the one place where I always seemed to find myself again, a home away from home.

Finally the rain slackened enough for us to talk. "So do you?" Elaine was the first to speak.

Still balancing in my chair I shot her a confused look. "Do I what? Want to buy you a new chair before this one kills me," I added with a grin.

"No, do you want to ride? We can hook you up, but there's a catch." She paused, waiting, "its dressage, not eventing."

I should have known. I couldn't recall having ever met an eventer that dressed like Deanne. The art form of keeping over priced riding clothes spotless while around horses could be found in only two riding disciplines as far as I was concerned—hunters and dressage riders. The hunters or hunt seat riders, whom I fondly referred to as Hunter Princesses or HP's for short and the Dressage Queens or DQ's were in my estimation not much more than pretty ornaments perched on horses that did all the work for them, ineffective riders in equally boring disciplines.

As my trainer had told me years ago, sit pretty equals ride shitty. I could be a very effective rider when on a cross country course. Translation, I wasn't what you would refer to as a pretty rider. No one could ever mistake me for either a DQ or an HP. Looking pretty had no place out there among fixed jumps that could flip you and your horse over and send you head first into the ground and then to the hospital. The danger of your horse hanging its leg on a jump and causing a rotational fall was all too real. Cross country riders had more of an edginess about their riding style, a get it done attitude, balls to the walls, if you will. But, I had to admit I wasn't sure how long I would last without horses around me, and I did have fun today. "Go on."

"Deanne, Rachel, and I ride at a private barn. Well, actually our trainer's boyfriend owns it. She moved here a few years back and we've been riding there ever since. She is an incredible rider and trainer. Anyway, when we met you the other day, we thought it might be more your style than this." She waved her hand to include the barn around us.

The rain stopped completely and we could hear a car's tires crunching on the gravel drive heading towards the barn. A dark blue Toyota coupe pulled up next to where we sat and parked.

"Perfect timing as always," Deanne pushed off the tack trunk and stood up.

The car door opened and an oval face with fine features and brunette, shoulder length hair popped up over the roof of the car. "Hey, sorry I missed you this morning Troy asked me to go over and help AJ with some billing stuff. Did you ride before the rain hit?"

"Made it back just in time." Deanne reached for the passenger side door. "Rachel, this is Lauren," she jerked her head in my direction as she climbed in. "Elaine is talking her into joining us at Colleen's barn."

"Oh, hey, that's cool. See you there." With that, her head disappeared, only to reappear behind the wheel. The car door *thunked* behind her and the Toyota's engine came alive. As she drove off a slim arm shot out of the window with a perfunctory wave, and then they were gone back down the drive.

Turning back to Elaine I asked, "So what's the deal?" "I mean, how did you guys end up here, in Panama."

"Oh that, that's easy." She smiled an easy smile. "The U.S. government has had a presence here in Panama since they built the Canal. There are actually a fair number of people, like me, who grew up here when the U.S. still controlled an area of land alongside the Canal, which was called the Canal Zone. My grandfather, for example, came here as a civilian to work as a surveyor and stayed. My parents both grew up here." She shifted, making herself more comfortable on the bucket. "When control of the Zone fell back into the hands of the Panamanians a lot of Americans left, my parents chose to stay."

"So, you are an American citizen, but you live and work here." Before moving I hadn't given much thought to exactly what I would find in Panama, but a bunch of American ex-patriots living and working here wasn't what I had expected at all.

"Yes and no. I have dual citizenship. My mom is Panamanian."

"Oh, what about Deanne?" I could envision Elaine and her life here much better than I could with Deanne. She seemed completely out of her element.

Elaine chuckled softly. "Deanne is close to her dad and he works at the consulate. That is the only reason she is here, her desire to learn classical dressage from someone who really understands it, well that is icing on the cake for her. She's a bit of," she paused, taking a moment to frame her answer, "a daddy's girl." Reaching over to the tack trunk she gathered up her half chaps and spurs. "Rachel," she motioned towards the gravel road, "she doesn't live here." "Her husband and AJ, you'll meet him tomorrow, are in a similar line of work. She rides with us when she flies down to help with the business." Noticing a look of mild surprise on my face she continued. "Didn't quite expect to find so many Americans here did you?"

Caught off guard by her perception, I stumbled a bit. "N-no, actually I am surprised. I guess I just never gave it much thought." Actually, I had been so numb and preoccupied with trying to wake up and function day after day to think much about anything. But I kept that to myself.

Elaine stood up and turned. Eyeing me she said, "So, I guess we'll pick you up tomorrow. Where do you live?"

Before I could reason the idea of riding again to death, or change my mind I quickly told her that I lived on the Point.

She nodded approvingly. "Nice place. Fancy. Did you know it used to be a leper colony?"

"No kidding! Well, the lepers had a heck of a view of the Bay. Didn't they?"

Elaine's face split into a grin. "I don't think I'd take leprosy in order to have a view like that! Seriously, the Point is very nice. Let me guess, does your mom or dad work for Avitar Defense?"

"How'd you guess?" I carefully extricated myself from the plastic chair without incident.

"It's a small world down here. Besides, there have been a lot of new technology and defense companies coming here lately to set up shop. I had heard that Avitar bought some real estate up that way."

As we made to leave I gave Elaine the address and she gave me a time. They would pick me up tomorrow at 1 pm.

**

It rained again that afternoon, but luckily I had already made it home, so I spent the rest of the afternoon curled up on the couch thumbing through a box of old pictures I had brought with me. There were horses of every imaginable color and size, but the face on their backs was always the same. From red pigtails tied with bows, jodphurs to stock ties, safety vests, and everything in between they were a catalog of happy times, even when we lost. Not a single picture held anything other than a smile spread from one side of my freckled face to the other. Sighing, I dumped the memories back into the box and settled the lid squarely on top. It was no use. I had to be around horses. I felt it to the core of my being. Out of habit, I sniffed my hands, searching for the familiar scent of eau de horse before I remembered that I had taken a shower. Winston Churchill was quoted as saying that "there is something about the outside of a horse that is good for the inside of a man." I couldn't agree more and it was a favorite quote of mine.

While I definitely wanted to ride again I wasn't at all sure I wanted to delve into the stuffy world of dressage. The word dressage essentially meant 'training'. It was a precise world of etiquette and tradition that existed within the confines of a rectangular arena, which was three times as long as it was wide. Letters were placed along the edges of the arena to serve as guideposts for the rider, a road map of sorts. Additional 'imaginary' letters existed in the middle of the arena, but for obvious reasons you couldn't actually place a physical marker with a letter 'X' emblazoned on it smack in the center of the arena. There were plenty of acronyms to help riders find their way through each test. I had been taught **A**ll **K**ing **E**dward's **H**orses **C**an **M**ake **B**ig **F**ences. These were the basic letters, however as you moved up the levels they added additional letters along the side (V, S, R, P). If that wasn't enough letters to remember there were also additional imaginary letters (D, L, I, G) added in the actual arena. In eventing, you must compete in dressage first, and then either the cross country phase or the stadium phase follows although usually the stadium is last. So, when I had been forced to ride dressage in order to be allowed to event, or rather, allowed to move onto the next phase, I had always memorized the shape or pattern of each movement in the arena, rather than the letters. I was just simply too 'blonde' to remember them all. But then again, I still could be caught counting on my fingers, I thought wryly.

Glancing at the clock on the wall I decided to fix dinner for Dad and Haley. Carmen and Roberto had the weekends off. I used to love to cook, but I hadn't felt that creative desire to invent something in a while. Never one for cookbooks I had a knack for 'salvaging' as Jake had called it. I could dig through just about any pantry or fridge and come up with a meal of gourmet proportions. To me it was a challenge, one that came naturally. Pulling myself away from the comfort of the couch I padded to the kitchen in my socks.

Dinner went well. Missing home after thumbing through the photos I had decided to go Southern; making fried chicken, mashed potatoes, gravy and cornbread. I had made sure that Granny's ancient cast iron skillet was packed when we moved. There simply was no better cornbread than that which comes from a cast iron skillet. Collards or turnip greens were not to be had easily so I settled for corn.

We ate until our bellies were full at the kitchen table, talking about our day. Dad had asked about the stables and I told him about my chance to ride again and he seemed pleased. Haley was excited to be joining the children's choir at church tomorrow. Since moving, Dad hadn't shared much about his job with Avitar Defense and tonight was no different. I shrugged it off, guessing that he must not have much to talk about.

Afterward, we curled up with popcorn and a movie. It was a good night to be with the ones I loved, and for the first time in quite a while I actually slept through most of the night and felt more rested in the morning than I had in a while. The nightmare still haunted me, but thankfully I woke up before I became pooled in sweat.

COLLEEN

True to her word, Elaine and the girls pulled up at 1 pm. Deanne was driving a sleek black Mercedes sedan. As the car pulled to a stop at the end of the driveway I noticed there was a guy in the passenger seat, a very good-looking guy. Even though he was seated I could tell he was tall. As I walked up to the car he rolled down the window and flashed a big grin at me. He was tan with thick, wavy black hair and liquid brown eyes. His face was chiseled and aristocratic.

"The girls suckered you into this, huh?" His eyes twinkled in mischief and I liked him immediately.

"Yeah, they did, you, too?" I shot back at him, opening the rear door.

"Nope, I am a sucker for four hooves and a good looking forelock any day." His smile widened at his joke, suddenly making his face appear boy-like. "Nice to meet you Lauren, I'm Hamish." There was a very faint hint of an accent to his speech, but I couldn't quite place it. *American with a hint of... northeast? Hmmm...*

I slipped in next to the girl who had picked up Deanne the day before. "Hi, Rachel, right?" Elaine sat on the far side behind Deanne.

"Hey," she replied, scooting to the middle seat.

The drive to the barn took about thirty minutes. Rachel and I were the only ones not wearing riding clothes so I assumed everyone else would be riding. The drive gave me a chance to get to know everybody a little better.

Just as Elaine had mentioned, Rachel was here on business from her home in Florida. She normally rode with the gang, but today she was just hanging out. In her 'former riding life' as she called it, she had ridden western. Growing up on a cattle ranch in Texas, she had learned how to cut cattle and competed in reining events. She had met her husband while at college in Texas. His business eventually took him to the East coast and she had left riding behind her until she had discovered dressage. I liked her immediately. She was open, honest, and forthcoming.

Hamish was originally born in Scotland. I would never have guessed his nationality because he sounded so very American. He was also very easy to talk to and seemed at ease with himself. He was dressed casually in a pair of tan breeches, a solid, brown tee shirt that accented his muscular torso, and paddock boots. Watching from the back seat I could clearly see that Deanne was smitten with him. The way she leaned over towards him, flashed her smile, and lowered her eyelashes was like a flashing neon sign to anyone who paid attention. The fact that Hamish didn't seem to notice made me wonder if he was gay. After all, most men who rode dressage in the States were gay. Eventing was the one English riding discipline that had mostly straight men within their ranks. The odd thing was that in Europe riding was considered a perfectly manly sport, but for some crazy reason, in the States riding English seemed un-manly. Western, on the other hand was in large part a men's world, or at least, the manlier of the two.

As we drove, the wall of green jungle along the road became more solid and the towns we passed grew smaller. Here and there a small, often shabby wooden houses built on stilts would flash by, breaking up the view. The asphalt road was crumbling at the edges with the occasional pothole for Deanne to avoid.

The Mercedes slowed as we approached a stop sign in the middle of nowhere. Deanne turned left onto a narrow gravel road as we left the paved road behind us. "Almost there." Deanne said, obviously for my benefit.

The narrow, winding road was covered with large, graphite colored gravel chunks, some as big as my fist. The thick, lush tropical vegetation had found its way to the edges of the gravel and there it stopped abruptly. Unlike the roads we had just been on, this one looked well maintained. In the front, Deanne was chattering away while Hamish politely listened.

Rachel leaned towards me and whispered, "No, he's not gay," in my ear. I couldn't help but smile. I felt a little better that the thought of Hamish being gay had crossed someone else's mind. Glancing at her I saw a knowing smirk on her face.

We pulled to a stop outside what appeared to be a fortress, a really old fortress. The grayish-green walls soared above us more than thirty feet. Here and there chunks of stone and plaster were missing from the exterior façade, giving it a pock marked look.

"Let me guess, cannon balls?" I muttered to no one in particular.

Rachel snorted through her nose and Elaine rolled her eyes, "No silly, we are too far inland for cannon fire."

I guess that was supposed to make sense so I nodded. I turned my attention back to the imposing wall.

"This fort was built in the 1600's by a wealthy Spaniard, and the jungle just isn't very forgiving," added Rachel. "At least that is the story I heard."

We shut the doors of Deanne's Mercedes and the thick jungle around us absorbed the sound like a plush carpet. Two massive black wrought iron gates hung together at what appeared to be the only entrance and sat recessed slightly into the wall. Thick, weathered wood was attached to the backside of the gates and the patina caused by the elements gave a warm and welcoming feel. Before Hamish even reached for the gate latch, one of them swung open smoothly.

"Buenos dias!"

"Chi-chi, how are you today?"

A short, thickset Panamanian man with a shock of white hair on his head smiled up at Hamish. Grinning from ear to ear, he clasped hands with Hamish and they thumped each other on the back.

"Muy bien, and eeven beetter now that you are heeere." The genuine smile and warmth that radiate from Chi-chi was palpable. "Senoritas, you look more bonita eevry day!"

Chi-chi patted the girls on the shoulder and then stopped to take me in. "Flaca zanahoria," he said with a twinkle in his eye.

Rachel snorted again and Hamish laughed out loud.

"What, what did he say?"

"He called you skinny, a skin-," Deanne said between giggles.

The giggling got louder as Deanne struggled to finish what she was saying.

"What!" I demanded.

"C-arr-ot," squeaks Rachel. "It's your hair." Rachel let out a snort as she tried to catch her breath, "he called you a skinny carrot. You have to admit Lauren; it does fit." She eyed my red hair as she spoke. "I think he does it to keep everyone straight in his head, as he gets older. Word association or something like that."

Hamish, unable to hold back, joined in. After a moment, he wiped the grin from his face and smiled at me.

"Great," I muttered.

Chi-chi laughed along as if he was part of an inside joke.

"He gives everyone a nickname," adds Elaine. "And, no we are not telling you ours!"

Just inside the gates, there was a lush garden, fragrant, white gardenia, bright red hibiscus with their yellow throats, and birds-of-paradise spilled over the confines of the edge of the garden to our right. Several different species of orchids hung in moss-covered baskets from the branches of a tree just inside the old wall. A two-story house with wide verandas on both floors sat to our left. The walls of the house were the same greenish gray as the outer wall behind us, but the texture of the stone and masonry was slightly different. The disparity in the stone seemed to point to the house having been built at a later time, but it was hard to tell with all the foliage growing along it. Hot pink bouganvilla climbed the walls and accentuated the Spanish style archways. The red ochre, tile roof looked identical to all the other's I had seen since coming to Panama.

Beneath our feet, a small flagstone courtyard. Leading away from the gates were two flagstone pathways. One led to the house on the left, the other straight ahead. I followed Rachel and the others down the pathway that led away from the house. About thirty yards past the gates, the pathway bent to the right just past a large banyan tree, its gnarled roots reaching up beneath the flagstones, leaving behind large cracks and shifts in the stone.

Out of nowhere a large stone wall, about chest high, which appeared to be part of the original fort, rose up in front of us. Large steel posts just on the other side of the wall supported the roof of an immaculately groomed indoor riding arena. The metal roof and support girders were all modern in style and a gigantic fan hung from the middle of the arena, spinning lazily around. The fan was easily twelve feet in diameter.

"This is where I leave you lovely ladies. I need to get tacked up. I drew the short straw." Hamish bowed gallantly, excusing himself, and with a wink he headed down a smaller path that led around the side of the arena.

The floor of the arena was illuminated by a combination of natural light from two open sides of the arena and from evenly spaced skylights above, which cast rectangular patches of sunlight across the arena floor. Florescent lights hung from the ceiling as well, but sat dark. In the center of the arena a huge black horse cantered towards us. As we watched, it slows. Dust motes from the arena danced in the sunlight, creating a haze just above the surface as the horse moves closer. The canter became more uphill and lofty with each stride. As they reached the center of the arena, the entire front end of the massive gelding seemed to lift higher and higher.

His hindquarters lowered and his hocks bent beneath him as he transferred his weight to his haunches. He began to pirouette to the left. Never once did he hesitate, slow, or become uneven. The tall rider on his back sat calmly, unmoving. Tall and thin, she gave the appearance of flowing with the huge black gelding rather than riding him. Incredibly, her aids were invisible. He moved out of the pirouette, and cantered toward the corner nearest us where he performed a flying lead change. The lead change was light and buoyant, almost as if he were skipping on air. They moved off the next corner on the short side of the arena and headed across the diagonal.

Skipping along, he switched leads with every stride of the tempi changes, his rider sitting ramrod straight able to pick up the barely imperceptible aids she was giving the gelding. Lightness, harmony, and palpable energy flowed from the pair—mesmerized I watched, I had never seen dressage like *that*. "This is your secret?"

"Correction, our secret weapon," Rachel grinned.

"Who is she?"

"Colleen Mudd. She trained in Germany," added Deanne. "She is simply brilliant isn't she." It was clearly a statement not a question.

"Yeah. I've seen upper level dressage before and it didn't look anything like *that*!" I jerked my head in the direction of the horse dancing in and out of the beams of sunlight.

Rachel smiled at my response, "there's dressage, and then there is *dressage*. True classical dressage is a horse of another color, if you will."

Elaine rolled her eyes, "pardon your pun."

I turned my focus back to the arena to think for a moment. "But I don't understand. If Colleen is so good, then why stay here? Why Panama of all places? She could go to Europe or back to the States. I've never seen riding like this. Surely she could compete and do very well."

"Alejandro," said Rachel.

"Yeah, Alejandro," Deanne murmured with a dreamy look.

Following Deanne's gaze, I glanced over to the edge of the arena. One side of the arena had been left open to catch the tropical breeze. The other side sat up against an old stone wall. Standing in the dim light of the arena was a man. I hadn't noticed him until now. He stood quietly, arms crossed, intently watching Colleen ride.

As we watched, Alejandro bent to pick up a long dressage whip at his feet. Then he unfolded and moved across the arena with a cat-like grace. He immediately reminded me of the jaguar we had seen at the Summit Zoo. He exuded confidence; knowing whom, what and where he was at all moments. Standing tall, but not gangly, he reached the side of the gelding, and without having to reach up, he handed her the whip. His dark brown hair was sun kissed with lighter shades of gold, short on the sides, and slightly longer on top. He passed up the whip, then, absently ran his hand through his hair while his other hand rested lightly on Colleen's thigh. As they talked, his azure, blue eyes flashed up from his aquiline face, as if she were the only person around for miles.

AJ was GQ personified. He was the full page glossy ad for something you just must run out and buy for your ordinary man back home. I hadn't even met Colleen, and I could see why she liked AJ. *Who wouldn't?*

"AJ is the reason she stays. His mom lives in the city and he looks after her. I think his dad died really young or something. Anyway, his older brother moved to New York to train thoroughbreds for the track and AJ stayed behind."

I listened to Rachel, nodding my head, but kept my eye on Colleen and AJ. There was clearly a deep connection between them.

"It's a Latin thing."

I turn to look at Elaine, "a what?"

"A Latin thing, you know making sure his mom is well taken care of. Latin men simply dote on their mothers."

"Oh." I took her word for it, not fully understanding what she meant. *Hmph, must be a cultural thing.* "So, is that her horse?"

Elaine nodded, "Gold Herr. Bavarian, she imported him sight unseen on a friend's recommendation. She's had him for a while now." We stood there leaning against the wall watching the rest of Colleen's ride. Loosing track of time, eventually Rachel tugged at my shirt to get my attention, then turned and started to walk away.

"Come on, I'll introduce you."

I followed her and the others along the wall to the left. Rounding the corner, a small stone stable, nestled within a stand of ancient mahogany trees came into view. The huge trees offered a welcome respite from the heat, and I could feel the temperature drop a few degrees. The quaint stable blended well with the Old Spanish architecture around it. I noticed the barn was attached to the arena by a dirt path.

We reached the entrance of the stable just as Colleen exited from the side of the arena walking next to the big gelding, which looked even more impressive up close.

"Hey, you guys are here early." Colleen had run up the stirrups and loosened the girth of her saddle before exiting the arena. She paused to take in the group before her, helmet in hand, and smiled. Without her helmet I could see she had a round, expressive face with a rose petal complexion and cornflower blue eyes. She wore her medium length blonde hair braided neatly at the nape of her neck. She looked to be in her late thirties and unlike some riders who spend hours on end outdoors under an unforgiving sun, her skin still looked smooth and fresh. Glancing down the barn aisle, she seemed to be looking for someone. "Maria, could you please take care of Gold Herr for me."

A sour faced girl with jet-black hair and dark olive skin stepped out from the barn aisle, effectively ignoring all of us. She was dressed even more DQ than Deanne, if that was possible. Fawn colored full seat leather Pikeur breeches, a sleeveless cream colored riding shirt with a mandarin style collar and boots polished to a mirror-like shine. If not for her sour expression she would have been very pretty. She took hold of Gold Herr's reins and led him down the barn aisle. Watching her sashay back into the barn, I couldn't help peeking down the barn aisle to see if there was any dirt on the floor. Her boots were way too clean to have actually been worn in a barn. Sure enough, the barn aisle was immaculate, not a piece of hay anywhere. Standing in the shade sweating, Maria left me wondering how in the world both she and Deanne stayed so clean. Being around horses was a dirty proposition, but when you added the dank tropical humidity, it was a recipe for sweat and grime of the highest degree. Feeling suddenly self-conscious, I squared my shoulders and took a cleansing breath. *What in the hell are you doing here, Todd?* Rachel pulled me from my thoughts.

"Colleen, this is Lauren, I told you about her the other day. She is interested in taking lessons."

"Oh, right, why don't you hang around and watch my next few lessons, and then we can talk afterwards."

Just then, Hamish came out of the barn leading a gorgeous dapple-grey mare. The large silver dollar sized dapples faded into dark steel grey knees and legs. Her generous forelock hung down the front of her face just shy of her soft black nostrils. She had a feminine face and doe-like eyes.

He stopped in front of me. "Lauren, I'd like you to meet the love of my life, Patina." Hamish placed a tender hand up under her thick grey mane and scratched. Reaching around, she nestled her soft muzzle in his other hand.

"Oh, Hamish, she's lovely," I exclaimed. "Lusitano?"

Startled, he looked up. "Yes, yes she is. You're good."

"Hmm, Andrade bloodlines by any chance?"

He stepped back to look at the mare. "How can you tell, I mean…."

"My mom was no horsewoman, but she loved the classic look of the Lusitano in all of the horse books I had growing up. We would flip through them and pick our favorites." I smiled at the memory of the well-worn books full of color pictures with horses of every color and size gracing the pages. "Anyway, she planned a vacation to Europe when I was twelve and bribed me into going by including horses as part of our trip." Absently I ran my fingers through Patina's forelock twisting and straightening it in turn as I recalled that magical day.

"A friend of Mom's at the University was from Portugal and knew the Andrade family so we got a tour of the stud farm. I'll never forget when the head trainer showed us this gorgeous chestnut stallion standing in his stall. He walked into the stall, flicked his whip, clucked to him and the stallion did piaffe right there in the stall. No reins, no bridle, nothing but a whip and a verbal cue. That was the first piaffe I ever saw. I'll never forget it." I let out a sigh. With a final pat I stepped back, "Besides, silly, I can see her brand." I winked at Hamish.

Colleen chuckled, "She got you Hamish."

We walked back to the arena, following Hamish through the side entrance. Just to the left sat a wooden picnic bench. Elaine and I perched on top, our feet resting on the bench seats, to watch Colleen work with Hamish. Hamish spent the first few minutes walking and trotting Patina while stretching her in a long and low frame around the perimeter of the arena. His contact with her mouth was light and soft, and Patina seemed to revel in the stretch, swinging her back softly. Her pure white tail swayed rhythmically behind her. Picking up the reins, gradually Hamish asked her for more engagement from behind at the trot, while maintaining a consistent and steady tempo to her strides. She was like a metronome. He then began to elevate her front end, using her engaged, hind end, until she was travelling in a lovely, soft frame. With soft half halts he pushed the energy from her haunches to his quiet hand. I watched as her frame compressed and her back rounded even more. Her tempo stayed the same. The loftiness of each trot step and the pushing power from her haunches were incredible. This mare had airtime, or what riders call suspension. Patina stayed soft and relaxed through her jaw, and her poll was clearly the highest point of her neck.

As Colleen entered the building she sat on an old wooden bar stool next to the letter B. Abused and battered, the bar stool clearly had seen better days, but must have been comfortable enough to keep around. Settling in, she set a foot on the footrest and crossed her other leg. She wore a pair of dark brown leather boots, the insides and soles worn smooth from years of riding. Her eyes never left the pair in the arena.

Hamish moved into a serpentine pattern, making three equal loops from one end of the arena, to the other, and back again. Colleen watched quietly from her stool until Hamish had completed his third trip down the arena. "OK, let's go to leg yields starting at the center line. I don't want to do pirouettes today since we worked on that hard the other day."

Without hesitating Hamish transitioned Patina when he reached the next corner on the short side, then started down the quarter line. Patina moved off Hamish's aids and was on the rail well before she reached the letter B. He repeated the same pattern from the opposite side of the arena, reaching the arena edge before the letter M.

"OK, very nice, change direction across the diagonal with a lengthening and let's get her engine going."

With almost no visible aids, Hamish sent Patina across the diagonal in a lovely, forward lengthened trot and then repeated the exercise from the opposite direction. Patina's legs carried her feminine frame across the arena with incredible pushing power. From what I could see, it looked like Hamish had to work at keeping her from shifting gears into an extended trot.

Colleen smiled knowingly. "Her back seems to be nice and warmed up, so move to sitting trot and leg yield from the corner to X, circle and then half pass to K."

The grey mare crossed her legs fluidly with each stride. Next came renvers and travers. Coming back across the diagonal towards us, we could just see the tips of Patina's horseshoes as she exploded into the extended trot. Bringing her back down, the pair took a walk break. Hamish let Patina cool down a bit and walk on a long rein.

"Pablito!" Colleen spoke loudly.

A tall, thin Panamanian who looked to be in his late teens materialized next to the wall where we had stood watching Colleen ride earlier. He wore a pair of work gloves and had a tool belt slung around his waist. "Could you please turn on the fan."

Pablito nodded, and then headed to a switch on one of the steel columns. I watched him stalk across the arena much the same way as AJ had earlier. The resemblance was startling. The huge fan overhead began to spin. Thirty seconds later the entire arena felt about ten degrees cooler.

"So Lauren, what is your riding background?" Colleen asked without glancing over her shoulder.

Had Elaine not nudged me I might have missed the question all together, as focused as I was on taking in my surroundings. "A small bit of Pony Club as a kid, and then I started eventing at fourteen. I was a working student for Ralph Hill for a summer as part of a young rider team. I rode with Jimmy Wofford as much as I possibly could, well every clinic he gave within driving distance. It's a good thing he didn't think I was a stalker." Elaine and Colleen chuckled. "I was bringing my off the track Thoroughbred up the ranks when we moved."

"I used to event. That is how I got my first taste of dressage, through the back door, so to speak. Those were the days when you needed a good jumper rather than a good mover to do well in eventing. Nowadays you need both. My God that was eons ago. I knew both Ralph and Jimmy. Nice guys and true horsemen. What level were you competing?"

"We had moved up to Intermediate and had three recognized events under our belt. We weren't placing in the ribbons yet, but we were still learning to finesse some of the cross country questions." She listened to me, her focus still on Hamish who had slowed and was performing a half-turn on the haunches along the rail. "Well, that and we were leaving the dressage arena with higher scores than I would have liked," I added, glancing in her direction. In eventing, much like golfing, the lower your score the better.

"Hamish, let's put her to work now. Go ahead and pick up your right lead canter around the entire arena and warm her up with some twenty meter circles."

We watched as Hamish and Patina circled to the right at the letter A a few times. As he crossed the center of the arena, Patina swapped leads effortlessly to the left as he put her on a twenty-meter circle in the center of the arena. He repeated the exercise again, then swapped leads back to the right and circled at C before heading down the long side of the arena. Once again, like in the lengthened trot, Patina seemed eager to stretch out in the canter, but Hamish held her back. As he rounded the corner he had a big smile on his face.

"Nice, she is eager today, huh? When you get to K, volte, then half pass from K to R, watch the flying change as she will try to anticipate, then repeat going to the left. In fact, ask for the flying change a stride or two before the rail so she really is listening to you."

As Elaine and I watched, Hamish worked on extended trot work and four tempi changes. Patina exuded feminine grace from her nose to her tail with one exception: her ears. So relaxed and happy was she that the grey tips of her beautiful ears flopped up and down on either side of her poll. Ears that remain relaxed and soft are often a good indicator of relaxation in a horse, but on Patina, they were almost donkey-esque. As they finished their lesson with extended trot coming right towards our picnic table, I had to stifle a giggle at the expression on Patina's face.

Her eye was soft, and she seemed to float across the arena, her ears flopping softly in rhythm with every step she took.

Deanne rode next on a very elegant chestnut mare with a white blaze and only one white sock. Her name was Nicola, and Elaine told me she was a ten-year old, Dutch Warmblood. Like Hamish, Deanne spent plenty of time warming Nicola up slowly with a lot of stretching. In dressage it is very important to develop a horse to use its hind end as the driving force, like a rear wheel drive car. When you push from behind you get more potential energy and power. A front wheel drive car tends to pull itself along the road. Every horse I watched appeared to have incredible rear engines. Nicola was all lightness and grace under saddle. Both she and Patina were small in height. Each seemed to be about 16 hands, but while Patina was solidly built and appeared much bigger in size, Nicola was feminine and light of build.

As the lesson progressed, Deanne worked on canter pirouettes. Elaine was right—Deanne could ride very well. Much like Colleen, you rarely saw her move in the saddle or give a cue to Nicola. Nicola slowed into a school canter as she passed us and headed for C. Turning up centerline, Deanne started a pirouette to the left. The first half of the movement was flawless.

Beside me, Elaine whispered, "Watch this."

As the pair completed the circle and started to move off down the arena Nicola suddenly exploded. The picture of harmony crumbled as Nicola bucked, flinging her hind legs out behind her in a display of amazing acrobatics. As her hind legs came back to Earth she then bolted forward for several strides until Deanne regained control.

"No, she can't come out of the pirouette and into the flying change if she leaves her inside hind leg behind. You have got to make sure that it is under her before you ask" Colleen had shifted to the edge of her stool and slid one leg onto the ground. "Again, and don't forget the inside hind. Let me hear you."

Picking up the left lead canter again, Deanne headed down the long side of the arena. As she passed us she appeared calm and composed. Clearly the buck hadn't rattled her.

"Does she always do that?"

"With just a pirouette, no, but she has been trying to add the flying change at the end for the last week. Nicola is very sensitive and once she decides not to learn something new or if she thinks it is too hard she gets stuck in a rut. You know that old saying, it takes a thousand times to correct a bad habit, but it only took one time to create it. That's Nicola. Like a scratch on a record, she will go round and round without advancing until they have another break through. Deanne will get her out of it though."

As they entered the corner I glanced at Deanne. Her jaw was set and she looked focused. About a stride before the pirouette, Deanne started talking out loud. "Inside hind, inside hind, inside hind," She repeated the mantra over and over again. Just before they reached the end of their pirouette, Deanne gave the cue and sent Nicola out of the movement early, heading for the far corner instead of back down centerline. This time when she asked for the change Nicola gave her a big hop, but accomplished the flying change and continued on. Deanne reached down and patting the inside of her sweaty neck, praised her fervently. Reaching the far corner, Nicola smoothly swapped again and continued on around the arena.

"Yes! That's it. Great job out smarting her, now do it again the exact same way. Only this time your transition should be smoother now that she has figured it out. And watch that you don't lean forward."

Deanne repeated the exercise several times until she was able to put it all together and complete the pirouette. As she was cooling off Nicola, she and Colleen reviewed the lesson and what Deanne was to work on before her next ride. When they walked back to the side entrance where we sat, Deanne slipped off the mare and loosened the girth.

"That only works with blondes you know." Elaine said sarcastically.

"Ha! At least this blonde can ride and talk at the same time." Deanne shot back with a gorgeous smile. "Besides, I need all the help I can get riding this little red bottle rocket, so if talking out loud helps, I'll be screaming out loud in Wellington."

While we stood talking, the dark haired girl named Maria came into the arena behind us leading a mare. She had pulled her jet-black hair into a tight bun at the nape of her neck, and not a single hair escaped from under her helmet. Slipping on her gloves, she glanced around the arena as if looking for someone. I got the immediate sense that Maria wasn't well liked.

"He went to the feed store with Chi Chi." Colleen said with finality.

Maria whipped her head around as if stung. Recovering, she smiled sweetly and said, "Who are you talking about?" Her bright red lips parted, revealing perfect white teeth.

Lipstick? Really? Who in the hell rides in lipstick?

Colleen nearly snorted at her answer. "Pablito, you know damn well who."

Her eyes flashed briefly, and then thinking better of it Maria shifted gears again. "Colleen, I have no idea what you are talking about. He said he would fix that loose bucket in Mariposa's stall. I just wanted to make sure he was doing his job."

"You let me worry about Pablito." Tension hung in the air between them. "I need to talk to Lauren here for a minute, so go ahead and warm up. I will be right back."

With that Maria turned on her heal, yanking her mare's head around as she stalked off towards the mounting block. Deanne and the others were already heading back towards the barn so I followed them.

When we reached the barn, Elaine disappeared into a stall at the far end, Deanne headed towards a wash stall about half way down the aisle, and I followed Colleen into the barn office, which sat to the right, just inside the barn door. Motioning me towards a chair, Colleen slipped around behind a shabby, little desk covered with neat stacks of paperwork.

"My filing system," she said ruefully. "I intend to clean it up every weekend, and then Monday comes before I know it."

I settled into an office chair. "This is a really nice barn. If you would have told me a few months ago, that I could find a gem like this in the middle of a jungle in Panama I would have laughed."

"Yeah, that's what everyone says. AJ's brother calls it Area 51 after the secret military base in Nevada." She added dryly. "It does kind of fit though." Resting her elbows on the desk she grew serious, cutting right to the point. "Listen, what we have here is really special and my time is very valuable to me. Elaine and Deanne both tell me you have a good seat and can ride, which is a plus. More importantly though is your desire. I need to know what you want to get out of this." She spread her hands out to either side of her, by way of explanation.

"I need to ride." After the words left my mouth I realized how lame they must have sounded. Swallowing hard I went on. "Listen, to be honest, I haven't ridden for nearly three months, but before that I trained five days a week. I sold my horse and nearly everything else before we moved." I fought to keep my fingers from twisting together in a show of nervousness. *Oh, God, I need to ride again.* "I didn't realize until yesterday's ride that I just can't walk away from riding." Pausing, I added, "It is too much of who I am, so you see, I need to ride." *Geez, Todd. That sounded lame.*

Colleen tapped her index finger on the cracked Formica of the desk. "You said you trained five days a week. That's a lot of lessons." I felt her eyes studying me from across the stacks of paperwork.

"No, I took two lessons a month. I said 'training' because every time I swung a leg over my horse, I trained him. I had to because I couldn't afford more lessons." *That and I was a mental basket case for the last eight months or so.* "That's just how I ride."

She paused, thinking. "Everybody here is equal. We help each other tack up, cool down, rinse horses, and we occasionally ride each other's horses so that we can learn from them and vice versa. I only want riders who are serious about learning classical dressage. There will be no over bent necks, hand riding, or gadgets used. I don't tolerate that stuff. You will learn to ride according to the German principles of horsemanship even if that means I have to break down your bad habits before you move on." She paused to let her words sink in. "I have big plans for the students I work with so please don't think I'm being a hard ass." She spread her hands out again in explanation, "I do this for the love, not for the money, so I can be choosy about whom I welcome here."

I nodded. I liked her bluntness. Colleen was very black and white, and I could respect that. "One problem, I don't have a horse."

That's okay, I would want you to ride mine until I can see what we need to fix. He is a Grand Prix schoolmaster with a lot of knowledge to share. Trust me, he will let you know if you are doing something wrong, do it right and he will also reward you in spades." There was a hint of laughter in her voice.

"Okay, thanks." We stood and moved towards the office door.

"I better get back to work."

Deanne and I watched Maria's lesson while we waited on Elaine. Elaine did not have a lesson today, but instead took her horse, William, for a short hack around the property. Maria was a fine rider, but she clearly lacked the patience and finesse of Hamish and Deanne. Watching her, I got the sense that she was trying to force her riding, rather than allowing it to happen and working with her mare. According to Deanne, Maria's mare's name was Mariposa, which meant butterfly in Spanish. She was a lovely dark bay with black points. A small snip of white on her nose was the only white spot on her.

As Maria's lesson ended, I made arrangements with Colleen to ride Tuesday morning.

**

I arrived at the barn just after nine in the morning to meet Colleen. Pulling the collapsible saddle rack from where it lay against the wall in the tack stall, I set my freshly cleaned saddle with its cover on the metal frame. Sliding my girth off of my shoulder I laid it across the saddle. I had spent last evening on the back porch oiling my tack. Although I had cleaned and oiled everything before it was packed up for the trip, it had been several months and cleaning tack was always a very zen thing for me. It was much like picking a stall, mindless work. However, they both granted me time to think and reflect about something or to clear my mind and think about nothing. Both of which could be therapeutic. I hooked my helmet by the chinstrap on an empty peg, then walked around the barn and visited the horses before Colleen arrived.

I gave William, Mariposa, Gold Herr, and Nicola each a pat on the neck and one of the soft melt away mints I had brought with me. Approaching a large stallion stall on the end, a large white face hidden beneath a frothy white forelock popped out of the stall. The stall plate read 'Macho'. The white stallion was clearly a Baroque breed with his short, thick crested neck, over abundance of mane and tail, and his prominently shaped Roman nose. He was built like a bulldog with his bulging muscles. Like a bulldog, he was also slobbery and sweet. His pink and black mottled muzzle with its large black nostrils searched my hand gently for the mint. After a final pat, I moved on down the row to what looked like a young horse. He was slight of build and lacked the muscle development of a horse that is regularly ridden. Stopping to scratch under his jaw I noticed his haunches were quite a bit taller than his withers, a clear sign he was still growing. A dark liver chestnut with dapples, his mane and tail were a silvery flaxen. A white face and four, tall white socks made him look very flashy.

"Hey there, handsome; are you looking for a mint?" After seeing every other horse in the barn enjoy their mint he was bobbing his head in excitement, watching me unwrap the mint.

"That's Stitch," Colleen walked up beside me dressed in a pair of workman like chocolate breeches and a black polo shirt. "A friend of mine found him for me in Argentina of all places. His dam was imported from Germany in foal. They kept the mare and sold this guy."

"What is he?"

"Hanoverian. I plan to start him and then take him with me to Florida on my next trip. I haven't decided if he is a project horse or if I want to keep him. Either way, I'll have to take him to the States if I want him branded." Turning, she headed for the tack room and I followed.

The tack room was neat and clean. Bridles hung on wooden pegs in a row along one wall. Black and white plastic nameplates sat just above each peg, announcing to whom they belonged. Further down, wooden saddle racks full of saddles jutted out from the same wall. Some had fitted saddle covers and others were covered with a towel. There was even an old sidesaddle. A shelf full of clean well used saddle pads in a rainbow of colors sat above a washer and dryer. The opposite wall had several large tack trunks set under a long countertop. Twelve long wooden dowels stuck straight up from the countertop in rows. Pairs of brushing boots, one tucked within the other, had been stuck on each dowel. Here, the plastic nameplates listed the sizes of each pair of boots; S, M, L or XL.

A couple of plastic chairs sat around an old coffee table upon which a bootjack lay. All in all, it was an efficient space without being fussy and made me feel at home. I had taken lessons from dedicated dressage riders in order to improve my dressage when I evented. Every one of their barns had been a showcase of marble, brass, polished oak, and pristine white saddle pads and polo wraps. They always seemed to make a social statement. A metal rack hanging from the wall above the brushing boots held several pair of polo wraps. I hadn't used polo wraps in years. They were a pain to put on, a pain to take off, and never remained white for more than one ride. Not to mention the fact that you had to roll them up after every use. From the looks of these wraps, Colleen must feel the same way.

"What width is your saddle?" Colleen had stopped in front of the saddle wall.

"A medium wide, it's a County Connection."

"Too narrow for Gold Herr, go ahead and use mine when you ride him, but you should be okay for the rest of the horses." She pulled an old brown Passier dressage saddle covered with a light pink towel from a peg. The girth lay across the towel. "Grab his bridle and a pad."

I found his bridle and grabbed a pad from the top of the pile, following her out a side door to the grooming stall. She set the saddle on another rack and handed me a halter. "Go ahead and tack him up. We use boots on all four legs. I need to take care of something in my office and I'll meet you in the arena."

Depositing the plain snaffle bridle and pad, I headed down the aisle to get Gold Herr. The tall gelding was a perfect gentleman with impeccable barn manners. I had him groomed and tacked up in no time at all. I slipped on my helmet and gloves. Heading past the office, Colleen hollered through the door to let me know she was right behind us. We headed down the dirt path towards the arena.

Colleen came in behind us, a cold Coke can in her hand, and climbed aboard her stool at the edge of the arena. "Go ahead and get on. I want you to walk him around the whole arena just giving him time to stretch over his back."

Picking up the reins I headed towards the edge of the arena. As we walked, I asked him to stretch his head forward and downward. A horse that is used to stretching is much like a person who stretches on a regular basis. They are supple, limber, and tend to injure themselves less. And so it was with Gold Herr. His walk around the arena was ground covering and smooth. When asked to stretch, he easily snaked his nose down to the floor of the arena and I could feel his back muscles lift the saddle beneath me. After one circuit of the arena, Colleen instructed us to change direction and this time to get more out of his walk.

As we changed direction I began asking him to use his hind legs more and to reach up underneath me with each stride. Apparently he had another gear, because his new walk was just as ground covering and smooth, but this time I felt him use his hind end more with each stride, until I felt as though I could ask for a medium trot at any moment and he would bound up into it, springing off his legs. I was learning quickly that Gold Herr responded to the subtlest of aids. Rather than physically asking for an aid, it was almost as it if I could think it and he knew what I wanted. No doubt he had been trained from the start with lighter aids than I was used to giving. Frowning, I concentrated on trying to lighten my aids.

As the lesson progressed, Colleen had me move Gold Herr in and out of medium trot and lengthen trot, each time asking for more energy and step from behind until I felt a lightness I had never experienced before. She had me work on shoulder in and haunches in, as well as leg yields. I had the feeling she was putting me through my paces and assessing my riding.

Gold Herr felt like butter beneath me. He was moldable, pliable, giving and soft all at once. When Colleen instructed us to canter, I felt as though I was sitting on a fully fueled rocket, which was set to launch at any moment. The power beneath my seat was mind blowing, and yet, the huge gelding remained soft in the bridle. As we cantered around the arena, Colleen asked me to shorten his stride and ask him for even more from behind. Not quite believing it possible, I gave a light half halt with my ring finger, asked for more from behind with my inside leg, and suddenly we were suspended in mid stride. Michael Jordan didn't even have hang time like this!

We worked through counter canter and flying lead changes before Colleen called us over. Getting up from her stool she entered the arena. "Walk him around me for a minute."

I slipped Gold Herr the reins and walked him on the buckle in a twenty-meter circle around her. She stood thinking for a moment, her eyes following us as we circled. Finally she spoke. "You have pretty good basics, a stable upper body, your hands are soft and quiet, and I think you have a good sense of 'feel'. Your seat and legs, however, need work. We need to lengthen your leg and plug your seat into your horse better. Your lower leg will stabilize and improve when we fix your seat. I hope you are up for some work without stirrups?"

I nodded, knowing she was right about my lower leg. Personally, I thought I had a good seat, but I nodded again as she spoke.

"How often can you ride?"

I pushed the end of the reins up through the leather keeper and back down with my thumb, thinking. "I am taking some online courses so other than picking up and dropping my little sister off at her school, I am pretty much free." *Actually, I have no life to speak of.* Gold Herr was striding out beneath me. Reluctantly I thought of my finances. I did have some money saved, but without a job I was loath to spend it. I liked having a cushion of cash for emergencies. I hadn't planned on staying in Panama any longer than necessary. I would do my best for Dad and Haley, but I knew that I would have to move on with my life eventually. I shivered involuntarily, apprehension running up my spine. "I guess it would depend on how much you charge for lessons." I shrugged, jamming the leather back down with my thumb.

"We can work it out, I could use some help with Stitch. Are you any good with young horses?"

"I used to help my trainer out with off the track thoroughbreds that came to us through a rehab program back home. I would think it's pretty similar."

"Alright, let's plan on having you ride four to five days a week for now." Colleen peered up at me. "That's enough for today let's plan on the same time tomorrow. Since you don't have a horse of your own, I'd rather you get started on Gold Herr, and if you are going to ride with me I would like to work with you several times a week in the beginning. I am going to change some of your habits and your position."

"K." I guided Gold Herr towards the edge of the arena and dismounted.

**

The lessons with Colleen were mind blowing. I could hold my own as a jumper and my dressage scores always placed me somewhere in the middle of the field of competition, but her classical approach and attention to detail were something totally new for me. Each little step along the way, each movement had to be done correctly or we did not move on to the next thing. I began to live on a twenty-meter circle.

Some children play with colorful wooden blocks that fall down at the slightest touch. Colleen built with Lincoln Logs. Each step in my training had a definite beginning and an end and it wasn't until we moved to the next step that I could clearly see how the foundation and the pieces locked into place. Once she built on a concept, it became clear just how it fit into this puzzle that was dressage. She was far more methodical than any dressage trainer I had ever encountered.

The work in the beginning was painstakingly slow. I was used to the agility and speed that came with eventing, and was now faced with what seemed like remedial riding. Each lesson involved quite a bit of time in the saddle, however I also learned about the musculature of a horse and how to develop it slowly and correctly. I thought I knew a lot, but she was able to open my eyes to new information. With Colleen's instruction I was able to collect Gold Herr and harness the energy of his hind end engine in ways that I had never imagined, much less experienced.

Mentally exhausted, I led Gold Herr back to the barn after our lesson. Today we had worked on maintaining straightness while executing a flying lead change. Gold Herr was such a finesse ride, that the slightest tweaking of my seat bones or shift in my leg would signal him to move beneath me, causing the flying lead change to be abrupt and a bit chaotic. Of course Gold Herr knew how to execute a perfect lead change, but he was making me learn how to ask nicely. When I managed to keep him straight and stay light in the saddle he would comply, no doubt with a smug look on his face. After discussing our lesson, Colleen suggested some exercises to improve the core muscles of my abdomen so I could use my body more effectively. In a hurry to keep an appointment in the city, she had bolted out of the arena, through the barn, and headed for her car.

After un-tacking Gold Herr, hosing him off in the wash rack, and putting him in his pasture for a few hours of down time, I trudged back to the barn. Every muscle in my body ached lately. Lost in my own thoughts and reviewing my lesson in my head I headed for the Land Cruiser. I had a few hours to myself before I needed to pick up Haley.

Half way down the gravel road, classic rock music blaring from the radio, I realized that my sunglasses were back at the barn, most likely sitting in the tack room where I had left them. No wonder I was squinting. Cautiously turning around on the narrow road I headed back to retrieve them. I made my way around the side road that led around the property to the backside of the barn near the pastures. Leaving the engine running and the door open, I headed back in.

Reaching the tack room door, I noticed the door leading from the barn aisle was shut. That was odd, I thought. Maria's car was still outside, and the door was rarely closed during the day. Shrugging it off, I reached for the handle and started to open the door. The unmistakably earnest and lustful sounds of two people having raucous sex came from the other side of the door and I stopped dead in my tracks, flushing five shades of red.

Embarrassed, slowly I allowed the door handle to turn until it clicked softly back into place. Backing up, I quietly exited the barn, leaving my sunglasses behind. Stepping clear of the cool shade behind the barn, I headed across the grass toward the Land Cruiser.

"Hey there, you must be the new girl." The man I had seen in the arena with Colleen the first day came striding cat-like up to me with his hand outstretched. He looked like he had stepped out of the pages of GQ magazine or, a Polo ad. His dark hair was slightly tousled and he exuded a manly charm.

Still flustered from the unexpected tack room incident, it took me a moment to grasp his name from the recesses of my brain. "AJ, right?" I shook his hand. "Lauren."

"Yes, welcome to our little piece of paradise." His voice held just a faint hint of a Spanish accent. "I am sorry I haven't had the chance to meet you before now, but I have been busy with work." There was a smile on his face when he mentioned his work.

"Oh, that's okay. What is it that you do?" Not sure if AJ was headed towards the barn or not, I decided that small talk couldn't hurt. Especially if whoever it was in the barn wasn't quite done. I felt the tips of my ears turn pink at the thought.

"I broker ships. That means I buy them from one customer, and resell them to another customer quickly. Or at least that is the idea," he paused. "It doesn't always work out quite so smoothly, but it is a challenge every day." His blue eyes sparkled.

I could see why Colleen was drawn to him. He exuded a nice mixture of confidence and charm, not to mention, he was super model gorgeous. His attention drifted past me for a moment and he lifted his hand to wave. Coming towards us from the barn was a young man. I had seen him from a distance several times before. It was Pablito. AJ said something to Pablito in Spanish and he headed our way, but not before glancing nervously back towards the barn. Finding myself tongue-tied, I was glad when AJ kept talking, this time in English.

"Lauren, have you met my little brother Pablito?" AJ slapped the young man on the shoulders proudly. He looked to be around seventeen years old, a bit young for Maria I thought. I found myself wondering if AJ knew about them. Then I remembered Colleen's comments the day I first came to the barn. No, I thought, this wasn't a good thing at all.

Pablito had AJ's blue eyes and slightly darker skin, which only served to make his eyes stand out even more. Like AJ he was tall and lithe. He wore an old T-shirt with the sleeves cut off and a pair of denim shorts. I knew that he worked around the barn doing odd jobs and by the look of his upper arms they were the kind of jobs that required strength.

We exchanged pleasantries briefly before I offered up an excuse and headed back to the Land Cruiser. I most certainly didn't want Maria to know that I had any inkling of her relationship with Pablito. Something told me it would be best to keep her anger focused elsewhere.

**

"You are dropping him in the transition. He stayed up the first time because he knows his job. That time you dropped him. Do it again."

I picked up medium trot again, collected Gold Herr with a balance of half halts and leg. He moved into collected trot, then, I asked for passage. His back swung under me rhythmically. His tempo remained constant—one, two, one, two. After a few strides, I exhaled and let my body ask him for a transition back to collected trot, driving him forward with my seat and legs while keeping his front end elevated. I was learning to lighten my aids, thanks to his help. His stride lengthened and he moved out of passage.

"Better, but do it one more time," Colleen said approvingly. "This is so important. I need you to learn how light and responsive upper level dressage is meant to and needs to be so you can strive for it and hopefully recreate it on other horses."

Nodding, I again moved him through each transition in a circle around her. This time, I nailed it.

"Bring him back to walk and let him stretch and relax."

After bringing Gold Herr down to a walk I exhaled and allowed myself to relax. As we circled past the end of the arena I felt a pair of eyes following me. Turning in the saddle I saw Hamish talking to a man I had never seen before, and since neither of them appeared to be gazing my way, I shrugged it off, returning my focus to the swing of Gold Herr as he moved beneath me. We circled the arena.

"Okay, pick him back up," Colleen directed from where she sat on her stool.

Gathering my reins I glanced up into the eyes of the same man. He met my gaze with a bold, but flattering intensity. Our eyes locked and held. In those few moments, the world around me slowed as we held each other's gaze, unmoving. Even Gold Herr had come to a stop beneath me. Then, as if in challenge, one sandy-colored eyebrow shot up. Or was it more of a question? I wasn't at all sure. It was only then that I noticed his startling green eyes and I nearly gasped. Feeling my face flush in embarrassment, I moved Gold Herr off my leg. I could feel his eyes as they studied me. Feeling my heartbeat quicken, I gripped the reins tighter in my hands as I sought something to hold on to. *This is* silly, I thought as my palms began to sweat in my gloves.

As we completed a lazy circle at the walk, I tried to see him better in my peripheral vision. Oh God, he was gorgeous. Not in the pretty sense, but in the rustic manly man sort of way, the kind of rugged man that can start a fire with sticks and his good looks. *Crap! He is staring at me.* Suddenly I felt open and vulnerable as his eyes found mine again. He was staring back at me, his face impassive. I made a concerted effort to gather my wits and looked away. But not before I had the chance to get a better look beyond those eyes. He was tall, medium build, and yes, very rugged looking. *That's it tall, medium and rugged?* But that was what my eyes saw, my body, well that was another matter all together. I found myself feeling flustered by this strange man. I wasn't at all pleased that his presence was invading my lesson and I tried to focus, by putting Gold Herr back together at the walk.

"Okay, let's move along. I need to see a walk not an amble," Colleen added.

Self consciously, I glanced down at Gold Herr, trying in vain to focus. When I looked up he had turned and was walking quickly away with Hamish. The T-shirt he wore hinted at but didn't quite reveal broad, muscular shoulders. The two men spoke heatedly to one another as they walked away from the arena wall toward the house, and I turned my focus back to Colleen's voice.

As usual, my lesson with Colleen left me exhausted. It wasn't until I was hosing Gold Herr off that I had the opportunity to think of him again. He'd left me feeling unnerved, like he was analyzing me with those green eyes, especially since I didn't even know him. He obviously knew Hamish though and by the looks of it they knew each other well. Trying again to push him out of my mind and concentrate on the task at hand, I felt my palms begin to sweat, forcing me to tighten my grip on the water hose.

Horses are funny creatures and many of them have certain idiosyncrasies. Gold Herr, while he would stand in the cross ties facing the barn aisle to be saddled; he wanted no part of being hosed off that way. I had no idea whether his hang up had to do with facing the outer window of the wash stall or having his haunches exposed to the window. Either way, a set of cross ties had been hung at the rear of the stall for His Lordship and Colleen had been insistent that he face outward. It was a chore to not spray any passersby in the barn aisle with water. Lost in thought, I bent down to aim the hose up under Gold Herr's inside hind legs.

"Hey watch it, gringa!" Maria growled as she stalked past the wash rack.

"Sorry," I retorted, still preoccupied and reached to shut off the water. *Oohh, she was such a bitch.*

SAN BLAS

I could feel the frosty air around me on my skin and as it burned my lungs when I inhaled, cold as ice. My lungs ached with each breath. Smooth, shiny metal was everywhere around me. It ran half way up the walls, draped every cabinet, and supported the bed and light fixtures. Intense bright, white lights hung from above in the shape of fat globes and long, sleek cylinders. The strong acrid smell of antiseptic clung to everything around me.

Voices, muffled voices moved in and out around me, buffeting me like a gentle breeze, words without form, shapeless and soft. Steadily they grew louder, reaching a crescendo. They became more intense, hurried, strained and eventually rose until it peaked. No longer did I find myself buffeted, but rather tossed around like a rag doll. Every fiber of my being wanted to escape, run, but I couldn't. I opened my mouth to scream and nothing came out. Transfixed, I knew I must stay rooted to this spot. I had been trained to stay. Suddenly white lights grew harsh then were gone in an instant. In their place was a red glow. Red was everywhere.

The familiar swoosh of the automatic glass door caught my attention and as I turned to my left, the flight medics rushed into the room. The stretcher rolled between them on silent black wheels. Their orange uniforms blended in with the sea of red all around me. The white and orange of their helmets bobbed nauseatingly up and down in front of me like some twisted carnival ride as they bent over the stretcher, then straightened to reach for something and down again. I wanted to get off this roller coaster. Someone please stop.

I reached down, frantically grabbing at the cold metal lap bar that held me firmly in my seat, but instead my hand found the cold, round rail of the stretcher. NO! NO! My fingers recognized the feel of the rail through my gloves and with a soft "click," instinct took over and I released the lock. It collapsed quietly. My heart hammered in my chest and my palms grew damp with perspiration in the cold room. Aching, my lungs stung with every ragged breath I took.

It wouldn't stop. I could hear it again, the only sound not muffled, it rang clearly in my ears, "male, 29 years old, MVA, car versus tractor trailer on Camp Road.... The voice rang clear and loud for all to hear. NOOOOO!

Staring down at the scissors in my hand, I was horrified. No, stop. I had to stop this. I cried out in anguish but my voice was lost in the chaos around me. The pitch of the background noises rose suddenly, mercilessly drowning out the timbre of the loud clear voice. Finally, it became lost in the cacophony of chaos that surrounded me.

I bolted upright in bed, my hands clenched in the damp sheets. Did I scream? I waited, listening but my heart was pounding hard, reverberating between my ribs and spine so loud I couldn't have heard anything else if I had wanted to. The dark house around me was quiet. Oh God my chest hurt. Falling forward I clutched my knees and curled into a ball, dragging the crumpled sheets with me.

The alarm found me asleep again at 7:15. The rumpled top sheet lay strewn across my body with the majority of the soft, caramel hued, cotton pooled on the floor next to the bed. I shivered and rubbed my cold feet together, searching for warmth. The soft creams and caramels of my room greeted me. No red. Thank God! Taking a deep cleansing breath I pushed the remainder of the sheet over the side and rolled out of bed.

**

The gang had talked me into a few days off from riding. Actually, Colleen had somehow finagled a way for all of us to take a short trip. They picked me up at 7 am with instructions to pack two day's worth of clothes and my bathing suit. Deanne's Mercedes cruised down the narrow road at breakneck speed. Glancing over my shoulder at Rachel I asked again, "Where are we going?"

"To the islands," she replied airily.

"Got it, but do they have a name, something else to go on maybe?"

"Didn't she say 'San' something or other?" Deanne chimed in. "Or was it 'Los' some thing or other? Down here everything starts with one of those. It's a Spanish thing," she said absently.

"Just how the two of you manage to function in a foreign country without an international incident is beyond me," Elaine quipped. "Okay, one more time. The San Blas Islands are an archipelago located off the Caribbean coast. They are mainly inhabited by a native tribe of the same name and are only accessible by boat or air. No causeways. They sell coconuts, lots of them. In fact they were considered a currency until recently. Now they have shifted to tourism. Also, the Smithsonian museum has an island base here that they use for archeological research in the area."

Encyclopedic Elaine prattled on for a few minutes reciting area history, folklore, and fauna although we had all tuned her out. It was nice to have her local knowledge, but at times I just wanted to be a dumb tourist and mindlessly soak up the gorgeous tropical views that were everywhere here in Panama.

The car slowed as we approached a four-way stop sign. Out of the corner of my eye I thought I saw what appeared to be the head of a pony extended over the cab of a rather rickety truck as it rolled to a stop at the intersection. At first, too stunned to speak, I pointed disbelievingly at the truck as it crossed in front of us and continued on down the road. "What in the heck is that?" The original red paint of the truck had faded to an odd shade of pink, at least where the panels from the original truck remained. The hood was white, the driver's door a faded blue, and the requisite statue of the Virgin Mary sat on the dashboard for all to see. Wooden rails had been added to the sides and along the tailgate of the truck. In the bed, quietly standing tied with a rope around its neck to one of the side rails was a thin, grulla pony. "Now I have seen it all!"

Giggling, Deanne piped up, "That was pretty much my response, too, when I first saw the third world version of a horse trailer. But, you do have to give them points for creativity even if we find it abhorrent." Deanne made a right hand turn. "Horse trailers are simply not practical for ranchers down here. They are too poor and the local ponies fit nicely in the trucks."

"But, how in the world do they get them in there?" I asked incredulously.

"You know, I am not sure. I never gave it much thought," Deanne answered, continuing down the road. Shaking my head, I leaned back into my seat.

A few minutes later, the Mercedes slid up to the side of a large green and white airplane hanger. The tiny airport sat just off the main road. There appeared to be only a single runway, a control tower, and a few metal hangers. We climbed out of the car, grabbed our bags from the trunk, and headed around to the entrance. Huge metal doors had been rolled back to expose a cavernous interior which was brightly lit. Florescent metal lamps hung in neat rows from the exposed trusses of the roof. In the center sat a sleek white and grey plane with its ladder door open on the side. From the smooth, rounded nose to the angular tail it appeared to be in pristine condition. Well, at least to an untrained eye like mine, and if I was going to get on this plane I guess I felt better that it looked airworthy.

The shiny metal of the single propeller reflected the rays of the sun as it rose behind me. I blinked hard and took a step closer to avoid the glare. Looking again I saw several small square doors opened along the underbelly of the plane, between the wheels and below the wings. The long, narrow storage compartment arose from just beneath the cockpit, and ran all the way back to the just beneath the last window where it gently tapered upwards to meet the fuselage. Seven windows, including what I assumed to be the cockpit, ran the length of the plane. All in all, it resembled a fat, squat bird.

Grabbing my arm, Deanne urged me forward. "Come on, it's not that bad."

Swallowing hard I bent to grab the bag I had dropped at my feet and followed her. Planes I could handle, big planes. Small planes, not so much. However irrational it may seem to others, to me, with regard to planes, size definitely mattered. Little dinky planes made me nervous. Elaine was handily tossing bags into the storage compartment and I passed her my burgundy duffle bag.

She quickly stowed it along with the rest, and the small pile of bags at her feet disappeared into the compartment. With a loud *click* she shut each door of the compartment and started up the steps to the plane.

Glancing up, I could see AJ and Colleen in the cockpit. AJ waved us up with one hand and turned back to what he was doing. *Here we go.* I followed Deanne up the steps with Elaine close behind.

The interior of the plane was plush. A smoke grey carpet graced the floor of the cabin. The bucket seats were a lovely cobalt blue with a light periwinkle blue floral pattern running down the middle of each seat cushion. There were four chairs arranged in two pairs, each facing a small cocktail size table. Deanne had settled in the one on the right side of the plane, directly behind the cockpit. Elaine was just across from her and closest to the door. I settled in next to Elaine, and left the open chair for Hamish. I received an appreciative smile from Deanne as she recognized my effort to seat them together.

"Hey guys," Colleen called back. She was leaning over the arm of her chair and had slipped her headset down around her neck. "We're just waiting for Hamish and then we'll get going. He is usually at least ten minutes late for everything." Grinning, she turned back around, reaching absently for her headset with one hand while checking her watch.

"The flight itself is only about an hour and a half long and there isn't much to see other than the top of the jungle canopy or the hills that have been cleared for cattle and farm land. When we reach the coast though, the clarity of the water below us will just blow you away, or at least it did me. Anyway, it's the landing that is the most fun. The runway is on the largest island, but that isn't saying much, because the runway starts and ends at the water's edge. I mean really, we come in so low that you think we are landing on water. Then he touches down and has to slam on the brakes before running off the end and into the water again. On the first trip, I could see the end of the runway and then the rocks and water below my window when AJ turned the plane around to head back down the runway."

"He's here," interrupted AJ from up front. Elaine stopped talking to peer out her window.

Turning to glance out my window I saw Hamish talking to someone at the entrance to the hanger. "Hey, that's the guy from the barn the other day. Who is he?" I kept my eyes glued to the window. Now that I had the chance to look at him without being noticed, I wanted to study him closer. They stood facing one another talking intently, much as I had seen them before. He was a tad bit shorter than Hamish, but considering all six feet of Hamish's height, he was still tall. He had sandy colored hair with slight hints of red throughout. I hadn't noticed the hints of red before. As I watched, he reached up and ran a hand across his chin. Solidly built, but not thick, he was clad in a pair of denim shorts and a white T-shirt that showed off his well-muscled arms and broad shoulders. I clearly recalled the look of those shoulders as he and Hamish had walked away from the arena. His legs were tan, well muscled and he sported a pair of brown leather flip-flops. Everything about his appearance and demeanor just screamed "outdoors." If AJ was Mr. GQ, this guy was Mr. Rugged and I couldn't take my eyes off of him.

Deanne leaned across the table next to me and bent to see out of my window. "Well I'll be darned. Hey, Lainey, have you ever seen Craig twice in one month before? That boy never comes into town. Wonder what's going on."

Peering out of her window, Elaine watched the two men talking, "Whatever it is, I'm sure it's big. He never leaves the resort. What a shame too, he's just plain hot."

As they talked, Hamish glanced towards the plane and Craig's eyes followed him. It was really hard not to notice the intensity of those green eyes again. His tan face looked rough, unlike last time, as if he hadn't shaved in a day or so. I watched mesmerized as he ran his hand over the stubble on his chin again, and I found myself wanting to touch his strong face. Flexing my fingers in my lap, I felt a warm flush wash through my body. *This is insane, I thought.* He looked to be contemplating something, or maybe it was worry that crossed his face, either way, his mood had shifted. Nodding his head in curt acknowledgement, he turned his focus back to Hamish, clapping him on the shoulder.

He stood there, unmoving, as he watched Hamish gather his bag and head for the plane. Turning on his heel, Craig made his way towards the hanger entrance. Stopping suddenly he turned back towards the plane and his eyes met mine through the Plexiglas window as if he had known all along that I was watching him. A knowing smile spread across his strong rugged features, and then he winked at me.

Crap!

The warm flush of embarrassment at being caught staring raced up my neck, across my face and to the tips of my ears. Swiftly, I turned away and pressed my back into my seat. Looking up, I found both girls staring at me. Deanne's bright pink lips hung agape. "He keeps doing that," I said defensively, jerking my head in the direction of the window.

"Doing what?" Elaine asked, clearly confused.

Just then, Hamish climbed onto the plane and pulled up the ladder door. Deanne quickly scooted back to her chair. As Hamish passed her in the aisle, she put on her brightest, most angelic smile for him, lowered her eyelashes coquettishly and I was mercilessly forgotten for the moment.

"Hmph!" Elaine snorted and rolled her eyes.

As we buckled up for take off I snuck another peak out of my window to see if Craig had already left. He was gone and I felt the plane begin to roll beneath me.

I had to admit the flight was really very pleasant. AJ had guided the plane out of the hanger and down the runway to a smooth and flawless take off. We climbed slowly into a powder blue sky. The interior of the plane quickly fell silent as everyone became glued to a window. The lush tropical foliage of the jungle canopy rolled out below us like a rich, green undulating carpet with scarcely a break.

Thirty minutes or so into the flight the landscape changed to mostly grassland full of the grey and white humpbacked shapes of Brahma cattle. Eventually the azure blue and aquamarine waters of the Caribbean came into view, edged by a sparkling white sand beach. The coast fell behind us and before long the timbre of the engine changed as AJ slowed the plane and brought us in for a landing. From my view there was only ocean and a few small islands visible. Elaine wasn't kidding; it felt as though we were landing directly on top of the water.

Noticing the apprehension on my face, Hamish reached across the aisle and tapped me on the shoulder. "Don't worry, Lauren, there really is an island in front of us. It is just so narrow that you can't see it from where we sit," he said while looking past me at the ocean below.

Just then the nose camp up, the wheels hit the tarmac, and a palm tree popped into view. After touch down the plane stopped quickly, then turned and headed back up the runway. Halfway up the runway, and just across from a small control tower, AJ turned the plane off the runway and onto a small patch of gravel. Pulling up next to a small, single engine plane, he parked and went through his post flight checklist while we set to work unpacking our stuff. Balancing our bags, several coolers, and some snorkeling gear, we trundled over to a small dock and climbed into a small white and blue sport fishing boat for the trip to the hotel.

The Isla Hotel was a very short boat trip from the airport island. Actually, according to Colleen, it was the only hotel in the whole archipelago. Painted bright red and white it sat on the north end of the main island. Constructed of two stories and built so it extended partially out over the water, the hotel had a rustic charming third-world quality. Bamboo screens graced the windows and thatched palms covered the roof. As we made our way up the stairs at one end of the building to our rooms, we passed a communal balcony with a small grill. Several colorful woven hammocks hung from wooden support beams along the edge of the porch.

Deanne and I were sharing one room. AJ and Colleen had a suite, if you could call it that, at the far end of the building. Hamish had his own room, and since Rachel was arriving later tonight by boat, Elaine would stay with her. Our room was sparsely furnished with two double beds, a table, only one chair, and a bathroom with a walk in shower. Fresh air flowed through the open windows of the room as we entered. A small back porch overlooked the water below. The door to our room was unlocked. Reading the doubt on my face, Deanne informed me that nobody locks anything on the island because crime is non-existent due to strict tribal laws. I had images of tattoo faced tribal chiefs cutting off the hands of tourists who broke their laws and smiled to myself, enjoying the comical aspects of my thought patterns, thanks to the indelible images from movies like Pirates of the Caribbean and Joe VS the Volcano. I couldn't help but chuckle at the hilarity of it all.

We had all agreed to meet downstairs, so after dropping our bags in the rooms, we changed into our swimsuits, grabbed a few towels, and then Elaine, Deanne, and I headed back downstairs. A small outdoor dining area with a thatched roof sat just to one side of the hotel. Next to the dining area was a manmade tidal pool. Slipping off our flip-flops we eased down onto the edge and dipped our feet into the warm water. Rectangular in shape, the tidal pool had been constructed of a mixture of concrete and stone, and was stocked full of tropical fish. Opposite us, a section of the wall had been designed to be about a foot and a half lower than the surrounding walls, allowing fresh seawater to wash into the pool. It was really quite genius. Barnacles, burgundy, brown and orange sea fans, sea urchins, and a myriad of other reef dwellers clung to an artificial reef submerged in the center. Brightly colored tropical fish in every color imaginable flitted in and out of the rocks. While we watched, the familiar orange and white stripes of a clown fish darted across the barnacled rocks. Smiling to myself, I made a mental note to tell Haley that I had found Nemo.

Once Hamish, AJ, and Colleen arrived we were planning to spend the day snorkeling, swimming, and just enjoying the tropical sun on a nearby private island. Grabbing our gear, we headed down to a small beach near the hotel. The men behind brought up the rear carrying a cooler slung between them. The worn, wooden shapes of dug out canoes and battered old fishing boats with their faded paint were pulled up haphazardly on the white sand. A short distance down the beach, a group of local men with dark cocoa colored skin weathered by life spent under the sun sat in the shade of a palm tree mending their nets and talking. An ancient battery powered radio sat precariously on a rock nearby, transmitting a mixture of Spanish rhythms and static.

Our island transportation would be one of the dug out canoes. An old man with the face of a raisin smiled cheerily in greeting as he met us down by the water's edge. Flashing all six of his teeth when he talked, he bartered with AJ over the price of our transportation. Finally, he motioned two of us into his cut out boat. The rear of the well-worn wooden boat bobbed up and down gently with each oncoming wave. AJ, ever the gentleman, paid our fare and said he and Hamish would follow in the last boat. Glancing dubiously around at the larger, sturdier appearing boats, I hesitated. Colleen settled herself into the rear most seat and waved me in. As I climbed in behind her, careful not to rock the small dugout, dirty water from the bottom sloshed over my toes. I had worn flip-flops since we were headed for the beach, but right now, I wasn't so sure I had made the right choice. I wiggled my brightly painted toenails in the warm grimy water. Grimacing, I settled onto the remnants of a small metal chair. Lacking a back, it sat perched in the front third of the boat. What remained of a once shiny metal chair was now coated with thick, orange rust.

The raisin faced man motioned for us to hold on as he pushed the boat free of the sandy beach. As he clamored into the rear of the boat, Colleen and I leaned in the opposite direction to prevent the boat from tipping. He expertly started the engine and with a large puff of grey and white smoke, guided his taxi out into deeper water. I followed Colleen's gaze as we pushed through the onshore waves, back towards the shore to see the rest of the crew climbing into similar boats. Okay, I thought, maybe the dinky plane wasn't so bad.

The hot sun beat down on the water. The salt spray splashing off the bow felt cool on my face and arms. We skirted around several small islands that were occupied by the local Kuna Indians. As we passed each island that was inhabited, the scantily clad Kuna children would rush to the shore to wave. On one island, a skinny dog tried to chase the boats, running alongside us until he ran out of sand and the boat pulled away in the water. Dipping my hand into the crystal clear water to cool off, I was astonished to see islands of coral reefs appearing beneath the water at random intervals. The water beneath the boat was a most lovely shade of aquamarine, and I could see the ripples in the sand below us. We rode on for about ten minutes before the bow of the boat slid onto the white sand shore of a small island. As our taxi driver pushed back from the beach, Elaine and Deanne came ashore, the guys followed right behind them.

About three hundred yards long and maybe one hundred yards wide, our little slice of uninhabited paradise had a stand of coconut trees at one end. Rimming the island was a crystalline sand beach, which sparkled in the sun and made me glad I had thought to bring my sunglasses. Tall spikes of sparsely growing green grass formed a spine down the center crest of the island. The guys dragged the red cooler up the beach and set it in the sand beneath a coconut tree while Elaine unfurled a few beach towels onto the sand.

"Okay, who would like a drink? Let's see, we have beer, water….um, beer, Gatorade, and did I say water?" AJ cracked open the cooler and dug for a cold beer.

"What do you think?" Deanne quipped. She wore one of her winning smiles on her face and had a well-manicured hand placed on her slim hip. She wore a pair of faded denim cut off shorts and a pink bikini top.

Smiling, AJ passed out cold beer to several waiting hands. Colleen stuck an ice-cold beer into my outstretched hand. Expertly twisting the top I took a long swig. The ice-cold liquid left a trail down my dry throat. The words on the green bottle of beer were in Spanish. *Hmm, pretty good for a local beer.*

Hamish dug through one of the bags we had brought and dumped some mismatched snorkeling gear onto a towel. There wasn't much to choose from. Grabbing a snorkel, mask, and a pair of fins from the pile he slipped off his flip-flops and shirt. "The water is calling me," he exclaimed with a childish grin before heading back towards the blue water at a trot, the muscles of his back rippling across his tall frame. Deanne sprinted after him, stripping down to her hot pink bikini as she followed.

"Yeah, well, the sun is calling me," Elaine dropped down onto a towel face down in her bikini. Reaching behind her with one hand she deftly tugged the strings loose on her top, exposing her back, and closed her eyes. Her bottle of water sat in the sand next to her towel.

Surveying the beach, Colleen jerked her head to the right. "Come on let us see how long it takes to walk around our little slice of paradise."

We walked in silence, cold beer in hand, to the furthest end of the island where Colleen paused to look back. From where we stood, Hamish and Deanne were no longer visible in the water. We watched the scene for a moment, enjoying the beauty of the crystal clear, blue water. The way in which the foamy white surf crashing along the beach blended to aquamarine and flowed out to the darker blue of deeper water reminded me of a watercolor painting. Every possible shade of blue blended to create a breathtaking palate of color. The tops of the green palm trees swayed with the ocean breeze.

I hadn't realized the stress I had been carrying around with me and slowly, with each retreating wave, I began to relax. Although the sun sat overhead, the constant island breezes kept the day pleasant.

Just then a bright spot of hot pink broke the surface as Deanne's butt rose out of the water. I knew Hamish had to be close by. "Funny, for someone who is being chased, he never runs off or allows himself to be caught," I said aloud, not really expecting an answer. "It's like a never ending stalemate."

"Who, Hamish?" Colleen had turned to look down the beach.

"Yeah, what is up with those two? It's almost like they prefer the game rather than the prize. Even then, it is lopsided. I mean, she does all the chasing and he does all the dodging." I paused, taking a sip of my beer. "Although, he doesn't seem to run, just dodges."

"You got that right. They will figure it out one day."

Sinking cross-legged down onto the sand, Colleen slid down next to me. The plaintive cry of seagulls and the waves slapping against the shore filled the air. Closing my eyes behind my sunglasses I tilted my head back and enjoyed the peace around us. The sun was warm and bright and I could feel the heat sink all the way through to my core. "Damn, I forgot my sunscreen," I muttered. *Dang!* I had no doubt I would fry in this tropical sun. *Lucky me.*

"There's something I've been meaning to talk to you about," she said at last. "I plan on taking my students to Florida for the winter circuit. We need to get enough qualifying scores if we are going to have a shot at the Games."

I turned my head abruptly. She had really gotten my attention. "The Games?" I began, "the Olympics?" In my head I was frantically trying to calculate when the next Olympics were going to be held. It didn't matter as Colleen interrupted my math.

Choking on her beer, Colleen gasped for air and bent over her knees as I slapped her hard on the back with the palm of my hand. Straightening she looked at me, her face a bright shade of red. She coughed. "Wow, you like to aim high," she sputtered.

Slightly embarrassed, I turned my focus to peeling off the label from my beer.

"I'm sorry," she went on. "Actually, I am very flattered but no, I was thinking more along the lines of the Pan Am Games. They will be held in Lexington, Kentucky next year and if we qualify I had hopes of fielding a team to represent Panama."

Intent on removing the label I swallowed hard. "That's really awesome. But why go all the way to Florida?"

"Fact is this part of the world has limited opportunities to get the qualifying scores that we'll need. I mean, we aren't exactly located in a hot bed for dressage," she said dryly.

The back label was off and I drained the last sip of lukewarm beer. *Ugh!* Making a face, I turned the bottle around and attacked the other label.

"Besides, it would be much cheaper for us in Wellington since we can stay with Rachel. She has enough stalls for us and there's a small cottage on the property. With her and Troy's help we can really cut down on expenses."

"When will you guys be leaving?" The melancholy had started to creep back, boiling out of the pit of my stomach and spreading outward. Here we go again, I thought. Just when the ground beneath my feet started to level out, and I found myself actually breathing again, fate comes along to shake things up. I was really getting very weary of the hand that fate was dealing me. I had settled into this new life, the rhythm of the barn and made new friends, just in time for things to change. Fate, hell, maybe it was Murphy's Law? "Blame it on the Irish." That's what Uncle Joe always said, but then again he was Irish. Well, that and he had an unusual sense of humor. Uncle Joe and Mom were only second generation Irish born in America. Personally, I'd like to choke Mr. Murphy. Distracted for a moment, I turned my attention back to Colleen.

"Well, not for two more months, maybe three. The season really starts in Wellington around the end of October. We have to arrange air travel for the horses. I will need to figure out which shows have the qualifying classes as well." Swiveling her head in my direction she added, "And we need to find you a horse—and fast." I stared wide-eyed at her, mouth agape.

"Catching flies? Come on, it's not impossible. The Olympics, now that is impossible, this is improbable maybe, but I think we have a real shot. Keep in mind that the Pan American Games include riders from this side of the world. Our toughest competitors will be the American and Canadian teams. There will be no powerhouse German, British, or Dutch teams to contend with. Everyone else on this side of the world is usually a wash." Pausing to think she added, "Team wise that is, some countries can field some really good individuals for the games." She paused, tapping her finger on her chin. "Mostly those who already live in the States, but claim their native countries for competitions."

"You say that like it's a cake walk! Do you really think we have a chance? I don't even have a horse. I haven't even ridden dressage for very long." A long list of excuses ran like a ticker tape through my head, winding in and out with no clear logical explanation or direction.

"Never say never, Lauren, I learned that early on. Besides, we won't know until we find you a horse. And yes, you have ridden dressage and you've been doing it for years. I just have to clean you up a bit and get visions of coffins and tables out of your head. Well, that and work on fixing your seat. You have all the elements of a good rider and I think with a dynamite horse you can do it, especially since you have a real sense of feel. That is hard to come by. Some riders are born with it, some learn it painstakingly over time, and still others never get it." She sighed.

"So, here's the deal, we need to find you a horse, like yesterday, train like hell and then get our butts to Wellington. Most of the riders that represent the smaller countries actually already live and work in the States so they have an advantage over us. Listen, you're a good enough rider. If we find you a horse are you in?" Her cornflower blue eyes met mine in an obvious challenge.

"You do know you guys are crazy, right?"

"Certifiable," she replied grinning. "Come on, let's go." She stood up, brushing the fine sand from her shorts, "I want to get in some snorkeling while we're here."

We made our way around what was left of the island, and then joined the others for ice cold drinks and sandwiches. The remainder of the afternoon was pure bliss. We snorkeled, swam, and lazed away on the sand. The sun kept time overhead, but none of us really paid her any attention. The fine, white sand of our little beach, gently sloped into the water and a small coral reef sat just twenty yards from shore. I had the urge to pinch myself more than once, and thought Calli would kill me if I didn't call her tonight and email pictures. I pulled my camera out of the bag I had brought and started snapping away. Studying the images on the back screen, I frowned. The camera just didn't do this place justice. On a whim, I held up my camera again and began filming the scene around us. I smiled, proud of myself. That way I could send it to Calli and she could really experience this beautiful place.

I scanned from left to right, filming a large panoramic circle around where we sat. As I turned my back to everyone on the beach in order to film behind us I noticed a man staring at me from behind a pair of binoculars. His dark olive skin and short black hair, stood out against the white collared shirt and trim pants he wore. Clicking the button on top, I adjusted the zoom to get a closer view. A bit overdressed for boating, I thought. He stood on the bow of a long, sleek cigarette style boat. *Okay, so you obviously have money with a boat like that.*

On a whim, I waved at him. Rooted in place, he simply stared at me from behind his dark shades. Either he was ignoring me, or wasn't watching me at all. Giving up, I continued filming until I had come full circle. After I had clicked the camera off and slipped it back into my bag, I turned to see if the man was still there. Without the zoom on the camera, he was harder to see. No longer on the bow, he was behind the wheel of the boat. Within moments, he put the boat in gear and pulled away from the island. He headed out to deeper water, the noise of the engine lost in the breeze.

Later that afternoon we made the trek back to the main island by water taxi, showered, changed, and met downstairs yet again, this time for dinner. The cool island breeze settled around us as night fell. A fingernail moon started its journey across the star studded sky above us while we ate. The sheer number of stars visible when away from civilization never ceased to amaze me. Famished, I dug in, devouring with gusto every bit of fresh seafood placed in front of me. Halfway through our meal, Rachel arrived full of news about her trip. The conversation around the table was light hearted and Hamish's antics kept us laughing throughout dinner with his impersonations of Bill Clinton, Arnold Schwarzenegger, and Billy Crystal. He even had a George Morris that was spot on. We all agreed that he should try stand-up comedy as a back up career. Although, I had to admit I really didn't know what Hamish did when he wasn't riding. Making a mental note, I decided to find out.

With our bellies full, we once again settled on the edge of the tidal pool, cold drinks in hand. Ten pairs of feet dipped in the cool water. After dinner, AJ begged off with an excuse about work and slipped away to handle a problem with one of his ships.

"So Rachel, what's new in Welly World?" Colleen inquired, a cosmopolitan balanced on her knee.

"Right now it's nice and quiet. I haven't decided if I prefer the calm summers or the crazy winters and all the drama they bring. But, I must say, I am pleased that we bought a place and don't have to make the annual trek from Virginia anymore."

Wellington, located on the east coast of south Florida had become a horsey playground for the uber rich and famous. During the winter months, the town swelled with an influx of northern-based equestrians fleeing the cold, dreary winter of their home states, exchanging it instead for the balmy breezes, bronze tans, and year round riding of Florida. Well, the show circuit and the gossip were big draws as well. Although Wellington wasn't exactly well known in eventing circles, most riders knew of it. It was to Wellington that Colleen had suggested we go this coming fall. Our conversation today seemed like a strange dream, something that happened to other people, not me. Lost in thought, Colleen nudged me with her elbow.

"So, what's your story, Lauren? This is the first time we've had away from riding and I realized I don't know much about you at all."

"I, for one, think mystery is very alluring; foreign country, a new life where nobody knows you." Rachel, obviously on her way to getting drunk was slurring her words. She was sunburned from her boat trip today, and the wrinkles at the corner of her eyes formed little white lines. She must have been squinting her eyes while in the sun today.

"Good God, Rach, alluring? She is not a sex kitten!" Elaine laughed so hard she nearly fell into the tidal pool. Thank goodness Hamish thrust his elbow out in time to keep her upright.

"Okay, mysterious. Does that work for you?" she shot back with a grin.

"Don't mind them, Lauren," Colleen added between chuckles, "they are working on becoming plastered. Ten bucks says that Elaine goes looking for a karaoke bar before the night is through."

"Here?" My mouth dropped open. I thought of the island we were on and threw Colleen a questioning look.

"Give her time; she won't know where 'here' is before long. But seriously, how did you end up in Panama?"

"My dad got a job, and here we are." I replied, peering at my feet under the water in the moonlight. *Keep it light, Todd.* My red toes glared up at me. Calli had mailed me several bright shades of nail polish as a joke. She knew I was riding again and probably thought my feet looked like hell. Funny thing was, I was really enjoying wearing sandals and flip-flops every chance I got. After a moment of silence I looked around to find everyone looking at me. "What?" I was beginning to feel the effects of the alcohol I was drinking.

"Hmm, I'm not buying it," Deanne said, shaking her head dubiously while balancing another full drink that the bartender handed her.

Colleen jumped in, "Yeah, me either. I'd believe the sex kitten thing before I fell for that lame explanation. We're not that drunk on Panamanian rum. Try again, Sista."

"You guys are a tough crowd. How can I possibly stay mysterious with the likes of you?" I tried my best to look offended. Instead they just waited for me to continue. Failing, I gave in. "My mom died last summer, June actually. My dad needed help with Haley so when he moved, I came along." I shrugged my shoulders then took a long sip of my rum and coke. *That should hold them. After all, it was the truth, just not the whole truth.* I blinked innocently up at them, struggling to keep my face blank. It would have to do for now. I wasn't drunk enough to talk about Jake to anyone. I bit my lower lip, testing to see if it was numb yet. *Close.*

Elaine spoke first, turning serious. "Oh, I am so sorry, Lauren. None of us are thinking straight. We sure didn't mean to upset you. I am so sorry about your mom."

The group had grown quiet. "Thanks Elaine. It still hurts." I had altered the mood of the party without meaning to. This was just what I had been trying to avoid. I didn't want everyone's sympathy. I didn't want them to look at me differently because each time they did it just reminded me of everything I was trying to move on from. *Crap!* I took another sip, glancing down to avoid their gazes as I did.

"So, you just up and quit your job and moved here?" Deanne pressed. "What did you do back home?"

With a sigh, I gave in. I was going to kill Deanne when I got the chance. "I was a trauma nurse." A big black and white angelfish with beady eyes was inspecting the bright polish on my toes, tilting its body at an angle to get a better look at them. I slowly wiggled my toes and the angelfish moved in closer. Changing my mind, I tucked my feet up onto the wall beneath me. The angelfish darted away in a flash.

Hamish whistled, "I am willing to bet you've seen some serious stuff. Trauma hospitals get it all, burns, gunshot wounds, car accidents. There is this show on satellite TV that is all about trauma hospitals. That's not for me!"

"Me, either," I mumbled into my drink. I was beginning to feel the rum creep through my body, slowly numbing my lips and dulling the pain that comes with memories of the trauma room. I took another big swallow of my drink. *Can we just lay off the inquisition? Please.*

"Drunk drivers, too. Thank goodness there are no cars here in paradise." Rachel was just too far-gone to be serious. At least she lightened up the mood with her joke and everyone went back to partying and ignored me.

Taking a moment to stuff my emotions back into their box, I took a few deep breaths and studied my painted toes in order to buy time. Finally glancing up, I saw Colleen studying me. Quickly she changed the subject, "Tomorrow we thought we'd go into the village to the local market. Does everyone want to go?"

"Works for me," piped up Deanne. "It's not designer, but they sell some neat homemade stuff. Rach, Lauren, Elaine, are you gals in? Hamish?"

Everybody agreed to meet poolside again in the morning, at the same spot, and then head out to the market before it got too hot. Even with the ocean breeze blowing cooler air off the water around us, the island could get really hot and miserable this time of year. We would be back in time for an early lunch and then have time for another island hop. Beating the heat was the name of the game. Besides, swimming in the heat of the day made the water feel even better.

The night wore on and the group thinned out, until Rachel and I were the only ones left. Like me, she sat on the edge of the tidal pool with her legs over the side. Only her toes could just barely reach the water.

"So, Rachel, what's your deal? Colleen said your husband has an import business?"

"Troy, yeah, he imports and exports things to different countries, mostly to Central America and the Caribbean. He usually works in Miami, but our home is in Wellington so he commutes to Miami only when necessary because he hates the traffic. Besides, most of what he does can be handled from home, or by his office staff."

"And you?" The coast looked clear and the angelfish had long ago moved on, so I slipped my feet back into the tidal pool. *Oohh, that feels so good.*

"I mostly stay at home. I really do like Florida." Pausing to sip her drink, she continued, "You know it's crazy. Most of the people I know travel to Wellington, Aiken, or big horse hot spots to ride with famous trainers and here I fly to Central America! Go figure. To most people it wouldn't make sense, but it is hard to find trainers who are classically trained. I mean the real deal. Lots of trainers go to Germany and then hang a sign out saying they were trained there, but it is more than that. The German training system really works. There is a reason it has lasted this long. There is a reason that horses trained correctly according to the training pyramid stay sound longer." Her voice grew serious.

She became more animated as she talked, adding her hands for emphasis. Thank goodness her drink was half empty, I thought, eying it as it came closer. "If you think about it, the sole purpose for dressage was to create riding mounts and war horses which soldiers could depend on. They had to last many years, stay sound, and be capable of many feats. Nowadays people just bring them along too fast, and crank their heads and bodies into strange shapes to make them travel a certain way, all in the name of the dollar. Either that or it is just stupidity. Everybody wants to rush their training. Rush their horses up the levels when they aren't ready. It used to take years of methodical training to reach Grand Prix—never mind keeping your horse sound for a lifetime."

Frowning, she drained the last drop from her glass, "You know I too could go to Germany and train with Colleen's mentor, or one of the classical dressage greats, but instead I oversee our business here in Panama. Coming down here makes better financial sense." Smiling, she added, "especially to my non-horsey husband and his wallet."

We sat for a moment; pondering dressage and watching the fish swim below us, illuminated by the glow of the bohio lights. Rachel set her empty glass down on the ledge beside her. "Not only that, but personally I have found it hard to find a trainer with the right mix for me. She isn't afraid to tell you like it is, both good and bad. And she absolutely loves to take away your stirrups, reins, whatever it takes to make you a better rider no matter how long it takes or how much it hurts." She rolled her eyes for emphasis, "Hell, I think she likes torturing us!" She stretched out her leg and with a kick, managed to send a spray of water half way across the tidal pool.

Working on draining my drink as well, I thought about all of the trainers I had ridden with or observed over the years. Some were wimps and didn't have the guts to tell their students the truth and others were just plain mean and hateful. For each rider, the choice was a personal one. First you had to know what you wanted from your riding. For me, as a type A individual, excelling was the only option. I reveled in trainers who could push me enough to keep me interested and challenged on a regular basis. Heck, I even liked it when they took me out of my comfort zone when I least expected it, in order to make me a better rider. I had to agree with Rachel, Colleen was a good fit for me as well and the more I thought about the possibility, however remote, of making it to the Pan Am Games, the more excited I became. *What the hell else do I have to do?*

The bartender was closing shop for the night. Rachel managed to sweet talk him into fixing us one more drink before he left. We sat in companionable silence for several minutes, enjoying the tropical night. The nearby village was quiet and dark. After the bartender left, the night around us grew even more serene. Occasionally a gentle breeze would blow across the water towards us, bringing with it the salty aroma of the sea.

"Hey, are you really serious about this whole Pan Am Games thing?"

Rachel was lost in thought, staring at the pool full of fish. After a few seconds she answered, "Yeah, I am. If Colleen thinks we have a chance, then we do." She sounded more confident than I felt.

"Oh," was all I could manage.

Suddenly a thought occurred to me, "Wait a second, how can you compete for Panama? You live in Florida," I blurted out. "Don't you have to be Panamanian to ride for the team? If so, where would that put me?"

Giggling, Rachel glanced up at me, "Good question, Sherlock."

She giggled some more, clearly drunk, "I was born here." She pointed emphatically downward with her index finger to make her point clear. "Well, not *right* here, but here," she waved her arm in front of her, hoping to clarify.

"Oh." The alcohol was clearly beginning to kick in for the both of us.

"My dad was in the military and he was stationed here at Fort Clayton. Because I was born here," there went her arm again, waving to and fro, "I can claim dual citizenship."

"I can be multiple things, American and Panamanian," her eyes nearly crossed, as she thought hard, "Oh, wait, that's just two things."

She wrinkled her face in obvious confusion, "Two is not a few...," she recited in a singsong voice. "Oh crap, I can't remember how it goes. Is multiple the same as two, 'cause three can be a few?" Suddenly her countenance brightened, "Just not to be confused with multiple personalities." She laughed at her own inane joke. Oh wow, was she ever drunk. "But don't worry, I think you can ride for Panama if you live here."

"Oh."

Eventually the two of us found our way back to our rooms for the night. Not one to get drunk often, I had an ulterior motive tonight. I was hoping to keep the nightmares at bay. The last thing I wanted was to freak Deanne or the others out in the middle of the night. The open windows and thin bamboo walls of our hotel room really allowed sound to carry and I had every intention of sleeping through the night.

Once in our room, I changed out of my clothes. Slipping on an old T-shirt and a pair of cotton sleep shorts, I rinsed my face, and climbed into my bed. As I skirted her bed, I saw Deanne lying sprawled out, her arms spread wide, mouth agape. Her face was covered in a lichen green facial cleansing mask. To top it off, the sound that escaped her mouth was unlike any snoring I had ever heard, it was deep, guttural and nothing like Daytime Deanne. How in the world could someone so beautiful sound so awful? I thought to myself, trying not to giggle and wake her up. She reminded me of a croaking frog. Pulling down the thin sheet, I climbed into bed. Within moments of my head hitting the pillow, I was out myself.

Had the early morning sunlight not awakened us, the noises coming from the island around us would have. Through the windows floated an early morning breeze and the mournful sound of a lone barking dog. My head was pounding. I lay staring at the wall for a minute, collecting the nerve to roll over and face the day. I could hear Deanne moving around in the room behind me. She had woken early. *Damn, my head hurts.* Slowly, I rolled over and faced the day.

Standing across the room, Deanne was immaculately dressed in a red and white cotton top and white Capri pants, spotless and sparkling clean as always. Naturally she had packed a matching purse and sandals.

I let out a groan when I saw her perky outfit and made up face. Refusing to wake up, I rolled back over and buried my face back into my flat hotel pillow. Unfortunately, I hadn't slept well at all. Although I wasn't awakened by a nightmare, I felt exhausted. My pounding head didn't exactly help the situation either. Giving up, I propped myself up on my elbows. The top sheet from my bed was no longer tucked neatly under the mattress, but instead lay haphazardly across my legs. My brightly painted toes stared balefully back at me. *Ugh!* I must have tossed and turned all night. With a sigh, I swung my feet over the edge of the bed careful not to jar my head, and padded past Deanne on my way to the shower.

The hotel shower sat to one side of the back balcony. Perched over the water it consisted of a tile floor with a drain in the middle. A faded, yellow and blue shower curtain hung limply by the occasional plastic shower ring attached to a metal rod at the entrance. An antiquated shower head dumped what I soon discovered was tepid seawater onto my head. Apparently there was no hot water heater at the Isla Hotel.

I stood with teeth gritted against the cool water flowing down my back and stared at the drain in horror. I cut off the water and listened. I could hear the water from the shower drain dumping into the ocean below. "That can't possibly be good for the ocean," I muttered.

Getting back to the task at hand, I reached for the soap. So much for feeling clean, I thought, as I tried to scrub up without using too much soap. After a few minutes, I gave up on trying to keep the ocean clean, when I realized I still had to shave my legs. "Sorry Nemo," I muttered.

Once out of the shower, I quickly threw on a pair of denim shorts and a T-shirt over my green bikini. Stopping by my duffle bag, I grabbed my flip-flops on the way out the door. Deanne stood by the front door, waiting patiently for me. As I headed for the door I noticed she was studying me intently, "What?"

She stood barring the door, arms crossed with her matchy-matchy handbag dangling from her wrist. Her eyes bore holes in mine. "Did you sleep well?" she asked pointedly.

Remembering her inquisitive questioning from last night, I played it safe, all the while wondering if I really had kept my mouth shut while sleeping. "Yeah, great, and you?" I feigned lightness, smiling back at her.

She just nodded, still studying me. I felt like she was expecting more from me. She waited, appraising me, her eyes linked with mine. After a few moments she gave up. *Geez, what's with the interrogations?* I hoped I'd had enough to drink last night. Thinking hard, I tried to recollect whether or not my nightmare had paid me a visit last night. Giving up, she turned and reached for the doorknob. Shrugging it off, I smiled pleasantly at her back as she opened the door to our room and stepped out into daylight. I managed to slip on my sunglasses before stepping out into the sunlight that streamed across the balcony.

On the stairs we ran into Rachel and Colleen. The rest of the gang was already under the bohio by the tidal pool, in our usual spot. When we arrived, Hamish set to work passing out bottles of water for everyone. "Thanks," I mumbled, taking a proffered bottle.

The market was a short walk from the hotel. The streets throughout town were unpaved, but regular foot traffic kept the dirt packed firm beneath our feet. There were no cars on the island and only an occasional bicycle passed us by. The Kuna Indians mostly kept to themselves, coming and going carrying woven baskets full of everything from coconuts to brightly colored fabrics. The Kuna carried the baskets by a long strap that ran across their foreheads, leaving their hands free. Their nut-brown faces were round and weathered, much like the coconuts they carried.

Brightly colored strands of tiny beads forming geometric patterns were wrapped around their calves and forearms. On their heads, they wore bright red and gold patterned scarves. As we moved through the market, I noticed that some of the women wore gold nose rings, some wore red face paint, and still others had both. They wore loosely fitted, peasant style blouses and skirts in a barrage of bright colors and patterns, which were mixed and matched haphazardly. On the Kuna, the overall effect was one of unique style. Had I tried to mix so many patterns and colors in an outfit it would have ended in disaster. But here they wore it with ease.

As we walked along, I made sure I finished the bottle of water. Before long my headache started to fade, although it never totally went away.

On one side of the street there were stalls set up with wares for sale, mostly to the few tourists that stayed at the hotel. Elaine showed me the brightly colored fabric panels, created from multiple layers of fabrics that were on display. They were identical to the ones hanging on the walls of our new home. She explained that they were called molas. Giving me a quick lesson in molas she pointed out that the intricacy of the design and the fineness of the stitching separated the traditional hand made mola designs that the Kuna women actually wore, from those created in bulk for sale to the larger number of tourists back on the mainland.

Eventually we split up, each getting lost in our shopping. Before long I found myself alone and at a table set just on the end of an alleyway. An elderly Kuna woman nodded at me. I politely nodded back, not knowing what to say. It was then that I noticed she had the milky white skin and ginger colored hair of an albino. Digging through a pile of molas on the makeshift table I found a pair of matching designs. They had stylized sea turtles on them. I quickly decided they would make a great gift or souvenir. Folding them neatly in front of me I dug into my pocket for money. Reaching across the table to pay the old woman, she began chattering away.

As I dropped the money into her outstretched palm she grabbed me from below by the wrist, placing her other hand over mine, effectively keeping me from freeing myself. Confused and thinking I may have counted out the wrong amount I tried politely to free my hand, pulling back gently. Clinging to my hand, she started to babble at me, while making a jerking motion over her right shoulder with her head. I couldn't understand a thing she said. Growing nervous, I tried harder to free my hand. Holding me fast, she reached for my hair, running her gnarled fingers over my wild curls. "Shee, shee," she said running my hair between her thumb and forefinger. My heart beat a frantic tempo and panic began to set in. I scanned the crowd looking for a familiar face.

A younger Kuna man dressed in ordinary street clothes slid up next to the old woman. At this point my palms were sweating and I tried again to free my arm. The old woman was much stronger than she appeared. Seeing the growing panic on my face, the man gently pried the old woman's milky white hands from my arm. *Oh, thank God.* She continued to prattle on in her native tongue, gesticulating with her hands.

"I am sorry, my grandmother was just trying to tell you something and she was worried you would walk off before she had the chance to talk to you." The young man spoke fluent, if halting English. "You see she is a wise woman in our tribe and very revered. She has the skin of the moon and that makes her very powerful," he said with pride in his voice.

Self consciously, I pressed the molas against my chest, and again searched the market for one of the gang. Giving up, I turned back to the young man. He smiled at me.

"She is of the old religion and sees trouble around you." Tipping his head, he listened intently to the old woman as she formed words around what little teeth she had. When she finished speaking, she glanced sheepishly up at me. With her hands in the air, she drew a circle around me.

Hesitating he added, "She wants me to tell you that you are strong like the coconut palm. You bend with the wind, but you will need the strength that is inside of you to come back to the middle where you belong."

He listened intently to her, "There are winds coming. These are evil winds. Wicked winds. She begs that you be careful."

He glanced earnestly up at me. "These winds will blow unexpectedly and try to break you." He nodded in understanding, "They seek to uproot the strongest of palm trees." As he said this she pointed at me. "She thinks you can weather the storms that are coming, but warns you to be careful of those that will do you harm."

A look of surprise crossed his brown face as he listened to her again. Clearing his throat, he continued, "She sees a halo of red around you." He glanced back at the old woman, who urged him on with her hands, pointing repeatedly from him to me.

He hesitated, shifting his feet, eyes downcast, "She feels the red represents blood or death." His words hung, suspended in the tropical air of the market place around us. The old woman spoke again and the young man added, "Please try to be very careful."

My breath caught in my throat and I had to concentrate on breathing the salt filled air. Frantically, I glanced around for a familiar face.

Ignoring his grandmother by his side he said, "Look, I know this must sound crazy, but my grandmother," he glanced down at the top of her graying head, "she is very gifted. She wouldn't have made a fuss if she didn't think it was important." His deep chocolate eyes met mine, and I felt as though he could see through me.

The hustle and bustle of the market faded around me until I felt lost in a universe with just the three of us. The earnest look on the old woman's face relaxed, as she patted the man's shoulder with her gnarled hand, then smiled at me. He immediately patted her tenderly on the shoulder. The wrinkles in her pale face reminded me of the ripples of white sand that waves leave behind on the shore.

Again the old woman spoke and the young man looked boldly up at me, "She said you have a man, and he is a good man. Keep him close and he will keep the winds away." He winked at me, his chocolate eyes twinkling.

Numb, I realized I still had the money in my hand. Tentatively I reached out and dropped it into the old woman's hand. She nodded then turned her attention to another customer as her grandson set to work tidying up the table of wares. Pulling myself away, I wandered out into the street where I ran into Rachel and Deanne.

"Hey, there you are. We've been looking for you." Deanne was chattering away but nothing she said was registering. My mind was still on the old Kuna woman and her ominous, if somewhat confusing, warning.

"Lauren, are you okay? You are white as a ghost." Rachel stepped directly in front of me. She took in the pallor of my skin and the molas clutched to my chest she spoke a little louder. "Lauren, are you okay?" she repeated.

"Hmm? Yeah, I'm okay." The sights and sounds of the market reached me and I could hear Deanne's voice nearby. Turning, I glanced behind me, scanning the line of vendors, but the old woman had disappeared. I shuddered even though the temperature was climbing steadily. Blinking, I tried to focus on what the girls were saying, but it was a jumble of meaningless noise.

"…then I found this really great mola of a butterfly for my grandmother. She just adores butterflies so I thought I would—" Deanne was holding up a large mola in front of her chest for me to see.

Tuning her out, I glanced at Rachel who was still staring at me, the white cream of her sunscreen streaked across her worried pink face. "Sure, that's nice," I offered. "Where's everyone else?"

I wanted to leave the market behind me. What had started out as a fun shopping trip had left my nerves shot to hell. Standing up on the tips of my toes, I caught sight of AJ. Thank God he was heads above the locals and tourists and easy to spot. At the same time, Rachel grasped my elbow and propelled me down the dirt street back towards the hotel. Deanne obliviously followed behind us, folding her mola as she walked. Leaning in Rachel whispered, "What in blue blazes happened back there?"

"I ran into a really spooky old lady."

Rachel shot me a sideways look, but kept walking. "Don't know about you, but spooky old ladies have never scared the crap out of me. And you, girl, looked really freaked out."

"This one was a Kuna wise woman, who basically just told me that someone is out to get me! Some crap about a palm tree, blood and someone trying to uproot me," I paused to glance back again. "Is that spooky enough for you?" I heard cackling behind me. "On top of that, she was an albino!"

"I'll get you and your pretty dog, too." Just a step behind us, Deanne had overheard our exchange and was cackling like a witch. "Oh, Lauren, you kill me, she was probably trying to make some extra money off of you." She snorted again with laughter. It reminded me of how she had sounded while snoring the night before and I found myself relaxing a bit. On second thought, it did seem a bit unreal. *Just a freaky old lady, Todd, that's all.*

Chuckling, I added, "You know, you are right. She did say something about my man and I clearly don't have one of those, although by all accounts he sounded like a keeper." This made everyone laugh and we walked along while Deanne discussed exactly which men she thought were worthy of being 'keepers'.

We caught up with AJ and Hamish who were looking for Colleen and Elaine. Joining forces, we finally found them buying colorful strands of beads at the far end of the market. The Kuna made beaded bracelets and anklets by threading several different colors of beads onto a thin cotton string. What appeared to be randomly placed colors actually formed geometric patterns when wrapped around a limb. Elaine wanted to find a way to incorporate the beads into the headbands of everyone's bridles for the Games.

Hanging back, I watched them sift through the selections, glad to have a diversion. I was still digesting my conversation with Colleen yesterday. The mere idea that any of us could actually qualify for the Pan Am Games, much less find the cash, or in my case a horse and the cash to get there seemed like a trip to the moon. But here I stood watching them act as if we were a sure thing.

Last night at dinner Colleen had announced to everyone that she had invited me to be a part of their scheme. She asked everyone to scour the Internet and keep their eyes open in the hopes of finding a suitable mount for me. I had a general idea how much an upper level dressage horse would cost back home and I knew that my budget wouldn't stretch that far in a million years. However, Colleen seemed undaunted when I pointed this out. It didn't seem to faze her that I didn't have a job at the moment, either. What I did have was a lump sum of money from Mom's life insurance policy. Jake and I had talked about putting it down on a house when the apartment lease ran out. While taking a shower this morning I had come to the conclusion that if a horse could be found, then I would take the plunge and go to Wellington with everyone. Chances like this just didn't come along very often.

We wandered back to the hotel and had a light lunch of fresh fruit, some of which I didn't recognize, and sandwiches under the bohio. Afterwards, we headed by dug out canoe to a small beach on another nearby island. This time we had a different cab driver and a much more stable wooden bench to sit on.

This island was similar to the first, with the exception of more trees and a wider beach. Just off the leeward side of this island sat a reef, which was almost twice the size of the island itself, and made for great snorkeling. The crystal clear waters and rainbow colors of the fish were breathtaking and I found myself wishing my camera was waterproof so I could share this adventure with Haley. Oh well, I shrugged, at least I got some great video of the island yesterday.

I snorkeled until my legs ached and my lungs burned with salt water. I had to admit I wasn't very good at keeping the snorkel above water. More than once, I found myself getting distracted by the colorful fish and momentarily forgetting that

I was still tethered to the surface. After sucking in a mouthful of water, I would come up gasping for fresh air. Hamish was kind enough to give me some pointers. I was growing fond of Hamish, not in a sexual way, but his gallant manners along with little things I heard him say made me realize what a great gentleman he was. They just didn't seem to be many guys like him anymore. Deanne better act quick or she would surely lose him to some other girl.

Taking a break, I plopped down on a towel laid out on the hot sand. Closing my eyes I turned off my thoughts, stilled my brain, and tried to feel the world around me with my other senses. After a moment, I could feel droplets of salt water run down the side of my body until they could no longer hold on and the laws of physics took over. One by one they broke free, only to fall onto the towel below. I could hear what I thought was a seagull. A sad smile crossed my face and I knew I had a wrinkle in my brow just above my nose. Jake had often placed a finger just there and told me how much he loved my frown lines. *Not now Jake, I implored, later, but not here with everyone around, please.*

I fought to clear my mind again, relaxing my face. He had also taught me just what I could feel and hear without my eyes. We used to lie together in a pasture on his parent's farm and fine-tune our senses. Thanks to him I could feel the direction of the wind across my face and tell a blue jay from a robin. Right now I could hear the palm fronds gently rustling in the breeze behind me. *Oh, Jake.* My heart clenched in my chest just as the light above me changed. Through the red gauzy haze of my eyelids the sky above me darkened for a moment. Spreading out her towel, Deanne plopped down next to me. "Mind if I join you?" Her voice was hesitant; as if she wasn't at all sure she should be asking.

Taking pains to slacken the muscles of my face, I forced a smile, "Hmm, not at all. Given up on Hamish?" I kept my eyes closed and my face blank while my heart slowly relaxed and let go of Jake.

"Obvious isn't it?" She wiggled around on the towel to create a mold of her body in the sand beneath it. "I just don't get that guy. I mean, look at me. I am not exactly hard on the eyes and I'm available. For most men, that would make me irresistible." She wiggled some more. "I mean come on; most men aren't exactly the deepest, most sensitive creatures on God's planet."

I tried not to smile. Deanne was absolutely gorgeous. With her stunning, long golden hair, flawless skin, and size six body she was indeed what most men desired. "'Are you sure he isn't gay?" I felt another droplet slip from behind my knee.

"No, he had a girlfriend when I first met him. Man was she frumpy. I never could picture them together. Anyway, he *isn't* gay," she added with emphasis.

"Maybe he likes frumpy women," I offered. *Or maybe she was his cover up, a distraction.*

She thought for a moment, and then let out a sigh. "Maybe," she said, not quite sounding convinced. "No, my gut tells me he is not gay."

I simply nodded and kept my mouth shut. We lay there soaking up the warm sun for a few minutes. Occasionally the onshore wind would send the whooshing sound of someone clearing a snorkel full of water in our direction.

"Deanne, can I ask a personal question?"

"Shoot."

"Are you serious about going to Wellington? I mean, how on earth are you going to afford it? If you don't mind my asking?" I nibbled my lower lip, hoping I hadn't gone too far in asking about her finances. I knew very little about Deanne's personal life.

"Yes, I am dead serious. As for your second question, I am rich." She let the last statement sink in before continuing. "Not quite the filthy variety, but still rich." She was chuckling to herself softly.

I nearly choked. Coughing to clear my throat I sat up. "Sorry." Thoroughly embarrassed by my outburst, I lay back down again.

"No, seriously, I am rich, so the money won't be an issue. Well actually, my dad is, but it will be mine someday and until then I am sitting pretty. See, my dad was a big time attorney back home. He met the right people through his job and ended up becoming a diplomat. Although, I am still not quite sure how that happened." She paused, "I was away at college. So, I packed up and moved here to be with him. Guess you could say I am a Daddy's girl." She smirked, "Anyway, he bought me a condo downtown so we can live our own lives. He lives in another section of the city and works non-stop so I rarely see him."

"Where is your mom?"

She giggled, "Which one?" "Most of them sucked. Dad has been married four times. The first one is my mom, but the other three tried to be surrogate moms. Number three really sucked at the whole 'mom' thing," she added sarcastically. "Mom and Dad were high school sweethearts. They got married right after graduation, and I came along when Dad was still in law school. After he graduated, Dad got a job in New York City at a very prestigious law firm, but my mom wasn't about to leave Georgia, she is a country girl at heart. Anyway, the marriage didn't last long after that. I adored my dad so I went with him. You know, I've been blessed with the best private schools and college that any girl could dream of." She started to chuckle.

Opening my eyes I looked at her lying next to me. She was trying really hard to control her laughter. "What's so funny about going to good schools?" I asked, thoroughly confused.

"You just don't get it. I have a degree from Georgetown University in architectural design and here I sit in a third world country on a beach, without a real job, no prospects for a husband, and I am just wasting away." A look of disbelief mingled with consternation crossed her face, causing her pretty little features to crinkle up. "I am twenty-six years old and a full third of my life is behind me. Don't you find that to be the least bit ironic, or maybe even a bit sad? I mean, what the hell am I doing here?"

I had no idea how to respond and the minutes ticked by. I had the feeling she was trying to think of a good answer just as I was. *Or maybe she wasn't really looking for an answer.*

Finally she spoke up, "Honestly, I am spoiled by my Dad and I really do like the finer things in life. Truth be told, he and I have always been best friends and as long as I am with him, he would buy me the moon." She turned up on her elbow facing me, "Do you think that makes me shallow?"

Her eyes met mine, then thinking better of it; she rolled onto her back and closed her eyes. "Don't answer that." With a distinctively feminine huff she shifted on her towel trying to get comfortable.

"Deanne, I don't care how much money you have, or whether you think you should be doing more in life than you currently are. You've been nice to me. And no, I don't think you are shallow. I do, however, think Hamish is a lost cause," I said, jerking my head in the direction of the surf.

Deanne adjusted herself, smoothing out the towel beneath her, trying once again to get comfortable. "Maybe," she said softly.

Tactfully changing the subject I moved on. "Oh, and one more thing, I don't get the whole three hundred dollar breeches thing. What is up with that? Really girl, that's just wasteful. How in the hell do you keep them clean?"

"My maid works her magic. Just think of me as the Imelda Marcos of breeches. Some girls buy overpriced purses, some go for the expensive lingerie, but me, I need therapy for my breech habit." She thought for a moment, "On second thought, I don't want therapy!"

"Who needs therapy?" Hamish stood at our feet, droplets of water dripping down his tan body. I couldn't help but notice his well-defined six-pack of abdominal muscles. *Hell, it was more of a fourteen pack.* With the body of a god, I could see why Deanne was drawn to him. His grey and white board shorts hung low around his hips, showing off the tantalizing V shaped muscles of his lower obliques and hips. In fact, the muscles of his lower abdomen, obliques, and thighs came together in perfect harmony to further accentuate the shallow indentations his hip bones made as they met the tops of his thighs. A trace of short dark hair trailed down and disappeared just out of view at the top of his waistband. *Oh my!* With his dark hair and easy smile he was most certainly an Adonis. When you added his cheerful personality and love of horses, he became as tempting as the forbidden fruit in the Garden of Eden. Yep, I could see why Deanne was smitten. Hamish was hot. Not my type, but hot none the less.

Deanne had been enjoying the view as well. When her senses finally returned she said, "Maria, she needs therapy." She smiled sweetly up at Hamish, one hand shielding the sun from her eyes so she could see him all the more clearly. With one hand I pulled my sunglasses off of my head, slipping them neatly onto my nose.

"You're not kidding. I try very hard to be polite to her, but she nearly ran Patina and me over in the barn aisle last week. She seems to think she owns the place." He made a grunting noise from deep within his chest. *Oh my!* "I wouldn't mind one bit if she packed up and left," Hamish mumbled from behind the towel he was using to dry his hair and face.

"What is her deal anyway? I am surprised Colleen puts up with her." I glanced past Hamish to make sure Colleen and AJ were out of earshot. It wouldn't do to have her hear us talking.

"All I know is that she is Columbian and from a very prominent family. She runs part of the family business here in Panama. I have seen her at some of the diplomatic parties, but I'm not sure if she is there as a guest or if her husband is a diplomat. To be honest, I avoid her like the plague." Deanne reached for her water bottle, which she had set next to her.

"She's married?" Hamish looked stunned.

"She's married!" I found that hard to swallow.

"Why, is she your type?" Deanne purred. Her face looked pleasant enough, but her eyes bore into his.

Swinging the towel over his head casually, he settled it around his neck and smiled wickedly right back at her. "No, she isn't. I am just shocked that anyone would be brave enough to marry her. It must be like sleeping with a she-devil, always having to watch your back and all." He winked at her, "I don't mind a little mischievousness, as long as it is in fun." His point made, his face became bland.

Deanne, either didn't notice, or chose not to rise to the occasion. "Her husband is much older than she is. In fact, I've often wondered if it was an arranged marriage. Or maybe she is the black widow type? Either way, there doesn't seem to be much love between them."

"Then what is the deal with her and Pablito?" I asked.

Deanne glanced towards the water where Colleen and AJ were swimming before continuing, "I don't know for sure, but I think she is having an affair with him. What ever you do, don't say anything about them around AJ. I think he suspects, but I personally wouldn't want to be the one to bring it up. He is incredibly protective of Pablito and hates Maria. Especially since Pablito is his younger brother and he is a father figure to him."

"Oh."

After a few hours we headed back to the main island and the hotel. After a quick shower we once again met up for dinner. Tired from a day spent having fun outdoors, the mood this evening was more subdued and our tongues were tired. It was a good thing, as my headache had returned. Avoiding the alcohol, I instead opted for bottled water. Rachel and I both begged off from the group with headaches, no doubt from dehydration, and headed back to our rooms early. For the most part I slept fitfully and could not recall having any nightmares. That was a good thing.

Sunday morning arrived, bringing with it wind and a light misting rain across the island. AJ moved our departure time up by an hour to avoid some storm clouds rolling in off the Caribbean. Deanne and I hastily packed our things and hurried downstairs to check out.

The flight home, while not as pleasant and smooth as the arriving flight, was still enjoyable. We left the rain behind us twenty minutes into our flight and the sun greeted us on landing.

CRAIG

Damn! That phone. I raced back into the bathroom and snatched it off the back of the sink where I had left it. "Dad, I am coming! I can't get out of here on time if you keep calling me!" The phone sat precariously between my ear and shoulder while I tried to stab an earring in the other ear.

"Sorry, honey, but I forgot the present on the dining room table. Bring it when you come. And Lauren, slow down, I haven't even picked Haley up yet and the ceremony starts at five."

"Okay," I muttered hanging up. I reached to drop the phone on the bed and heard the unmistakable sound of my earring bouncing across the wood floor and then nothing. "Crap. Crap, crap, crap" I pulled up the hem of my russet colored, linen sheath dress so I wouldn't wrinkle it, and dove for the ground in search of my wayward earring. Just great! After a moment of frantic searching I caught a hint of gold beneath my bed. Wedging my left arm all the way up to my shoulder, I stretched my fingers as far as they could go just barely hitting it. "Crap!" I planted the side of my freshly made up face on the floor and tried again. This time I snagged it.

From somewhere above me, my phone began ringing again. Extricating myself I leaned against the bed and snatched the phone with my other hand. "What is it?" I snapped.

"Bad timing?" It was Colleen.

"Dropped my earring, sorry. What's up?"

"I have a minor emergency I was hoping you could help me out. AJ and I are stuck on one of his ships."

"Stuck on a ship?" I said incredulously. "How in the heck did that happen?"

Laughing, Colleen continued, "I went out with him this morning for a shake down cruise on one of his newest purchases and um…one of the propellers broke or something. We are waiting for a tugboat to tow us back to port, and I have no idea when we will get to the dock, much less home. Would you be able to bring the horses in and dump their grain?" She paused.

I swallowed hard, trying to calculate in my head if I had the time to stop by the barn on the way to the wedding. Finally I said, "Sure."

"Oh, Lauren, you are an angel. I owe you one. Their feed is all labeled and the hay is already in the stalls, all you need to do is bring them in and dump the grain. Hey listen, I gotta run, AJ needs me. I'll check in later, bye."

With that the phone went dead. Deflated, I crammed my pearl earring in the hole, shoved the back on tightly, pushed off from the bed and stood up. Glancing at my watch I ran the time through my head, calculating. I might be a few minutes late if I left this instant. Snatching up my phone and high heels off the bed I did a quick check in the mirror to ensure I was indeed dressed and ready. The deep, rich russet color of the dress complimented my fair complexion and set off my red hair. My freckles stood out against my pale skin, almost a perfect match for the earthy tone of my dress. My hair was hastily pulled in back into a loose chignon at the base of my neck and thick wavy strands fell about my made up face and neck. My Akoya pearl earrings and single strand necklace had a slight golden hue to them, which made them pulsate against my skin. Satisfied, I left the mirror behind, grabbed an old pair of socks out of my dresser and raced down the hall for my purse and keys. Locking the door behind me, I jogged to the Land Cruiser barefoot, purse, shoes and cell in one hand, and the keys in the other.

I made it to the barn in record time. After yanking on my socks I reached down onto the passenger side floorboards for my rubber boots. Leaving my purse and keys behind on the seat, I spun sideways on the seat so I could pull my rubber boots on.

Once in the barn I headed straight for the feed room. The barn and feed room were silent since all of the horses were turned out and nobody else was around. No wonder Colleen had called me, I thought to myself. In an effort to stay clean, I slipped on Colleen's ugly barn apron and tied it behind me. The pink and yellow calico apron looked like something from the 1950's, but would definitely do the job of keeping the front of my dress clean. Grabbing two lead ropes, I headed out to the closest pasture.

William and Patina, then Gold Herr and Nicola were brought in without incident or horse smudges on my dress.

Macho's paddock was closest to the house and he greeted me at the gate with incessant bugling. Standing at his gate, he impatiently tossed his head up and down. His long, thick, white forelock fell over his big brown eyes, making them nearly impossible to see until he tossed his head again. I swung the gate inward and slipped in alongside him. Clipping the lead rope to his leather halter I gently asked him to back away from the gate. As a stallion he had pretty good manners, but he still liked to be a bully when he thought he might get away with it. Today, he responded by leaning his big, meaty chest heavily on the pasture gate, making it difficult to open. "Back up, you knuckle head," I scolded. Macho was all show, but I didn't have time to play his stallion games so I swung the end of the lead rope against his muscular chest with a loud *whack*.

He snorted. Giving in, he stepped back from the gate so I could swing it open. Once out of the pasture we headed down the dirt path behind the barn. Twice on the way back to the barn he tried to drag me and I quickly corrected him. Finally I had to plant my right elbow against his neck to keep him off my dress and out of my lap. "Watch it, buddy. I need to stay clean today, and you don't belong in my lap." Frowning at him, I realized I'd have to wash my arm before I left the barn. Dad wouldn't be happy if I smelled like a horse at his boss's daughter's wedding.

I had met Emily once just after we arrived at a company picnic. Nice girl, but I had no doubt we had been invited so Charla, her mom, could find me a suitable boyfriend. Dad also had to keep up appearances at his new job. "So, lucky me, I get to go to a wedding single and face the humiliation of Charla and every other meddling woman trying to find me a man," I grumbled aloud. Feeling my mood, Macho pricked his inside ear at me and sidled sideways a few steps. This probably meant there would be more parties to attend in the future. I groaned aloud and Macho eyed me from beneath his forelock. "Sorry, buddy, it's not you." I lowered my elbow since he was behaving himself now.

"Hmph! I don't need a man," I said aloud. There was no one to hear, but I felt better hearing the words actually come out of my mouth. "I mean, what am I, defective or something, just because I am twenty-eight and not married?" Macho snorted and black stringy horse snot spattered across the front of Colleen's apron. I was glad I had put it on. "See, you agree." We reached his stall. After walking him in and turning him around I slipped off his halter, unclipped the lead rope, and headed back out for Stitch.

Stitch had the furthest pasture all to himself because he was such a troublemaker. He would continually pester the other horses until they hauled off and kicked him. Inevitably he ended up used as a whipping post by the other horses or was lame and couldn't be ridden, so Colleen kept him on his own. This way he couldn't get into mischief and stayed sound. As I reached the pasture gate, my heart sank in my chest and my empty stomach did a flip flop. Where was Stitch? He always met me at the gate. I called out his name a few times and tried desperately to imitate Colleen's whistle while loosening the chain on the gate. Standing there for a minute I jingled the metal gate chain against the metal gate, hoping the sound would bring him running. Nothing. Shutting the gate behind me I stopped and called again. Nothing.

"Now what?" I said through clenched teeth as my watch glared at me. 4:37 pm.

Turning on my boot heel I traipsed down the left side of the fence and began a pasture search. I decided to loop around the pasture once, covering the perimeter, then, if I still couldn't find him I would work my way in. The front section of the pasture was set on a slight rise, which fell away down a small hill about half way down the fence line. The pasture was mostly grass with small groups of bushes scattered throughout which limited full visibility. Since it was late in the afternoon, the humidity was high and my freshly ironed dress began to cling to my body and wrinkle. *Crap!* Reaching the left hand corner of the pasture I ran my hand across my damp forehead then turned right and followed the back fence.

I was trying my best to perform a fireman's search, or that was what one of the fire medics I knew at the hospital called it. When searching a burning building you pick a direction, say left, you then stay on that path, keeping the wall of the burning building on your left until you can't go left or straight any more, then and only then do you turn right, all the while keeping the wall on your left side, repeating the process. In an enclosed space, this tactic always leads you back to the door, or in this case, the gate. I called again. I became more agitated between the late hour, missing the wedding, and finding Colleen's horse. That and I had never been this far back in Stitch's pasture before.

Somewhere along the back fence, just after I had turned right once more I heard something big thrashing around in the over growth. It came from an island of jungle foliage about ten feet from the fence line. As I reached the edge I clearly saw the white blaze on his worried face. When he saw me he started to struggle again in panic and I waded in to reach him. His big lustrous brown eyes locked on me and he tried to whinny, but a coarse throaty sound was all that came out. *Crap!*

"Easy, Stitch. Whoa, buddy." I lowered my voice and focused on soothing him. As I made my way through a tangle of vines he pricked his ears at me and let out an exhaustive sigh. "Good boy," I praised in a calm voice.

Cautious of where his hooves may be I made my way towards his head and laid a hand on his sweaty neck. Thick green vines lay across his neck and shoulders like a spider web, holding him down. Surveying the dense jungle around him, I had no doubt that thrashing around had only made the problem worse. It was doubtful that he had gone into a full-blown panic mode or the scene would probably have been worse. Nickering at me, his voice sounded like fresh sandpaper.

"Hey, buddy, I'm here. Easy, let me take a look, huh." Rambling on with soothing nonsense I kept my voice calm and even. He lay on his left side, but not completely flat. That was good since I had no clue how long he'd been here. Horses weren't meant to lie on their sides for extended periods of time. They were grazers and as such needed to move. In fact, most horses slept for short periods of time throughout the day while standing with their knees locked.

A jumble of bushes, vines, and who knew what else appeared to be keeping him partially upright so I moved on to his legs. His right hind leg was stretched out behind him at an odd angle. Nervously I sent up a quick prayer request asking that I would find his leg intact and not broken. Keeping free of his other legs, I forced my way through the thicket until I could see his hoof.

"Crap!" I muttered. Hearing the change in my voice, Stitch started to thrash again. Mad at myself for upsetting him, I switched back to my soothing rambles and reached down to touch his right flank, hoping to calm him. As I talked, he relaxed and I stood trying to assess the damage. Slowly, I pulled a branch aside to expose his hind hoof. Two of the outside nails of his horseshoe had been loosened just enough that an old piece of metal fencing was stuck between the shoe and the hoof. I ran my hands gingerly across the bottom of his foot, making sure he stayed calm. The metal fencing was firmly wedged underneath both sides of the horseshoe. Unfortunately, with his hind leg stretched out and his hoof bent backwards, the wire exerted too much force for Stitch to free himself.

Out of sheer habit I reached for my cell phone on my right hip only to find empty space. "Crap!" I muttered more softly this time. My cell phone was on the passenger seat of the Land Cruiser where I had left it. Upon hearing my voice, Stitch raised his head and regarded me with his right eye as if to say, "Is there a problem?"

"You're a funny guy, you know!" I admonished him with sarcasm, hoping it would lighten my mood. No luck. Stooping lower, I gently slid my hand down his leg until I reached his hoof. I felt him lift his big head again to peer at me. Grasping the wire firmly in my hand, I rocked it back and forth trying to free it. No luck. The tension between the hoof and wire didn't give me much room to work with. Hiking up my skirt so I could move better, I stepped gingerly over his outstretched leg, tramping down the vines with my boots. "Don't get any ideas and kick me." Readjusting my grip, with one hand on either side of the hoof, I tried again. As soon as one side started to loosen, the wire on the other side slipped farther between the shoe and hoof wall.

Frustrated, I stood up. "Okay, plan B. I need a plan B. Think, Todd, think!" Talking through things or singing out loud had always helped me relax, sometimes I would even sing. When I had ridden with Ralph Hill one winter in Ocala he had made me sing songs out loud while galloping cross country fences. I soon discovered that George Thoroughgood made for a good rhythm on course. Without even thinking I started to hum, and before I knew it I was having a one sided conversation with Stitch while I worked to free him. Following the wire away from the hoof I tried to loosen it up from the ground. No luck there. Stitch laid his head back down with a weary sigh and let me work. Tendrils of hair that had framed my face earlier now stuck annoyingly to my chin. Impatiently I tucked them behind my ears with dirt stained fingers so I could see what I was doing.

After a few minutes of struggling I gave up and moved back up to his head. Gently pulling back his lips, I checked his gums. They were pink and moist. That was a good sign. Pressing firmly I pushed my thumb against the soft wet tissue of his gums, and then released. Good capillary refill. Okay, he wasn't dehydrated yet. Running my eyes over him again I checked for puncture wounds or bleeding. The only blood I saw appeared to be where the vines had torn his skin.

"All right, you stay here nice and quiet like while I head back to the barn. We're gonna need a pair of wire cutters." He flicked a big ear towards me, but didn't move. With a final pat on his sweaty neck I set off for the barn. Three strides later and before I could even navigate my way through the dense brush, Stitch became frantic and began thrashing violently.

"Shit!" In a flash I had a steadying hand on his golden neck. The panic began to ebb from his body. Slowly his eyes softened, and then licking his lips he nuzzled my arm. Light puffs of warm air and the soft whiskers from his muzzle tickled my air. With a sigh he laid he head back down on the tangle of vines.

"Okay boy, so maybe I won't leave you just yet." I checked his pulse again—55 beats per minute. I would have been happier if it was less than 50 beats per minute, but it could be worse. Resolutely I went to work on the vines which held his neck and shoulders. A few minutes later I was able to slip a few of the looser vines over his head, the rest clung tenaciously to him.

"You are one lucky boy. Good thing I came along when I did." A quick glance at my watch revealed it was 5:15 pm. Dad would start to worry before long. It was too bad he didn't know where I was. I hadn't bothered to call him after I had heard from Colleen. "Dumb move, Todd," I spoke louder than I had intended as my nerves started to get to me. Lord only knew when AJ and Colleen would make it back to the docks. Surely someone would see the Land Cruiser, and empty stall, and figure it out. The question was, when? With a sinking feeling, I remembered the empty barn. It was doubtful anyone would be out tonight to check on the horses, especially on a Saturday night.

I went back to work with a purpose. Twisting and twirling the fibrous vine between my fingers got me nowhere. I even tried to dig my nails into the flesh of the vine. They simply bent and folded despite all my efforts. They were just too green to snap or break. Before long I was back to babbling at Stitch in order to keep my mind occupied. Ever so often, I would reach over and check Stitch's gums and pulse to make sure he was okay. Occasionally he would life his head and sniff my arm. As the afternoon waned, the daylight began to fade into night, casting long shadows through the thicket.

Glancing up, I tried to work a kink out of my neck, stretching it from side to side, then backwards. The neck strap of Colleen's apron dug into my skin. Pulling up on the front, I tried to loosen it. My shoulder muscles ached with the effort and my tight knees begged to be straightened. Using the back of an earthy smelling hand, I wiped the sweat from my brow and noticed bats swooping through the dusky sky above us.

So silent were they, I had not even known they were there until I looked up. "I hope they are fruit bats and not vampire bats," I said rather loudly. I clearly remembered the pinched faces and sharp teeth of the vampire bats at the zoo and shivered. *Don't even go there with your imagination.* Even though they mainly feast on animals, it didn't make me feel warm and fuzzy all over to have them swooping around looking like little red-eyed demons from a bad horror movie above my head. I shook my head. *You've seen way too many vampire flicks lately.*

Lowering my head, I went back to work once more on the vines. Before I realized it, I was telling Stitch about Mom, the move, and Pogo. *Pop.* A vine snapped free. Thank God, I thought. The joints of my hands were starting to ache. I took a moment to lean against Stitch as I flexed my aching fingers and shook my arms trying to release the tension in my muscles. I could feel the blood rush back into them, easing the discomfort a bit. Cramming a broken fingernail between my teeth to chew off a rough edge I tasted the metallic taste of blood. Spitting out the chunk of nail I had bitten off, I let out a heavy sigh.

As night settled like a heavy blanket around us I could no longer see well enough to check his gums, but I was able to slide my hand up his neck to his jawbone, and feel for his pulse. Without a light on my watch I resorted to feel and gut instinct. Right now, his pulse felt about the same as it had last time. That was all I could do.

Still searching for a Plan B, I mulled over my options. There was simply no way I would ever be able to free him without wire cutters or another set of hands. A light would have been welcomed as well. *Think about what you can do, not what you can't, Todd.* I certainly couldn't leave him to thrash around and cause himself harm. Without being able to get him up to evaluate him I had to go on the fact that he would stay calm if I stayed. There had been no obvious signs of trauma, lacerations, or pools of blood. He was simply very, very stuck. At least with me here I could keep him calm, besides, there was no way I could find my way back in the dark, and even if I did follow the fence line it would probably take me a while to find it again. Wandering around this pasture in the pitch dark wasn't the most appealing of ideas either.

Resigned to staying put, I peeled off the ugly apron, spread it on the ground near his head then eased myself down onto my makeshift seat. Not willing to give up quite yet, I again attacked the vines, sliding my fingers along them until I found what felt to be a thinner section to work on. Curled up on his side, he could now manage to keep his head upright with more ease, and the bottom of his chin rested on the ground in front of him. The stark white of his legs and blaze stood out in marked contrast to the darkness around us.

Talking aloud to ward off the creepy noises of the jungle around us I began to tell him about Jake. I spoke hesitantly at first. Funny, I thought to myself, there was no one around to hear except for my captive audience of one horse. *Hmph!* I stopped early on in the telling of my story when I realized I had never even said many of these words aloud until now. *Todd, you need a shrink and a couch. That's what you need. Instead you decide to bare your soul to a trapped horse. How nuts is that?* Getting up the courage, I continued. In fact, not a soul alive knew the whole story, not even Dad. I told Stitch how good Jake had been to me, how much fun we'd had, I even laughed out loud when I told him crazy stories about us. All the while, Stitch listened patiently, especially when I found myself in tears.

I lost complete track of time as it related to minutes and hours, instead I measured the passage of time in aches and defeated vines. My knees were numb, almost beyond feeling. Shifting often, I finally sat next to his neck. Easing my long legs straight, one by one I wiggled my toes in my boots, trying to increase circulation and bring back some feeling. With a deep sigh, Stitch lowered his head onto my lap. "You're welcome," I said, patting his neck. My mouth and throat felt dry and thick like cotton when I spoke. Swallowing hard, I cleared my throat.

Now that I had slowed down, I noticed just how badly my legs, arms, and face itched. God only knew how many bugs and mosquitos had made a meal of us. Poor Stitch had grown too weary to even swat his tail.

Although exhausted, I knew I needed to dig deeper and keep working on the vines. "Come on, Todd, you need to kick on," I muttered aloud, trying to give myself some verbal encouragement. Suddenly, my hands stopped and I smiled tentatively. A trainer I had ridden with had given me the best advice ever about two minutes before I rode my first preliminary cross country course. When he saw how worried I was about moving up a level and tackling bigger, bolder, more technical jumps he had laid a hand on my knee while steadying my horse and told me that each jump would come up before us, no matter what. "Remember," he said, "the difference is how you prepare for the jump. You know how to do this. Just set your horse up properly then once you are over it, just kick on to the next. Before you know it, you will cross the finish line." Squaring my shoulders, I decided to kick on and tackle the next vine.

I worked on into the night, completely losing track of time. The remaining vines were as big around as my wrist and no amount of work had made a dent in them. Exhausted, I slumped over his warm neck, one outstretched arm slung across his neck, the other bent into a makeshift pillow on his shoulder. Absently playing with his mane, twirling it between my fingers I started to tell him more about Jake. It was as if the floodgates opened and, at last, I was able to verbalize everything I had hidden within me, every ache, every pain, every lost opportunity, everything. I told him about looking down at the stretcher and seeing Jake looking up at me. His eyes had never really focused on me and I still to this day don't think he ever really saw me. I blinked back tears and Stitch waited patiently for me to continue, his big goofy ears turned in my direction now and again in encouragement.

Jake's eyes had been like pools of nothing behind half closed lids. No depth, no spark, nothing. I confessed aloud about my inability to do my job. I had failed, frozen up, and been unable to help him. The one person I would have given anything to be able to save was Jake. But I had been useless. I couldn't help him. After all my training at a career that he, Jake, had encouraged me to pursue, I couldn't help him. The irony was just too much and warm tears streamed down my face.

Doctor Hammond, the trauma surgeon, had no idea that the broken body on the stretcher was the love of my life, my best friend. Continuing on, he barked orders directing the physician's assistant, trauma room nursing staff, and radiology staff. Oblivious to everything around me, I had frozen, unable to move. I later found out that I had been screaming at Jake to wake up, to look at me. Of that, I had no memory. It had taken Hal, a member of the flight crew, to pull me away from Jake's side. Hal's daughter rode in pony club with Elena. He had known who Jake was when they picked him up in the helicopter. He just hadn't known I would be on duty when they landed. Hal's huge arms had been there to hold me up as he somehow managed to half carry, half drag me in shock from the trauma room. That was right after the trauma surgeon had officially declared Jake's time of death for the record. That was when everyone stopped working to save a life.

My memory of that day returned to me in bits and pieces over the following weeks and months. As I told Stitch the story, tears continued to flow down my face. I distinctly remember that no one would look at me. The nurses and staff that I had worked with so closely wouldn't or couldn't make eye contact. I also clearly remember opening my locker in the break room to get my purse, but after that my memory was a complete blank. Well, at least until I saw Calli's face. She had found me in the barn, and still to this day, I have no idea how she found out about Jake. Somehow she had, and knew just where I would be.

The scent of horse filled my nostrils as Stitch and I lay entwined in the muggy night. "I knew he was gone the moment I saw him. After you've worked in trauma long enough you begin to see it. Usually it's the eyes, they are empty," I said aloud. Whether for my benefit or for Stitch's I didn't know. The jungle, although not exactly a quiet place at night, seemed especially eerie since I couldn't see much beyond where Stitch and I lay. Although I had been crying, suddenly, the floodgates opened even wider and the tears poured down my cheeks as sobs racked my tired body.

Stitch nickered, a raspy sound that reverberated through my body. As I wiped the tears from my face, he nickered again, this time in earnest. His ears pricked forward, and then I heard it, too. There was movement in the bushes on our left. Tensing up, I watched Stitch's expression, hoping to gauge if it meant danger. He nickered again, and I exhaled with relief. My throat dry from sobbing, I coughed while trying to inhale.

"Lauren, are you in there?" came an unfamiliar voice, a man's voice. A bright beam of light appeared from the same spot in the brush through which I had entered hours ago.

"Here, over here. Stitch is trapped," I croaked. Quickly I wiped the tears away.

The figure of a man burst through the brush. "Ach now, let's have a look," the voice had an accent to it that I couldn't quite place and the beam of light bobbed as the voice came closer, nearly blinding me. Blinking hard, I tried to focus but black dots danced in my vision. *Who the heck?* Try as I might I couldn't see the man behind the voice and spotlight clearly.

"His hind leg is caught in a wire and his front end is tangled in a bunch of vines," I offered, my voice cracking again, thanks to my dry throat. The dark silhouette behind the spotlight was tall, broad shouldered and moved through the thick brush easily. The back glow of the light cast shadows against his face, revealing strong masculine features. I vaguely remember his face, but couldn't quite place it. Stitch shifted, his ears followed the voice, and I managed to extricate my legs from beneath his neck. Balancing, with one hand on his neck and the other grasping his mane, I righted myself. They tingled as I stood up, and for a moment, I thought I might fall over.

"Hmm, let's see your back leg, ol' boy." His voice became softer and reminded me of water rushing over rocks. His consonant and vowels seemed to flow together, lightly nudging each other. He surveyed Stitch with the spotlight, shining it from head to tail until he saw Stitch's outstretched hind leg. Slipping cautiously towards the hind end, he bent to study the wire. Flicking the light back in my direction he studied me for a long time, taking in the dress, pearls, rubber boots, and grime, "You okay?"

"Umm, yes," flustered I straightened my shoulders, smoothing my dress out with my grubby hands. His gaze made me uncomfortable, though I couldn't quite put my finger on why.

"Hmph," he made a noise that was more grunt than words. "Weel then, if ye weel hole the torch I'll be cuttin' him loose."

"Torch? Oh right." Reaching for the spotlight I fumbled in the dark for the handle. Electric sparks shot through my fingers as they brushed his and I nearly dropped the light. My eyes searched for his in the dark, but I still couldn't see him clearly. What I did see was strong masculine features highlighted by shadows from the back glow of the spotlight.

"Are ye sure ye're okay?" he asked again, eyeing me rather skeptically. He had one eyebrow cocked upward as his glaze swept from my boots to my face.

"Fine," I stammered as I shook my head to clear the fuzziness creeping in the edges of my sight. Damn, I was tired. The tingling sensation in my legs and feet just wouldn't go away and was becoming annoying. Hidden by my boots, I wiggled my toes madly, trying to gain circulation. Stitch nickered impatiently as if to say "What about me!"

Just then his cell phone lit up and started to hum against his hip. Clearly distracted, he turned from me and answered with one hand as he dug into his back pocket with the other. As he reached behind him I could see the grips of several tools that he had shoved into the back pocket of his shorts. He had come prepared. Deftly he pulled out a pair of wire cutters and set to work clipping Stitch free. A sharp *pop* followed by a *twang* was all it took to free the wire on one side of his hoof.

"Aye, he's in a wee bit of a jam," he replied to the muffled voice on the phone, "Back side of his pasture, yeah, towards the old homestead on ta the south side. Just bring me Jeep." He looked up at me considering, then added, "She'll be needin' a ride back tae the barn."

"I said I was fine," I blurted out. The thought of stomping a foot to make my point crossed my mind, but I still couldn't quite feel them and I was not about to land on my butt in front of this man, whoever he was.

Effectively ignoring me, he went back to work. *Pop!* The remaining wire gave way and he pulled it free of the metal horseshoe. Stepping over Stitch's tail, he moved up to his withers and made quick work of the sinewy vines while I followed him with the light. I held my breath, waiting for Stitch to get to his feet, and then chaos hit me.

Without warning, my vision started to waver, becoming blurry along the edges like the wavering image in an old mirror. Annoyed, I gave my head a quick shake to clear my vision. Just then Stitch lurched to his feet. From somewhere in the background, although I wasn't sure from where, I picked up the sound of eager voices coming from the brush behind me. Suddenly I felt a pair of strong arms around me as the mirror went black.

I could feel the cold creeping along my spine, inching higher and higher up my back, until I shivered involuntarily. The cold room was enveloped in wavering shades of red, crimson, and burgundy, all the shades of blood. Sweat broke out on my palms and my body shook again, violently, as I shivered. Everything around me felt oddly familiar, but somehow out of place. Instead of the sharp tang of antiseptics I smelled the fresh scent of the sea. And then it was gone, replaced by the sharp smell of blood. An ominous sense of déjà vu settled in the pit of my stomach. Something wasn't right, something was out of order.

A shifting sea of red began to build all around then started to recede as brighter, white lights appeared overhead. No! I had to run, escape. Deep within my core, in a place known only to me, I knew I had to fight the lights. I knew what the lights foretold. No! Panic set in. Turning, I ran, trying to keep the bright lights behind me, but every time I changed course they reached out, groping for my arms. No! I screamed with every fiber of my being. Jake! No! Oh God, please don't let this happen. NO!

"No!" I screamed aloud as I sat bolt upright, a combination of tears and sweat blurring my vision. The nightmare still gripped me. Its weight clung to my forearm like a vise and I sought to free it. Jerking my arm hard, I gasped when it actually slipped free. This time, the nightmare had felt so real.

"Lauren," a soft voice drifted in shattering the remains of the nightmare. Blinking to focus, I recognized the old worn out furniture of the barn office. "Lauren?"

I followed the sound of the voice and was met by an intense pair of green eyes. I gasped, the sound of my voice, catching me off guard. *Mr Rugged? What was his name?* Caught in his gaze, I felt the breath leave my body as the myriad shades of green within his eyes lured me deep into their depths. Suddenly my head swam and I reached for something solid to steady myself. I felt him slip his muscular arms under my shoulders and around my back, holding me up. He smelled of salt air and the sea.

"Dehydrated, most likely, here, this weel help." His voice was impassive, controlled. Pulling one arm free he reached for the table next to him. His remaining arm balanced my weight with ease.

A cold bottle appeared in my right hand and my fingers closed reflexively around it, as he slowly released me. Taking a sip, the Powerade slid down my dry throat.

"Thanks," I croaked and took another swallow. I was slowly returning to normal. The green eyes staring back at me were framed with long, generous auburn colored eyelashes. Biding my time with smaller sips, I studied the man in front of me. His skin had a healthy outdoor glow and I could feel the warmth of him long after he let go of me. Butterflies danced the rumba in my stomach and I felt my cheeks turn a deep crimson as I realized he was staring back at me. We sat in an awkward silence, neither of us willing to speak first.

His green eyes never left mine as the butterflies in my stomach picked up the beat. Finally, breaking the silence I asked, "Stitch?"

"Ach, weel I'm thinkin' he'll be okay. Colleen and AJ brought him in. No doubt he'll be a wee bit sore, as weel you." He added, studying me with those green orbs.

Glancing down, I could see the extent of my adventure written all over my once gorgeous linen dress. Nearly every inch of the fabric was pilled and wrinkled. Dark chocolate and reddish brown smudges and stains covered the entire front of the dress. There was no telling if they were dirt or dried blood.

Lifting my free hand, I turned it in the light, peering at dried blood crammed under what was left of the fingernails of my thumb and index finger. My arms and legs were covered in scratches from the brush and red welts from insect bites. Mortified, I turned my focus back to my drink. Taking another sip, I rested the plastic bottle on one knee. Nervously shifting the Powerade to my other hand, I was startled to see that my right hand was perfectly clean.

Glancing at the ground, he cleared his throat, "I needed tae see if it was yer blood or his." He shifted uncomfortably in his chair. *Oh my! He had cleaned my hand while I was passed out. The thought of his touch made me jumpy.*

"Thanks. Thanks for finding us. Er, I mean…uh…thanks for everything." Embarrassed, I focused on my hands in my lap, trying in vain to smooth the wrinkles out of my dress. I could feel his eyes on me.

Just then, the door to the office swung open and in glided Colleen, looking exhausted. She managed a smile, "Hey, Sleeping Beauty, you're awake! I left you in good hands I see." Her gaze swept between us, an odd smile on her face. "Craig here is going to see you home tonight. I already called your dad to let him know you were okay."

Crap. Dad was probably freaking out by now. "Thanks Colleen. How's Stitch?" I was feeling more like myself as I nursed the cold blue liquid.

"No problem. I called the vet, but honestly he's so far away that I went ahead and started a bag of saline on him just in case, especially since we don't know how long he was stuck. He's a bit stiff in that hind leg and I may have the vet x-ray his stifle just to be sure. Either way, both of you could use some rest."

Numb, I nodded. Every part of me ached, just begging for a hot shower and sleep. I flexed my right hand, feeling my stiff joints.

Craig. I rolled his name over in my mind feeling the taste of it without speaking.

"I can drive myself home, really," I blurted out, not sure I wanted to be babied any more. Besides, I couldn't think straight when Craig looked at me, and right now my brain felt like bran mash. Not to mention the butterflies had moved on to the tango in my belly. I didn't need anything or anyone fogging things up even more. Emotionally and physically drained, I wanted desperately to climb into bed.

Craig cocked an auburn eyebrow in my direction, studying me with those eyes. Lips pursed, he just shook his head slowly from side to side in response.

"Well, I'll leave you two to work this out," and with that Colleen was gone.

"Come now, yer Da is waitin' for ye, no doubt pacin' the floor."

I really was tired. Besides, I rationalized it would take too much energy to argue for my independence. Reluctantly I gave in. Standing up, I headed for the door, my knees knocking as I walked. Stepping alongside me, Craig slipped an arm around my waist and matched my shaky stride. The smells of warm earth, sun, and salt air, reached my nose, a very heady and manly combination to be sure. Automatically, I glanced up at him, the smug look on his face seemed to say, "I told you so."

Craig's Jeep was parked next to the Land Cruiser. I stopped to grab my stuff. My purse and phone sat right where I had left them. After retrieving them I settled into the passenger seat of his Jeep. He started the engine and pointed the short hood of the Jeep back down the gravel road that had carried me here hours ago. According to my cell phone it was 10:14 pm and I had no less than twelve missed calls. Too tired to deal with them I dropped it back into my purse. Once on the road, Craig remained silent.

I tried to fill the silent void of the cab with small talk, "Thank you again. I guess we skipped the introductions, my name is Lauren Todd."

"Craig Duncan, your knight in shinin' armor, at your service, madam." Turning, his eyes met mine with an unmistakable twinkle. The corner of his mouth turned up slightly as he suppressed a grin. *His accent was less noticeable. What was it? Irish? Scottish?*

As exhausted as I was, I couldn't help but smile, "How did you know how to find us?"

"AJ left me some paperwork in his office. I stopped by to pick it up before I leave town tomorrow. I guess Colleen got a call from your Da when you didn't show up at the weddin' tonight. When she found out I was headin' to the house, she rang me up."

The dark jungle walls on either side of the gravel road made it hard to see his face. "Your truck was parked by the barn and not by the house, so I didn't see it when I first pulled up. I did, however, hear the horses making a heck of a strammash in the barn. Boy, they were pissed!" He chuckled softly.

Then it hit me, Duncan, of course. "So you're Hamish's brother?" I blurted out. There was no resemblance that I could see between Hamish's dark smoky looks and Craig's ruddy auburn complexion, but I recognized him as the man Hamish had spoken to at the barn, and again in the hangar. Any doubt as to whether he was indeed Mr. Rugged evaporated.

"He's my little brother."

"Oh," was all I could muster. As tall as Hamish was, the word 'little' didn't seem to apply to him at all.

"Now, mind telling me where you live?" There was a hint of laughter in his voice.

My cheeks burned with embarrassment and I silently gave thanks for the dark interior. "I live at The Pointe. Do you know where it is?"

"Aye," he cleared his throat, "I mean, yes."

We exchanged short bursts of small talk for the next ten minutes or so, at which point we were approaching the Bridge of the Americas. The timbre of the asphalt beneath the tires changed to a hollow sound and as we started across the concrete and steel span. Steel girders flew past my window, casting long, eerie shadows across our faces. A few minutes later we rounded the corner to my street and I pointed out my house. Swinging into the drive, Craig shut off the engine. Before my feet hit the driveway he was there again, with an arm around me. Dad met us at the foyer. After seeing that I was in fact in one piece, he let me excuse myself. I politely thanked Craig again, and headed down the hall towards my room.

The door shut firmly behind me, I caught a glance of myself in the mirror and moaned aloud. My gorgeous linen dress looked worse than I could ever have imagined. What little hair remained in the chignon was full of leaves and dirt while the rest of my hair stood out around my dirty face, making me look like a wraith. My legs, between the tops of my garish, pink rubber boots and what remained of my dress were scratched and filthy. Bright red, swollen bug bites dotted my skin. My pearls, still intact, glared indignantly back at me, defiantly out of place with the rest of my disheveled outfit.

Ugh! Too tired to care I set to work getting undressed. My muscle weary arms struggled with the zipper on the back of the dress. Finally, I managed to free it, and with my last bit of energy, I slipped it over my head. As I did, my nose caught an unfamiliar scent clinging to the fabric. Bringing the dress up to my nose I inhaled cologne, along with the manly scent that was Craig Duncan. I hadn't realized he was wearing cologne. All I could recall from the office was the earthy, salty, mixture of scents. My stomach fluttered again as I dropped the dress on the bed and headed for the shower.

**

Exhausted, I had slept past noon, which was very unusual for me. Dad and Haley had gone to church without me and had plans to stay afterwards for a meeting. I hung out at home, enjoying the peace and quiet of an empty house.

Home alone with nothing to do, I found myself wondering about Craig. What little I had learned on the plane from Elaine and Deanne only served to pique my interest. I spent the day trying to tell myself that it was merely curiosity that made me want to learn more about him, but each time my thoughts drifted back to that night, my body would simply hum. When he had his arm around me in the barn office my body had responded to his touch in a way I had never experienced before. It was new and confusing. With Jake, I had felt a deep connection, but never had my body responded to him the way it had when Craig's arms were around me. *Oh good grief, Todd!*

Thoroughly confused, I set to work cleaning the already clean house in an effort to keep Craig off my mind. While sweeping the kitchen, I made up my mind to forget about Craig, especially since it was just too early to even contemplate dating again. Besides, I wasn't at all sure I wanted anything to do with a man who made my heart leap in my chest and butterflies tango in my belly. Not yet anyway, I had worked too hard at cordoning off my emotions since Jake's death. *No, I wasn't ready.*

So, I put Craig on the back burner and decided to focus on my riding. That was until I began doing laundry, at which point the feeling of Craig's arms around me and his soft reassuring voice came back to me and I found myself daydreaming instead of matching socks. While wiping down the bathroom I was back to my original and safe plan of avoiding Craig completely. Unfortunately, when I stepped out onto the veranda and caught a whiff of a fresh onshore ocean breeze, my body remembering his touch, changed its mind again. *Ugh!* And so it was all day long until Dad and Haley came home.

It was Tuesday before I made it back to the barn. Colleen had reassured me that Stitch would be okay when I spoke with her by phone on Sunday. Luckily, he did not appear to have any tendon or ligament damage to his hind leg. His quiet nature probably had a lot to do with the fact that he hadn't struggled to the point of injuring himself too seriously. Today I had a lesson on Gold Herr scheduled at 9 a.m. so I dropped Haley off at school and headed straight for the barn.

The barn was empty when I pulled in. The horses and been fed and a few of them were already in their pastures for their morning turnout. Opening up the tack room door, I flipped on the iPod docking station and chose country music from the playlist. The Zac Brown Band filled the barn with the soulful, Southern sounds that reminded me of home.

Leading him from his stall, I set to work getting Gold Herr ready. It felt really good to be back at the barn again and before long I found myself singing along to the music. Gold Herr stood in the grooming stall next to the tack room, quietly waiting for me to groom him. Someone had cleverly thought to put a pass through in the wall, with a sliding pocket door between the tack room and the grooming stall. This saved me from having to constantly duck under cross ties and walk back out into the barn aisle to get back and forth. I liked the set up so much I filed it away in my brain for when I built my dream barn.

After polishing his dark black coat to a shine and brushing out his mane and tail, I put oil on his hooves. Still singing out loud, I ducked back into the tack room for his saddle. Reaching up on the shelf, I grabbed a clean saddle pad, Colleen's saddle, and girth. Balancing the gel pad on the top of my pile I managed to scoop up Gold Herr's bridle, using a free finger.

Colleen's Passier dressage saddle was absolutely ancient, the seat hard as a rock, and it weighed twice as much as mine. Like many riders, her saddle was very much a reflection of her. A saddle can often make a subtle statement about its owner. Some riders like lots of extra stuff such as extra leather blocks made to hold your leg in place, expensive leathers like buffalo hide, or the latest saddle style modeled by some rider who happens to currently be en vogue. Not Colleen, her saddle was basic, smooth brown leather. There were no huge knee rolls, or thigh blocks. It was functional and simple. It was clear to me, that many memories clung to the well-worn brown leather. Once broken in, there were few things in life as comfy as your favorite saddle. My saddle didn't quite fit the contour of Gold Herr's back so I was forced to use her saddle when I rode him and boy could my butt tell the difference between her saddle and mine.

Still singing along to the music, I headed for the pass through. The gel pad started to slip off of the saddle as I reached the door. Glancing down to adjust it, I rebalanced my load, lifting one knee and shifting the weight in my arms. Once I had everything rebalanced I headed back through the opening in the wall where I ran smack into the well-muscled chest of a man. Saddle, pad, girth and gel pad went tumbling to the floor at our feet.

"Crap!" Frustrated, I glared up into the face of Craig. His emerald green eyes were alight with humor as he smiled down at me. My heart skidded to an abrupt halt then leapt back to life, pounding out an erratic rhythm in my chest.

"Looks like you could use a hand," he said. Kneeling down, he scooped up the dressage saddle by the pommel with one hand. The bridle hung in a mass of twisted leather from his other hand. He was casually dressed in a pair of denim shorts and a white T-shirt, which he wore very well. On his head was a tan colored visor with Brisas del Mar stitched across the front in dark blue. His hair, although short, stuck out in all directions and I was reminded of how much I had wanted to run my fingers through his hair. Today he had on a well-worn pair of leather deck shoes instead of flip-flops. His sunglasses were slung backwards around his tan neck, hung by a black nylon cord, their dark lenses staring sightlessly behind him. He swallowed and I watched the muscles of his neck slide beneath his skin.

Oh geez.

Flustered, I bent down to grab the rest of my gear from the concrete floor of the tack room. "Ah, thanks." *Crap, Todd, pull it together.* The butterflies started their warm-up routine in my belly. Blocking the entrance like the massive trunk of a tree, he stood his ground, watching me with those cool green eyes. He seemed to be savoring the moment, and a slow smile crossed his face.

"I um…thank you again for the other night. Thanks for helping me with Stitch and driving me home." Standing close to him I could feel my pulse quicken. Pulling his gaze from mine, he blinked, breaking the connection. For a moment, I thought he seemed suddenly unsure of himself. "No problem. Where do you want these?" He held up the saddle and tangled bridle.

Regaining my composure, I took a deep breath. "There's a rack just on the other side of the door," I motioned, "to the right." He stepped aside, allowing me to pass, then followed me. His hair was wind blown and I inhaled the very manly scent of his cologne mixed with salty sea air as I brushed past him in the narrow space. *Does he feel it, too?*

He swung the saddle up onto the rack. With his free hand he tried to make sense of the bridle, shifting it from one hand to the next, frowning. A furrow appeared across his brow and I watched as it grew deeper as his frustration mounted. Finally he thrust the black leather mess in my direction, with a scowl on his face.

Wordlessly I took it in one hand and laid the rest of the tack on top of the saddle. Saving the bridle puzzle for later, I reached up and hung it by one of the bit rings on a wooden peg jutting out from the wall. I squashed the urge to immediately sit down and untangle it. Tangled bridles drove me nuts; pet peeve number 49, or was it number 46? *Why can't I think straight with him around?*

Just then Elaine came down the barn aisle, a halter and lead slung over her shoulder. We hadn't heard her coming with the music on. She stopped dead in the aisle at the sight of Craig. Glancing from him to me, her face split in a slow smile, "Hey Craig, it is good to see you again. How's business at the resort?"

"Boomin', I came back to civilization to pick up a few things before flying out tomorrow. You still with that American GI you were seein' a while back? Was it Jeff? From Kansas?"

Setting the saddle pad on Gold Herr's back I started the job of tacking him up while listening to them talk, grateful to be forgotten for the moment. Smoothing it out, I placed the gel pad on top. I listened to their conversation while I worked. His accent was much less noticeable than I remembered.

"Jack. No, he ended up being a loser. Although he wasn't a GI, he was a pilot with a nice ass and a flight suit to boot." She smiled wickedly. "Still, he was a certifiable jerk. Good riddance," she quipped. "Guess I am still looking. But then, that's the story of my life." Looking straight at me, she added, "The really good guys are few and far between." Her tone of voice caught my attention and, looking up, her eyes met mine. "Well, I have to go get William. See you guys around." And with that she was gone back down the aisle.

Lifting the saddle from the rack, Craig handed it to me backwards. "Thanks," I turned it around and set it down on top of the gel pad, pulling both up under the pommel to give Gold Herr's withers some room to move. I turned, searching for the girth. Craig handed it to me with a smile. As I ran the billets into the buckles I could feel his eyes staring at my back. "So, you work at a resort?" I slipped under Gold Herr's neck to his other side in order to attach the girth.

Stepping around to the front, he rubbed Gold Herr's face with the palm of his hand, "I own a fishin' resort south of here on the coast. Marlin, sailfish, dorado, you know; sport fishin'.

Tightening the girth I smiled, "I used to fish a lot with my family off the coast of North Carolina. We had some friends of the family that lived on the Outer Banks. Haley, my little sister, gets sea sick, so my dad and I would go while Mom stayed onshore with her."

The vacations spent at the beach house with family and friends, were some of my best memories. I smiled to myself and slipped the billets into the keepers. Glancing up, I found him watching me with those green eyes.

"Listen, I stopped by to see how you were doin', but I also wanted to see if I could take you dinin' tonight?"

"Dining? Oh, you mean out to dinner!"

He just laughed softly, "Yes."

Chewing on my lower lip, I thought it over for a moment. Truth was I didn't feel right turning him down after all he had done, but a part of me wanted to run, screaming, down the barn aisle as fast as my legs would go. Craig was a piece of my new life I hadn't quite counted on. He was a man. One that was certainly easy on the eyes, and he was definitely polite, which meant I was my only hang up. "Sure," I blurted out, not at all convinced I had made the best decision. The butterflies started to tango now, making me slightly nauseous.

Giving Gold Herr a final pat between the eyes he said, "Great, then I'll pick you up at six o'clock." Gold Herr flicked his big ears forward and nudged Craig with his nose, leaving a brown smudge on his shirt. With that he made an about face and strode down the barn aisle. Leaning around the wall I watched him go. Unlike AJ's feline grace, Craig moved with a warrior's stride, confident and strong, someone who was sure of himself and his surroundings. Leaning my head against Gold Herr's neck I inhaled eau de horse, hoping to ground myself in all that was familiar. *What the hell are you doing, Todd? You are in no position to handle this. It's too damn soon. It's too fresh, too raw.* My butterflies picked up the tempo ignoring me.

I was late getting on Gold Herr for my lesson. I had been forced to unbuckle every single piece of the bridle and then reconstruct it before slipping it onto his head. Even then, I had to make a few adjustments as his bit sat too low in his mouth. Thank goodness the bridle leather was well cared for and supple. It didn't help that Craig had left me a bit jumpy and my fingers wouldn't follow simple commands. Thank goodness Colleen was in a good mood.

By three o'clock I was dragging my feet. Colleen worked Gold Herr and me really hard. She focused mainly on our trot work, especially the half pass. She also had me ride Macho and Patina, back to back. Afterward, I helped her clean tack and strip Stitch's stall. The poor guy was stuck on stall rest for the next week and he was all too eager to tell us how unhappy he was. In order to strip his stall, Colleen had to put him in an empty stall to prevent him from knocking us around while we worked. He wanted to walk in circles and neigh out loud in complaint to anyone who would listen. By the time we were done, my head was pounding from all the racket.

Jumping in the Land Cruiser I raced to pick Haley up from school on time. The air conditioner had quit working on my way to the barn so Haley and I rolled down all four windows to get some relief from the stifling heat. Sore, hot, hungry, and tired, I pulled into the driveway. The clock on the radio read 4:06 pm and I was starting to regret my decision to go out with Craig. I had not been on a real date since high school. Jake had been my first, my only, and my last. What had I gotten myself into? I knew that I would have to take the plunge into the world of dating eventually and that was okay, but now, so soon? Tonight? Really? What was I thinking?

Haley jumped out and headed into the house, her backpack bouncing against the back of her knees. Leaning forward I rested my forehead on the hard plastic of the steering wheel and tried to come up with an excuse to avoid tonight, but my brain was too hot and too tired. The last thing I wanted to do was to hurt Craig. He seemed so genuine and he did, after all, rescue Stitch and me. "Come on, Todd; put your big girl britches on. It is only one night," I muttered at the dusty dashboard. "Besides, he never said the word 'date' now did he?" A tap on the windshield jerked me out of my thoughts. Flustered, I looked up into Dad's face.

"Lauren, you okay?"

"Yeah, yeah, I'm fine," I replied, wondering just how long he had been standing there. Turning the key one click in the ignition I powered up all of the windows. Removing the key, I gathered my cell phone, dropped it into my purse and climbed out. "The A/C died today."

"That's what Haley said. Let me see the keys, I'm going to check it out." He took the keys then reached in to pop open the hood. Without a backward glance, I headed inside.

Heading for the kitchen, I grabbed a couple slices of Colby-Jack cheese from the fridge to tide me over. Carmen was stirring something that smelled heavenly on the stove while Haley set the table before doing homework. "Mees Lauren, you hungry?"

Carmen's eyes ran from the cheese in my hand and down to my waist rather disapprovingly. One hand on her hip, the other holding a wooden spoon, she waited expectantly for my answer. Carmen thought her new job in life was to put weight on me. Lately I had been successful in my attempts to avoid her. However, having been unsuccessful with me, she had recently turned her focus on Dad. I hadn't heard him complain yet. "No thank you, Carmen, I am going out with a friend."

"Flacca, men don't like skeenny weemen. They want someteeng to hol on to." She waved the spoon like a wand from her bosom to her ample hips illustrating her point. "If you want a man, you must eat. I tell you this because it ees true."

Much to my annoyance, Carmen, like Chi Chi, had taken to calling me Flacca, which meant skinny. "Whoever said anything about a man," I retorted over my shoulder before heading for my room. I could hear her laughing quietly to herself as she went back to work. Shutting the bedroom door behind me I stared at my closet; too tired to even think about finding an outfit for tonight. Giving up, instead I headed straight for the shower, peeling off my sweaty shirt and sports bra on the way.

DATE

The clock on the table read 5:15 pm. I had been sitting on the end of my bed with my feet tucked under me. I was still wrapped in a damp towel and had been glaring at my closet for the past 15 minutes while my hair dried naturally. Or that was my excuse. What in the world should I wear on a date, that isn't really a 'date', with a man I hardly knew? *Ugh! What did you get yourself into?* It didn't help that I had no idea where we were going. He hadn't told me in the barn, and I had been too flustered to ask.

With a sigh I shifted, stretching one leg out so it reached the floor. Maybe if I sat here long enough something would scream, "Pick me!" Several more minutes passed without any inspiration. Finally, after mulling over my options, I decided that something in the middle of the road would be best. Prying myself from the bed I pulled out a white pair of cotton Capri pants and a white peasant style blouse with several shades of green embroidery around the sleeves, neck, and bottom. A pair of dressy white flip-flops completed the look. Since arriving in the tropics I had learned that everyone had a large selection of flip-flops and there indeed was a difference between your everyday casual pair and those reserved for dressing up, or rather, the tropical version of dressing up.

Never one for a bunch of make up I kept it simple and fresh with a light foundation, powder, and some blush to brighten my fair cheeks and break up the monotony of my freckles. After all, this wasn't a real date. Running my fingers through my curls, I decided to leave my hair down. Jake had been a fan of Ralph Lauren's signature perfume; aptly called Lauren. I had worn it for as long as I could remember. With Jake's death, the thought of wearing it, and all of the memories that were attached to the scent was just too much for me. I had thrown away what was left of the perfume and I hadn't worn anything for several months now.

Reaching into the bottom drawer in the bathroom I pulled out a beautiful pink and silver box with 'Romance' on the front, and smiled. Calli, God love her, had given it to me as a going away present at the spa that day. It was still a Ralph Lauren scent, but something fresh and new, unburdened by memories. Prying open the box I pulled out the clear, square glass bottle and misted the air above the sink. It was a light, floral scent. Best of all, it was the new me. "Thanks, Calli," I said aloud, and then misted my wrist and neck before heading downstairs.

As I passed the entrance to the kitchen, Carmen, spoon in hand, thrust her head through the door. "Flacca, you smell good for a date weeth a friend." Chuckling, she disappeared back into the kitchen.

Hearing his Jeep pull up out front, I dashed out the door, hoping to speed things up in order to avoid an inquisition by Dad. Even though, I was clearly an adult and able to care for myself, he had become more protective over the past year. I really couldn't blame him, Haley and I were all he had left. But, I did miss my own space, especially the apartment Jake and I had shared.

I wasn't fast enough. Craig was talking to Dad, both bent intently under the hood. As I walked up, Craig glanced past Dad and smiled, "You look nice."

"Thanks. Um, are you ready?" I shifted my feet, ready to get going.

"Nice to meet you, Mr. Todd." Craig reached out to shake my Dad's hand. Straightening, he headed for the Jeep. Reaching the passenger side door, he opened it for me. Shutting the door neatly behind me, he rounded the hood and climbed in behind the wheel. "So, where are we goin'?"

"Italian?" he asked.

"Sure." He fired up the engine and we headed out.

As the sun began to set, Craig headed through the city towards the Bay of Panama. Parking in an alley lot with a guard on duty, we walked the short distance downhill to an open-air Italian pizzeria perched on the bay. The yeasty smell of dough found its way to our noses as we approached the restaurant. The place was busy, even though it was a weeknight. Craig found us a table next to a low wall, at the front of the restaurant.

The view from our table was incredible. From where we sat, I could see the huge ships transiting the Canal. We were on the north side of the bay; almost exactly opposite from where my house sat. On the opposite side, the lights of the city curved back out towards the bay. The restaurant was a cozy place and overflowed with people from all walks of life and ethnicities. The back wall was composed entirely of red bricks from floor to ceiling. There were three cavernous brick ovens set into the brick wall. Black soot, from years of use, lined the inside and outer rims of each brick oven. Boisterous cooks, with long handled wooden spatulas reached in and out of the oven shifting pizzas around as they cooked; removing and adding them in dancelike motions. Once again, I was amazed at the diversity of Panama.

We ordered a pizza to share for dinner and on Craig's recommendation, we also ordered an appetizer of fresh clams in a white wine and garlic sauce. He was quick to point out that the clams came straight from the Bay. Craig also ordered us each a locally brewed beer. Sipping my cold beer, I started to relax and enjoy myself.

The twinkling lights of boats floating in the dark waters of the Bay bobbed and shifted, creating an ever changing scene. Soft ocean breezes from the bay gave the small restaurant an airy feel. Red and white checked plastic tablecloths and old wine bottles plugged with half burned candles adorned each table. It was a décor that could be found in a million different Italian restaurants around the world and yet, here I sat in Panama across from …

Interrupting my reverie, Craig set his bottle down with a soft *thump*. "So, you ride with Colleen." It was more of a statement than a question.

Pulling my gaze from the Bay, I reached for my beer. "Yes, I just started. I rode quite a bit in the States. Well, I jumped a lot, but she concentrates more on dressage." I wasn't sure just how much Craig new about horse sports so I tried to keep things in general terms.

"Jumpin', like you see on TV with the wooden poles and fancy jumps?" he asked.

Okay, so he has a general idea. Not bad, not bad at all. Now, let's see if it stops there.

"Sort of, I evented." As always, when talking to someone who didn't ride, about horses I got a confused look, so I continued, "Eventing was originally started as a form of military training. Since horses were the mode of transportation in the battlefield for centuries you had to be able to cross-train them and that is where eventing fits in."

He waited patiently for me to continue. Just then the large bowl of steamed clams and fresh baked bread arrived. The white wine and chunks of fresh garlic smelled like heaven. Medium in size, they sat open, waiting for us to savor. Setting down our drinks, we grabbed our forks and dove in. Chasing a steamy clam with a sip of beer, I continued, "Okay, it's like a triathalon. Over three days we do three different things. Day one is dressage."

"That's what Colleen does, then? The dressage bit."

'The dressage bit'. If only it was that easy.

"Yes, she gets much more in depth then what I used to do. Day two is the cross country course. This is similar to fox hunting, only there are no hounds." Pausing to make sure I hadn't lost him, I added, "Actually, there are no foxes either, but the style of jumps is much the same; solid, wooden fences, ditches, stone walls, and water obstacles. Things you would find in nature or galloping across the countryside a hundred years ago. The trick here is to complete the course of jumps and obstacles in a certain amount of time. Go under and you get penalized, go over, and well you get a speeding ticket."

"So, what makes day two so hard. Sounds like a jaunt in the woods."

I nearly choked on a clam. *Jaunt, huh?* Setting down my fork, I continued, "Well, for one thing, the jumps aren't made to fall down like the ones you see on TV. If you hit them wrong, you and the horse can flip, break a leg, or worse."

His eyes grew wide and he paused, his beer halfway to his lips. "That's why we wear medical arm bands and safety vests. There are also medics on hand for every show, just in case."

Reaching for another clam, he stopped, raised a sandy hued eyebrow and studied me for a moment. Slowly, the clam finished its trip to his mouth, "Go on then."

I watched again as the muscles of his neck slid beneath his tan skin and my body began to hum. *Oh geez.*

His eyes held mine and the butterflies in my stomach started to tango. Swallowing, I continued, "Day three is the stadium jumping. The idea behind the third and final day is to see if you and your horse are both talented and fit enough to get around the course without knocking down a fence."

"So these are made to fall down? Why?" He tore a chunk of the bread and dredged it through the sauce.

"Well, the horses are tired after day two so the slightest rub can send the jump crashing down. They use shallow cups to hold the jump poles in place. The cups are specially designed to allow the jump to fall if knocked too hard."

He thought for a moment, dragging another thick slice of bead through the rich sauce, "Safety vests, sounds dangerous. Have you been hurt?"

Have I been hurt? I evented for goodness sakes. I stabbed a clam with my fork, stalling. Jake had understood my eventing, but that didn't mean he loved it as I did. He knew I was both good and careful. Still, I had several broken bones, an assortment of torn ligaments, an untold number of bruises, and one concussion on my eventing resume. The fact was, you could be the most talented and careful rider in the world, but you couldn't control everything around you. Eventing was in many ways a sport of chance, even with the addition of newer jumps, in recent years, that were designed to break upon impact. Horses were unpredictable creatures. They were and forever would be a prey animal, and with that came a set of flight instincts that could pop up at the most inopportune time.

I smiled, remembering Pogo's flight instincts and a nearly broken nose. On one sunny day in particular a photographer positioned near one of the last fences on course dropped something. Innocently bending down to pick it up, they had instantly morphed into a fire-breathing dragon, or at least in Pogo's mind that is what happened. You would have been hard pressed to convince him otherwise at the time. Two strides out from a huge wooden table jump he leapt sideways to avoid the dragon. He nearly collided with the poor jump judge sitting under a tree. The judge shrieked and Pogo, thinking there must be another dragon after him hopped back in the direction we had come from. All this happened while still travelling toward the jump. At the last second I kicked him firmly and sent him over the jump, which looked quite a bit safer than the two dragons. We barely made it to the other side.

I hadn't had much time to think about or prepare for the jump because of Pogo's behavior. As a result, when he landed on the other side of the jump my upper body had shifted forward and I whacked his neck hard with my nose. I had been so full of adrenaline that I had no clue my nose was bleeding until we crossed the finish line. I wiggled my nose, remembering the pain. Glancing up, I noticed Craig was patiently watching me, "It's hard not to get hurt around horses." That would have to do for now, I thought.

Dinner arrived and we talked between mouthfuls. The brick oven style pizza was incredible. Lost in conversation, we enjoyed the meal and each other. Craig was easy to talk to and I found his interest in me flattering. As the night wore on, I began to relax and before I knew it, I was opening up to him. We chatted our way through a myriad of light topics, never delving too deep into any one in particular. *Keep it light, Todd.* On more than one occasion I found myself pausing to think before speaking so as to avoid any mention of the last eight months of heartache, which was difficult considering how much of my life had included both my mother and Jake.

On one occasion I nearly said Jake's name. Catching myself, I half halted, rebalanced and continued the conversation. My emotions zinged just under the surface. Reading a change in me, he leaned back, balancing his chair on two legs and studied me with those green eyes. "So what brought you to Panama?" he asked.

Other than the brief explanation I had given the gang on the San Blas trip, I'd not been faced with this question since arriving. That had been a definite plus to starting over in a new place. No explanations. No need to tell the truth, or even lie for that matter. Anonymity, I was finding, was a great hiding place. But to keep my privacy, I would need to tell the same story to everyone. *Keep it light.* "My mom passed last year so I came along to help my dad take care of Haley." There, that was neither lie, nor the whole truth.

"I'm sorry." His green eyes narrowed slightly, appraising me. "You seem passionate about your eventin'. You gave all that up to come here?" The front legs of his chair hit the tile floor with a soft *thud* as he leaned his elbows on the table. He held his beer between both hands.

Damn, he was hot. "Yes," I said with less conviction than I felt. He glanced down at his beer then raised it to his lips, draining the last bit of liquid before setting it aside. *He isn't buying it.*

"So, are you workin', I mean other than takin' care of your sister?"

It was an innocent enough question, but one that rankled me. I had always worked and supported myself. I'd started my first job at sixteen giving riding lessons at a summer camp and hadn't stopped working since. I shifted my empty plate, setting it aside and stacking the empty bowl of clams on top. I gathered up the silverware next, placing it in the bowl, both to buy time and think of a good answer. The sad fact was I didn't have an answer, at least not one that I liked. Not one I wanted to admit. *Hi, I'm Lauren and I'm a basket case since nearly everyone I've loved has died lately and I can no longer work in my field because I had a break down and the smell of antiseptic or the thought of an emergency room makes my palms sweat.* "I'm in a career change. Right now my focus needs to be Haley, although I am taking some online business courses."

Thankfully, he ended the inquisition and moved onto lighter conversations. It wasn't until Craig had paid the bill and we were heading for the Jeep that I realized that although he had lightened up on the personal questions, he had, in fact, kept me talking for most of the night. At the end of the night, I found that I didn't know much more about him than when he picked me up. On the drive home through the city lights, I tried to turn the conversation around without much luck and before I knew it we were home.

The Jeep came to a stop at the end of the driveway, and Craig turned off the engine. Silence drifted through the cab. For the first time that night it felt like a real date and I could feel myself starting to pull away. Sensing a shift in the fabric of the evening, Craig slipped out from behind the wheel. Grateful to have avoided an awkward moment in the dark cab of the Jeep, I gathered my purse.

I watched him stride across the beams cast by the headlights. The shifting shadows and light made him look even more rakish then he did in natural light and my body began to hum again. As he rounded the corner of the Jeep, the shadows played across his strong face and he looked up, meeting my gaze. I couldn't deny it, he was incredibly sexy. Deep within my belly, what began as a hum became a smoldering fire and I felt my pale skin flush and turn hot in the dark cab. Suddenly embarrassed, I glanced down at my purse lying in my lap, trying to hide my emotions as he reached for my door.

After opening the car door he walked me up to the house. Pulling out my keys, I clutched them nervously in my hand. *Oh Lord, here we go. I'm not ready for this.* I could feel my palms begin to sweat. He smiled down at me; his eyes dark pools of emerald green in the dim yellow glow of the front porch light. Leaning in, his hand grasped mine and he gently pulled the keys free. His touch made me jump.

"Which one?" he was thumbing through the keys.

I let out a breath. "Hmm?" I hadn't realized I had been holding it.

"Which key is for the front door?" His eyes danced with mirth, the tension between us thrummed.

"Oh, ah, the silver one with the green rubber thingy on it," I was glad he had the keys. I didn't want him to hear them rattle together in my shaky hand. Even more, I didn't think I wanted him to touch me again. He stepped past me to unlock the door and I caught a whiff of his cologne mingled with the salty, earthy, fresh breeze scent that was Craig. My heart pounded in my chest and my breath caught at his nearness.

He unlocked the front door, and handed me back the keys. My pulse quickened and hummed as his hand brushed mine. Before I realized it, he leaned closer slipped his hand around the nape of my neck and slowly pulled me in until his face was inches from mine. *Oh my.* His skin was warm, his big hands gentle. My heart continued to thud in my chest and I felt like an inexperienced teenager waiting for her first kiss. *Oh Lord he smelled good.* My eyelids slid shut waiting, expecting, but nothing happened. Flustered, I opened my eyes to see him watching me. His green eyes appeared even darker, more hazel in the yellow glow of the porch light. Our faces were within inches of each other. Changing course, he gently kissed my forehead then whispered, "Good night." With a smug look of satisfaction, he smiled, stepped back and opened the door for me. As I stepped inside I hoped he couldn't hear my knees knocking or my heart pounding. "Good night. Thank you for dinner, it was lovely."

"It was my pleasure." He sounded so formal. "I'll see you tomorrow before I leave."

"See you tomorrow then." I shut the door, hearing the soft *click* as I turned the lock. I slid down the inside of the door with a thump. *Dumb, dumb, dumb!* Embarrassment mingled with incredulity filled me until I thought I would burst. "He must think me an idiot," I murmured to the foyer. "Ugh!" Finally, I stood up and for the first time noticed the warmth of his kiss as it lingered on my forehead. Reaching up with one hand, I gently placed a finger on the spot. It was still warm. "You need one hell of a half halt, Todd," I muttered to the quiet foyer. "You need someone to sit you on your ass with a half halt."

**

Jake stayed away for most of the night. Near dawn, he managed to find me again and I greeted the morning in the usual way. Well, usual for me I thought as I pulled the damp sheets off the bed to wash them.

True to his word Craig stopped by the barn the next morning. Just as I swung my leg over to dismount from Gold Herr, I saw him come up the path from the house with a large brown bag in his arms. "Afternoon," he said with a sly smile as he walked briskly past us in the aisle. Setting the bag down in the office, he headed towards the arena.

I stopped Gold Herr in front of the wash rack. "Um, hey," I said to his retreating back. "Well, okay then," I muttered to Gold Herr. "Wonder what he's up to." Turning Gold Herr around, I slipped off his bridle and exchanged it for a halter. As I pulled the saddle off his back, Maria came down the aisle with Mariposa. "Have a good ride," I offered as they passed us.

"Always," she purred as she halted Mariposa in the aisle.

I peeked back down the aisle, saddle in hand just in time to see Craig enter the dark shadows of the indoor arena.

Following my gaze, Maria caught sight of him as well, "What in the hell is he doing here?" She snapped, her mood suddenly swinging the other way. I swore I could feel hot rage coming off her. Deciding not to deal with her I simply shrugged my shoulders and headed for the tack room. I had yet to figure Maria out. She seemed to always be in either a foul mood or sweeter than honey. Although in my opinion she most often leaned towards the foul side. Feeling her rage, I put some distance between us. Her mood swings were annoying as heck, but this was the first time I had seen blatant rage. From what I could tell she was a very miserable person, I just couldn't understand why, nor did I particularly want to.

As I set the saddle down on its rack I glanced back and saw her staring down the aisle, a look of pure hatred on her face. Snatching up the reins she marched off, dragging poor Mariposa behind her.

I made quick work of rinsing Gold Herr off. After sharing a carrot with him I walked him down the aisle and returned him to his stall. I still had Macho and Nicola to ride and my stomach was complaining. Heading back to the tack room, I grabbed a fresh saddle pad and Macho's bridle when Craig popped in behind me. "Put the tack back, you need lunch."

Chuckling at him, I headed for the door. "Yeah right!" I shot back as I reached the doorway. "I've got two more horses to ride today."

"You did, I brought you some lunch and told Colleen you were training too hard, besides, I am willing to bet you haven't eaten all day." He paused, "I'm right, aren't I?"

I could hear the laughter in his voice and I stopped. Turning around, I leaned casually against the door frame, bridle and pad in hand. He stood across the room with the large brown bag in his arms. "And just what did you bribe her with?" My stomach grumbled, deciding that half a carrot wasn't good enough and Craig's brow shot up as he gave me a knowing look.

"Fresh fish, or at least a promise that I would brin' her some next time I get to town. She has a weak spot for ceviche and Chi Chi makes the best ceviche around." Shifting the bag to one arm he pointed to the tack on the wall. "Put it back." He tried his best to look stern and I tried not to smile.

"Okay, fine. Is this a picnic?" I hung the bridle on its peg and put the pad back on the shelf.

"Yes, so let's get movin'." He grabbed my hand and headed out of the barn. We walked along the dirt road by the pastures. As we reached the end of the large pasture where I had found Stitch, the road narrowed and became a trail leading into the jungle. I hadn't even noticed, before today, that it was there. As we entered the jungle canopy he released my hand and I slipped in behind him. He led the way up a small hill. Here and there medium sized boulders jutted out from the clay and leaves that covered the jungle floor. The path wound around them and continued on upwards. Halfway up the hill I realized I was still wearing my half chaps and my riding gloves were tucked into my belt at the small of my back. Oh well, I thought, I would still be able to squeeze in a ride when I got back.

Reaching the top of the hill, Craig started back down. Even though we were in the shade of the trees, the humidity was thick as a knife and the sweat began to trickle down my face and back. I noticed damp patches on the back of Craig's shirt in front of me. A few strands of hair had come loose from my ponytail and I absently tucked them behind my ear. In his rush to leave, Craig hustled me out of the barn and I hadn't had the time to think about my hair before leaving. Groaning inwardly, I could just imagined what my 'helmet hair' looked like.

We walked for quite a ways, Craig shifting the bag from one arm to the other, until finally we reached a clearing overlooking a small lake. My jaw dropped at the view. On one side of the clearing sat the remains of an old building, its weathered stones lay strewn about. Thick vines covered the one remaining wall. No doubt, I thought, holding it up. My experience with the thick vines in Stitch's pasture had shown me just how strong they could be.

"Wow, this is gorgeous," I muttered, taking it all in. Crossing the clearing ahead of me, Craig headed for a cluster of taller stones that looked like grave markers. The grassy area around the headstones was well maintained, the jungle kept at bay. As I stepped up behind him I noticed one stone in particular was in the crude shape of a cross. Bending down to get a closer look, a few wild curls fell across my face blocking my view. Tucking them behind my ear, I studied it closer, running my finger along the weathered numbers. My fingers ran over the smooth stone. "702?" Puzzled, I looked up at Craig.

"1702. The first number is illegible, gone with time, just like his name."

"That's amazing. I can't believe it survived this long in the jungle. Who maintains it?" I glanced around realizing what a chore it would be to regularly travel the path we had just left in order to keep the site maintained.

"Chi Chi." He must have read the confusion on my face. "He is a devout Catholic, as are most Panamanians. His family lives nearby and they have maintained this site for many, many years. I seriously doubt they are related," he said, pointing to the gravestone. "I don't know, maybe they maintain it out of respect." He shrugged. "Besides," he added, "it makes a great picnic spot."

I spread a blanket that Craig had packed under the shade of an ancient mahogany tree and we dined on ham sandwiches, potato salad, and iced tea. Again we talked about small stuff, safe stuff, and I told him about Colleen's crazy idea to field a team for the Pan Am Games. He asked some questions but didn't seem as shocked by the idea as I had been.

"Sounds like a great idea on paper, but one small thing."

"What's that?"

"I don't exactly have a ride."

"A ride?" He looked lost for a moment, "Oh, you mean a horse."

I couldn't help but giggle, "It is sort of important."

His green eyes danced as he laughed aloud. "Not sure how I missed that point?" Still chuckling, he leaned on one elbow, studying his hands. After a moment, he grew serious, "Can't you borrow one?"

Flopping onto my stomach, my arms propping me up, I crossed my ankles. "Not that easy." How do you explain to a non-rider the bond between a horse and rider? Tucking another errant curl behind my ear I jumped in. "Not that simple. Riders at the upper levels spend countless hours developing a bond with their horses. A nudge with a leg becomes more of a thought than an action."

He regarded me for a moment, "Two become one?"

Wow! "Yes, that's it." *Impressive Mr. Duncan.* "But in order for two to become one, there needs to be two to start with."

"So how do you find a horse?"

"Good question. Colleen seems to think it is doable…" I left the rest unspoken and rolled onto my back, studying the clouds above. The storms would be building soon.

"I take it you are not convinced." He shifted, sitting upright, one strong arm wrapped around his bent knee, "Why?"

We talked for a while and I told him that the biggest hurdle for me, which happened to be the most insurmountable of them all, was finding a horse capable of upper level dressage. Colleen had been checking with her contacts in South America, Europe, and the States. I explained to Craig that finding the perfect horse dressage wise that also fit within my meager budget and in time for the qualifiers was likely not going to happen. He listened intently as I talked; laughing when I told him I needed to find a $100,000 horse on the clearance rack for the bargain price of 70 percent off.

Glancing at my watch, I sat up, "I'll need to get going soon."

"No worries, Colleen isn't expecting you back for a while." I threw him a questioning look, which he returned with a bland expression. "Besides, I was just beginnin' to relax and forget about everythin' I have to do today." A wistful smile crossed his rugged face. Absently, he plucked at the blanket with his thumb and forefinger.

"Work?"

His brows creased in thought and his eyes grew dark for a moment before he recovered. "Just some stuff going on at the resort that I need to sort out." He tried to keep his voice light, but something in his tone made me think there was more going on than he was telling me. "You're right, we better get goin'. I fly back to the resort early tomorrow. We have several large groups arrivin' in the afternoon."

"Sounds like the resort is a busy place. Do you manage it alone?"

He nodded, "Busy, yes. Hamish handles the bookings, internet stuff, and supply side. I manage the day to day stuff and the boats." A grey cloud, heavy with the prospect of rain drifted overhead, blocking the midday sun and offering a brief respite from the heat. Craig glanced up, watching it for a moment. I had the feeling he was calculating in his head, although exactly what, I wasn't sure. "It works out pretty well, especially since Hamish isn't one for the water." He grinned a boyish grin and turned his focus back to me. "I get to fish nearly every day. I'm guessing that would be the same as riding every day for you." It was more a statement of fact then a question.

I nodded. We sat in silence for a few more minutes while the fat cloud moved off to the south. Eventually I started to pack up. It was almost two o'clock and we both had things to do. Scooting up onto my knees I wrapped up the leftovers and gathered up our trash, placing everything back into the worn out brown bag while Craig held it open for me. As I dropped the last napkin into the bag he reached up to tuck another wayward strand of hair behind my ear. Electricity shot through me and I could still feel his touch on my ear after he had pulled away.

Smiling, he said, "Did you know that the red in your hair brings out the amber in your eyes." He fingered another loose curl at the nape of my neck, sending tiny pulsating shock waves along my skin. My breath caught as his hand slid slowly down my neck triggering goose bumps everywhere his fingers touched me. He blazed an electric trail along my neck and my body began to hum. Trying to catch my breath, I shook my head slowly, my eyes never leaving his. Sliding his hand beneath my chin he leaned in until his lips met mine, soft and gentle. We explored each other slowly, lips parting to allow for that first taste. Giving in, I slipped my arms under his and urged him on. Finally stoked, the smoldering fire began to spread through me as he pulled me tight against his body, crushing the brown bag between us. *Sweet Jesus.* My body responded to his touch and once again I felt the heat of desire coursing through me.

Craig pulled away slowly. Pausing for a moment, he gently kissed my upper lip, moving on to the tip of my nose and then my forehead while I struggled again to catch my breath. The humidity and heat between us left my lungs aching. Sliding my palms down his chest, I supported myself on shaky knees. Beneath my right hand his heart thumped strong and sure. *Oh Lord, Todd, what are you doing?* Before I could pull away he caught a long curl in his fingers. Smiling, he toyed with it, rolling it between his fingers. I watched mesmerized as his pulse bounded beneath his temple as he turned his head and slipped it behind my ear.

"We better get goin'," his voice was thick with emotion as he stood. Offering a hand, he helped me up. The crumpled bag between us fell over onto the blanket. Reaching down, he scooped it up while I gathered up the blanket. Yanking the blanket off the grass, I shook it hard, buying a moment to collect my brain cells and my breath. The ends of the blanket made a popping noise each time I shook it. As I rolled it up and tucked it under one arm I felt his eyes on me. Suddenly self-conscious I blushed, my fair skin turning a deep rose red.

Without a word, he slipped his hand in mine and headed for the edge of the jungle. His hands were strong and calloused, those of a working man. Once again, after a few steps under the jungle canopy he let go of my hand and took the lead back up the hill. As we walked in silence I struggled to play the part of mediator between my heart and my head. Being around Craig was like holding on to a live wire, once attached it was hard to let it go. But, a large part of me wanted to run far and fast away from the danger he posed to my heart. *Danger, Will Robinson. Danger,* kept playing over and over in my head. If only it were that simple.

Before we reached the dirt road, Craig stopped. So intent was I in mediating between my heart and head, that I nearly ran smack into the front of him. Without a word, he pulled me in for another kiss. "I'll be in touch, but cell service at the resort is spotty at best."

"Okay," I said wondering why it sounded as if he was making an excuse for not being able to call. Uh oh, here goes, he is pulling away.

"No, the phone company is rebuildin' and refittin' the cell towers and land lines along that section of the jungle." He said, as if reading my mind. *How does he do that,* I thought to myself? He ran his thumb along my cheek, pulling my thoughts back to him. I nodded.

We exited the jungle canopy and headed down the road. As we reached the back of the barn, he took the blanket from me, his hand brushing mine. Turning on his heel, he headed towards the house. Rather than go back into the barn I decided to avoid any questions about Craig and head for the Land Cruiser instead. It was about time for me to pick up Haley.

**

The matte black hands on the wall clock told me it was 12:56 am. Closing my eyes I tried again to shut down my mind and body so I could wind down and let sleep in. Unfortunately, it wasn't working and I lay there a bundle of mixed emotions. I had held it together, with my game face plastered on, until everybody had gone to bed. I wanted to keep these jumbled emotions I felt for Craig to myself for a while longer. I knew it was no use to even climb into my bed. I was just too keyed up to fall asleep right away, so I plopped down on the couch and channel surfed while trying to unwind.

A part of me still tingled from the memory of his touch, could still taste him. My body responded, even now, hours later to the thought of him. Why then couldn't I still my mind? I punched the button on the remote, shifting upwards through the channels. This was exactly what I had feared would happen when I built up an iron wall around my heart. There was a chink in my armor and a man had found it. "Not just any man," I muttered to an infomercial as it flipped past.

Deep in my core, I knew the answer. Oh sure, I could tap dance around it all night and into tomorrow. In the end, I just had to admit it. I had it in my head that if I acknowledged it, then like some mythical Kracken it would surface and wreak havoc on what little peace I was carving out for myself. *Too late for that now isn't it? He found the weak spot in your armor.*

I punched the down arrow on the remote, deciding to flip through the channels once again. I had always been a strong willed, independent person, but Mom's slow decline and death had taken their toll on me. Somehow I had lost myself along the way. Thank goodness Jake had been there and had pulled me out of the blackness, which sought to drag me under. He had been my light, my reason for surfacing again. He had pulled me through with his kind soul and love, combined with his sheer determination to see me get back my sparkle, as he had called it. With his help I had kept my head above water.

In the days following Jake's death no one had been able to reach me like he had when Mom died. For the second time in less than a year I had lost all feeling, all sense of time and space; all purpose. I lost my light. In retrospect I had little doubt that Dad's supposed job change had really been orchestrated to shock me back into reality. I must admit, it had worked. I had been doing fine, or at least I thought so until Craig came along.

Suddenly my palms began to sweat. Setting down the remote, I wiped them on my blanket. "I can't do this," I said aloud, shaking my head. I closed my eyes, shutting out the nothingness that was late night TV. I didn't want to lose what little I had of Jake, even if all I had were memories. Afraid the raw wounds wouldn't heal again if torn apart. I wasn't sure if I could love again, or if I even wanted to try. I had to admit, lying there staring at the back of my eyelids, I wasn't sure of anything anymore. *Crap! Face the facts, Lauren. You are scared to death of what could happen with another man, or for that matter, loving again.*

With a groan, I pulled myself into a sitting position and, picking up the remote, I turned off the TV. What to do about Craig? Should I pull a Forest Gump and run far, far away? That would be the easy way out, the safe way. My body, though, might disagree. I couldn't ignore the way Craig made me feel, the way he made my insides jump, my body hum. It had never been quite like this with Jake. Alone, in semi-darkness, guilt began to creep in. *But what about Jake?*

I awoke just after four in the morning only to pry myself from the couch, stumble over the remote control where it lay on the floor, and climb into my bed. Several hours later, the alarm clock roused me from sleep before the nightmare had the chance to begin.

MONKEY ISLAND

Over the next several days I settled into a new routine of studying online in the morning, dropping Haley off at school, riding, picking Haley back up and then getting online to study again. I didn't hear from Craig and a part of me was relieved that I wouldn't have to worry about my heart. Problem solved. And yet, there was the other part of me that willed him to call.

Finally, on Friday, my cell phone lit up as I was driving Haley home from school. My heart lurched in my chest when I answered and heard his voice. He would be back in town on Sunday afternoon, and we made plans to spend the afternoon together after I got home from church. Although he wouldn't tell me what he had planned, he at least told me to wear something casual. As I hung up the phone, Haley nudged me in the shoulder with a finger. "What?" I tried to sound innocent. I still very much wanted to keep my feelings for Craig on the down low.

She giggled, "You're smiling."

"Yes, yes, I am." I had to admit, Craig made me smile. The next day crawled by. Haley, much to her credit, never brought up our conversation or that she knew I had a date.

On Sunday I left Dad and Haley at church and drove home to change. Now that Haley was singing in the choir and stayed late on Sundays we drove separate cars. Craig picked me up at the house. He was dressed casually as usual, with denim shorts, a T-shirt, flip-flops, and his visor. I had opted for something similar, sans visor.

Climbing into his Jeep I tried to pry out of him a destination, but he just begged off with a smile. We crossed the bridge and headed down the main highway towards the direction of the zoo and the Albrook Stables.

With the sides and top of the Jeep open, conversation was nearly impossible, except at stoplights. After a few minutes he pulled off into an industrial area with large warehouses lining one side of the road. At the end of a row of mundane tan buildings, he swung into a parking lot attached to a small marina and parked the Jeep. Climbing out, he reached into the back and grabbed a duffel bag.

As I stepped around the back of the Jeep I heard a deep thrumming sound coming from the marina. As I looked up, I saw a massive ship as it slowly passed the marina. Even though it was a good ways out into the Panama Canal, its size made it appear much closer.

"Skiing?" I stopped short as we approached the dock. "You didn't say to wear a bathing suit," I shot him a reproachful look

"Nope, come on," he reached for my hand. Slipping my hand in his we headed down the sloped concrete that led to the docks. Craig made a beeline for a small white ski boat with a red stripe running down its side. Straddling the boat and the dock with ease, he tossed the duffel bag into the bottom. Small waves from the huge ship sent the ski boat bobbing against its mooring lines. "Here, give me your hand," he said, steadying the boat with one foot.

His hand wrapped around mine, strong and sure as I stepped down into the boat. Reluctant to let go of his grip, I slid my hand free and grasped the edge of the windshield for balance. It was hot to the touch and I glanced up, gauging the weather. The sun blazed overhead, and the afternoon storm clouds had yet to build.

Reaching the console, he lowered the motor into the water. With the turn of a key the engine roared to life and I could feel the boat vibrate and come alive beneath my feet. I was comfortable around boats and knew my way around them. At his signal I untied the bow line and sat down on a bench seat next to him while he pulled clear of the dock.

With the ease born of practice, he moved the boat out into the deep water of the Canal and turned left. I had seen the canal nearly every day since arriving, but the view from within was unique and my eyes sought to take it all in. We cruised along the Canal, its saw grass covered banks growing steeper the farther we travelled. The long green blades of saw grass on the hills and banks danced each time the wind blew. Here and there bright patches of orange clay and rich chocolate earth broke through the sea of green. I still found myself amazed at the lushness all around me here in the tropics and I never grew tired of my favorite color; green. The water of the Canal became murky beneath the hull of the ski boat as we rounded a curve, no doubt churned up by the ships passage.

Craig tapped my shoulder and pointed toward the bow. Just off our starboard bow loomed the gigantic black and white bow of another ship. This one was definitely a cargo ship. Long streaks of bright orange rust stood out against the black paint beneath the forward anchor ports on either side of the bow. The convex curve of the metal bow plowed through the water, several stories above us. The roar of its engines reverberated around us in the narrow passage. Tilting my head backwards as we passed, I caught a glimpse of several deck hands waving from above so I waved back.

We passed one more ship, this one smaller, before the waterway opened up, forming a small lake to our left. Leaving the canal behind, Craig pointed the bow towards several small islands in the middle of the lake.

Much smaller than the San Blas Islands, these were covered by lush tropical vegetation. The tops of the trees blended one with the other in a never ending canopy of green. The trunks, when you could spy them were rich shades of mahogany. Ever present vines wound their way through the greenery. The sweet, sticky smell of some sort of tropical fruit permeated the air around us. When we reached the second and larger of the islands, Craig pulled within about twenty-five yards of it and shut off the engine. Drifting to a slow stop, he raised the engine from the water and clamored forward to drop the anchor. Without the background noise of huge ships passing by or the steady throb of the ski boat's motor I could clearly hear a high pitched shrieking coming from the island directly ahead of us.

"What in the heck was that?" I exclaimed as another shriek ripped the air around us. The sound was primal and eerie all at once and made the hair stand out on the back of my neck. Thoughts of Jurassic Park went through my mind.

Smiling, Craig leaned against the center console of the boat. "Watch, you'll see." A boyish grin split his face. It was clear he was enjoying himself.

Wary, I turned back toward the island. Out of the corner of my eye I saw something move along the low branches of a tree which hung out over the water. Without a beach, the water lapped up against the jungle. I immediately recognized a howler monkey. Its long black hair and grayish black face stood out among the varied shades of green foliage around it. It looked just like the ones at the zoo that Haley and I had seen. As I watched, fascinated, several more howler monkeys made their way along the bank, swinging and hopping from branch to branch.

"They hear the boat motor and come out to the edges of the island to check us out. There is a tour company that brings tourists out here to see the monkeys. They aren't dumb, the monkeys I mean," he chuckled. "They have been conditioned to associate the sound of smaller boat engines with the possibility of free handouts."

"Wow, this is amazing. They are so close."

We settled in on a cushion in the bow to watch the afternoon show. The chattering and shrieking from the island grew as more and more monkeys made their way to the water's edge. Craig pointed higher up in the trees. "See the smaller ones with white faces and necks? Those are capuchins. If you travel to the interior area of Panama you'll see native Indians sellin' baby capuchins in hand made bamboo cages along the road. A lot of people down here keep them as pets."

"They are amazing. How did they get out on this island? Can they swim?" Swinging my head around in both directions I surveyed the area. I had forgotten my sunglasses so I shielded my eyes with the palm of my hand. With the exception of the few small islands and the shore, which was quite a ways off, there wasn't much dry land around.

"Here," Craig pulled his sunglasses off of his face and passed them to me.

"Thanks."

"No, monkeys don't like the water, at least not these guys." He shrugged, "To be honest, I'm not sure how they got here." His brows came together in thought. "Never thought to ask." Getting up, he made his way to the console and, reaching under it, came back with another pair of sunglasses. "If you look closely you'll see another type of monkey. It has a white chest with red draped across the back of the neck. The tail is reddish in color also. They are smaller than the others."

Slowly I scanned the palette of green jungle foliage, searching. After a few minutes I felt as though I was lost in a 'Where's Waldo' picture. "I don't see it. Are you messing with me?"

"No, it's a Tamarin monkey. Keep lookin'." Several more minutes ticked by. I watched as the monkeys cavorted, leaping from tree to tree. Occasionally they would get into a fight and the shrieking would escalate in timbre.

Eventually Craig stood and pulled the anchor up from the muddy water. Setting it down on the bow he said, "Pass me that pole."

Held by a couple of brackets, a metal pole lay tucked along the inside wall on the side of the boat. Popping it free I passed it to him. He twisted it a few times until it doubled in length. Using it to push off from the bottom, he guided the boat slowly around the island. Finally, on the far side of the island, facing the Canal, we saw a trio of Tamarin monkeys playing in a tree.

We sat and watched the playful antics of the monkeys until Craig's cell phone rang. The tone of his voice changed and he was all business, talking in clipped tones. It sounded like it was work related and after a moment he moved to the back of the boat to talk and I turned my attention back to the monkeys. Small snatches of conversation floated my way.

"Again? What the hell is going on?" Glancing back, I saw him run his hand along his chin in a motion I was becoming more familiar with. Something was clearly bothering him. "….no, don't say anything…"

After a few minutes he returned to the bow. "We'll have to cut the monkey watchin' short." His green eyes were dark and worried.

"Oh, okay." I didn't want to pry. Craig made quick work of lowering the engine and starting it up. They monkeys screamed in complaint as he backed the boat away from the island and pointed the bow of the boat back down the canal. The return trip seemed to go by faster somehow and before long I saw the familiar dock come into view.

After tying up the boat we made our way to the Jeep. "Everything okay?"

The crease across his brow smoothed out, "Yeah, sure. We have a bad batch of milk at the resort."

Bad milk? I wasn't convinced. Somehow that didn't quite fit with the worried look I had seen on his face.

He tossed the duffel bag into the Jeep. "We have to fly most of our food supplies into the resort to make up for what we can't get locally. I might have to fly out tonight."

"Oh," I said climbing into the passenger seat, my heart sinking.

After dropping me off at home, Craig left with a promise that he would try to stop by the barn tomorrow. On the ride home he seemed to withdraw into himself although when I asked, he assured me everything was okay. I hated to admit it, but I was bummed at the prospect of not seeing him again for a few days.

At least I had my riding, which was really starting to click. Many of the upper level movements were unfolding beneath me in a way I had never imagined, movements that before had seemed beyond my knowledge and riding ability. There was something to be said for a good schoolmaster.

**

Once again I cooked for Dad and Haley. Carmen was an exceptional cook, and had I asked she would have cooked on Friday and put it away for our weekend meals. Lately, however, I found myself craving tastes from home, especially on Sunday afternoons. Those were the days that Mom would always go all out and make the most scrumptious home made dinners. Jake had been a Sunday dinner staple. Even when we lived together he would find a reason to stop by my parent's house on Sundays with me in tow. I used to tease him, telling him that I was trying to get out on my own, and dragging me back for Sunday dinners wasn't helping. He would just smile and laugh, knowing full well I liked nothing better than time with my family.

I stood in the bright poppy kitchen, my fingers no longer visible in the cold meaty mess of Mom's meatloaf recipe, feeling the ache of two huge holes in my heart. One by one the tears I had been holding back made their way down my face. Hearing footsteps behind me, I brushed my wet cheeks against the sleeves of my shirt. I put on my game face. "Hey, Dad."

Never one to show too much emotion, I could feel him grow awkward in the small confines of the kitchen. Reaching for the fridge, he pulled the door open and grabbed a cold bottle of beer. "Onions?"

Although we both knew that onions had nothing to do with the situation at hand, leave it to Dad to do the two-step around a crying female. Actually, it was one of the qualities I liked best about him. One of the traits I had inherited from him. Trouble was, I had lost it somewhere along the way. We rarely cried around each other. It just wasn't our style. "Uhuh," I mumbled. "Dinner will be ready in about an hour." *Sniff.*

"Want a beer?"

I nodded, my hands still icky from the meatloaf mixture. He pulled out two bottles. Deftly twisting off the caps, he set one on the counter. As he turned to leave he briefly placed one hand on my shoulder and I went back to work, dry eyed.

Losing two people that were so close to me within a year had been devastating, and although friends had assured me that the pain would fade; I had yet to experience it.

By all appearances, Haley seemed to be coping well with Mom's death. The first few months were the hardest, of course, but whether it was her age, inexperience, or naïveté, I wasn't sure. Dad, ever the rock, would have liked the world to think of him as a tough guy. He never allowed himself to shed a tear in public. I knew that he had been a mess in the weeks following Mom's death.

In the beginning I would make the trek from our apartment to my old home several times a week to make sure the house was clean, laundry done, and there was sufficient food in the fridge for both of them. I was the one who pulled tear stained sheets off of both beds. I was the one who had to clear Mom's clothes out of their closet when Dad was away at work. In my heart, I knew he just didn't have the strength to remove her things. Maybe that was why I was so shocked when he told me of his new job in Panama.

Lost in thoughtful memories, I busied myself with cooking way too much food for the three of us. After dinner Dad offered to do the dishes. Declining his offer I plunged right into the dirty mess, pushing the envelope of exhaustion. Jake usually stayed out of my dreams if I went to bed exhausted or tipsy. Since I didn't want to become a statistic, I chose exhaustion;

it had been my medicine of choice lately. Well, except for margarita nights, but those were sacred. Either way, Colleen seemed to make sure I had a healthy dose of exhaustion every day I rode.

**

The next morning I had a lesson on Gold Herr at 9 am. Colleen continued to focus on effective and subtle aids. I could feel my seat and position changing on a weekly basis. My reactionary skills seemed to improve as well. I was discovering that DQ was definitely a misnomer. There was no doubt in my mind that tackling a really tough cross country question required skill and quick thinking. This I knew from experience. But, I was learning that both skill and quick thinking were imperative in order to transition from a canter half pass to a flying lead change and straight into another half pass going the other direction. Getting the feel of the slight changes in bend and straightness that could throw off a movement was, for me, a revolutionary experience.

More than once I felt as though I was flailing like a monkey on Gold Herr's back. My legs, shoulders, and head felt as it they had a mind of their own, none of which belonged to Gold Herr, who day in and day out, ride after ride, put up with me. For some inane reason, the more I tried to minimize my aids, the harder it became to actually lighten them. My brain would kick in and before I realized it, I had 'over thunk' the problem. I had Colleen to thank for my new phrase.

Gold Herr remained a saint throughout. Thank goodness he usually chose to ignore my really bad aides and completed the movement he was taught to perform. I was beginning to think he was half human. On more than one occasion I would stop him in order to discuss something with Colleen and before we went back to work he would crane his big head around and peer at me with those liquid brown eyes as if to say, "Did you get all that?"

As I was tacking up Stitch for Colleen to ride, Craig came striding down the barn aisle. He looked very much like the cat that swallowed the canary. "Uh oh, what are you up to?" I asked.

"I came to claim a kiss before I set off into the afternoon sky with my precious cargo of dairy." He smiled, his eyes twinkling.

"Did anyone ever bother to inform you that you have a knight in shining armor complex?" I shot back mockingly. "Running around saving this, rescuing that…"

"Ah, but I am just so damned good at it." He leaned in for a quick kiss on the lips. "Is Colleen around?" My lips tingled pleasantly.

I was caught off guard by his public display of affection. "She doesn't need rescuing, Sir Craig. I, on the other hand, do. Pass me the fly spray."

He scooped up the bottle of home made fly brew that Colleen concocted and tossed it at me. Laughing, I caught it with both hands, "Hey, watch it!" Just then we could hear Colleen coming into the barn, the loose doorknob on her office door making a jiggling sound as she opened it. "Be right back," Craig strode down the aisle and disappeared into Colleen's office.

Leaning around the corner I noticed he had shut the door behind them. Hmm, that was curious, I thought. Pushing aside the thought, I went back to work putting boots on Stitch's legs and then grabbed his bridle off of the peg where it hung. Like a pro, he accepted the bit and stood patiently while I slipped the headstall over his ears. "Good boy." He gently mouthed the bit, then opened and closed his lips with a *fwopping* sound. Stitch had only been under saddle a handful of times before getting trapped in the vines and Colleen had been careful to ease him back into work.

Some horses come by their names, whether show names or casual barn names, honestly, and so it was with Stitch. It didn't take me long to realize how he had gotten his moniker.

When Haley was little she had been in love with Nemo from the movie *Finding Nemo*. Her second love had always been the cartoon *Lilo and Stitch*. Stitch, an errant alien who found his way to Hawaii, was forever causing a ruckus wherever he went. He was simply an accident waiting to happen, a catastrophe waiting to strike. Stitch, the horse, could have easily given that cute little alien with the funny teeth a run for his money.

Although a dark cloud of foreboding disaster was never far from Stitch, he seemed to bounce through life with great aplomb, oblivious to his destructive ability. I wasn't yet sure if that was a good thing. At any rate, he could always be seen smiling. Well, if horses really do smile. I tended to think they could and did. During my time with Stitch I had also learned that when he behaved like you expected, well then, you better watch out.

As I buckled his noseband, he blinked innocently at me. His left eye had quite a bit of the white sclera showing which made him at times resemble Beaker from the *Muppets* and I laughed aloud at him. He was in essence a dork of the highest order and I liked him a lot. He was also a dork with a lot of promise and three fantastic floating gaits. In fact, he had 'air time' that would have made Michael Jordan envious.

Adjusting his headstall, I heard the office door open and Colleen and Craig came around the corner of the tack stall. Colleen reached up and affectionately pulled Stitch's forelock out from behind his brow band.

"Thanks for tacking him up. Why don't you meet me in the arena before you leave, I want to talk to you about something."

"Okay." Colleen led Stitch down the aisle. Stretching as far as his reins would allow, she reached into her office and came out with her helmet in hand. Stitch waited patiently for her then fell in step beside her as they headed for the arena.

Returning to work, I grabbed the manure fork from its hook on the wall and scooped up the fresh pile of manure Stitch had left behind in the tack stall. Dumping it in a bucket I hung the fork back up and started for the tack room. I jumped when Craig snuck up behind me and wrapped his arms around my waist. I could feel the soft bristle from his chin along my neck and a warm pulsing sensation ran through my body as I melted against him. "I hate to go, but I will be back early Wednesday mornin'," he whispered in my ear.

What's with the sudden change? Last time at the barn you were less touchy feely. "Hmm," I nearly purred as he pulled me even closer against him. Once again, my body responded to his touch and for a few moments I let myself go, dropping the steel curtain that kept my heart hidden. His warm lips brushed the side of my neck just below my jawbone. *Nice!* My skin leapt at his touch, yearning for more as my pulse quickened. We stood there for a moment wrapped in each other.

Reluctantly he pulled away and gently turned me around to face him. His long auburn eyelashes dipped low, making it harder for me to see his eyes. Slipping his strong hand beneath my ponytail he pulled me in for a kiss. My arms settled around his waist. Slowly at first, his tongue teased mine, tasting, playing as we kissed. *Hmm, very nice, indeed.* Unsteady beneath me, my legs grew weak and I leaned into his body for support. Hearing a noise down the aisle bounced me back to reality and I quickly pulled away, breaking the spell he held on me. Flustered, I felt my cheeks and neck flush red.

Recovering quickly from the awkwardness of the moment he smiled and said, "I'll see you on Wednesday bright and early."

"See you then, bye." Still flustered I ducked into the tack room to grab my helmet and gloves, just in case I needed them, and headed out to the arena. With Colleen, I was learning to be prepared at all times. "Oh, what you do to me," I murmured quietly, the taste and feel of him fresh in my mind.

Passing Maria in her stall crooning to Mariposa, I stopped. Lately I had been making a concerted effort to break through the glacial ice that was Maria, although why, I wasn't sure. Perhaps it was a challenge? "Hey, Maria, do you have a lesson today?" I tried to make my voice sound cordial and light. I could hear Craig's Jeep start up in the back lot behind the barn.

"Yes, right after she gets done with Stitch," she almost sounded giddy. "My new saddle arrived and I just know it will help my lower leg." Maria had ordered a brand new dressage saddle several months ago. The temporary high she got from spending money seemed to make her a little more tolerable and slightly more pleasant to be around. Hey, whatever worked, right? We had all been hearing about her magical saddle for way too long and it would be a relief to ride her newly discovered wave of excitement for a short while. In time, her mood would certainly sour again. Of that I had no doubt. In my estimation it would be the moment her 'magic' saddle fix quit working.

I groaned inwardly, "That's great. Have a great ride." I walked away, desperately biting my tongue in order to keep myself from saying something I would regret. Only Maria would think that a new $5,000.00 saddle would magically fix her wickedly poor lower leg. Well, at least it made her happy for a little while. God bless Mariposa. The poor mare did more to cover for Maria than most other horses would ever put up with. Surely there must be a special place in heaven for horses like her. Shrugging it off, I headed towards the arena.

When I arrived, Colleen was just about to mount Stitch. Lately she had been lunging him before her rides in order to better judge his mood and work out any demons he might imagine were chasing him. "Oh, good, could you hold my other stirrup while I mount. If you would, go ahead and grab a hold of his bridle, too."

I steadied her right stirrup as she put her weight in the left one, pushing down gently to counteract her weight in the saddle as she smoothly swung her right leg over his back. Stitch stood calmly. "I think he is wearing his brain today, Colleen."

"Yeah, he seems to be having a good day. That is at least until a fly farts near him and he comes unglued," she chuckled. That was one of the best analogies I had ever heard and I couldn't help but laugh. Flies most assuredly could not pass gas, but if they did Stitch would no doubt be the one to hear them and react. "Oh, by the way, I think I may have found you a horse." she added casually.

Colleen had been busy searching high and low to find a horse capable enough and within my budget for me to compete. Several times she had shown me a potential horse on the internet, but they were either out of my price range or sold before we had the chance to inquire about them. The gang would be leaving for Florida in September and time was running out for me to find a horse to compete. There was also the issue of bonding and trust. I needed the time to get to know my new horse.

"Really? Where?" I had cause to be skeptical. I had spent some time yesterday scouring the internet and had finally opted to turn the computer off before I chucked it through the French doors in frustration.

"Long story, but we need to go look at it tomorrow. I am not sure how long it will take. Can you get someone to pick up your sister from school for you?" Stitch stood quietly, although I could tell Colleen had one eye on him while she spoke.

I ran through a few ideas in my head before responding, "Most likely, let me go make a few calls." What I needed was time to think. The reality of actually finding a horse for me was so far removed from the basic facts of life such as 'how in the hell would I afford it?' Or, 'how could I manage to go back to the States, ship a horse from God knows where, and afford to compete at the upper levels?' I needed to ground myself for a minute, pull myself down from fairyland.

"Well, this sort of happened overnight so we have to work fast, really fast in fact." She had started walking Stitch in a circle around me. Every few strides she would pull back gently on the inside rein, asking him to soften his jaw and give to the pressure of the rein. When he got it right she rewarded him with a scratch on his neck.

"Okay, let me go make a few calls."

"All right, but let me know as soon as possible. I will need to change my schedule around tomorrow as well."

I left Colleen and Stitch behind and headed for the barn. After making a few calls, I made arrangements for Haley to get a ride home with a neighbor tomorrow and let Colleen know. Getting back to work, I lost track of time while cleaning Gold Herr's tack. Thankfully, I had the timer set on my phone so as not to forget to pick her up today from school. For a red head, sometimes I could be so blonde. It wasn't until I was getting ready for bed that it occurred to me that I hadn't even asked Colleen about the horse she had found. Oh well, beggars couldn't be choosers, could they?

CRONOS

We drove deeper into Panama City than I had ever been before. Traffic careened around the narrow corners of the Old Town section of the city. At every stop light young kids, mostly boys, would race up to our car and try to wash the windows with grungy buckets full of mud colored water and filthy rags. Afterwards, they would ask to be paid for their efforts. Craig handed a taller boy a few coins. Then he thanked them for the job as the light turned green.

"Tough way to earn a dollar," I mused aloud.

"Yes it is. Some people pay them not to wash their windows, but as silly as it may seem, I think there is honor in being paid to do a job, no matter how poor you are or whatever the job."

I nodded as he accelerated across the intersection.

We crossed through Old Town, passing some early Spanish ruins along the way. Colleen, sitting in the back seat, explained that the city had sprung up around the walls of an old fort, hence the name 'Panama Viejo' or 'Old Panama'.

About fifteen minutes later, we left the narrow stone streets behind and entered a more modern section of the city dotted with high-rise buildings. These buildings were spread out a little bit more. The alleys between the buildings were wide enough to drive down, unlike the narrow alleyways we had seen in Old Town. Stepping on the brakes, Craig swung the Jeep down one rather wide alleyway. At the entrance were two policemen standing guard in front of a large chain link fence. A large loop of concertina style razor wire was wrapped along the top of the fence.

Both guards were armed and wore very sour expressions. The short fat one on the left cautiously eyed the Jeep as we pulled up. His dark eyes darted to his partner standing across from him and back to the Jeep. Out of the corner of my eye I saw the second guard purse his lips beneath his dark mustache and tighten his grip on the AK-47 he wore slung across his chest. Glancing around, I felt a stab of uncertainty. *What in the hell?* Moving my head slowly, I peered over my shoulder at Colleen. After all, I didn't want to get shot by accident.

Colleen placed her hand on my shoulder and shook her head from side to side as if to say, "Keep your mouth shut."

Leaning out of the window, Craig started a conversation in Spanish with the short well-fed guard. The guard nodded tentatively a few times while I watched Craig turn on the charm. He could go from serious businessman to one of the guys in the blink of an eye, a silver fox with a silver tongue. The guard smiled, nodded again. He glanced over his shoulder, then back at Craig. A big grin crossed his meaty face and Craig reached out of the window and shook hands with him. A small wad of bills passed expertly from one hand to another. A quick nod towards the second guard and the gate swung open.

"What just ha—."

Glaring at me, her eyes huge, Colleen just shook her head silently and squeezed my shoulder in a vise-like grip. I turned in my seat and tried to focus straight ahead. Probably better if I didn't know anyway, I thought.

Once inside the gate, Craig parked the Jeep along the side of the building. He turned to Colleen as he shut off the engine. I could hear the metallic *click* of the gate echo down the alleyway behind us, causing the hair to stand up on the nape of my neck.

"OK, here's the deal. We have less than an hour. Apparently the Chief has gone to lunch. We timed it just right. The mare is in the last lot on the right, past the warehouse."

We both nodded, although I still didn't quite understand. Hesitating, I asked, "Where will you be?"

His eyebrow shot up and a mischievous look played across his face, "Playin' cards and tryin' my best not to get drunk." He grabbed the brown paper bag he had left at my feet, gave me a quick kiss on the lips and was out the door in a flash. I watched his back as he strode purposefully to a side door of the building. Without looking back he squared his shoulders and walked into the building.

Colleen had climbed over the back of the Jeep. "Let's go," she urged, grabbing the saddle and saddle pad. I climbed out with the rest of the tack in hand, my lips still warm from his kiss. We hurried down the alleyway. The heavy metal door slammed shut behind him with finality, making me jump.

The last lot on the right was rimmed with another chain link fence. A sign on the gate in Spanish and English read **Compound Lot**. Through the links in the fence I could see a dirt lot, which was full of every make and model of vehicle you could think of. A candy apple red Ferrari, a white Maseratti, a handful of sleek BMW's, too many Hummer's to count, sexy cigarette boats, a mini submarine laying on it's side, and a tank.

"Is that really a submarine?"

"Yeah, crazy isn't it?" Colleen unlatched the metal gate and rolled it back so we could enter. "They use them to smuggle drugs."

Stepping through, I rolled the gate shut and followed as she started off across the lot.

A nicker greeted us from a shed row in the middle of the lot and I nearly jumped in surprise. Neither Craig nor Colleen had bothered to tell me just where the horse that we were looking at was kept before we left the barn. *Can you blame them, after all who the heck would have believed this?* A dark bay mare with a white star and a snip on her nose looked eagerly in our direction. She was in a small, ramshackle metal shed constructed of corrugated roofing material. Her big head could be seen sticking out of the small shed. As we drew closer, I could see a pair of brown ears rimmed in black pricked in our direction and she nickered again. From the looks of things, this wasn't the first time the compound yard had seen a horse. The door of the shed was propped open with a brick. A faded, webbed stall gate hung across the entry. The metal snaps were rusty, and several of them dangled freely from the webbing. The mare ducked her big head and stepped back into the dark interior.

I followed as Colleen unclipped the bottom snap and slipped under. Once inside, the smallness of the shed became overwhelming. Dungeon-esque was more like it. The shed was roughly eight feet by eight feet and I could easily touch the roof if I stretched my arm up over my head. Poor girl, it was no wonder she kept her head hanging out of the stall. She took up nearly the entire space. The floor of the stall had been strewn with dirt and old musty hay by the smell of it. A single water bucket sat on the ground towards the back. It was hard to tell how big she was in the little shed. Her warm nose eagerly searched out the front of my breeches. She was looking for treats.

"Let's get her out into the light. The clock is ticking."

I found a halter hanging on a hook just inside the shed door. The mare's warm, brown eyes lighted on the halter and she dove her nose into it. "Good girl," I murmured. Slipping the crown behind her ears I led her out into the light.

She eagerly followed me out of the shed and I had to move to the side so as not to get run over. Bringing her to a halt in the sunshine, she shoved her warm nose into the small of my back and nudged me gently.

"Walk her out and back." Colleen watched her walk from behind with a critical eye as I led her away. Her coat was dirty, but you could tell she had been well kept in the not so distant past. She was a lighter bay than I originally thought, with dark points on her legs, ears, and muzzle. Two white socks graced the front and hind legs on her left. "I forgot a brush," I said by way of apology as I turned her around and walked back towards Colleen.

Her eyes never left the mare's legs. "That's OK, just use the underside of the saddle pad as a towel and wipe the big stuff off her coat. It will do for now. Here, I'll hold her."

She danced a little in the sunlight, shifting her feet around in a small circle, while I quickly went to work brushing her with the pad and the palm of my hand before saddling her. She was tall, 17 hands if she was an inch. Taking stock, I noticed she had horseshoes on the front feet only. While not overly long, she could stand to be trimmed by a farrier.

"Here," Colleen passed my helmet to me while she put the bridle on and adjusted the fit, making sure the bit sat at just the right level in her mouth.

"Ummm… where do you propose I ride her?" Glancing at the parking lot around us, I pulled on my gloves. This was hardly an ordinary ride in an ordinary pasture or arena. Frowning, I studied the gravel and asphalt footing beneath my boots.

Colleen walked around the shed until she found a small area between the tank and a blue Volvo. A rectangular area slightly wider than a twenty-meter circle and twice as long, sat directly behind the shed. Here the footing was a mix of dirt and coarse gravel. Small patches of grass had taken a random hold wherever they could. "I want to stick to the basics, she is out of shape. Just walk her a minute and try to get her to stretch. Then we will see if she is sound at the trot."

"-K." Colleen gave me a leg up. The mare stood quietly. Picking up the reins I clucked. She moved promptly off my leg and walked. I asked her to stretch to my hand and she nearly yanked the reins out of my grasp, rooting her nose down towards the ground. I caught the buckle before it slid out of my hands and down onto her neck.

"That's OK, we'll fix that later. I can't really blame her for wanting to stretch after being crammed in that shed." We walked on. "Now, pick her up." Colleen directed after a few circles at the walk.

I shortened the reins and asked for a trot. Her trot was smooth, rhythmical, and uphill. Out of the corner of my eye, I thought I saw a grin on Colleen's face as we passed her the first time, but I couldn't be sure. After a few circles, I found myself getting lost in the lofty suspension of her trot. She floated across the lot. We worked to the left and then the right, changing leads across the tiny diagonal between the tank and the Volvo. My friends back home would never believe this one, I thought as we rode around. I began to play with her, asking for a leg yield and then a half pass. The area was too small to do much canter work so I stuck to the trot. Besides, all I needed was for her to slip on the gravel and go down with me on her. As we worked, the minutes ticked by, revealing just how much the mare did know.

"Bring her here." I halted in front of Colleen. Square. Beaming, I glanced her way, but Colleen was staring down at the mare's legs and I couldn't quite discern the look on her face. She had her game face on.

"Let's kick the tires, shall we." She ran her hand across her chin thoughtfully and said, "piaffe." The shock on my face said volumes. She met my eyes then focused her gaze back on the mare and repeated, "piaffe."

"I… I… I'm not sure," I stuttered. "What about passage, would that be easier?" I wasn't at all sure I could accomplish either of them without Gold Herr.

"Nonsense, you have the tools, use them," she was curt and to the point. "Either she knows it or doesn't. Let's find out." She glanced nervously towards the direction of the gate and the alleyway beyond. "We don't have much time."

Oh, Lord. I had done one piaffe in my life and that was on Gold Herr just last week. *Deep breath, Todd. You can do this.* I picked the mare up and made a smaller circle in front of Colleen. *Really? A piaffe on a strange mare in an impound parking lot next to a cigarette boat and a tank. Sure, no problem. Coming right up! I'm sure riders do this on a regular basis!* Clearing my head of distracting thoughts I prepared for piaffe.

"Now, don't forget your driving aids, you have to push her hind end forward and into your hand. Alternate your leg pressure and sit up. Remember, it's back to front always, and keep her light in your hand. We just want to see if she has any idea what we are asking. Does she understand collection?"

The upper level movement of piaffe requires much more from a horse in terms of muscle development, control, and connection with the rider than anything I had ever done. Much like a spring, coiled and ready to expand, a horse is able to create its own version of potential energy in achieving the perfect balance that is piaffe.

As the haunches of the horse sink behind the rider, the horse's back rounds up beneath them, pushing the saddle upwards. The massive shoulders swell, reaching a point that is higher than the rider's seat. Muscles on either side of the neck bulge outwards as the neck elevates, the crest forming a lovely scythe-like shape. All the while, the horse must remain in balance as it steps off the two beat rhythm of the trot. All this happens while either staying in the same spot or taking barely imperceptible steps forward.

In the act of harnessing such raw power, the opposite effect is achieved, one of overall lightness and grace, a prima ballerina, dancing across a stage, while entirely en point, is another good analogy. While not able to hold the pose for too long, when done right, it can be amazing, even mesmerizing to watch.

With a clear vision of a light ballerina in my head (albeit using an impound lot for a stage), I sat deeper with my seat, signaled a half halt with my fingers, and compressed her walk. The mantra played over and over in my head—*create the engine from behind, get her under you, half halt and lift her abdomen with your seat and legs, half halt, lift, one-two, one-two, left-right.* And then, like magic it happened. Her haunches sank and I could feel the power in her back and haunches as she stepped off the rhythm of piaffe. Although she only managed three steps before falling apart, it was a clear rhythm.

"Well, at least someone has introduced her to the concept. She is not the finished product," she said, hiding her smile behind her hand, "but she'll do. OK, let's put her up, we're cutting it close." She glanced over her shoulder toward the direction of the Jeep.

I didn't want to stop, much less leave the mare behind in the ramshackle metal shed. Dismounting, I slipped off my saddle. Colleen replaced the bridle with her halter and walked the mare back to the shed. Looking around, we couldn't find a hose with which to rinse her. Handing my saddle to Colleen, I managed to fill her water bucket from a spigot along the fence. With a cursory pat on the nose we headed for the gate. As we shut the gate behind us the mare nickered again, this time in distress.

"Ugh, I hate this," Colleen's voice was gruff.

"I know, I don't want to look back for fear I'll try to steal her or cram her into the back of the Jeep and take her with us." I picked up the pace as the mare nickered again, effectively wrenching my heart. "Do you think Fatty at the gate would notice if we went galloping down the street?" I said. Colleen just grunted.

We reached the Jeep at the same time as Craig. He smelled of cheap liquor, but his eyes were clear. Glancing at his watch he radiated a sense of urgency. We threw the tack into the back and climbed in. Reaching behind him, Craig passed a manila envelope back to Colleen then cranked the engine.

Fatty and Grumpy nodded at us as we passed through the outer gates. Craig nodded curtly at them. We drove in silence through the city streets with only the wind, tires, and ambient city noises around us as we absorbed the events we had just witnessed. Somewhere in Old Town I finally turned in my seat, unable to take the silence for another minute, "Can someone please tell me what just happened?" My voice started to shake. Turning to me, Craig smiled and jerked his head over his shoulder towards Colleen. Focusing his eyes on a spot above my head, he smiled.

"What?" My eyes darted between them, demanding an answer.

Colleen broke into hysterics and slumped sideways in the back seat. Craig, no longer able to keep a straight face, joined in.

Thoroughly aggravated, I turned around to see what they were looking at. When I did, the chinstrap of my helmet swung freely, bumping me on the side of the neck. I reached a hand towards my head. *Helmet.* I was still wearing my helmet. With a look of disgust, I slid it off my head and hit him in the shoulder with it.

"Hey, watch it," he said swerving. He straightened the Jeep, all the while chuckling.

"You watch it! Is someone going to fill me in on what just happened?" There was a pause as Colleen and Craig acknowledged each other with conspiratorial looks. "No really, what just happened back there? Where did that horse come from?"

We had stopped at a light. "A drug cartel," giggled Colleen, pulling herself upright with the roll bar.

My eyes widened as I took them both in, "Come again? A drug cartel? Are you serious?" Neither of them answered me, but instead stared straight ahead, grinning. "You guys are certifiable."

Another fit of laughter took hold of Colleen, "You tell her, I – I – I can't."

"A drug cartel, just like she said," he smiled then turned back to the road ahead, changing lanes to avoid a bus that had stopped to load and unload passengers.

"Okay, back up. You just bought a horse from a drug dealer?" I paused to let the idea sink in. *Wait a minute, since when do drug cartels use Grand Prix dressage horses to smuggle dope?*

As if reading my thoughts, Craig answered. "No, you have it wrong. She was taken as a seizure from a drug raid in the interior of the country. A drug kingpin known as Carlo owned her," he was trying hard not to laugh. His green eyes sparkled as he struggled to maintain composure. "I heard about the bust from a friend."

"Actually," Colleen continued, "The drug guy bought her as a gift for his girlfriend. She wanted a horse so he went out and bought her one. Crazy what idiots with money will do," she shook her head, clearly dumbfounded.

"So, the kingpin's girlfriend was a dressage rider," I reached across and slapped Craig on the shoulder again to keep him from laughing. He really could be annoying. It didn't work. This whole thing was getting more ridiculous by the minute and I had to keep my sanity. Especially since it was clear I was the only sane one in the Jeep. If Craig started laughing, I knew the gig was up and I would slide with him into a fit of mildly hysterical laughter. I crammed my lips together tightly trying to keep from laughing at the absurdity of it all.

"No, she just wanted an expensive horse and liked to play dress up," Colleen said sarcastically. "Who knows?" her voice was dripping with contempt. "An agent of Carlo's came to me earlier this year asking a lot of questions about horses. I think he saw me doing dressage and naturally assumed that dressage was what people did when they weren't racing Thoroughbreds. Who the hell knows? Around these parts, horse racing is all people do know. Anyway, at the time, I didn't have any idea what he was really after. He just asked a bunch of questions and acted like he was trying to impress his girlfriend or something. I never saw him again." She shrugged as if that explained everything.

Craig jumped in, "Fast forward a few months. A friend of mine called me yesterday to tell me that the Garda had a horse from a drug raid. Usually they confiscate the Thoroughbreds, but he said the police chief didn't know what to do with this horse, as it obviously wasn't built for racin'. They normally sell the Thoroughbreds just like the Ferrari's, diamonds, and other stuff that drug lords collect. So, I called in some favors and thought it would be worth checkin' out." He winked at me then glanced over at Colleen. I looked at her expectantly. Waiting.

"So," she continued, "Craig's friend checked out the paperwork that came with the horse. It was in German so he couldn't read it. He brought it by the office the other day to show me. I thought that might be a good sign." Her eyes twinkled and she held up a piece of paper, "I was dead on."

"Her name is Cronos. And get this—she has Coriander as her grandsire. She is a 10 year old registered Holsteiner." She slapped the paper with one hand, "Shazam!"

"Jackpot," he grinned. We were making our way down the gravel road, the sound of the Jeep's tires echoing against the jungle walls.

I pondered what they were saying and digested it for a mile or so. "What now?"

"That is up to you," she shrugged, "most contraband seized in drug raids is auctioned off."

I caught the inflection in her voice, "Most?"

We pulled up at the barn and Craig cut the engine. Fiddling with his keys he took a deep breath, "Well, as she said, that's up to you."

"Me, I can't afford a horse like that, even if she were to be auctioned off." *Or could I?* I crossed my arms and stared at my knees to keep from shuddering. God only knew where she would end up if she were to be put up for auction.

His hand brushed my cheek, sending a shiver down my spine and I shuddered anyway. Gently he lifted my chin and smiled at me. His warm fingers slid down the back of my neck. "I called your Da this mornin' when I found out about her."

My eyes flashed in anger, "No way, noooo way. Uh, uh, the last thing my dad needs…"

Just then, Colleen's cell phone rang. "I'll leave you two alone," she grinned wickedly, "don't kill each other." Taking the short cut she eased out of the back seat and climbed over the side of the Jeep. I watched her walk towards the gate, talking on her cell.

As she reached the main door to the compound he turned towards me, "I've already paid for the mare." His green eyes searched mine. Probably looking for absolution, I thought. "I wasn't sure if she would work, but I knew you'd be upset if she went up for auction."

"Wait a second… I thought Colleen said she *would* be auctioned off?" The smell of cheap liquor found its way to my nose again. It must be on his hands, I thought. Suddenly, things became a bit clearer. "What exactly did you do back there?" I sniffed again, "you reek."

Stifling a grin he said, "A form of third world dealin', if you will," His eyes danced. While his tone was mocking, there was no mistaking an underlying seriousness to it. As if trying to distract me, he cocked a sandy colored eyebrow up and shot me a challenging look. "Look, I simply made arrangements for Cronos to avoid the auction block," he added.

I saw his eyebrow and raised him one. "Come again? No wait. I don't want to know, do I?" *What in blue blazes did you do, Craig?*

He shook his head slowly from side to side, "Nope, you don't," he said with finality. Those darn green eyes sparkled and whirled in mischief. He was trying very hard not to smile.

With an exasperated sigh, I gave in to him yet again. It felt nice to be taken care of, to have someone who actually wanted to take care of me for a change. He opened his door and climbed out. Not waiting for him to open my door, I climbed out, gathering my purse before I shut the door. A frown crossed his gorgeous face and I couldn't help but smile back. Although it was gallant of him to open my door, I was feeling a bit confused at the moment. *Railroaded was more like it.* And I felt the need to flash my independent side. The wrinkle in his brow faded as he helped me gather up the tack from the back of the Jeep. I let him wrap a strong arm around me, and we walked up to the barn, both lost in our own thoughts.

**

The deal was complete. Cronos would be delivered tomorrow. I had visions of her being squeezed into the bed of a dilapidated pick up truck, but Colleen assured me with a laugh that AJ had access to a horse trailer through a friend at the racetrack downtown.

Today, I had a lesson on William, Elaine's gelding. I was quickly learning that Colleen didn't do anything willy-nilly when it came to working with her students. She was inventive with her training methods and no matter how odd the initial idea may appear, the end result was always crystal clear. I had a feeling I was about to have an inventive lesson.

Tightening the girth, and tucking in the billet straps, I stooped in front of William to stretch out each of his front legs. My mind drifted as I wondered just what Colleen had in store for us today. I had never ridden William before, but Elaine could make him dance. He also had one of the most amazing uphill canters of any of the horses at the barn.

Planting his nose in the small of my back, William politely lifted his left front leg before I had the chance to ask. Pulling gently up and straight out with my hands behind his knee, I stretched his skin smooth under the girth. "Good boy, Will." Reaching for the other leg I tried another nickname on for size, "Bill? Nah, how about Willy? You need a nickname because calling you William is just way too formal." William just blinked at me, then made a *wuffling* noise in response. "Doesn't she call you anything else big boy?"

"William it is. All of her horses have had men's first names and she never uses nicknames," Deanne had come up behind me, halter and lead rope in hand. "Her last gelding was Walter. Not Wally, just Walter." Reaching up, she ran a hand along William's forehead as he dozed contentedly in the crossties. "I guess we should be glad she hasn't had a Leroy or Aloysius! Those are really awful."

Sliding off his halter with one hand, I deftly slipped the bit into his mouth and set the headstall behind his ears. William was indeed falling asleep, his head drooped almost to his knees and his lower lip hung loose, exposing the soft seashell pink of his gums. "You riding today?" I finished with the noseband and checked to see if the bit was level in his mouth.

"In a bit, but I don't have a lesson. Nicola's back was out so I am taking it easy on her for the next couple of rides. She hasn't been out in a while, but I've noticed her bracing to the right in her neck so Colleen took a look at her for me. I see you get to ride the Magician today."

Before I could answer a slew of Spanish cuss words flew out of the tack room. It hadn't taken long for me to learn that most of what came out of Maria's mouth in Spanish wasn't good. Deanne rolled her eyes, laid the back of her hand on her forehead, and let an exaggerated sigh escape her lips. She continued to pantomime her distress like a silent film star. Struggling not to laugh at Deanne's antics, I slipped on my helmet and gloves. Clucking to William, I woke him up and made a beeline for the arena. By the grace of God, I was lucky enough to avoid Maria and her drama du jour as it was headed in the other direction, away from the arena.

Once on William, I took a few moments to warm him up and get to know him. Colleen came in and settled onto her stool while I was trotting him around. His trot was forward and uphill with good suspension. I smiled to myself, enjoying the ride. We went through the usual warm up routine of serpentines, leg yields, and transitions from working trot to collected trot and back again. He was very responsive and light to my aids.

We picked up the right lead canter and immediately William felt different under me, almost as if we were slogging through mud. I asked him to go more forward with my legs first, but only got a moderate response from him. Again I asked, this time using more leg. Wondering where the forward moving horse I had ridden in the trot had gone, I touched him with the whip. This time I received a bit more of a forward feeling, but I still felt as though we weren't going anywhere. Before I knew it, I was red in the face, using my seat and legs, and still nothing. Pulling up in front of Colleen I noticed her grinning from ear to ear.

"So, what just happened?"

"He won't go anywhere in the canter. I mean he is stuck in one gear and it's first." I hadn't realized how out of breath I had become trying to push the seventeen hand beast beneath me. I was confused to say the least.

"Is he?" she asked.

Sensing a trap, I thought through my ride at the canter, evaluating the steps I took to get him more forward, before responding. "Well, something is not right. He has no 'go' button at all. Obviously it's me or you wouldn't have put me on him," I said, satisfied with my response.

"Exactly," Colleen adjusted her seat. "So, is he not forward or not fast enough for you? Which is it?"

"Both, I feel as though we are slogging through mud. The more I ask, the less I get."

She smiled a satisfied smile, "Believe it or not, William here has one of the best canter gaits of any horse in this barn. The collected work and pirouettes are easy for him. What you are feeling is his lack of motion beneath you. But do not confuse that with his lack of forward movement. What you are used to is fast. These are not always the same. That is the eventer in you coming out.

"Let me guess, you feel as though you are not covering ground based on how he feels beneath you. The difference is that William's canter is so awesome and uphill that you don't really feel him move beneath you at all. But trust me, I will tell you when he is not working beneath you. When riding his canter, you could probably carry a glass of wine and never spill a drop. With him, it is just that smooth. He also has a huge stride so when you combine that with his uphill nature you actually cover a lot of ground without feeling like you are." She paused, giving me a chance to soak up what she was saying. "Make sense?"

I nodded, still out of breath.

"Your core, your seat, in fact most of your body, literally doesn't move, he does all the work. What you need to do is allow him to work beneath you and recognize the difference between uphill and forward versus fast. Welcome to the world of truly wonderful school canters."

William reached down to scratch his nose on his front leg, while I digested this new idea.

"You've ridden so many Thoroughbreds that his movement is something unique and new for you," she snorted. "Pick up the canter again, this time I want you to sit very chilly on him and don't try to physically push him along. Completely relax your seat. Trust me, he is uphill and forward. And there is no drop fence, bank, or coffin coming up in front of you, I promise. This is a school canter, not a cross country gallop or even a jumper canter. Just completely relax everything from your chest down." Rolling her eyes for emphasis she added, "You eventers! It's not always about speed."

Laughing, I picked up the reins and put William together at the walk. After a stride or two I asked him for a canter depart. Again, we felt as though we weren't covering ground. Stagnant.

"Quiet your seat. Quit pushing so much. Loosen it, and then let him carry you. You have been effectively blocking his back with it. He is used to a lighter feel on his back. Think feather soft."

I took a deep, cleansing breath heading into the long side of the arena and made every effort to reset my body to the rhythm beneath me. William's big red ears perked up, flicked back at me, then relaxed and I heard him snort.

"Okay, now are his shoulders up?" Colleen asked as we cantered past her.

"Yes, he is uphill." We started down the short side and I had to focus very hard in my attempt to not push him with my seat. I hadn't realized just how much I used my seat at the canter when riding him.

"Do you feel him beneath you? Is he stepping under himself?"

I did feel him stepping beneath me with each stride and I did a mental check of the rest. He was stepping under himself, his haunches were lower than his shoulders, his back was round and swinging beneath me, the front of his face sat just at the vertical, and he was light as a feather in my hands. It was all there. It had been there. I just couldn't really feel it until now. The light bulbs started going off in my head as William taught me to ride with a lighter seat. Everything beneath me felt right, even then I had to check myself every few strides, less I tighten up and fall into my old habit which would once again block his back. Although Gold Herr had taught me to ride with a lighter seat, it became glaringly obvious that I could still use a lesson or two on developing an even lighter seat.

"Now, come across the diagonal with tempi changes every four strides, and for his sake, don't change a thing in your seat from what you have right now."

Turning across the arena, I pointed his nose toward the far corner and began our changes. *One, two, three, four (switch), one, two, three, four (switch).* We made our last change and rounded the corner.

"Now in threes and keep your seat quiet. Don't over think or over ride it. Just ask him and allow him to do his job. Your job is to keep him up hill, and for God's sake don't nag him."

Thank goodness she hadn't asked for the two tempis, I thought as I turned the corner. Every three strides I thought about the change rather than ask for it and William skipped across the arena, swapping strides smoothly. I would conquer the dreaded two tempi changes on another day. We rounded the corner again.

"Again, and then lengthen down the long side."

Again, the tempi changes flowed, we rounded the corner and William skipped into them again. I was so caught up in the tempi success that I never took the time to worry about the lengthening. Rounding out of the last corner, I opened my hip angles, nudged him with my spur and he exploded down the long side. His canter stride felt gigantic beneath me even though his rhythm remained the same. Grinning from ear to ear with light bulbs going off in my head, I brought him down to a walk in front of Colleen.

"Congratulations, those were some of his best tempi changes ever. Looks like you both figured it out together. William will always tell you when you are using your seat too much by shutting down. So, do you get it now? You wanted forward, but you really kept asking him for faster until you pestered him to death. That is what happens when you, she pointed at my chest for emphasis, over think things."

"When you ride a really good horse on cross country it feels like you have this never ending engine beneath you. It is about speed and power—that power that lies in reserve and ready for the next jump, I know, I have been there. With dressage it is less about speed, although you still have that power beneath you, it is refined, has more depth."

Turning him in a circle to give him a break I added, "Even though his canter is so uphill, it felt as though we weren't going anywhere."

"Trust me, you were, and he has several gears, but you were blocking his back and chasing him with your seat. Most horses don't have his canter, but what I wanted him to teach you today is to lighten your seat at the canter so whichever horse you do ride will be able to feel and respond to a lighter aid from you. From the ground, you look like you are pumping him two strides out from a giant four-star fence at Rolex. It's actually quite funny to watch!" Her eyes danced with laughter as she stood from her stool. She tucked a loose strand of hair behind one ear.

Craig came striding up the path to the arena smiling, "You'll have to show me what to look for so I can join in the fun." He stood at the edge of the arena in his usual T-shirt, shorts, and flip-flops, looking decidedly delicious. "What's all this about 'pumping him'?" His eyes sparkled with mischief as I turned three shades of embarrassed.

Ignoring his innuendo, Colleen turned her back to him, "I would rather you observe and leave the riding to the pros." She winked at me.

"Well, Colleen, you have to give him credit for sticking around. Most men run like Forrest Gump when they meet a woman with a horse, much less one that competes and takes this 'horse thing' seriously," I added, innocently batting my eyelashes.

"See, I'm no galoot. I scored points just for showin' up today! Actually I came to say goodbye, I need to get back to work. We have two large guest parties arrivin' this week. I put the paperwork that AJ wanted on his desk up at the house. I had to hustle in order to make it out before Chi Chi tried to feed me," he said patting his belly. "Are you ladies done with all your horsey stuff?" He smiled back at me, trying his best to bat his eyes like I had.

Catching him out of the corner of her eye, Colleen tried to swat him with her hand but he scooted out of reach just in time, "Yes, that is all I wanted to do today, any more and she'll start overanalyzing her ride." Colleen left her stool behind and headed for the barn.

As I swung my leg over William's back, Craig moved to help me dismount and I slid slowly into his arms. Damn, I couldn't think with him around. I hated to move away, but Maria was headed for the arena. Approaching us, she threw me a nasty glare as I ran up the stirrups.

"Please move your horse, I am on a schedule," she nearly stomped her foot, her dark eyes flashing.

Craig stepped away from me so I could move William away from the arena entrance. Feigning concern, Craig stepped aside for her, gallantly sweeping his arm in a bow. As Maria swept past him, he said, "Maria, how is your brother these days? I heard he left the country." He paused for a moment and I got the definite impression he was allowing his words to sink in, "When you see him please tell him I said hello." The tone of his voice brought me up sharply.

For a second I thought Craig had unleashed the furies upon himself. Maria's face turned ghastly white, then bright red as she fought to control her reaction. Her dark eyes shot daggers at him and then she swung them on me. Her eyes bored through mine with such hatred, the hair on the back of my neck stood on end.

"You watch your back," she hissed and then just like that she switched to Spanish, and gave him a tongue-lashing as she walked to the mounting block. Craig just shrugged, blowing her off. Grabbing me by the elbow, he guided me towards the barn and William fell into step next to me. Once in the barn aisle, we could no longer hear her ranting.

Just then Colleen popped her head out from behind the feed room door, "Really, Craig? Shit, now you are going to leave and I'll have to deal with her." Exasperated she disappeared back into the feed room and I could hear her mumbling to herself.

"What in the heck was that about?" Craig had started to help me un-tack William in the wash stall.

"Just some old business. Maria's brother Jose and I used to be friends. That is until I caught him smugglin' cocaine through the resort. It was right after I started runnin' the business," he shrugged. Looking around, he reached over and laid the damp saddle pad on a rack to dry. "Anyway, I have known her family for years, so when I caught him runnin' drugs through the resort I was stuck between a rock and a hard place. Because of me, he got busted. I found out later that there was a lot more going on and Jose left the country pretty quick." He stepped back into the aisle, "There is still a lot of bad blood there."

Cocaine? Really? Holy crap. Welcome to the third world, Todd.

Keeping my face hidden, I took a moment to regain my composure. It wasn't everyday you heard someone talk nonchalantly about cocaine smuggling. Turning on the hose, I rinsed William down. Maria's reaction to Craig had me uneasy, especially since she seemed to include me in her vehemence towards him. I bent down to rinse under his belly where the girth had been.

Craig artfully changed the subject. "Listen, I've got to run, but I will be back next week. Do you think you could get away for a few days?"

"Yeah, sure, what do you have in mind?" My palms started to sweat, or was that the water from the hose. *Oh Lord, don't get serious on me. No, no.* Switching hands, I ran my palm across my breeches, trying vainly to wipe it dry.

"I was hopin' to drag you out to see the resort. Maybe go fishin' off shore. I thought you might like that. The guests will be gone and we'll have the place to ourselves...." The last sentence hung between us. "I'd like to show it to you," he added quietly.

Swallowing, I shut off the hose and ducked under William's neck to get the metal sweat scraper. Craig handed it to me, and then gently pulled me in when I took the bait. His mouth found mine, soft, gentle. Unlike before, my body stiffened with his touch. *Why is there always a 'next step'? Can't we just keep this light?* Ignoring my brain, my body softened, giving in to him. He tasted of salt air and I started to melt further into him. *Oh Lord help me, the man could kiss!* The sweat scraper slid from my hand and *pinged* on the concrete floor next to us. Finding it hard to breathe, my body warring with my brain, I suddenly pulled away.

Craig stood there eyeing me for a moment. First a shadow of pain, then disappointment, crossed his face. Recovering quickly, he reached down for the sweat scraper. Offering it to me, he squared his shoulders and turned to leave. His face was blank, devoid of all emotion.

How does he do that? "Craig, wait!" My pulse was still racing from our kiss. Pulling the inside of my cheek between my teeth I bit down, trying to steel myself against the look I had seen on his face. I had never meant to hurt him. *I just...*

He came to a stop and slowly turned to face me, his face impassive. "Craig, I..I..," I stammered. I swallowed hard, the warm tang of blood from my cheek souring my mouth.

"Ach lass, I've no idea what ye hae been through, but it's no fault of mine. Can ye no see that I care for ye?" He spoke softly, in his thick brogue, his hands heavy by his side. His vowels rolled off his tongue thick and slow. His consonants blurred together. Gone was his clipped prep school English. I was learning that it faded when he got emotional, when he spoke freely, honestly... when he let his guard down.

His words hit me like a ton of bricks in the empty aisle. My lips moved, but nothing came out. Unable to meet his eye, I fumbled with the sweat scraper, turning it over in my hands, "It's just that, I…. um." It was no use. I looked him in the eye pleadingly. I still couldn't talk about Jake.

"It's okay, Lauren. I've no intention of harmin' ye on purpose or otherwise. Understand? I'll be back in a week and the offer is still open. I would really like to show ye my place." With that, he forced a smile and turning once again, he disappeared around the corner.

Frozen, I stood rooted to the floor, a weight pressing against my chest. *Damn, damn, damn.* Impatient, William began to paw in the wash rack, lifting the edge of the rubber mat with each flip of his hoof. "Quit," I scolded and I went to work stripping what was left of the water off of him. *Crap, crap, crap.* William picked up on my angst. Stepping away from me with his hind end, he tried to turn his head in the crossties, clearly distressed. "Sorry," I muttered and tried to calm my nerves. I took a few deep cleansing breaths to clear my head. Satisfied, he flicked an ear at me then went back to dozing. Unclipping the cross ties, I snapped on his lead rope and walked him back to his stall.

Swinging the door shut behind me, I slipped off his halter. Giving him a pat on his damp neck, I turned to leave. Stopping at the stall door I had second thoughts. I didn't have any desire to face Colleen or whoever else may be in the barn. From deep within me I could feel a myriad of pent up emotions bubbling to the surface, just waiting for a chance to explode. Not thinking, I again bit the inside of my cheek. Lately I had become darn good at squashing my emotions, hiding them, and plastering on my game face, but now, I just needed space. I needed to be alone. Heading to the back of William's stall, I sought sanctuary.

With my back against the cool concrete block I let my body slide down until my butt hit the shavings. The halter and lead fell from my hand into a jumbled heap next to me. Burying my head between my bent knees I lost it. Quiet sobs racked my body and warm, salty tears raced down my face. Unable to control the sobs, I slipped one hand over my mouth trying to stifle the noise. The other arm, I wrapped firmly around my legs, squeezing for all I was worth.

After several minutes, I heard the stall door open. Unable to hold my breath, my face hot with tears, I waited to be discovered. All the while praying that whoever was there would just go away.

The bolt on the stall door slid into place and I heard someone moving through the shavings toward me. Burying my head further into my tear soaked riding breeches, I listened as a soft shuffling noise grew closer, then stopped. *Go away.* Someone sat down next to me, back against the wall. Unwilling to surface, I slowed my breathing to a more manageable state and the tears slowly ebbed. The ceiling fan in the stall was off balance, creating a perfectly timed ticking noise. And the only other sound came from William's large molars as he enjoyed his hay. Still, we sat. A cold beer appeared in the space below my knees and I knew then it was Colleen. I also knew she wasn't going to go away.

Wiping my wet face on my breeches I surfaced for air, accepting the cold beer as I did. The tears had stopped and I managed a few clean breaths. Colleen sat quietly next to me, sipping her own beer and staring off into space. The cold, dark liquid felt heavenly as it slid down my hot throat. Neither of us spoke as the minutes ticked by, measured by the sounds of the stall around us. Finally I broke the silence. "Sorry."

Colleen remained silent next to me, and William continued working diligently on his hay. The soft munching sounds took me back in time to my childhood, and rainy days spent alone in the barn. We sat in silence, occasionally taking a sip of beer, but otherwise unmoving. I had to admit, I was grateful for the company, but still couldn't bring myself to talk. And still we sat.

"I don't usually lose it like this. I used to have such a handle on my emotions, but lately all I seem to do is cry. Somewhere along the way, well, over the last year I've become a sniveling mess." The sounds of the barn settled around us as we sat for a few more minutes. "Sorry, I get mad when my emotions get the best of me and that just adds fuel to the fire. Sorry." I laid my forehead on my knees as the minutes ticked by.

My head had started to pound, aching from the sobbing and it hurt like hell. It always did when I cried myself to this point. Time crept by, measured by the ticking sounds of the fan. Like gas on a smoldering fire, it was fuel for my headache. *Tick, tick, tick.* Somewhere deep within me under the maddening ache it hit me. With a calm certainty I knew it was time to go *there. What the hell do you have to lose, Todd? You've tried everything else. Crap! Well,* here goes… Lifting it I continued, haltingly at first, "His sister rode. Actually I gave her lessons. But that wasn't how we met."

Lifting the bottle to my lips, I downed the last swallow. Colleen, reaching on the other side of her, produced another beer. *Liquid courage, huh? Well, at least she came armed.* Taking it, I continued. "We actually met in school. We had a couple of classes together our senior year." Tilting my head back against the wall, I closed my sore eyes. I was emotionally spent. My cheeks, now dry, stretched tight where the salty tracks from my tears had gushed. "When we met, it was like I had found the other half of me. Only thing is I never really knew that it was missing."

"Hmm," Colleen offered and a few more minutes ticked by.

"We were just really good friends at first. Actually, for about three years, and then something… well, it just clicked. After that we were mad for each other." Pulling my heavy head off the wall, I traced circles in the loose shavings between my legs with the end of a finger.

Munch, munch, munch.

"Six years." I took in a lungful of air, willing my chest to expand and relax. Thankfully, the tightness in my chest had eased with each passing minute making breathing a bit easier.

Tick, tick, tick. The fan was beginning to drive me nuts. Taking another sip I went on, "I ended up in a stall like this one, with Pogo. Only there wasn't an annoying fan." With a wry smile I lifted the beer to my lips again.

Taking a deep breath, I plunged ahead, "Apparently, he swerved to avoid some logs that had broken free from the truck in front of him. Or so that was the official report." I shrugged, "On a winding mountain road, there was just nowhere to go." *Don't forget the ice and the visibility, and the fact that he was coming home early to surprise you.* The tears threatened to well up and spill over again. Blinking them back I saw the stall begin to fade in a watery blur, "The oncoming traffic swerved too, and well…"

"Ah," Colleen acknowledged. "Over six years, that's a long time, especially when you are young. You must feel like half your life was spent with Jake."

My head snapped up, "How did you know his name? I haven't…" I hadn't talked about Jake to anyone in Panama. I had been so careful.

"Deanne. Apparently you talk in your sleep. I guess you freaked her out when we flew to the islands. That's the only reason she said something to me." Colleen shifted the beer in her hand, "She thought maybe I knew what was going on or who Jake was. I figured you would say something eventually. Or not."

"Oh, I guess I wasn't quite drunk enough."

"Nope."

I could feel her smile.

"You know, I don't want to 'get over' him. That's not it at all, I just… well, I don't think it is possible to love like that again. I'm not sure I can open my heart up all the way for someone else. That wouldn't be fair."

"Fair? To whom? Is what you are doing to Craig fair?"

"I didn't ask for this, Colleen. I didn't *do* anything to make him like me. I wasn't looking. Don't put this on me." The circles in the shavings became squares as my index finger plunged deeper into the tiny, fluffy curls of wood. *You didn't stop it either?*

"Exactly, you weren't looking, and I know Craig. He sure as hell wasn't looking. As long as I've known him, he rarely dates and it takes wild horses to drag him from the resort." She let out an exasperated sigh, "It just happened. That's the point. You can run around avoiding men for the rest of your life, but sometimes it is not up to us. Call it God, fate, karma. Hell, just call it luck, but it found you twice so don't be stupid and run the other way." She took a sip of her beer. "Hell, I wasn't looking for AJ either. He found me, and now look at me," she spread her arms wide and glanced around the stall, "I live in

Panama! Who would have ever thought I would follow a man to a foreign country."

Munch, munch, munch...

"Listen, Craig is about as real and good as it gets. His life hasn't exactly been a picnic either. Hell, none of ours have, but the choice is yours, nobody else's. Living doesn't mean forgetting." She paused. Turning her beer upside down the last few drops hit the shavings next to her. "Besides, doesn't that accent just make you nuts? It does me!" Her elbow jabbed me in the ribs.

Smiling, I nodded my head. "It's like he's two different guys and both are sexy as hell. He can sound so... well, normal until he gets ticked." I shot her a sideways look, "I've found myself wondering what he'll sound like between the sheets."

Colleen laughed, "Please do tell!" Her eyes sparkled with mischief, "You know, he's grown up in so many different places; I guess he learned over the years to blend in and sound normal." Snickering, she added, "Get him drunk, I mean really drunk, and you can't understand a word that comes out of his mouth." The tension eased a bit and we both laughed. Before long she stood, her knees making a popping noise as she straightened them. "Damn, I'm getting old. I'm cracking like my Granny." She offered me her hand, "I've got to get back to work. Come on."

She pulled me to my feet. We gathered out bottles and with my game face back on, I followed her out of the stall.

**

The sound of the truck and trailer heading down the gravel road returning to the racetrack was music to my ears. I stood just outside the old fort walls, Cronos grazing contentedly on the lush grass at my feet. The dense jungle around us was quiet in the hot afternoon sun, not even the birds were chirping. She had unloaded from the trailer like a pro, glanced around once, and then immediately set to work mowing the lawn. Her fuzzy black muzzle worked overtime, eagerly pulling chunks of grass into her mouth. With a purpose, she moved on to the next clump, making quick work of it as well.

The mosquitos were already coming out for dinner, stirred up by our movement through the grass. There were dark patches of sweat behind her front legs, along her shoulder, and under her halter began to darken and spread. The afternoon rain had stopped minutes before the truck pulled up and the air was now thick and heavy with humidity.

I stood for a few more minutes marveling at my new horse until I couldn't stand the onslaught of bugs for another second. I let out a low five beat whistle that slowly rose in octaves. Pausing mid bite, she pricked her ears in my direction. It was the whistle my parents had used to get my attention when I was growing up, the same one I had used with every one of my horses. Lowering her head, she went back to work mowing the grass. With a contented sigh I made a clucking noise and pulled upward on her lead rope. She still wore the old halter she'd had in the impound lot, "We'll have to fix that now won't we?" I had visions of a new leather halter with a brass nameplate.

A dirt road ran around the outer wall of the compound, just skirting the jungle edge, to the backside of the stables. After making our way around, and sampling every thing that was green and within reach along the way, we reached the entrance of the barn. As her hooves clip clopped onto the barn aisle, Maria and Pablito came strolling in from the arena.

A big smile split Pablito's tan face. "Is this the new girl?" he asked, offering a hand for her to sniff before rubbing her face with his knuckles. "She is big."

"Yes, this is Cronos." Full of the fresh realization that she was really mine, I smiled back at Pablito.

Glancing over his shoulder, Pablito searched for Maria who had disappeared from his side. She stood at the barn entrance. The look on her face was one of utter disbelief, her mouth hanging open. For a brief instant I was shocked at just how vulnerable and child-like she appeared. Clenched at her sides, she slowly uncurled her fists as her expression returned to one I easily recognized, the usual Maria. As daggers flew from her dark eyes, she spun wordlessly on her heel and vanished from sight.

Bitch!

Thoroughly flustered, Pablito slowly lowered his hand to his side. Clearing his throat, he glanced at me with a look of surprise. I watched as his Adam's apple bobbed up and then back down in his thin neck, "I better get back to work." He shuffled off in the direction of the main house.

"What the hell?" I mumbled out loud. Pricking her ears, Cronos handily shoved her muzzle into my side, leaving a damp green smudge. Alone in the barn, I found myself at a loss for what had just happened, "That girl doesn't need any explanation other than the obvious one. She's crazy!" Cronos nudged me again. One thing was clear, Maria was beyond pissed, but why was a mystery.

Shaking it off, I headed for the empty stall on the right which Pablito had prepared for Cronos. Once inside, I removed the old halter and shut the stall door behind me. Rather than delve into the pile of hay in the corner of the stall, she stretched her neck over the top of the stall door, reaching for me. I wanted to leave her alone and give her a chance to settle in, so with a cursory pat on the neck, I headed back down the aisle, halter and lead in hand.

Cronos settled in nicely. She seemed to take her new surroundings in stride and we soon discovered that not much seemed to faze her. Colleen and I created a feeding plan to put some weight on her large frame. Like Gold Herr, she was a very keen example of the old style warmbloods with a good deal of bone and body mass. Many breeders over the last ten years or so had been breeding a lighter style of horse that could cross disciplines more adeptly, but personally I liked her imposing size.

Allowed to settle into life at her new home the first day, she spent most of her time with her head stretched over the stall door, watching life at the barn as it passed her stall. She had a naturally inquisitive but bold personality. I set to work pulling her mane, trimming her up, and bathing her.

Although it was evident to all that Cronos had some upper level, most likely Grand Prix training she was very much out of shape and had not been in consistent work for some time. It wasn't hard to guess that her former owner had not a clue what the mare was capable of, nor could ride for that matter. Our first goal would be to get her back into shape; the fun stuff like piaffe would have to wait. Rather than assume she knew more than she actually did, we would start fresh, from the bottom, building up her muscle and stamina. Then we would take one movement at a time to see what she really did know. I was simply giddy with excitement and anticipation. Not in my wildest dreams would I ever have thought I'd own a horse such as this.

Our first few rides consisted of nothing more than getting to know each other and systematically re-building the muscles along her top line and back by stretching her nose forward and downward. Often referred to as long and low; by maintaining a consistent metronome-like rhythm and push from behind using their hind legs and haunches, a horse will loosen and stretch their back and neck muscles. Much like a cat stretching or a downward dog pose in yoga, it feels lovely and before long Cronos was relaxing her back beneath my saddle and her hips swung freely behind me. She was unable to hold the stretches for very long at first, but in time her muscle memory would return.

It was becoming more and more evident to Colleen that she had been trained to use her body correctly, and all we had to do was refresh and recharge her.

The more I rode her, the more she amazed me. When I least expected it, she gave me moments of brilliance, a peak down the rabbit hole into her former life and training. On only our second ride I picked her up again after a walk break. We trotted around the arena once before I gave her a half halt to bring her onto her haunches some more and raise her front end. Instead, she shortened her frame and stepped lightly into passage. I had either given her an unknown cue that she recognized, or she simply wanted to show me what she could do. Either way, it was glorious and light. It would, no doubt, take time to figure out each other's signals and cues, but at least I knew she had it in her. Right now, that was enough.

Towards the end of the week, Colleen stopped by the arena to check on our progress. She was dressed up in a soft flowing, cotton sundress in a lovely shade of peach. The strapless top and waist had a fun pattern of rick-rack appliqué and detailed embroidery in shades of cream, ecru, and off white. The peach tones set off her tan and her blonde hair hung long and straight past her shoulders. I couldn't help but smile at her choice in footwear. Like a true horsewoman, she sported a pair of moss green rubber Wellington boots. The white cotton edges of her long socks peeked out over the tops of the boots.

"My, don't you look stunning!"

She struck a dramatic pose for fun. "AJ is taking me out for a date night. Troy is in town. Both he and Rachel flew in last night. I've no doubt they will talk shop, but at least it's a night out," she smiled. Everyone knew that AJ was absolutely in love with Colleen. While she may joke about him talking shop, we both knew that he thought the world revolved around her.

"Do you think I ought to go with the boots, or are they a bit much?" she said, her voice dripping with sarcasm as she stretched a long boot clad leg in my direction. Colleen scratched the crest of Cronos's neck, taking care not to get horse smut on her dress. Cronos leaned her honey bay neck into Colleen's nails, reveling in the feel of the scratch. Her large round nostrils vibrated with ecstasy. "You know, we are very lucky to have found a horse that is classically trained."

"How can you be so sure she is classically trained?" The intricate subtleties of dressage training were still beyond me. "We haven't had her that long."

"Her neck for one, if she had been ridden with her nose consistently behind the vertical plane and artificially cranked in, then there would be a break or hollow spot in her neck muscles here." She pointed to a spot below her coal black mane and about a quarter of the way down her neck. "She also uses her back correctly when she steps under herself with her hind legs. It is easy for her because that is what she knows. Her back comes up under you rather than dropping and hollowing. Another indication is that she travels with her hind legs up underneath her instead of trailing behind her. If her hind end is trailing, then it would be physically impossible for her back to lift up under you. It is another sign of a classically trained horse." She gave her neck another pat, pausing to squeeze the crest of her neck. "We won't need to spend time re-training her."

While there was more than one style of dressage training, Colleen stuck firmly to the German model. "That makes sense. I don't know Colleen. I have so much to learn in a short amount of time. Are you sure this is a good idea?" There were times when I thought I had finally grasped this whole upper level dressage thing, and then she would explain something to me that seemed so obvious and I would be left wondering if I really knew how to ride at all. Some days I was left wishing I had a bounce into a coffin jump or a skinny brush fence to a big corner fence. Heck, the course around Rolex would have appealed to me. Trying not to defeat myself with negative thinking, I changed the subject, "I think I would pass on the boots, although they do have a certain amount of sex appeal!"

"Ya think? Yeah, maybe I'll go for a sexy pair of strappy sandals instead," she smiled up at me. Giving Cronos a final pat, she headed back towards the barn.

The barn was empty when I walked Cronos up from the arena after our ride, or so I thought. Maria was still lurking about. I could here her in Mariposa's stall. I un-tacked Cronos, rinsed her off, and walked her back to her stall.

The atmosphere was damp and tingling with electricity. The sharp smell of ozone reached my nose and I knew a big storm was brewing. Glancing out of the window at the back of the stall I could see a steel gray sky overhead. Periodically, lightning branched out in bright, white electric splendor, travelling horizontally between the roiling gray clouds. *Hmph, the girl brings black clouds with her.* A loud crack of thunder reverberated through the barn, causing Cronos to jump straight up in her stall with a mouthful of hay. I scratched her back just behind her withers and she settled down enough to finish her mouthful, although her eyes remained wary. "Guess you don't do storms?" I murmured.

I glanced at my watch. I still had an hour before I needed to pick up Haley. In an instant the angry skies opened up and rain drops the size of quarters slammed down on the barn roof with a deafening roar. With a sigh, I decided to wait out the storm rather than trying to make a dash for the Land Cruiser. Most of the storms during rainy season rose with a vengeance then quickly faded out.

I had parked up by the house rather than next to the barn since I had dropped off some stuff for Chi Chi when I arrived. I certainly didn't want to run that far in the rain. Besides, driving in these tropical downpours wasn't much fun, especially when I couldn't see more than a few feet in front of the steel cow catcher on the front of the grill. I slid down the wall of the stall, prepared to wait it out.

I lost track of time with the overhead drumming of raindrops and watching Cronos move about the stall. You could learn a lot about a horse by hanging out in their stall. Riders who showed up at the barn and accepted the reins from a groom, who did all the work for them, really did miss out on the subtleties of their equine partners, in my opinion. With my back against the cool concrete blocks of the outer wall of the stall, I let my eyes rove over every inch of her body, studying her conformation. She was a far cry from the lighter, faster eventers I had ridden most of my life, but I kind of liked it. She was growing on me. I made a mental note to find out what I could about her on the internet. After all, I did have her papers even though they were written in German. I sighed, the sound muted by the storm raging outside. Colleen had trained in Germany, maybe she could help me decipher the paperwork.

Lost in my own thoughts, I heard what sounded like two voices arguing in the aisle. The feminine voice was unmistakably Maria's. The second voice was male, and I had trouble placing it. It wasn't the smooth tones of Pablito's voice, but there was definitely a Latin flavor to it. At first I tuned them out, but the voices grew louder and more insistent, until I found myself eavesdropping. They were arguing heatedly, that was for sure. Cronos's massive body blocked my view of the aisle, but then again, it kept me hidden. Sitting very still, I strained to hear the conversation over the rain as Maria and the man walked down the aisle towards me.

"-what in the hell are you doing here? You know he'll hunt you down if he finds out you came back," Maria's voice had a distinctively desperate tone to it. "You need to leave now, it's just too soon."

"I'm tired of running, and I won't let him control my life anymore." There was a pause, "Besides he's taken everything." The voice was rich with emotion as he snarled back at Maria. "I'm done running, it's time to turn the tables." They seemed to have stopped just outside Cronos's stall. "So far, I've been able to get a third of it," his voice softened. "But I can't do it alone. Are you in?"

"You are loco. He told you he would kill you and Ricardo will kill me if he finds out." she added a frantic edge to her voice. "Your last mistake really cost me."

Kill? Kill whom? Who in the heck was she talking to? I strained to hear as a clap of thunder exploded around the barn.

"…back this week. I'm not afraid of him. You forget I know him better than most people. Everyone has a weak spot, and I think I've already found his," he laughed, the sound sending a shiver up my spine.

The voices slowly faded as they walked away from me, though in which direction I couldn't quite be sure. In a rush, I let out my breath. I hadn't realized I had been holding it in while they talked. Lightheaded, I tried to fill my lungs with air. The rain started to slacken as quickly as it came and the damp atmosphere of the stall left me sweating, or at least I blamed it on the humidity. Beads of perspiration dotted my forehead. Absently, I ran my forearm across it in an attempt to dry it. *What in the heck was that?*

I hung around the stall as long as I could, but time was slipping away and I still needed to pick up Haley. Standing at the stall door, I listened for any hint of sound from the barn aisle. Cronos shifted in the stall behind me and shoved her soft muzzle into my side, searching for a treat. Her newly trimmed whiskers poked through the thin fabric of my shirt, tickling me. Gently, I pushed her away. I was beginning to grow anxious. Straining my ears, I listened. Hearing only the familiar sounds of the horses, I cautiously slid open the stall door and stepped out into the aisle. Glancing both ways, I quickly headed out of the back door of the barn, cutting across the grass towards the house.

I had no idea what Maria was up to, or who she was talking to. What I did know, without a shadow of a doubt, was that I didn't want to be involved. I resolved to leave the incident behind me in the barn as I sped through town towards Haley's school.

LAS BRISAS

There were only two ways in and out of the resort, by air or by sea. Well, actually there was another way; by land, but Craig was quick to point out that it was not a viable option. The cost of replacing axles, tires, shocks, and steering columns damaged by the rough clay road that led to the resort through the dense jungle was cost prohibitive. Therefore, the resort owned two planes, one for transporting guests, and one for the cargo and supplies needed to operate the resort. It was aboard the cargo plane that we climbed for our weekend together.

After the flight to San Blas, I was becoming more comfortable with flying in small planes, which was a good thing, because at first glance the matte silver cargo plane resembled nothing more than a big tin garbage can with wings. When I looked at it, all I could see in my mind were the matte tin roofs that seemed to cover most of the houses in the shanty towns which dotted the outskirts of the city. I swallowed hard, put on my game face, and climbed aboard. Once inside, it became clear that the plane was well cared for. Everything was neatly stowed away and the controls in the cockpit looked much newer than the exterior. Feeling slightly more reassured, I settled into the co-pilots seat. We flew out of the same small airstrip we had used to get to the islands.

There was a storm moving in off the Caribbean so Craig had called me at the last minute, while I was still at the barn, to let me know that we would have to leave earlier than planned, so here I sat still wearing my riding clothes and boots. It was a good thing I had packed that morning with the intention of showering at AJ and Colleen's after my work at the barn was done. Craig, in his usual attire of shorts, T-shirt, and flip-flops passed me a headset, which I put on. He went to work clicking toggles and flipping switches as I watched in fascination.

Within moments, bright metallic propellers, edged in red paint on each wing coughed and roared to life. After one last check of his instruments, he winked at me as the plane began to roll down the tarmac. Like a silver whale, the cargo plane lumbered down the runway until it finally picked up enough speed to pull itself free of the ground, leaving the tarmac behind.

Once in the air, the roar of the engines faded enough that we could talk to each other using the headsets. The engines were still too loud for any sort of conversation without them. Grinning like a kid, Craig said, "It is just short of a forty minute flight." "We'll head east over the jungle, then turn south once we reach the water. Panama City is just north of here." He pointed out of his window.

I nodded, "Okay, which jungle, the Darien?"

He looked surprised, "You've been doing your homework. Yes, the Darien. It is one of the most beautiful places on earth." He spoke with a sense of awe and reverence in his voice. "There are still some native Indians that live there, but there is very limited access to the interior of the jungle because of the drug corridors." He frowned, "It's a shame because they limit access for botanists and other researchers. The drugs that come up through the jungle from Columbia are usually transported by some very ruthless guys, which makes livin' there really tough for the native tribes as well. It doesn't exactly make for a tourist destination either."

As the plane banked heading away from the airport and toward the east, Craig's face was lit by the sunlight streaming through the cockpit, highlighting the coppery hued hair on his face. He took my breath away. Maybe Colleen was right, maybe it was possible to find love twice.

He added, "Have you seen the movie *Sniper?*"

I had, a young Tom Berenger, all sweaty and dressed in camo, wasn't exactly an image that was hard on the eyes, but then again, neither was Craig. I nodded. I had always liked manly looking men, ones that had rough hands that knew how to build things and work for a living. Metro-sexual men were definitely not my thing.

"The story line was based on the Darien."

"Oh, wow," I made a mental note to watch the movie again more closely now that I felt I had a connection to the story.

Craig banked the plane again and we headed south along the coast. A bank of ominous, dark, clouds were building off to our east, over the water as we approached the resort. The pitch of the engines changed as Craig slowed the plane. Off to our right, the dark grey of a landing strip sat atop a hill above the resort. Cut out of the jungle, it resembled a scar on the green landscape. Flying low, Craig started to circle the buildings below, tipping the wing of the plane on my side downward so I could survey the site.

"The big buildin' is the clubhouse. That is where we serve meals and get together when we aren't fishin'. There are a few guest rooms in it as well, although most of the guests stay in the cabanas."

A large, white, main building with a bright blue colored tile roof sat within a hundred yards of the shoreline. The blue of the roofs matched the deep color of the Caribbean water. A few smaller, matching cabanas were scattered around the property. A well-manicured lawn connected each cabana to the main property. The brown, earthy colors of a thatched bohio sat on a small rise near the water's edge. A long wooden dock stretched out across the lighter blue hues of shallow water until it reached the darker shades of deeper water where it ended abruptly. Several boats were moored on either side of the dock. Leveling off, Craig brought the plane around for a landing. With a bump I felt the landing gear lower.

Once safely on the ground, we were met by a member of the resort staff who off loaded my bag into a waiting side by side utility vehicle for the trip down the hill. Craig and I climbed in and the tires of the Rhino UTV crunched along the gravel path that led down the hill.

"I thought we could wind down tonight and just relax. This storm should pass in a couple of hours, leavin' us with some gorgeous fishin' weather tomorrow."

I was beginning to see a shift in the man sitting next to me. He was markedly different from the one who had met me at the airport, more relaxed, more at ease. It was as if he had changed mid-flight. Nodding, I smiled to myself, and then turned my attention to the gorgeous grounds of the resort. We passed several gravel pathways on either side of the main one that led to isolated bungalows along the way.

As we reached the bottom of the hill, the crystal clear waters of the Caribbean stretched out before us. To the right was the main building. Just behind us, and to our left, was an outdoor dining area covered by traditional bohio, or thatched roof. Another gravel path ran to our immediate left and parallel to the shore. Craig stopped the Rhino in front of the clubhouse and climbed out.

The building welcomed the ocean vista with a large, open air porch. At the top of a small set of steps was a glass storm door. A thin, mousy woman met us at the door, opening it for us. The cool rush of air conditioning felt good after the hot ride down the hill. It was difficult to gauge her age, as hard work and the sun appeared to have taken their toll on her face and arms. She was almost as black as the night and wore her curly grey hair very short. Thin and wiry, her short legs jutted out from below her petite body. She was wearing a pair of navy blue chino shorts, a white polo shirt with the Las Brisas logo, and a pair of navy deck shoes. Taking Craig's face in her hands she kissed him warmly on the cheek, muttering something in Spanish. Taking both of her hands in his, Craig turned to introduce us.

"Lauren, this is my Clementine." His affection for the old lady was obvious. "She *is* Las Brisas and I would be lost without her."

"Hello," I offered my hand, but instead she gave me a warm hug, leaving me little time to raise my arms to embrace her. Her thin arms held me tightly, belying her petite stature.

"Lauren, so nice to meet you, you must be very special." She winked conspiratorially at Craig. Her Panamanian accent was light and her voice had a bird-like quality to it which clearly matched her appearance. "Come now, you two go have fun, Ganso and I will take care of the luggage." With that she shooed us towards the cool interior. As we left, she called down a long hallway in Spanish and a young Panamanian man in his early twenties came out to help her with the luggage.

With his hand tucked in the small of my back, we headed towards the open air porch. The large porch sat beneath a white washed, vaulted ceiling. Large wicker ceiling fans spun slowly overhead. In each corner sat a small collection of plants in terra cotta pots of varying sizes and shapes. Natural wicker lawn furniture with bright cushions in a banana leaf motif dotted the porch. Stepping back out into the moist tropical air, we could feel the storm fast approaching. Black clouds rolled towards us from directly over the dock, making the white fiberglass of the boats look dull and grey. My hair shrank another half an inch as my curls drew up in the humidity. Craig motioned me towards a small couch in the center of the space. Just as we sat, the rain started to fall.

You could almost set your watch by the afternoon rains; they fell like clockwork nearly every day. It hadn't taken long for me to come to the conclusion that the raindrops here in the jungle were easily three times the size of the raindrops in North Carolina. I was also getting used to the idea that if you were not inside a well-insulated building when it did rain, then you could forget trying to have any sort of a conversation over the roar of the rain as it hammered the roof. And so it was at this moment. Craig wrapped his arms around me, pulling me in to his chest. I could feel the radiant heat from his body through the fabric of our clothes. Resting my head on his broad shoulder, I stretched my long legs out until my boots dangled over the edge of the couch. I let myself relax, sinking into him.

The young man, who I assumed must be Ganso, popped his head out of the door behind us, nodded to Craig, and then disappeared. We sat together for quite some time, each absorbed within our own thoughts, while the rain pelted down around us. An occasional gust of wind would reach under the eaves, sending rain droplets skittering inwards from the edge of the porch. It was a good thing that we sat in the middle of the porch.

After a few minutes, Ganso reappeared with a tray of cold tapas and a glass jug of iced tea rimmed with large slices of lemon, which he set on the coffee table in front of us. Before he disappeared back into the clubhouse, Craig thanked him.

Eventually the rain slackened and a steamy mist descended like a veil around the property. The air all around us was heavy with moisture. Wet from the rain, the grass on the lawn was a deeper shade of green and the tree trunks a darker mahogany brown. Pulling free of the couch, Craig leaned forward and poured two glasses of tea, handing me one.

The ice cold tea felt heavenly as it slid down my throat. "Ganso? That's an odd name."

"Aye, it is. It means goose in Spanish." There was a faint hint of mischief to his voice and I liked it.

"Goose? Please tell me it's his nickname."

He nodded, "My Da gave him the nickname, his real name is David." He took a swallow of tea. "You see geese are pretty smart, mind you. They are also territorial. What most people don't know is that they are quite good at navigatin' long distances. Ganso's da was one of our boat captains and Ganso used to go out with us when he was younger. He has this sixth sense about him when it comes to findin' his way on the water. Like most fishermen, we use a navigational system to find our fishin' spots. Ganso," he shook his head in wonderment, "can set us down on those spots without the help of navigational systems. Don't get me wrong, he uses them, too, but in a pinch, he knows his way around every one of our fishin' spots."

Setting down his tea, Craig ran his hand along his chin. The stubble made a scratchy noise and I had to keep from reaching up to touch it. I could see the expression behind his eyes shift. His mouth twitched briefly as if he was trying to frame his next words. "He is also quite the guard dog," the mischievous boy was back.

"How so?" A deep rumble from my stomach startled me. "Whoops, guess I better eat." Sitting up I reached for the tapas. I picked up a thick slice of crusty bread covered with green olives and what looked like goat cheese. Popping an olive in my mouth I offered one to Craig. He shook his head and reached for his tea.

"You asked me why Maria hated me so much."

"Yeah," I reached for a shrimp roll. *Smuggling wasn't it?*

"I used to work with her brother, Jose. My Da originally hired him as a deck hand, you know, someone who helps the clients with baitin' hooks, reelin' them in, that sort of thin'. Anyway, we were great friends. Durin' our downtime we would go spear fishin' or surfin' together." I felt his body tense against mine. Glancing up, I caught him staring out at the water through the mist. A deep sadness crossed his face. After a few moments he cleared his throat and went on as if nothing had happened.

"I noticed him acting odd off and on for several weeks. I thought he was maybe havin' trouble with some girlfriend or somethin'. Anyway, I never could nail it down, so I blew it off. One day, my Da flew him into the city for supplies, said he needed Jose's help." The dark clouds started to part overhead and beams of sunlight stubbornly pushed their way through the misty air around us. "We only had three guests, so I took Ganso offshore with me. Everythin' was goin' fine, the marlin were bitin', and our guests were havin' a heck of a good day. This one guy had his line snap and we lost the hook. Part of

Jose's job was to make sure all the gear is stocked and ready to go."

He let out a deep sigh and I could see the events of that day playing behind his eyes as he remembered. The ice in his glass *clinked* as he drained the cool liquid. Reaching for the jug, I poured him some more.

"Thanks. I remember being pissed. It was so unlike Jose to screw up like that. Lucky for me, I kept an old tackle box shoved away in the cabin so I went searchin' for it. The marlin were runnin' and I was in a hot hurry to get the customer's line back out in the water so I just started diggin' through the cabinets." He paused, turning his focus on me, "I found over a hundred kilos of cocaine instead."

"Crap! On your boat? Was it his?"

"Yes and no. No it wasn't his, but yes he was smugglin' it. He was a mule. And, he stood to make a good deal of money."

I had no idea what a hundred kilos of cocaine looked like, but I had no doubt that the street value for such a haul would be incredible. I pictured images on the evening news of drug busts with black hooded DEA agents standing proudly, arms crossed, faces masked, behind row after row of brown paper wrapped bundles while the anchor talked about relative street value. "What in the world did you do?"

His mouth twitched, "I found the hook, put the coke back, then went back to fishin'." He grabbed an olive from one of the tapas and popped it in his mouth. Finished with the olive he added, "I had no choice at the moment, and I needed time to think. After we got back to shore, I told Ganso that I wanted to take the boat out because I thought one of the engines was missing when it idled. When I was out of sight, I pulled the coke out, slit each bag open, and dumped them overboard. It was almost half a million dollars worth."

I let out a whistle. That was a lot of money. "Thank God you didn't get caught with it. So what happened when Jose found out?"

"I threatened to turn him in, but he didn't know that all the evidence was already gone. I was tryin' to scare the shit out of him." Setting down his tea, he stared at his upturned palm for a moment. "I don't know, scare him straight or somethin'." Clenching his fist, he shook his head, a sad look on his face. "He thought I still had the drugs, so he made a break for it and left Panama that same night. I told him I would give him a twenty-four hour head start because we were friends. I haven't seen him since. He didn't have the cash to cover the drug loss, so he has been on the run since. I sent him to purgatory, so to speak."

"No wonder Maria hates you. Her brother is on the run for the rest of his life."

Nodding with assent, he added, "Not to mention the damage to the family name. His family is very well known in Columbia and Panama for bein' good upstandin' businessmen and citizens. A hard thin' to find in this part of the world," he added wryly. "Ganso, well he took offense to what Jose had done and fiercely defended me." Moving to get up, Craig set his drink down, "Come on, I'll show you my boats now that the weather is clearin' up."

We traipsed down to the long wooden dock where I marveled at his two boats. He was very proud of his latest purchase, a brand new thirty-nine foot Contender fishing boat. The sleek white fiberglass and shiny stainless steel of the boat sparkled in the sun, nearly blinding me. Climbing aboard, he showed me all the extra features he had added to make this the best boat in his fleet.

After poking around for a while, Craig walked me to my bungalow. I had wondered about my accommodations on the flight here. Not wanting to sound like a prude, I had kept silent, hoping that what I knew of Craig so far would be a good indicator. It was. He was a perfect gentleman and acted as if it had been his intent all along, that we have separate accommodations. I didn't want to be a foregone conclusion. At least this way, the question of 'what next' remained unanswered. The bungalow sat next to the main building, nestled in a small stand of trees. It felt a million miles away from civilization, when in fact, the path from the front door led straight to the main path which was lined with islands of tall bamboo, fragrant frangipani, along with a host of other tropical plants.

Turning the brass knob, Craig opened the door and stepped back to allow me to pass. My bags were already sitting on the floor, just inside the room. The room had a nice mixture of natural wicker and wood furniture, some of which appeared to be hand made. I had seen something similar at a circular, outdoor market in downtown Balboa. The fabrics were pale shades of ecru with the occasional soft green motif of a banana plant leaf. An abstract watercolor on the wall depicted a bunch of ripe bananas hanging from a long stem. This same banana yellow accent color popped up in the room on the throw pillows and bathroom accessories. Neither masculine nor feminine, it was a nice mix.

Craig pulled open the natural wood Bahama shutters, then turning, tossed me the keys. Catching them in mid air I held them up in triumph, a smile on my face.

"Good catch. I'll give you some time to clean up. Dinner is at 5:00. I thought we'd dine casually on the porch and watch the sun go down. Well, actually, it goes down behind us, but the colors on the water are really nice to watch." His voice trailed off, and he seemed suddenly embarrassed. For a moment, I thought I saw him blush. And then it was gone.

Smiling, I said, "Sure, sounds nice."

As he moved to pass me in the foyer, I turned to meet him. Standing my ground, feet firmly rooted to the floor, I blocked the door. Having nowhere to go, he stopped before me. Without thinking, I reached for him, pulling him into me, and for the first time I initiated the kiss. I caught him off guard, and my boldness surprised me.

"Wow, to what do I owe that lovely kiss?" his voice held a mocking tone but the corner of his mouth was turned up and his eyes sparkled with mischief.

"For getting me here safely in that tin can of yours, for taking me fishing, and last but not least, because it felt right."

"That works. I'll pick you up a few minutes before dinner." He gently pivoted me around until his back was to the door. With a wink, he was gone.

The neon green numbers on the bedside clock read 2:47 pm. Still in my riding clothes, although I had shed my half chaps on the plane, I decided to take a long hot shower and freshen up. Once out of the shower I collapsed exhausted on the bed with an oversized towel wrapped around me. My wet hair was wrapped in a towel and piled atop my head.

From where I lay on the soft bedspread I could just see out of the large picture window. Lush green grass fell away from the cabana towards the beach below. The cabana sat back far enough from the path and the clubhouse so as to have an unobstructed view of the water. The dock was just out of sight to my left. My suitcase sat open on one end of the dresser where I had left it, and my purse lay on the small table by the window. With a deep sigh of contentment I closed my eyes and listened to the silence around me. Between Haley, Dad, and Carmen at home, Ricardo didn't count as he rarely spoke at all, and my new friends at the barn, I hadn't had much silence in my life lately. I decided to enjoy the moment before getting up and dressed for dinner.

A gentle knock on the door roused me from my nap. Bleary eyed and slightly confused, I sat straight up in bed. It took a moment, and another more insistent knock, before I realized where I was. "Crap!" Leaping off the bed I jerked open the door one handed, the other clutched the end of the towel where I had tucked it in above my left breast. Craig, looking very amused stood on the stoop. His eyes travelled up from my bare legs to the towel wrapped snuggly around me, examining every inch in detail, until they reached my face.

With a snort of amusement he said, "I'd rather thought you'd dress for dinner, lass." His eyes sparkled with mischief as they ran down the length of my body once again. I felt his eyes through the cotton towel. *Oh, my!* The hungry look on his face spoke volumes.

The towel around my hair took this particular moment in time to unravel and slide off my head, tumbling towards my feet. A red cascade of damp curls fell across my face. Without thinking, I reached to catch it before it hit the ground, nearly losing the towel wrapped around me. Trying to juggle my grip on both towels, the one wrapped around my body began to slide precariously down. At the last moment I caught it just before my breast became exposed. The pale white skin stood out in sharp contrast to my tan line and freckles. The other towel hit the floor near my bare feet without a sound. Seeing the look in his eyes, I felt the heat of embarrassment snake up the creamy skin of my neck to my cheeks, turning my skin a hot shade of red.

Flipping my curls out of my face, I grasped for some semblance of composure. "I, uh, I fell asleep. If you give me just a moment, I can be ready." I took stock of his casual appearance of shorts, polo shirt, and flip-flops.

"Aye, I'll wait for you," he said, standing his ground.

Hurrying to my suitcase, I grabbed something to wear and darted for the bathroom. I could hear the door shut behind him, then the sound of the television as he turned it on.

Slowly, as I dressed, the red blush on my skin faded. Jake had been the only man I had ever been with, the only one who had ever seen me naked. Pulling on a short skirt made of light rayon, I found myself both flustered and, I had to admit, aroused. Before the blush could creep back, I pushed the thought from my mind and reached for my top. I brushed my teeth, ran my fingers through my hair and headed back to the room. He turned off the television as I grabbed a pair of sandals from my bag and slipped them on.

"Ready?" He tossed the remote on the bed. Shutting the door behind me, he tucked my arm under his and headed for the clubhouse.

Dinner was simple. Craig grilled a steak for each of us and pulled steaming hot baked potatoes out of the oven. Apparently the resort was empty except for Clementine, Ganso, and a few other employees whom I hadn't met, so we ate alone at a table on the porch overlooking the water. The sun set behind us, but the orange glow it cast across the water was a magnificent display of muted oranges, reds, and yellows. Craig had thoughtfully opened a bottle of Australian merlot for me and fixed himself a glass of Laphroaig whiskey.

Picking up the bottle, I read the label. "Is this from home?"

With a shrug he replied, "Where's home?"

"Hmph, never mind, with a name like Laphroaig, it must be Scottish."

"Aye," he lifted the glass up, studying the amber liquid in the light. "It was my Da's favorite. He took Hamish and I fishin' there once."

"Hamish? Fishing? I have trouble picturing that."

He laughed, "No, he never was the outdoors type like I was," He set the glass back on the table, "except for the horses." I saw memories flit across his green eyes. "Brown trout and salmon, that's what we were fishin' for."

"Well," I lifted my glass, "slainte."

Lifting his glass he grinned. "Do ye even ken what that means?"

"Nope, but I've always liked Irish pubs," I smiled back at him.

"Weel," his brogue was thick and he cocked one sandy colored eyebrow for effect, "'tis more Scottish than Irish seein' as how we owned the Gaelic first." I nearly snorted into my glass, which only served to egg him on. "Tae yer health, then," he reached over and tapped his glass gently against mine, making a faint *clinking* sound.

We made plans to leave the dock at 6 am, before the sun rose, in order to get in a full days worth of fishing. Both tired, and with a big day planned for tomorrow, we ended the evening early. After two glasses of wine and some good conversation Craig walked me back to the bungalow. I had to admit, I was tired. He gave me a short kiss goodnight and handed me a bottle of water. How romantic, I thought.

"Make sure you drink this tonight. You've had alcohol tonight and you don't want to get dehydrated tomorrow. We've got fish to slay."

"Hmm?" His lips moved, but I was distracted. This time his kiss had tasted of whiskey. "Um, yeah, got it, see you tomorrow bright and early."

Heading back down the path he hesitated. He turned around as I was shutting the door, "Lauren. Em, don't forget the alarm." A relaxed smile split his face.

"Oh go on you oaf," I shot back in my best British accent. I could never in a million years have imitated his Scottish brogue. With a *click* I shut the door, set the alarm, and headed for bed.

"Male, 29 years old, MVA, car versus tractor trailer on Camp Road…. The voice rang clear and loud for all to hear. NOOOOO!

Staring down at the scissors in my hand, I was horrified. No, stop. I had to stop this. I cried out in anguish but my voice was lost in the chaos around me. The pitch of the background noises rose suddenly, mercilessly drowning out the timbre of the loud clear voice. Finally, it became lost in the cacophony of chaos that surrounded me.

Large muscular arms wrapped around me, lifting and pulling me to safety. The red glow faded with a 'whooshing' sound, only to be replaced by sharp acrid smells of the ER and dull faces, eyes downcast to avoid looking at me.

"Lauren. Lauren, look at me. It was a grizzled face, covered with beard and mustache. The eyes were a smoky shade of greyish

blue. Voices began to creep in and snatches of conversation filtered through the smoky eyes in front of me.

"...shock.."

"..give her a moment.."

"..grab a cuff and check her blood pressure.."

"Lauren?"

My vision cleared and the smoky eyes steadied before me. Pulling free I...

The sounds of cicadas reached me through the glass window as I lay sweating between the sheets. The neon green lights of the clock mocked me. It was 3:52 am. Rolling stiffly out of bed, I changed into an extra T-shirt that I had brought, piled my damp hair up onto my head with a hair band and climbed into the other side of the bed where it was dry. After what seemed an eternity of tossing and turning, sleep wrapped me in its arms again.

**

Big, fat, white light bulbs strung along the railing of the dock showed me the way to the boat in the dark. Ganso and Craig were finishing up their preparations on board. A faint whiff of coffee caught my attention, "Okay, who's got the coffee?" Ganso offered a helping hand as I stepped over the port side.

"You can stow your bag there," Ganso pointed towards a storage box set inside the console in front of Craig.

"Mornin'," he looked totally at ease sitting behind the wheel. Grabbing me with one arm, he pulled me down beside him on the bench seat. As I settled in, he pulled a cup of coffee from a cup holder on the console and stuck it in my hand.

"Hmm, thanks." The aroma tickled my nose and my stomach growled.

"Well fix that in a bit," he said before turning his attention back to the myriad of toggle switches and gauges on the console.

Smiling back, I settled in as he fired up the engines. After letting them idle for several minutes, Ganso released the ropes that held us to the dock and we moved slowly out into the dark waters of the Caribbean. Using the GPS, we cruised along for about thirty minutes before he slowed down. The bow of the boat lowered back into the water as we came down from our cruising plane. Ganso had been busy rigging up the fishing poles during the trip. He made sure the leader lines, hooks, and jigs were all set up. As the boat slowed, Craig and Ganso switched jobs and I followed Craig towards the back of the boat. Ganso kept the boat idling along while Craig started to cast the lines.

"I thought we could try for some bottom fish; snapper or grouper. It is fun to catch the big billfish, but exhaustin' as well, and since we are here to relax…" The coffee had settled in my stomach, fortifying me for the day and I was ready to get fishing. "For the snapper and grouper we'll use jigs," his hands worked as he talked, selecting a bait fish from the live well, he slipped it on a hook, "but this is what I call insurance. I like to toss somethin' else over the side just in case we get somethin' interestin' to bite. You just never know."

"Sounds great…"

"We'll drop a couple of lines overboard and then Ganso will let the boat drift slowly over this area." He pointed towards the east side of the boat as the rising sun turned the waters around us from an eerie black to a yellowish shade of grey. The bright molten ball had cleared the horizon by the time Craig had all the lines overboard. Leaving his pole in the rod holder, he stepped across the boat to hand me mine.

"So you want me to keep the jig moving, right?" The saltwater rod felt good in my hand, solid.

"Yeah," he placed his hand over mine on the rod just above the reel, "like this." He raised then lowered the rod in a jerky motion. His hands were warm and gentle and I found myself remembering what he had tasted like last night.

Without warning, the boat rocked hard and he caught me with his other hand, pulling me against him. "Thanks," I said, regaining my balance.

Raising one sandy colored eyebrow he said, "I would have thought riders would have really good balance." His tone dripped with sarcasm.

"Not fair, I can see the jump and prepare for it. I couldn't see the wave coming." *Because you distract the heck out of me.* "Besides, I was distracted," I smiled sweetly at him, remembering to jig the line.

"Aye, likely excuse," he added, mockingly.

Out of the blue, the boat rocked hard again and he was thrown against me. Instinctively I reached for him, nearly dropping the rod over the side. Recovering faster than me, Craig managed to keep both of us upright. In one swift motion, he had the rod steadied in his hand. A scowl spread across his face and he shot Ganso a scathing look over his shoulder. Ganso turned sheepishly away, pivoting on his seat, but not before I saw the corners of his mouth turn up in a grin.

The first hour or so passed uneventfully as we jigged away. I had learned early on that most men who fish were not big on small talk. Mom, when teasing Dad, had said that talking had something to do with scaring the fish away. I highly doubted that theory, especially when salt water fishing. The fish were just too deep to hear my chatty self. No, I was sure it had more to do with male bonding, enjoying Mother Nature and the simple fact that men have less of a propensity for gab than women do, plain and simple. So, I relaxed, enjoying the peace and quiet while we fished.

Craig got the first bite. After setting the hook he quickly handed the rod to me, "Go on then. It's yours, bring it in." There was a childish urgency and excitement to his voice. Ganso snapped to attention at the controls, ready to move the boat if necessary.

Fumbling in my haste, I slipped my rod into a holder and took his. The fish, whatever it was, was strong. Ganso, working his magic, skillfully slowed the boat to reduce drag on the line.

"Pull up then reel down," Craig offered.

After a moment I found my rhythm. Slowly, painstakingly, I managed to bring the fish up from the reef below. Grabbing the gaff pole, Craig bent over the side of the boat, "Keep the line taunt." He slid one hand down the line just as the fish broke the surface a mere five yards from us. As it reached the surface, salt water cascaded over the shimmering red scales of a snapper. "Aye, that's it. Keep the pressure on," his voice was calm and reassuring.

As I kept reeling, the rod jerked, catching me by surprise. The snapper arched its muscular body in a last ditch bid for freedom. With the ease born of practice and long hours fishing, Craig slipped the metal hook on the gaff under its gills and flipped it expertly on board. With a wet *smack* the snapper landed at our feet then flipped and flopped around on the fiberglass floor of the boat, gasping open mouthed.

"Nice job. Not bad for our first fish. Looks to be about thirty pounds," Ganso had stopped the boat once Craig had the snapper on board.

"Thirty pounds, that's all!" I said with awe. "It felt like fifty."

Craig bent to grab the fish by the gills, "That's because it was thirty pounds of fight that you pulled up from the bottom. It all adds up to feelin' like more." Lifting up the lid on the large cooler, he dropped the fish on some ice.

We caught several more snapper and a grouper, which we threw back because of size. We only kept the first snapper. Craig explained how the bottom fish are easily over fished so he is very careful with what he takes home.

We took a short break for lunch, I had forgotten how hungry I was, then Ganso headed back out over more open waters and away from the reef. We spotted a school of tuna as they tore up the water chasing some bait fish and a few porpoises. Craig removed the jigs from our lines, attached a down rigger to each of them to keep the live bait deep, and cast them overboard. Within minutes I had a bite.

After what seemed like forever, the broad, squared off head of a dorado split the waters surface, and then with a flick of its tail, tried to escape back into the depths. I gasped at the sheer beauty of it. Incandescent shades of emerald green and yellow shimmered from head to tail.

"You caught a bull. Good job." Craig stood ready, gaff in hand. After hauling the fish aboard, he dropped it into the ice chest on top of the snapper.

I took a few moments to catch my breath then I asked, "A bull?"

"Aye," he lifted the lid of the cooler carefully so the fish couldn't flip out. "See the square shape of the head?" I nodded, leaning over to peer at my prize. "The females are more rounded here," he ran his index finger along the top of the fish's head.

As if on cue, the dorado arched his back hard. Quick as lightning Craig slammed the cooler lid shut and sat down on top of it, grinning like a kid.

By this time the afternoon sun was sinking so Ganso pointed the nose of the boat back towards the shore. Rather than head straight back, he skirted the shore from north to south while Craig pointed out various landmarks and tried to regale me with tales of pirates and their gold.

**

Fresh from a hot shower, I dressed quickly in a cream and white floral sundress. The linen felt soft against my warm skin and accentuated the freckles on my fair skin. Turning before the mirror, I peered over my shoulder, making sure the back looked okay. Craig had made sure I was doused in sunscreen on the boat and I shivered involuntarily as I recalled the feel of his big hands on my back and neck as he spread the lotion. I was sure his hands had lingered longer than necessary at the small of my back, but I had to admit, it felt good to be touched again. Tiny goose bumps popped up across my shoulders and arms and I smiled warmly at the thought. Turning back, I ran my fingers through my curls and frowned at myself in the mirror. We had made it back to the dock late and he said he would pick me up in less than ten minutes.

"Well, you're a little beyond trying to impress him," I told my reflection in the mirror. Shoving a few pins in my mouth, I twisted my hair up in a loose knot at the nape of my neck. With the pins in place, a few tendrils fell naturally around my face and neck. I applied my make-up with a light and natural feel to it, slipped on my sandals and rushed out the door.

I met him on the gravel path outside my room. His sun kissed skin glowed beneath his white, cotton buttoned up shirt. He was adjusting his collar when he glanced up and saw me. A pair of khaki chinos and brown leather flip-flops completed the ensemble.

"You look beautiful," he said softly.

Before I could mumble an answer, he kissed my forehead, grasped my hand, and turned up the path toward the thatched bohio. "Oh, somewhere different tonight?" Squeezing my hand in his, he nodded. *Oh, mysterious, this could be fun.* Small solar lamps illuminated the gravel that crunched beneath our feet as we made our way up a slight hill just off the main path towards the bohio. The square shaped bohio, or thatched hut, stood in a clearing with a view of the sea. The massive structure was supported by large, round wooden posts at each corner.

Leaving the path behind, we climbed a set of steps with natural wood handrails, leading up to the foundation. The wood felt smooth and cool to the touch. As we stepped into the soft glow of the interior I could see the exposed cross beams and thatching above us. The entire space was illuminated with soft candlelight. In the center stood two wood-burning grills, which were flanked on either side by a long wooden bar. This set-up enabled the chefs to grill while facing and conversing with the clientele. Nice.

Motioning to the chef behind the counter, he said, "This is Paulo, he is goin' to take care of us tonight." He winked at me and pulled a stool out from the long bar, motioning for me to sit.

"Paulo," I nodded, "thank you."

"I thought you might like to enjoy your spoils tonight," Paulo grinned back at me. He set two large cobalt blue margarita glasses in front of us and went to work grilling our fish.

The conversation between us flowed easily while we enjoyed an appetizer of fresh clams, steamed on the grill in a decadent wine and garlic sauce. It brought back memories of our first date at the pizzeria. This time, the clams were smaller and more succulent than the ones we had shared that night.

As we shared small talk, I realized once again that Craig spoke so little about his family. Other than Hamish, I knew nothing of his family, much less his past. While showering I had made up my mind that I wanted to know more about this man I was falling for. Step by step, I began to steer the conversation in the direction of his family, hoping he would open up.

Once again, Craig hesitated when the topic of his family arose. Seeing that I wasn't going to back down, he began to share his story. He spoke haltingly at first, then after a few moments he started to relax and tell me about his adventures growing up.

He told me how his father had worked for a large oil company discovering new reserves all over the world, and the family had travelled with him to several different countries when the boys were younger. Oil exploration was and still is big business, especially in this part of the world. His father's particular expertise was in high demand. So, while they were both born in Scotland, they had travelled the world with their parents, moving often as the jobs came and went.

As it turned out, he had spent time living on the coast of just about every continent. Older than Hamish by a year, Craig had chosen to attend college at the University of Florida, while Hamish had gone back home to Scotland to attend the University of Edinburgh. In time, work had eventually brought their father to the coasts of Central and South America, and he had fallen in love with Panama during one of those trips.

Paulo, with one eye on our meal and the other on our drinks, continually topped off our drinks as he worked. Enjoying the cool tropical night, I leaned back in my chair and listened. I wasn't sure if it was the aromas wafting from the grill, the cool drink in my hand, or the nearness of Craig, but I lost all track of time, and before I knew it dinner was ready. We moved to a small table at the edge of the bohio. It was draped in a white tablecloth and lit with a single candle. Craig, ever the gentleman, pulled out my chair for me. As I settled into the chair I could sense him lingering behind me. After a moment, he stepped away, trailing one hand across my shoulders, as he did. The sudden warmth of his hands against my cool skin caught me off guard and I nearly gasped aloud. His eyes locked with mine as he sat across from me.

Reaching for my margarita, my eyes never left his. My body was still humming from his touch. His green eyes were much darker, almost black in the candlelight, and I found myself lost in their smoldering depth. Breaking our gaze, he turned to acknowledge Paulo as he set our plates down in front of us. Taking a moment to collect my thoughts, I glanced out over the water where I could see the moonlight casting a silver glow across the water below. Paulo filled our drinks again, and then quietly disappeared.

The dinner was a culinary delight. The freshly grilled snapper we had caught earlier melted like butter in my mouth. Paulo had taken the liberty and added a few fresh lobster tails, which he split in half and grilled in their shells. The firm white flesh of the lobster was moist and positively succulent. A fresh, chunky mango salsa with touches of lime and cilantro added just the right amount of sweetness to complement both the fish and lobster. Sweet jasmine rice and freshly grilled vegetables rounded out our full plates.

I leaned back in my stool, margarita in hand. "This is wonderful," I said, running my finger along the corners of my lips to retrieve the excess salt left behind by the salty rim of my glass. "He makes a mean margarita."

He grinned up at me, "Yes, he sure does. Paulo is like family here." He reached for his margarita, "My Da hired him when he bought the place."

"Ah," I acknowledged. "So, where do your parents live now?" *Aha, another opening!*

Averting his gaze, he looked past my shoulder and out into the night.

Hmm, not what I expected.

I watched several emotions play across his face, hurt, anger, and helplessness. When he had control he turned back to me.

"Um, I'm sorry. I didn't mean to be so forward." I waved it off and reached for my glass so I could shove it in my mouth along with my foot. *Would both fit?* Clearly I had pressed too hard.

He smiled slowly as if remembering something else then met my gaze, "No, it's alright. Truth is, I don't know." Seeing the astonished look on my face, he continued, "You see, they have never been found."

"What do you mean? What happened to them?" I stammered.

"I'm surprised Deane didn't tell you all about it. Especially since she knows just about everythin' there is to know about Hamish," he paused, "and then some." He smiled ruefully.

Actually, Deanne rarely spoke to me about the personal side of Hamish. In fact, I didn't know much more about Hamish than his relation with Craig and his riding ability. Well, that and he seemed to be a really nice guy. I kept my mouth shut and simply nodded. I didn't feel this was the time to correct Craig.

"I was in my last semester," he paused, "actually I had one week worth of exams then graduation when I got the call. They had gone on a vacation to the Maldives, where Da had rented a sailboat. There was another couple with them, friends from when Da worked in Columbia. Anyway, near as we can figure, they rented the sailboat, set sail sometime after sunrise and…" he paused again. I could see his jaw tighten as he reached for his glass.

"I'm so sorry, Craig. Not knowing must be awful. I…. You don't have to go on." I concentrated on dipping my last chunk of lobster in the melted butter, avoiding his gaze.

As he pushed back his chair, it made a loud screeching noise and I flinched involuntarily. Thank goodness he didn't notice. I had hit a nerve without meaning to. I had pushed too hard.

He headed to the fridge behind the bar, retrieving the pitcher of margaritas. When he came back, his demeanor had changed. Reaching across me, he filled my glass, then his. I tried to remember just how many drinks I had had tonight, but couldn't. Biting down lightly on my lower lip, I had my answer. It was numb. I could feel the effects of the tequila in the numbness of my lip. *Better slow down, Todd.* "Thanks," I mumbled, releasing the hold on my lower lip.

"I flew out as soon as I got the call. We searched for over a week, but nothin'." Setting down the pitcher, he spread out his hands, palms up in supplication. He looked helpless. A part of me wanted to wrap him in my arms and hold him, but I had the feeling he wasn't done with his tale. Something about the look on his face made me think he needed to get this out.

His arms fell heavy by his side as he returned to his chair. Slipping onto it, he reached for his glass. Grabbing it by the stem, he slowly turned it in circles on the table, studying the water droplets it left behind on the white linen.

We sat in silence for a few minutes. I kept my mouth shut, afraid I couldn't fit my other foot inside of it. I wanted to give him the chance to speak first.

"Ach, now," he said pushing his chair back, "this isna verra romantic." He slipped into his brogue, as his eyes danced.

Not romantic? He had exceeded any idea of romance I had expected, what with the candles, ocean side dining, food, and of course, those eyes. "What do you have in mind then?" Out of habit, I licked the salt from my lips.

"A walk on the sandy shore, of course!" He slid my chair back, deftly removing the margarita from my hand and setting it on the table. "I think we should leave the poison behind, who knows what Paulo put in those drinks."

I had to agree. The margaritas had done their job of helping me to relax. Call it liquid courage. They served their purpose well enough to help keep the ghosts and doubts of my past at bay. They also calmed the niggling feeling that arose in the pit of my stomach whenever Craig directed those brilliant green eyes at me. I was becoming increasingly aware that I was alone in a tropical paradise with Craig. I could feel myself falling for him on so many levels and I was afraid. Just the thought of opening up my heart again, made me want to pull a 'Forest Gump', as Calli like to call it; to run far and fast without a thought in my head or a destination in mind, but rather just to escape. And yet, I couldn't deny that there was a growing part of me that wanted to run into his arms. The margaritas would slow my escape, I thought wickedly. *Blame it on the margaritas. Wasn't that a song, too?* Hooking one finger in the strap behind my heel, I slipped off my sandals. Standing up, I let him lead me towards the sound of the waves, his hand warm around mine.

We walked hand in hand along the desolate and dark shoreline. Phosphorescent algae in the water shimmered and sparkled as our feet disturbed the water surface and punched through the damp sand. Starting near the dock, we followed the half-moon shape of the inlet with only the moon to guide us. As we reached the curve in the shore, Craig turned around and headed back. We hadn't said a word, yet everything was spoken between us and I could feel an expectant tension building.

Returning to the bohio, he spread a bright red blanket on the grass, overlooking the beach below. I noticed that our table had been cleared, but glancing around, there was no sign of Paulo.

Not a cloud could be seen for miles and the full moon and stars illuminated the sky above us. We lay on our backs; shoulders touching knees bent, and absorbed the feel of the cool night around us. The heat of the day had faded to a radiating warmth, which in turn had cooled to a beautiful tropical night. Nestled against the mountains, the resort was lucky enough to experience a wider range in temperatures than places further inland. Now and again the wind would shift, bringing the fragrant smells of frangipani drifting our way. We hardly said a word. We didn't need to. Soft sighs and murmurs along with the occasional touch of skin was all that was needed. Every once in a while he would bump his left knee against my right one. The sighing of the ocean mingled with our breathing filling the night around us, and before long the two seemed to meld contentedly together.

I could feel the heat coming off him in waves as he lay next to me. He simply pulsed with it, even when he lay still. He bumped my knee again. Damn, he made my head fuzzy and all coherent thoughts go racing from my head when he did that. I bumped back.

Time passed by without our notice. If I'd known how to read the stars above, then maybe I could have known just how long we lay there. I sighed. I had no doubt that Craig knew each star above and how much time had passed. He was very much in his element here.

My sigh must have stirred him as he propped himself up on one elbow. Looking down on me he asked, "Are you happy?"

His brow creased and his green eyes met mine. They reminded me of the iridescent green on the dorado we had caught today and I smiled, holding the memory close. Watching him, I decided there wasn't a shade of green that I hadn't yet seen reflected in those eyes.

"Hmm, let me think about that for a minute." Teasingly, I closed my eyes and tried to look serious. When I opened them he was still gazing at me, but the crease in his brow was gone.

I closed my eyes again, "Let me see, you whisked me away to paradise. Add a point, although, you did make me bait my own hook today. Hmm, subtract a point." I made sure to exaggerate the pout on my face. "You drug me off on a covert operation into the bowels of the city to save Cronos from the auction block, point. You got my dad, of all people, to front the money to buy me a horse. A drug cartel king pin's horse, no less. That alone is worth five points!" I felt him stiffen slightly and I opened my eyes. "What?"

"Um, see, actually your dad didn't actually pay for Cronos," he stammered.

I covered my eyes with my left hand, then thought better of it and peeked through my fingers at him. "Oh Lord, Craig, did you steal her?" I groaned.

He glanced down at me sheepishly. "No, I won her," he whispered.

What started as a giggle quickly bubbled into an uncontrollable laugh as tears poured from my eyes. Before long his face became a blur as I put the pieces of that day together. Of course, now it made sense, the alcohol I smelled on him, and yet he wasn't the slightest bit drunk, and his evasive answers to my questions.

With a finger, he wiped the tears of laughter from my face. My breath caught in my throat and began to burn deep inside. The butterflies in my belly had begun to dance again. This time it was the slow erotic movements of a belly dance. His face hovered inches from mine as I marveled in the strong lines of his face. Studying the angle of his jaw, my gaze lingered on his lips. Reaching up, I ran a finger across the short stubble that he kept on his face. Following the now familiar terrain of his face, my eyes met his. Gone was the grinning boy I had seen on the boat. In his place was the unmistakable look of a man hungry for a woman.

Suddenly his lips found mine with an eagerness that was new and unlike anything I had ever felt. Electricity shot through me and the heat I had felt radiating from him a moment before became a fire that enveloped us. It was as if the air had been sucked out of me, and the sounds of the night around us instantly vanished. All I could hear was his heart pounding against my chest, beating stronger and surer than mine. I felt him hard against my thigh as he leaned over me. Earnestly his tongue explored my mouth, diving, cavorting, and teasing all at once. He tasted of salt and lime and smelled fresh and wild like the ocean. *Oh Craig!* His lips were warm, reminding me of our sun filled day. As we kissed, his tongue became more demanding and I wanted him. I wanted him now.

I reached for him and my hands found the soft warmth of the skin along the back of his neck. Eagerly, my fingers delved into his hair, and pulling him closer I urged him on with a silent plea, a need that desperately needed to be met. His hands sought the feel of me. My breathing became ragged. First, my neck, shoulder, then everything started to blur and I lost track of my body as it melded with his. Slowly, his lips found their way down my neck searching, exploring, until they reached the edge of my sundress. His skin was on fire, a fire, which ignited me past anything I had ever thought possible. I struggled for air, pulling mouthfuls of cool night air in past my salty lips.

Before either of us was aware, we were skin on skin under the cloudless night sky. Sprawled on the blanket, I stared up into those smoldering eyes, which had deepened from a dark shade of emerald to almost black in the night. Every nerve ending felt stretched to the limit as his body hovered inches from mine, teasing me. Slowly at first, I explored the landscape that was Craig. The curve of his biceps as they sprung from his broad shoulders to the auburn tinged hair, which ran across his chest, tapering as it neared his navel. He was more than ready. I could feel his eyes on my face as he watched my emotions blend from wonderment, as my eyes took in his perfect body, to a look of hunger as my body reacted to the feel of him.

Hammering in my chest, my heart felt as though it would explode with a desire I had never felt before. Shifting his weight to his knees, he seductively slid his hands along my skin, drawing out our dance. Our eyes locked, as he began at the base of my arms and slid his hands slowly upward. Blazing a trail across the skin of my arms, he worked his way past my elbows, gently slipping my arms over my head until his hands had reached the delicate bones of my wrists. And there he pinned me. His eyes held me trapped, as my breathing grew quick and shallow. Slowly, he nestled his face against my neck, inhaling my scent. I lay beneath him, stripped of my physical and mental armor, completely vulnerable.

Oh, God!

The soft stubble on his face teased my neck and I arched my body up to meet his. Without a doubt in my mind, I wanted him and my body thrummed with eagerness, all too willing to oblige.

The tiny hollow between my collarbone and my neck bore the brunt of his breathy assault and I could feel my skin jump each time he exhaled. The coolness of each blade of grass was magnified as they caressed my wrists. Letting my arms relax downward, they were free, finally, of the confines of the red blanket. Instinctively my legs parted for him and he gently lowered his body until it covered mine. At last, I could feel every inch of his hot flesh burning against mine, and again I arched up inviting him in. Pleading.

Without a word I urged him on with my body again. Responding to my call, he lowered his lips to my breast.

Pulling my nipple gently into the warmth of his mouth, he let his tongue dance tantalizingly across the tip until my other nipple grew hard and screamed out for attention. As he let go, I moaned in sheer pleasure as a cool ocean breeze blew softly across our bodies, tickling my wet nipple as it passed. Shifting his weight, he prepared to arch his body into mine.

And then he suddenly stopped. His breathing, still ragged, slowed as he fought for control. Confused, I lay unmoving beneath him, waiting. Slowly he raised his head, blinking hard, as if to clear his thoughts as his face changed. Those green eyes focused again on mine and I watched, mesmerized, as he grasped for control. Again I marveled at how his face could change in an instant. He looked amazingly vulnerable. His eyes were like mirrors in the light from the bohio, and I watched his emotions shift within them, disguised as a million shades of green.

"This is just between us," he muttered between shallow breaths, his voice hoarse. "Nobody else..." He paused then added, "Right?"

My brain, too muddled with desire to answer, followed the desires of my body. I had no idea what he meant but I knew without a doubt that I needed him. I needed him now. "Y - e - s," I struggled between gasps as I arched my body up with impatience to meet his. *Oh God, quick before I melt right here...*

**

As my senses returned, I could hear his steady breathing behind me. The length and breadth of him fit against me without a single gap between us. His body no longer burned, but rather had returned to the familiar warmth I was beginning to know so well. As we lay entwined on the red blanket, a multitude of cicadas offered up a chorus behind us in the jungle. Salt from the sea air had settled on our skin. The moon had continued its journey while we made love, keeping watch on time as it passed us by. Funny, but I could have sworn it had stood still.

The familiar sounds of the ocean sighing reached my ears as the tropical breeze picked up. We drifted off to sleep on the red blanket, curled up under the light of the moon.

Sometime during the night I felt him stir behind me. His body fit along the backside of mine like it had been made for me. Burying his face in my hair he inhaled, taking in the scent of me. After a few minutes he stretch languidly behind me then propped himself up on one elbow. I could feel his eyes as they skimmed along my body and I blushed. Suddenly, I felt exposed and vulnerable. Picking up on the shift in my emotions, he blinked hard, turning his attention to my hair. Reaching up with his other hand, he captured a curly lock, spinning it neatly around his strong finger. For a moment, he studied it intently in the moonlight. Finally he spoke, "Your hair suits you?"

"Hmm? Oh, you mean a mess?" The salt air, wind, and lovemaking had destroyed any semblance of order I'd managed before dinner. This late in the evening there would be no taming it.

"No, it's like molten fire," his voice had gone husky, "like that which you see from the earth." Releasing the curl he selected another one, "What lies below the surface is hotter than that which daylight sees."

I was momentarily taken aback. For such a manly man, Craig had a way with words. I was finding him to be not at all what I had expected. Leaving my hair behind, he traced a finger lazily up my right arm, along my shoulder, then down to circle my nipple. A low moan escaped my lips as my nipple answered his call and grew hard.

"We better get goin'," he whispered in my ear.

The warmth of his breath sent fresh chills down my entire body. Reminding me, that when I was with him my body was not my own. I slowly rolled onto my back and looked up into his rugged face. I ran my tongue across my numb lips—*alcohol or the stubble from his face?* A faint hint of salt lingered at the corners—*margarita or salt air, I wasn't sure*—"hmmmm?"

His eyes sparkled and he raised one eyebrow, "Come on, the staff will be up soon and we need to make our bed look like we used it last night." There went that eyebrow again, part question, part insinuation.

"Our bed..."

It was then that I noticed the sky was beginning to lighten. With the morning came the winds, and the fresh, clean smell of frangipani drifted over us. Craig quickly slipped on his jeans, and then grabbed the rest of our clothes up in one arm, neatly tucking them under his elbow. With his other, he shook out the blanket then wrapped it around me. Holding the blanket in place with one hand, he led me back to his room with the other, the red fabric trailed behind me in the grass as we started up towards the bohio.

Barefoot, we padded along on the grass next to the gravel path. This time we headed away from the direction of my cabana down a bamboo lined path to his bungalow. There, we made love again. This time we took our time exploring the varied terrain of each other's body. Those intimate places that are discovered one by one between lovers. Making love to Craig was like nothing I had ever experienced, a sublime high. And I wasn't at all sure I could get enough, my fill of him. Everything about him made me want him. He was strong, lithe, and utterly masculine, and best of all, when with him I could think of nothing else.

**

Clouds were building out over the water, suffusing the sunlight as it fell on the gravel path back to my room. We had dallied as long as possible, but I needed to return home and he needed to pick up supplies for the return trip tomorrow. I had left him to shower while I made my way back to my bungalow.

The birds in the trees sang their morning lullaby, hoping to get in their melodies before the heat of the day dampened their spirits. On the edge of the jungle, near the foot of the mountain I thought I heard the unmistakable chatter of monkeys and I smiled, remembering Monkey Island.

Caught in my reverie, I approached the door to my room, noticing as I did, that it was ajar. Cautiously, I placed a hand on the knob and pushed inward. The door swung freely on its hinges. At first glance, everything appeared as I had left it the night before. I let out a sigh of relief. The maid must have been careless and left the door open, I thought to myself. *Besides silly, you're in the middle of nowhere.* Shutting the door behind me, I headed for the shower, leaving a trail of clothes on the floor behind me. A short time later, I was dressed and ready, suitcase by the door.

My purse sat on the small table by the balcony where I had left it two days ago. As I picked it up, the sharp metallic smell of fresh blood hit me. Recognizing it immediately, my hand flew to my mouth as I gagged. A montage of images from my time in the trauma room flashed across my consciousness. My head spinning, I dropped my leather purse onto the carpet. As it hit the ground, the mangled head of a dead chicken fell out onto the floral carpet, its flat black eyes stared sightlessly back up at me.

Frozen and numb with shock, I stood stupidly staring at it, not quite believing what I saw. When I did finally scream, the sound filled the small room, resonating off the walls and back to me. Stumbling backwards, in an effort to escape, my knees slammed into the edge of the bed, pitching me backward. Back peddling across the bed in a panic, the door to the room flung open behind me, and Craig burst in.

"Lauren, are you all right?" His eyes ran around the room and settled on the dark, sticky pool of blood on the table where my purse had sat. In one smooth motion he pulled me to my feet and had stepped protectively in front of me.

"What the hell," he exclaimed.

By this time I could hear the gravel outside crunching underfoot as several of the staff arrived. The nearness of Craig brought me back to the present. My breathing slowed and Craig's eyes met mine. His eyes ran the length of me, a worried look on his face.

"I'm okay," I sputtered.

Stepping around the end of the bed he surveyed the mess on the floor and the pool of dark red blood on the table. It was beginning to coagulate and darken in the cool room. Carefully, he picked my purse up by the strap and carried it outside. Clementine's wiry body brushed past me with a few towels to clean up the mess. She bent down, reaching for the chicken head. Before she could scoop it up in the towel, she reared back in panic, her eyes wide with fear. Quickly she made the sign of the cross across her chest, dropping the towel in the process, "Aye, Dios mio!"

Alone, without Craig by my side, my knees began to shake. The look of horror on Clementine's face sent a shiver racing down my spine.

Pushing her aside, Craig knelt and picked up a small gold object covered in blood. As he unfolded and stood I could clearly see the hard lines of his face and the side of his mouth twitched. Barking an order in Spanish to one of the men, he scooped up the towel, wiped off the golden object, then shoved it into his pocket. Turning on his heel he crossed the room in two strides.

He slowed long enough to scoop up my suitcase. Clasping my hand in his, he propelled me out of the room. On the way out, he bent to retrieve my purse from the stone path where he had left it.

"Where are we going?"

"I've got to get you home, remember."

We were headed up the hill toward the airstrip at a fast clip. I struggled to match strides with him, still numb. A few times I tried to pull my hand free, but Craig ignored my struggles and kept on moving.

"But wait a minute. What was that all about?"

He ignored me for a few strides so I tried to dig my feet into the gravel to slow the pace. "Just keep movin'," he growled at me. "I will fill you in on the plane."

His tone of voice brought me up short and I gave in, following him up the hill.

He threw my bag up the steps and onto the plane. Bounding up in one stride, he reached down and helped me up. Still numb, I made my way to the copilot's seat and sat, waiting for him to run through his checklist. He never once spoke, although he kept glancing in my direction while he worked. Not once did he make eye contact.

Once in the air I could feel the anger slowly ebb from his body as he focused on flying. Although I was deeply curious as to what exactly he had shoved in his pocket, I found myself replaying the events in the room over and over in my head like a cheap horror movie. *What in the hell? Why would someone put, of all things, a decapitated chicken in my purse? I had no enemies here. In fact, I would be hard pressed to think of anyone whom I could call an enemy. Truth be told, I didn't have many friends either.*

When I could stand it no longer I ventured forth with a simple question, "Why?" I finally asked over the loud hum of the engines.

Craig frowned and I could see he was thinking hard before answering. "I honestly don't know," he shrugged. "Lauren, do you have any enemies? Anyone who would want to see you hurt?"

He didn't look at me. "Look at me," I wanted to scream.

"No. I have already been turning this over in my head and I can't think of anyone." I stared down at my hands clutched tightly in my lap. Loosening my grip, I turned to him, "Craig, what is that in your pocket?"

"A huaca," he said at last, a serious look on his face. "Originally it was designed as a form of pre-Columbian art. It is believed that warriors would wear a larger version as a chest plate when they went into battle." He still wouldn't look me in the eye. "Over the centuries it has decreased in size. Nowadays they are sold in a much smaller version, mostly to tourists. They are usually stylized after humans, animals, or both. Normally they are harmless pieces of art or jewelry." He finally turned to face me, "The one I found in your room was a war eagle. It symbolizes a warrior in battle, or in this case a warrior challenging someone to a battle."

I could no longer feel the warmth of the sun through the windshield as a cold shiver shot up my spine.

"We were the only people at the resort, there were no guests, so near as I can figure it can't be a case of mistaken identity. Whoever left it, knew we were there."

"Can I see it?" He shifted in his seat until he could reach into his right front pocket. He pulled it out and handed it to me.

It was warm to the touch. The golden figure was as big as my palm and depicted an eagle. The wings were outstretched with small coils of gold wire along the tips. The lower half of the body was abstract and tapered, before widening into a triangular shape of smooth gold. A small beak protruded outwards from below two menacing eyes. The eyes were set with small, dark green emeralds so dark they almost appeared black. *Like his eyes.* What appeared to be small, stylized ears arose from either side of the face and were fashioned from intricate gold coils. Had it not been for the menacing look of the emerald eyes, it might have been pretty.

I bounced it up in my palm and felt the heft of it as it landed, then turned it over, looking for a mark.

"Yes, it's real gold, and I would venture to say the emeralds are of a high quality." Craig reached for the huaca and I reluctantly turned it over to him.

The return flight was somber. Craig was deep in thought and hard to engage in conversation. I felt the magic of the weekend unraveling the closer we got to the airstrip. After unloading the luggage and setting my bags into the Land Cruiser, I paused, leaning against the door, keys in hand, waiting to say goodbye. After a brief conversation with a guy dressed as a mechanic, Craig stalked towards me, finally...I thought. The look on his face changed from one of deep thought to a forced smile, then back again, his brow furrowed as he stood before me.

"Did you have a good time, Lauren?" He wasn't really focusing on me at all. Preoccupied, his gaze strayed everywhere but upon my face.

Why won't you look at me?

When I didn't answer, he was forced to make eye contact. I shifted my keys from one hand to the other and looked into those green eyes, "Yes, I did. It was lovely. Look, Craig, I don't know who or what that incident in my room was about, but I have no enemies. Maybe this was just a prank or a sick joke. Maybe it wasn't really meant for me. I just don't want to think about it or have it spoil our weekend." I hesitated, searching his face, "Do you?"

"No, no, you're right," he shook his head as if to clear a thought and his countenance lightened. "I don't want it to spoil our weekend. I had a wonderful time, too." Reaching up, he placed his muscular arms on either side of my head, gripping the edge of the roof with his hands. "Close your eyes," he said moving his face closer to mine.

Weak in the knees, my breath came quicker as the scent of him enveloped me. He bumped the side of my leg with his knee, skin brushing against skin, and a shiver of anticipation raced through me.

"Close your eyes," he said softly, his eyes locked with mine.

I snapped my eyes shut, afraid if I waited any longer I would become lost in the sea of green just inches from my face. My heart pounded in my chest like a tympany drum as I felt him move in closer. His body never touched mine, instead he managed to remain mere inches from me, teasing me. And then, in an instant his breath was warm against my neck. I shivered and every hair on my body stood at attention then lay taut, waiting for the next onslaught of breath. Then he whispered in my ear.

"Aye, you are utterly amazin' and I had a magical time this weekend." Faint hints of his brogue slipped through his usually clean English. I felt his lips reach mine.

Numb, I gave in to his kiss and re-discovered his mouth, which was just as alluring as his eyes, especially when his eyes could no longer distract me. He was soft and gentle, leaving me wanting more. Pulling away, he quickly kissed my forehead. Swallowing hard, I opened my eyes to find him grinning at me, his arms still braced on the roof behind me.

"I've got to get goin'. Rachel has some supplies that Troy shipped down for me," he pushed off with his hands and stood back.

"Okay, I need to pick Haley up from a friend's house on my way home. So, um, I'll see you later then?"

"Absolutely, I'll call before I fly back to the resort. Cell service is still spotty out there." With that, his cell phone rang. Glancing down at the screen he quickly added, "Hey, Lauren."

"Hmm?"

"Listen, please be careful. I mean, keep your eyes open for anythin' unusual." I had the feeling he wanted to say more, but his phone kept ringing.

Nodding, I watched him turn on his heel, answer his cell, and head towards his Jeep. As I settled into the Land Cruiser I took a deep cleansing breath, then let it out. *What in the world was he referring to, the huaca? I thought he said not to worry. Damn, I can't think straight with him kissing me like that.* Involuntarily I shook my head to clear it, started the engine and headed to pick up Haley. Glancing in my rearview mirror, I could see Craig talking intently on his cell phone, the gold of the huaca shined brightly in his hand. A chill ran up my spine in the hot cab of the Land Cruiser. Nervously, I glanced at my ruined purse sitting on the floorboard in front of the passenger seat.

"You are going in the garbage the minute I get home," I said aloud.

**

Setting one booted toe into the stirrup iron I swung smoothly into my saddle. The black leather, long ago molded by countless hours spent in the saddle, recognized me. There were few things in this world that could make a rider feel as truly at home as their favorite saddle. With time, between the weight of your body and a good dose of sweat, the leather seat became yours. For the second time this week, I sent up a prayer thankful that my saddle had indeed fit Cronos's back.

Alone at the barn, I had plugged in my Ipod and let the unique mix of Celtic and modern melodies by Enya pour from the speakers at either end of the arena while I rode. Picking up the reins, I asked Cronos to move off at the walk. Today was my first ride on her since my trip to the resort. I was eager to start forming a partnership with her. Something had come up, and Colleen had cancelled our lesson so today it was just us.

We rode for nearly an hour. Nothing difficult or too taxing, but I wanted to refine my aids and get a better feel of her. My goal was to take what Gold Herr had been teaching me in regard to lightness and apply it to Cronos. Satisfied with my ride, I dismounted and, after loosening the girth, I ran up my stirrups, running the leathers neatly through them.

I had tried to keep my mind occupied and focused on anything but the incident with the huaca. It had been more than twenty-four hours since I had heard from Craig and although he had warned me about the cell service, I couldn't help thinking there was more going on then he had let on.

Peeling off my helmet, I tucked it under my elbow and headed for the barn.

THE HUACA

Colleen had grand plans for my riding this week. I was to ride Gold Herr nearly every day to work on my feel for the tempi changes. Flying lead changes I had done before, but tempis were something completely new for me. Although I wouldn't need to perform two or single tempis, Colleen and I both agreed that a rider could only benefit from schooling movements above that which they were showing. It helped to build confidence.

So far, the three tempis were easy for me, especially since, like most riders, I am attuned to the three beat rhythm of the canter. *One, two, three, one, two, three...* On the third beat I smoothly ask for and get the change. Two tempis made me anxious. For some crazy reason I was capable of counting to three, but not to two, so my timing was constantly off and Gold Herr was able to put up with me only to a point. To shake things up, Colleen gave me a Tuesday off from doing any tempi changes, and then during our next ride had me go straight into the single tempi changes. Shazam! Apparently I can count to one or three, but not two, go figure.

Cronos was coming along nicely. We focused on building up the muscles along her topline with a lot of stretching in all three gaits and then added transitions toward the end of each ride. She was clearly capable of doing much more, but since we had no idea how long she had been out of work, Colleen and I decided to bring her along slowly for the first few weeks. Either Colleen or I would ride her every day. Sometimes Colleen would teach lessons from her back rather than work her. On occasion, between teaching her lessons she would concentrate on working Cronos.

On Wednesday, Deanne was gracious enough to let me experience piaffe for fun on Nicola since she is a piaffe machine.

Colleen also had me help her leg up Stitch since he was cleared for more intense work. Because of his young age, I rode him with a light seat, while stretching him over his back in a long and low trot for most of our ride. This enabled him to find his balance without too much interference from my shifting weight.

With each passing day, the steady rhythm of life at the barn wrapped its arms around me as the days went by. That is, each day without a single word from Craig. Nothing. Nada.

Excuses ran through my mind day after day, and by the time Friday rolled around I couldn't hide it anymore. I had tried to leave him a message on Wednesday, but his cell phone mailbox was full. Colleen must have picked up on my distracted mood, she kept an unusually close eye on me and pushed each lesson until all I could do was go home and crash at the end of the day. My abdominal muscles ached as never before as she consistently worked on fixing our 'lazy eventing posture' and smoothing out our position in the sitting trot. Maria even made herself scarce around the barn.

Rachel had flown back to the States last week. Deanne had been in a sour mood all week with Hamish gone, and Elaine was putting fires out at her job. With no one around to talk to, this left my drive to and from the barn each day to worry, stew, get angry, cry, and then pull myself together before I arrived at my destination. For the life of me I couldn't fathom what had gone wrong. On the other hand, I was pissed at myself for opening up my heart. I should have known better.

Saturday dawned overcast and the thunderstorms hit hard by 10 a.m. After running the gamut of emotions and excuses all week I had arrived at my answer. Craig was a player, plain and simple. I vowed to put him behind me, and focus on my riding. I was still angry with myself for letting my guard down and allowing him to get close to my heart. After Jake, I had hung an 'off limits' sign on my heart. I had done my best to avoid the mere idea of dating again. Now, all I had done was brought more heartache on myself.

Today though, Dad had other plans for us. His company was having some sort of a corporate shindig to celebrate the previous year's huge increase in earnings and the expansion of some of their newest departments, Dad's included. On the downside it sounded pretty boring for Haley and me, especially since we still didn't know many of Dad's co-workers. On the upside, it was another chance to dress up, spend some time with Haley, and take a break from my riding for an afternoon.

After digging through everyone's closets I decided we were all in need of something fresh and new to fit the occasion. The party was being held at an estate along the coast, which belonged to the founder of Avitar Defense. Thankfully Dad's secretary, Rosa, had given me a heads up on the venue and expected dress code, which was a luau party. Since it started at four o'clock, Haley and I got dressed and headed out of the house just as the rain stopped. The smell of fresh cilantro growing wild filled the humid air around us as we climbed into the Land Cruiser for a trip downtown.

I had discovered the shopping in downtown Panama City was hit or miss when I had made several trips before to buy Haley some clothes. It was unlike back in the States, where there was a store on practically every corner. Here, there were a handful of medium sized malls with a small selection. Boutiques were where I would probably find what we needed. So, with directions from Carmen, we set off in search of a few small boutiques in a more upscale neighborhood of the city—keeping in mind, that upscale in Panama City meant better quality and selection, as well as stores providing their own security for residents and shoppers. In other parts of the city, street urchins would promise, for a small fee, to watch your vehicle while you shopped.

We found the boutique Casita del Sol, or Little House of the Sun, right where Carmen said it would be. A uniformed guard directed us to park behind the building and we walked through an awning-covered entrance into the store. A tall, elegant woman behind the counter turned when the small bell attached to the shop door rang softly to announce our arrival. She had a lovely, creamy café au lait complexion that complemented her hazel eyes and brunette hair. She wore her hair very short and modern in what could be considered a boy cut, but on her it was very becoming.

"Welcome, welcome, come in please," she exclaimed in very good English, moving from behind the font desk where she had been working on her laptop computer. She made a beeline for us with outstretched arms. Clearly, we were the only clientele in the shop. "What can I do for you today?" Although she had asked and waited for an answer, she was clearly sizing both of us up, judging size and style. Clothes shopping for me was borderline painful. I had to be honest, I felt much more at home in a tack store with the rich smell of leather and rack after rack of breeches. I shifted, slightly uncomfortable. *Here we go.*

"Hello, we need a few outfits for a special party tonight. Our mai… friend Carmen sent us here." Shoving the note with Carmen's directions on it into my front pocket, I squared my shoulders. I still couldn't bring myself to call her a maid even though that was her job, and she was indeed paid a good wage, it was just too rich for my blood. "We have a party to attend. It is a luau theme at a rather fancy estate, and she thought you might be able to help us."

"I bet you we can find something," she was clearly done mentally sizing up Haley and me with her professional eye. "Okay, let's get started shall we, my name is Ella. What I'd like to do is pull a few things off the rack to get you started, will you trust me?" Her tiny rosebud lips pursed as she waited for a response. I had the feeling she wasn't *really* asking.

Her question hung in the air for a moment. I had never had anyone pick my clothes for me and I wasn't at all sure about the idea. A quick glance around the interior of the shop confirmed my suspicion. This shop had a definite upscale flavor, which surprised me. I still tended to think of Panama as a backwards country and it had honestly never occurred to me that this city was just like any other around the world. Well, maybe a tad bit more third world I thought, remembering the guy guarding our SUV. I swallowed hard. I had a feeling this was going to be expensive.

"I do," piped up Haley. "I think it would be fun to have you find me a dress. You pick it and I'll tell you if you picked the right one. Do you want to know my favorite color?" To Haley, nearly everything was a game or could quickly be transformed into a game. Glancing up at me with a smile she said, "You can play, too."

With a fine boned fingertip softly tapping her chin, Ella studied Haley. "Hmm, I think pink?"

Glancing down, I could see a sparkle in her eye as she waited for Ella's reaction. Haley nodded mouth agape. On cue, Ella pointed us towards the far wall of the boutique where several small dressing rooms with curtains stood. A pair of mismatched love seats sat on either side of the curtains with a full-length mirror off to one side. We slipped inside our dressing rooms to wait. There was a lovely cornflower blue jacquard settee in mine and I sat fidgeting, while waiting for Ella's return. From across the wooden partition between us, I heard Haley whispering, "She is so smart."

My face grinned back at me in the dressing room mirror and I wondered if I should spoil it for Haley. After all, she was dressed in pink from head to toe today. "She is just really good at her job, that's all."

A few, nerve racking minutes later, I could hear Ella passing a few items through the curtain to Haley, then came my turn. The curtain pulled back just enough for Ella to slip in one dress.

"This is the one for you," she said from the other side of the curtain. Balanced on the tip of one long manicured finger was a gorgeous dress. Hanging from a white satin hanger, the dress had a simple halter style top and an empire waist, which flowed down into a long, elegant A-line skirt. Although simple in style, the silk and organza fabric of the dress looked and felt like a dream. The body of the dress was a patterned silk. From a distance the dress simply appeared to be blended shades of white, off white, and cream, but up close the silk revealed itself to be lightly printed with large Phalaenopsis orchids which cascaded down the left side of the dress, tumbled past the waist line, then fell at an angle across the front of the skirt. The large white petals and butter yellow throats of the flowers reminded me of a watercolor painting. An inch wide band of creamy white organza peeked out from beneath the skirt and at the lowest point of the V in the halter-top. Gingerly I reached out to take the dress, "Um, Ella, I think this is a bit much." I didn't even want to touch it.

"I don't, put it on." The curtain had swung shut.

Annoyed at being told what to wear by a sales clerk, I reached to pull back the curtain, only to have Ella's face pop into view at the end of my outstretched arm. She had anticipated my escape.

"This is a fancy party you are going to and that dress was made for you. Besides, Carmen called me before you came, she said, you need to find a husband." Her rosebud lips were set in a firm line, "That dress will do the trick." With that she stared me down.

"I don't need a husband, please and thank you. What I do need is a dress for an outdoor luau." *There was no way I would ever be able to keep this dress clean outdoors.* Gingerly I hung it up on a brass peg. "And why would Carmen call you anyway?" I shot back.

"She is my tia and she gave me instructions to make sure you are dressed for the event. Besides, what could it hurt?" She tried to pout, but the look was lost on me. Giving up on me, she disappeared again to help Haley.

Through the curtain I could hear Haley. "Tia means aunt doesn't it? I am learning Spanish in school."

Resigned, I stepped out of my clothes, slipped off my bra and stepped into the dress. The cool silk of the dress felt heavenly against my skin. Pulling it up, I hooked the halter around my neck and turned to face the mirror. The dress fit me like a glove. The halter style accentuated my chest and waist in all the right ways. Peeking over my shoulder at the mirror I saw my jaw nearly hit the floor. The back of the dress fell away in a dramatic sweep of fabric, exposing nearly all of my back. At the very bottom, a small insert of organza just above the waistline concealed just enough of my lower back to be decent.

Turning left, then right, the silk swirled around my legs. The hemline fell just above my ankle when I stood still. *Shazam! I did look good.* My body had changed since coming to Panama. Even though I was in shape when we arrived, the definition in my muscles since riding dressage were hard to miss. Studying myself in the mirror again, I noticed that my posture had even changed. Thanks to the combination of working without stirrups, riding so many horses in one day, and Colleen's tutelage, I now stood more erect and my shoulders no longer slouched. Pulling my shoulders back even more for effect, my abdominal muscles complained. Relaxing again, I smiled at myself in the mirror. Well, the dress looked stunning and I had to admit, it really made me feel good after all the angst of the past week. Maybe it was time to clear this jump and kick on to the next. Turning once more in the mirror, I smiled smugly at the reflection of my exposed back.

"Let me see, Lauren," Haley's voice came from outside the fitting room. Stepping out to meet her, I saw her spinning in circles in front of the larger mirror. She wore a rose petal pink short skirt and a white cotton peasant top with hot pink and light pink stitching around the neck and sleeves. She looked so much older and more grown up than when we had arrived. I felt my heart squeeze in my chest. This must be what it feels like to watch your own kids grow, knowing they will one day leave. Right now Dad and Haley were all I had and I quickly pushed the thought of Haley getting older to the back of my mind.

"Wow, Haley, you look so pretty."

Haley took a break from admiring herself in the mirror as I stepped up beside her. Her little jaw dropped open. "Whoa! Are you gonna wear that?" She exclaimed, eyes wide.

"It depends on what you think Kaboose. Is it a yes or a no?"

Haley bobbed her head up and down, "Definitely a yes."

From the corner of my eye, I saw Ella step out from behind a tall rack with a smirk on her face. "Now that will do the trick," she stopped to appraise me, casually leaning on a rack. "Now we need shoes, but no worry, I know just where to send you." With that she stalked off to the counter while Haley and I changed back into street clothes. After paying for our new clothes, we stopped at a shoe store down the street, a men's clothier, and then headed home to get ready.

**

The drive to the coast was pleasant enough, especially since we skirted the city. Haley was still enthralled with her new pink outfit. I had managed to dress Dad in a cool cotton button up shirt in a rich shade of coral and a pair of light tan dress slacks. Glad I had bought the dress, I had left my hair down and found the perfect pair of dressy espadrilles to go with it.

The home was perched on top of a hill directly overlooking the shifting blue waters of the Caribbean. Climbing out of the company car, we were greeted by a waiter wearing a bright Hawaiian print shirt and neat white cotton pants. He offered Dad and me glasses of champagne and motioned for another waiter to get a drink for Haley. The sun, a deep shade of tangerine, was slowly sinking into the dense jungle behind us as we made our way up the steps of the modern style home.

The stark white two-story home boasted seamless floor to ceiling windows on either side of the front steps. The architecture was sharp and angular, with clean lines. The glass front doors stood ajar, allowing the ocean breeze to flow through the house. After making the necessary introduction to quite a few of Dad's business associates whom I was sure I would never remember, I slipped away to enjoy the view of the ocean. Haley, meanwhile, had disappeared to explore a tree house with the two other children I had seen.

Making my way past recently familiar faces, I found myself on a large marble and stone terrace at the back of the house that led down to a lush green lawn bordered by a tropical garden, much like the one at AJ's home. The sweet smell of flowers mixed with the salty breeze drifted across the lawn, pushed by onshore winds. A Tiki bar sat to one side of the lawn, its back toward the garden. Opposite from the bar was a band; its members sat tuning up their instruments. Spread out on either side of a center dance floor were round tables covered in white linen tablecloths and adorned with orchids of every color and shape imaginable. Staff dressed in the same Hawaiian style uniforms that greeted us moved about the lawn with drink and appetizer trays. Tiki torches were just being lit as I started down the steps. Taking the last sip, I frowned at my champagne flute and headed for the bar. Before long the house crowd would make their way out onto the lawn and I didn't want to have to wait for a drink.

The bartender glanced up as I set my empty flute on the bar. Flashing a gorgeous, white smile in my direction he said, "You seem to have a problem." He was polishing a wine glass with a white linen towel. "Can I get you another drink?"

Squinting in order to see his bamboo nametag, "Gerry, huh? You don't look like a Gerry, especially one with a 'G'." Bored with the stuffed shirts in the house I was pleased to have found someone closer to my age and willing to talk about something other than the business of defense. He had a dark, rich tan, jet black hair, and blue eyes, which studied me for a moment. Not half bad, I thought.

"Gerardo," he said, but with his accent it sounded more like 'Gerrrarrrrdo' as he trilled his R's and winked at me. "And you would be?" He swept my flute off of the bar and began mixing a drink.

"Bored already. But I'm Lauren to my friends. I sure hope this night gets better or I'm going to have to jump off that cliff over there," I added sarcastically, jerking my head toward the sound of the ocean.

He set a tall margarita glass on the counter. On the rocks, it was rimmed liberally in coarse salt and garnished with a lime wedge. Smiling, he deftly topped off my drink with an unmeasured shot of Patron, straight from the bottle. "You'd have to come up with a plan B since there isn't much of a cliff. Just a gentle slope down to the beach, but you could always take the stairs." He chuckled, "Here, this seems more your style," and pushed the margarita towards me.

"Thanks, I'll check it out." Retrieving my drink I pulled a tip from my clutch purse and made my way towards the beach as the band started playing island music. The soft ocean breeze felt magical and I started to feel myself relax and let go after a week of worry. Dusk had faded into dark and the Tiki torches gave the party a definite Hawaiian flavor. As I walked away, I felt his gaze on my exposed back. Turning slightly, so as not to be obvious, I glanced back at the bar. Yep, he was checking me out. Ella was right, I felt good in the dress. *Sassy. Sexy.* Feeling bolstered by my fresh shot of liquid courage, I decided to make the best of the situation at hand.

Sure enough, the crowd begun to gather in the garden while I sipped my margarita. I scanned the faces for Dad or Haley. Not seeing them, I moved to a bench at the edge of the flickering torchlight. The mood of the party was picking up as more and more guests flowed out onto the lawn. Loud shirted waiters passed by occasionally with trays laden with canapés and hors d'oeuvres, which were rather good. Before long I found myself enjoying the music. It was hard to sit still when listening to Tahitian drums and my feet tapped gently on the grass.

Twice, I had invitations to dance, but politely turned them down. Dressing up felt good, but getting close to another man right now probably wasn't a wise choice. My heart squeezed in my chest at the thought of Craig. "Damn you," I muttered under my breath as the thought of him threatened to tip the balance of my evening. Resolutely, I pushed him aside and tried to focus on the music.

I closed my eyes, and inhaled deeply, mentally sifting through the scents of tropical flowers in the garden. Much to my chagrin, the salty sea air brought back the memory of that night in spades, along with the smell of frangipani. Frustrated, I shifted my thoughts, to what lay ahead for Cronos and me in Florida. My mind drifted back to Craig. With a sigh, I gave up. It was no use, all I wanted was to enjoy a night out without any lingering thoughts of Jake or left over pain from Craig. *Was that too much to ask?*

"Ahem."

Startled, I opened my eyes to find a waiter standing above me. Slightly embarrassed, and lost in my own thoughts, I blushed. No doubt I was the only one at the luau sitting alone with their eyes closed. *Dork.* Leaning down, he handed me another margarita, much like the first, picked up my empty glass, and set it on his tray.

"Gerry asked me to drop this off," he looked a bit abashed.

"Um, thanks." Setting down the glass, I grabbed a tip for each of them from my purse. He took it and quickly moved off into the dance crowd.

Two sips into my drink I had yet another dance invitation, this one from a tall, handsome Panamanian man. Politely refusing his offer, I slipped off into the dark towards the beach, hoping to avoid another invitation. I followed a path lit with tiki torches to a set of stone stairs that led down to the beach. The stairs were wide and illuminated by soft, yellow lamps set underneath the handrail. Slipping off my shoes, I left them along with my clutch purse on the last step. Scooping up a handful of my dress, I headed out across the still warm sand towards the water's edge. Tiny grains of sand massaged my tired feet as I walked toward the water. It had been a while since I had last worn heels and my calves were starting to complain. Colleen had worked really hard lately to get me to lower my heels further in the stirrups than I was used to, and walking around in the espadrilles tonight wasn't helping. The sea breeze made the curls in my hair skip around my face and the hem of my skirt flutter around my legs. The sound of the waves drowned out the party above.

I stood at the water's edge, lost in the rolling sound of the waves until my glass was empty and all the salt was gone from the rim. The ocean was dark and the soft yellow glow from the party on the hill was the only sign of life around. I tried to think of everything else but Craig. The scent of him, his emerald green eyes, the way he looked at me, I tried to push it all to the dark recesses of my mind and heart, but it wasn't working. "Go away," I muttered. All week I had managed to stay busy and keep the nagging thoughts at bay. I had thought the party would help, but it hadn't. Now with time on my hands to think, all I thought of was Craig. I stared for a few more minutes out into the dark water, brooding. Giving up, I decided another margarita wouldn't hurt. Besides, I wanted to check on Haley.

Making my way back to the stairs, I heard a pair of voices raised in a heated argument near the bottom of the stairs. Not sure if I should disturb them, I stopped, trying to decide what to do, and then froze as I heard the sound of Craig's voice. "…no, that's not it."

"But you love me, you always have. We were perfect together and we will be again." The woman's voice was close to hysterical. "Is there someone else? Is that it?"

Stunned, I stood there in the dark, palms sweating. I held my breath, squeezing the soft silk in my fist.

"Listen, Gabby, there is no need to do this. I have never lied to you. What we had..." His voice was lost to the wind and waves, but I had heard enough. They were at the stairs, now I could hear the sound of sand underfoot as someone made their way quickly up the concrete steps. I waited, giving them a chance to leave. Numb, I finally exhaled, my head spinning. Craig was here and with another woman. *Player!* I wanted to scream out loud, but instead I waited, the roar of the waves filling the emptiness inside my head. I stood for a few minutes, biding my time to make sure the coast was clear.

"Lauren, I know you are standin' there." His voice was tired, defeated.

Standing stock still, thoughts raced through my mind. *How in God's name did he know I was here?* Maybe he was just guessing. It was nearly pitch dark on the beach and I hadn't moved, I was sure of that. I was too numb.

"I can smell your perfume, besides a white dress on a dark beach sticks out like a sore thumb, and I knew you were here. Can we talk?" He kept his distance, waiting. In the back glow of the tiki torches I could see his outline. He wore a pair of light tan linen drawstring pants and a loose fitting linen shirt.

I exhaled, not realizing I had been holding my breath again, "I don't think we have anything to talk about." The sound of the waves had subsided between sets. In a moment, they would pick up again. He stood between me and the stairs, the only way back to the party.

"I think we do," he chided.

Thinking fast I replied, "Fine, you talk while I get my shoes." I moved to pass him and grab my stuff, hoping for a speedy exit back up the stairs before he realized I had no intention of sticking around to hear his side.

With a faint snort, he stepped between me, and the steps. "Aye, you will listen because this has everythin' to do with you." The darkness around us hid his features, leaving me unable to read his face, but I knew his eyes were a dark shade of green.

Annoyed, I started to push past him. He stood rigid and unmoving. At a stalemate, I let go of my dress, and crossed my arms in a huff, "Fine! I'll do the talking, and save you the time." Not waiting for a response I babbled on, my voice shaking. "The gig is up and I'm moving on. This was a mistake, and you used me." I started to tremble.

"Nay, it's nothin' like that. I came here to see you," he said. "Only you," he added softly.

How dare you! That won't work with me you, you... Pressing my lips together in fury, a thousand retorts ran through my head, but none of them formed clearly in my mind or made it to my mouth. Instead, they got lost along the way. Damn him for muddling my brain.

"It is true, Gabriela and I had somethin', but that was a long time ago and she is not one to let go or move on. I came here tonight because I thought it would be safe."

"Safe!" I nearly screamed at him, "Safe! Safe until you realized that another of your lovers would be here to muck things up for you. I can't believe you're..."

"Stop it! Just shut your gob for a minute and hear me out," he nearly shouted.

Simmering, I stood my ground, arms firmly crossed. I could feel hot red heat rising up my neck to my face even as a cool breeze blew across my skin.

"There have been some things goin' on around the resort and I had to find out if the huaca was really meant for you or if it was part of somethin' else."

He had my attention. A chill snaked up my spine making me shiver involuntarily. With all the excitement of the upcoming trip and trying to gel with Cronos, I had forgotten about the golden huaca. "What do you mean?"

We've been havin' some trouble with drug traffickers near the resort, in the Darien jungle. Usually the drug mules and traffickers keep to themselves and travel a central route, but lately they have been coming closer to the resort. We've had some odd things happen there lately. I needed some time to figure things out and the last thin' I wanted was to be connected to you." He paused to let his words sink in.

Odd things? "Go on."

"I couldn't call you because there was literally no cell phone service where we were and like I said, I didn't want there to be a trail linkin' me to you. Not until I sorted things out." He paused then added, "I had to eliminate possibilities. Lauren, I keep my personal life and my business separate, and other than your visit, no one there knew you."

"So why come here? Why risk my safety? If that is really what this is about?" I added sarcastically. *Got you.*

"Because, that huaca was meant for *you.* I just couldn't put the pieces together without talkin' to some local Indians and ruling out the cartels. I needed more information."

"I thought you said the huaca was pre-Columbian and really ancient? Besides, I don't have many friends here, much less enemies, and I sure as hell don't know anybody who deals drugs, so how could it possibly be meant for me?" *Aha!*

He was growing more exasperated. "It *is* a relic of pre-Columbian people, but the indigenous tribes have been here since that time period. While they didn't actually make them, they do have some bits and pieces of huaca lore mixed in with their oral history." He paused, trying to control his frustration. "The Kuna Yala or San Blas as you call them inhabit territories all the way to Columbia. While checkin' out the situation with the traffickers, I talked to the local chieftain near the resort."

"Okay, so someone really hates me, what does that have to do with Gabriela, Gabby, or whatever her name is?" I wasn't about to let their reunion on the beach go without an answer.

"Not a damn thin', but bad luck," he sighed, his voice softer.

"Hmmph," I offered with a glare.

"Look, I came to find you. I had no idea she would be here." He shrugged, lifting his palms upward as if pleading a case.

"Hmmph!" I retorted, not giving in.

"Good God, woman, are you no hearing a word I say." His anger got the best of him and he switched smoothly to his brogue, the vowels rolling heavy off his tongue. "Someone means tae kill ye and here we stand blatherin' 'bout some woman I care not about! That damn thin' was meant for ye!"

You could have cut the salt air between us with a blade. His words hung between us, the weight of them was heavy indeed. My head swam. *Me?* This wasn't making any sense. *Think, Todd. Think!* Finally, I spoke, "How do you know it was meant for me?"

"The warrior eagle alone didn't make sense." He spoke calmly now. "I couldn't put together all the pieces. I couldn't connect the huaca to the bloody mess of the chicken. It didn't make sense until Clementine found the knife."

His words brought me up short. "Knife? There wasn't a knife." Sifting through my memories of that morning, I couldn't remember a knife.

"It was in the bed." He ran his hand across his chin, and I could hear the rough sound of stubble on his face. "Under the sheets where you slept. That was Paulo that called me when we landed. Whoever did this must have put it there for you to find, only you didn't make it back to your room that night."

Stunned, I just stood there wishing I could see his face. So, that's why he acted so distracted after we landed. *Good God!* This was just too surreal for my brain to grasp. *If I had gone back, would someone have been waiting? What then?*

"No, I don't think someone would have been waitin' in your room for you," he said, reading my mind. "This was left as a warning. Of that I am sure, but I still haven't figured out the last few pieces of the puzzle."

"Who and why?" I quietly added. My voice sounded far away.

"I honestly don't know, but until we find out, you won't have much alone time. So, why don't we head back to the party so I can speak to your Da and make arrangements." It was framed clearly as an order and not a question.

I gave in, too numb to fight anymore. Craig's encounter on the beach with Gabby would have to wait until later. While it did still gnaw at my gut, there were more pressing issues at hand, like my life. We found Dad, and Craig pulled him aside to explain what had happened, starting at the beginning. Needless to say, since I had never mentioned anything about the incident at the resort, he was surprised. The surprise was short lived as he then became very upset at the whole situation. They both decided the four of us would stay at the party long enough to be polite. Craig and Dad also decided to keep the whole thing from Haley, which I agreed with wholeheartedly. We would continue on as if leading normal lives. Hopefully, whoever had it in for me would think the threat had not been taken seriously and this would encourage them to act again. Hopefully, with just another threat, but either way, it would draw them out into the open. Essentially I was bait.

At first I found it near impossible that my Dad would agree to this insane idea of bait, but since we didn't know who was out to get me, they both decided the local police could not be trusted. Besides, they assured me, if I was never alone, then I would be safe. The fact remained that this was a warning. Had someone really wanted to cause me harm, then they would have had ample opportunity during the last week when Craig was incognito and Dad was busy with work. So, before heading home, Dad surreptitiously gathered Haley to his side, and

Craig dragged me towards the dance floor for one last display of normalcy before we left the party.

The party had mellowed and the band, having switched to a more updated repertoire, was playing a slow song. Grabbing my hand, Craig drug me out onto the dance floor. All of a sudden, trying to act normal didn't feel quite normal. On our way, we passed Gerry at the bar who smiled and waved at me. Missing nothing, Craig pulled me protectively to him as we started to dance.

"You really shouldn't lead that poor bartender on you know." His mouth was mere inches from my ear, and his breath made the hair on my neck tingle when he spoke. Betraying my mood, my body responded to his touch. The smell of salt air mingled with his cologne and, I thought, a hint of whiskey.

I kept my mouth shut, ignoring him, and instead planted my heel firmly onto the top of his leather loafer in response. Grunting, he pulled back and studied me for a moment, his green eyes fixed on mine. "At least I finish with one man before moving on to the next," I shot at him. "You know, you are free to ask your girlfriend to dance if you'd like. What was her name again? Gaudy? No wait… Gabby," I smiled wickedly at him, enjoying the jab.

He picked up where he had left off and we began to move again, keeping time to the beat. "Hmm, jealous are we? I'll have you know, here and now, that I haven't even seen Gabby in over a year. Can I help it if she was mad for me?" Grinning wickedly, he grasped my hand, and spun me around until my back was against his chest. The heat of him radiated through the thin linen of his shirt to my bare skin. His strong arms encircled me, pulling me in tight. I could feel the buttons on the front of his shirt press into my exposed back and my body started to hum. The soft stubble on his face tickled as he nestled his chin in the crook of my neck.

As we turned, I caught site of a gorgeous woman with light mocha skin and jet black hair glaring at us from a nearby table.

Dressed in a skin tight black cocktail dress, her dark tresses hung in large curls on her ample chest. It was a wonder she could breathe. Fuming, she shot me a nasty look through her false eyelashes, just before Craig spun me back around again. *And you must be Gabby.*

The music faded and the movement on the dance floor slowed. Grabbing me by the hand again, Craig pushed his way through the crowd towards the house where we were met by Haley and Dad. We said our goodbyes and made our way out to retrieve our cars from the valet.

Craig ushered me to his Jeep and sent me a smoldering look when I objected. Not keen on being alone with him just yet, I protested by riding home with my arms crossed, staring out the passenger side door at the dark silhouette of the jungle as it flew by. The drive home was uneventful and quiet. Ever the gentleman, Craig let me wallow in my mood and didn't breach a single subject during the drive, which only served to make my blood boil even more. Once home, he unlocked the front door, did a cursory walk through the house, and then headed back out to wait in the Jeep.

Passing him in the hall, I shot him nasty look, "You can stop playing the knight on the white horse, you know."

Never missing a stride, he sailed past me. Just as he opened the front door he shot back, "Just as soon as you don't need rescuin'." With that he was gone.

Peering from the kitchen window I saw him sitting in the front seat of his Jeep. He stayed put until Dad and Haley pulled up, parking alongside him. It was several minutes before he finally drove off. No doubt they were planning the upcoming week of babysitting duties. I stomped down the hall, still fuming.

SECRETS AND CONFESSIONS

Sunday dawned dark and overcast. A tropical low was passing us on its way up the coast towards Belize. After such gorgeous weather the night before, I was surprised when the weather reports said they fully expected it to become a tropical storm by the time it reached the southern coast of Belize. For us, though, it meant an ugly wet day was in store. Dad drove Haley and me to church.

Shortly after arriving, Dad had found an Episcopal church within what used to be the Canal Zone. There were few churches that held their services in English, and only one that was Episcopal. Catholicism was king in Panama, as it was in most Latin American countries. Mom had been an Episcopal when she and Dad had married, therefore, so were Haley and I. I knew that both of my parents wanted to make sure that Haley spent her childhood involved in the church as I had, so while I didn't make it to services very often, I did make an effort for Haley's sake. And so, on this rainy and gloomy day, I pulled myself out of bed, got dressed, and headed towards the kitchen.

"Are you going to church with us today?" Haley was unrolling a hot fresh cinnamon roll on her plate and eating one small section at a time. The thick white icing coated her fingers. Passing her a paper towel from the counter, I pulled out a chair across from her and grabbed another hot roll from the pan in the center of the table.

"Yes, I wanted to hear you sing," I said.

"Hey, good morning. How are both of my girls?" Dad strode in and scooped up his favorite mug from next to the coffee pot and poured himself a mug full. "Lauren, I'm glad you are coming with us," he shot me a pointed look.

"As if you would have let me stay home," I fired back then shoved the soft moist center of a roll into my mouth. It was probably best not to say what I really felt. *Oh heck with it!* "Listen, Dad, I really don't think I need a babysitter. Good Lord, I am old enough to care for myself. I know that you have been there for me a lot this last year. And I also know that losing Mom was hard on you, too, but you can't watch over me for the rest of my life just because some sicko ..."

He cut me off abruptly. "Haley, why don't you go hop in the car, we'll be right behind you."

Haley's eyes were as big as the cinnamon rolls she had just devoured. "What sicko? Who is sick?"

"Go on, honey, and don't forget your music sheets." Dad smiled sweetly at Haley over his coffee mug. "Go on, run along." With a quick glance at me, then back at Dad, Haley trotted slowly from the room.

Crap, I had completely forgotten that Haley had no idea what was going on. We had agreed last night at the party, not to tell her anything. "Sorry, I wasn't thinking." The roll was starting to sour in my stomach.

Quietly setting down his mug, he crossed his arms. He stared at the white wall above me for a moment and then he spoke, "Have you stopped to think why my company would keep houses in the same neighborhood for their employees?"

Taken aback at the change in direction our conversation had taken, I was slow to reply, "Not really. Why?" *Should I?*

"You never thought that was odd, everyone working for the same company and virtually living on the same street?"

"I haven't lived in many foreign countries," I said sarcastically, "so no."

"Did you ever wonder why our family vacations weren't to Disney, or State Parks, or places that your friends always went on their vacations?"

Now he had me thinking and the wheels began to turn. Growing up, we had spent our vacations in places like

Washington D.C., Nebraska, Virginia, South Dakota, Portugal, and Canada, to name a few. I guess if I sat and thought about it, they weren't exactly where other families had gone. In fact, most of my friends had gone to the beach, or theme parks. "What are you getting at?"

He took a deep breath and shifted his feet. "Lauren, I need to make sure that somebody is not trying to get to *me* through *you*."

"That's pretty ridiculous," I snorted. "Why would anyone want…" and then it hit me. Everywhere we vacationed while growing up had been near military bases. In fact, he would often disappear, leaving Mom, Haley and me to sightsee together. When he did return, it was usually late at night, briefcase in hand. He used to make frequent trips up north, but for the life of me I couldn't remember exactly where he went, with the exception of Washington D.C. Certainly he wasn't in the military. Dad had served as a Marine before I was born, but I had never seen him in uniform other than in old pictures. Was he working for the military?

"What in the heck have you gotten us into? What kind of work are you doing down here? And don't come up with some crazy crap like 'I could tell you but I'd have to kill you'!"

His eyes sparkled as he watched me solve part of the puzzle in my head. "No, I can't really tell you, but what I can tell you is that I do work for the military, sort of, but as a civilian. And no, I am not a spy," he added with a smirk.

"Okay, so you are doing stuff I don't need to know about. I can handle that, but what does that have to do with allowing me to be my own person even though we live under the same roof." The idea last night that I would have to have a 'baby sitter' still rankled me. "I came here to help you with Haley, and I would never have moved if you hadn't asked me to. I had a life and friends back home. Moving to some third world country wasn't exactly in my life plans!" My hands were shaking as I tried to keep from screaming at him. While I knew that wasn't exactly the reason I had come I felt the need to hang on to whatever was left of my independence. Nobody wanted to be living with their father at my age.

"First of all, this whole business with the huaca does concern me because, like it or not, you are my daughter and I love you. That won't change no matter how old you are or whether you are married with kids. Secondly, it is not unheard of in my…er…business to have um…people want to get a hold of the work you do through family or friends. Does that make sense?" His neck had turned red while he talked and I knew he was trying to control his anger as well.

"Okay, so let me see if I got this. You are not a spy, but you do stuff you can't tell me about, and you won't let me out of your sight."

"Or Craig's," he interrupted, "him I trust."

"What in the hell does he have to do with this? Don't tell me he is a spy, 'cause I am not buying it." I glared up at him fuming. "And furthermore, you are using your daughter as bait to figure this all out. Does that cover it?" I spat out the word bait.

He took a long stride forward, placing his palms on the table in front of me, leaning in until we were eye to eye. I leaned back instinctively, creating more space between us. His neck and the tips of his ears had turned the color of a ripe tomato. "Believe me when I tell you that at no point in time will you be compromised. I will have some people I work with do some checking into this whole huaca mess. I trust Craig—."

"Well, at least someone does!" I spat back at him, crossing my arms in exasperation.

Taking a deep breath, he continued as the red crept all the way up his cheeks, "I have already contacted my office and things have been set in motion, so you will stop using the word bait!" Pushing off from the table he added, "You and Craig will continue on as if everything is normal until I can make sure this doesn't involve me or the work I do. Craig is still trying to work out exactly what all this tribal symbolism means." Turning on his heel he headed out of the kitchen, leaving me behind gulping air like a fish out of water. "And Lauren, this stays between the three of us." He added from half way down the front hall. "No exceptions."

**

The next day, Craig was waiting for Haley and me out front. Apparently he was my escort for the next few days. Haley was thrilled to see him again. On the way to Haley's school I let her jabber away with Craig while I made a point of blowing him off. Once Haley was gone, the inside cab of the Jeep became silent and uncomfortable. Finally Craig spoke up.

"Are you still pissed about Saturday night?"

Actually, I wasn't even sure what I was mad about any longer. I was just annoyed at the whole situation, annoyed with him and myself. I didn't need this right now. Just being near him jumbled up my brain and I felt the need to… *to what?* My anger with him finally deflated as we turned onto the gravel road leading to the barn, but I still felt jilted. "Can you see this from where I sit?" I pivoted in my seat so I could see him clearly.

"Yeah, actually I can. But the truth is, I didn't have a way of contactin' you and even if I could have, I didn't want any link to you if I could help it. I was actually thinkin' of you first," he added softly.

"Well, hopefully this will all be forgotten soon because we both have lives to get back to."

The Jeep came to a sudden stop in the middle of the road. The tires skidded across the gravel as I threw my arm out in front of me, bracing against the dashboard. *Crap!* I could just see the grey walls of the old fort up ahead. Craig sat quietly behind the wheel staring straight ahead while the engine idled. Stunned, I leaned back in my seat, waiting.

"Can I ask ye a question?" He turned his head and his eyes met mine. "And weel ye give me a straight answer fer my trouble?" His brogue was thick as syrup on a cold day and he was clearly thinking through each word carefully.

Caught by surprise, I hesitated to return his gaze. With a nervous hand, I tucked a loose curl behind one ear. Tentatively I nodded, waiting.

He took a few deep breaths before speaking again, and his brogue was gone. Just like that. "Who or what did this to you?"

"I'm not sure I understand." I chewed on my lower lip.

"One minute you cower from me, and the next minute you can't seem to get enough of me. This hot and cold is not my idea of a relationship. I've given up tryin' to figure you out, Lauren, so you better just tell me. That way I can sleep at night instead of tryin' to figure you out. I am not one for games." There was a cool finality to his voice.

"Y – you think I am playing a game?" I said incredulously.

"How 'bout you tell me. Why do you flinch when I touch you? Who did this to you? Damn it, Lauren, you won't let me in." His knuckles turned white against the tan steering wheel.

The surrounding jungle sounded flat through the hard top and windows of the Jeep, its normal melodies muted as if it knew to be quiet. The pitch of the engine changed slightly as the engine idled, and the cold A/C blew softer from the vents. A million thoughts, sentences, feelings, tumbled over each other in my brain, but none of them seemed to come together to form a coherent explanation. I had done such a good job of locking things away; I wasn't sure how to pull them out. It reminded me of my bedroom closet as a kid, so crammed with stuff that once the door was breached, chaos rained down around my feet. We sat for a few minutes facing each other, without either of us really seeing the other. Breaking the spell, Craig pulled his gaze away and stepped on the gas pedal.

"His name is Jake," I reached out and grabbed Craig's arm "was Jake." Craig stopped the Jeep, shifted into park and looked me straight in the eye. My lips were trembling and I blinked hard trying to keep Craig's face in focus while holding my tears at bay. Craig waited. I wanted more than anything to get through this without losing it, to get through this and have someone help lift the weight from my shoulders, the sadness from soul. *But this is your cross to bear, not his.* Better to be straight forward and stick to the facts, I decided. Staring at my hands, I continued.

"We were together for six years. We lived together and talked about marriage. He was a really good person, kind." I took a deep breath, wringing my hands. "I was on duty when they brought him into the trauma room." I could see the red and white lights and hear the noisy room come to life inside of the confines of the Jeep and I began to sweat despite the A/C. I inhaled again through my nose and exhaled through my mouth, slowly willing the tears to behave. Steeling myself.

"There was nothing that could be done to save him. He died in flight, but it is our job, my job, to still try. In the end, I couldn't save him, nobody could." I stared out the windshield of the Jeep at the gravel road ahead remembering the utter helplessness I had felt that day. "All I could do was look into his eyes and see the nothingness, he was gone. I loved him." I glanced down at my hands. "There was actually a time when I loved him more than life itself."

"One of the flight crew carried me out of the trauma room." My eyes found Craig's again. "I heard them call the time of his death for the record right before the doors closed behind us." To this day I still had chills when I saw 9:38 a.m. on a clock face. A tear had found its way out, sliding slowly down my face. Craig reached a rough hand out to wipe it away.

"I don't have much memory after that. Somehow I drove to the barn and my friend, Calli, found me in the corner of Pogo's stall. I was curled up in a ball, comatose." I smiled at my hands, recalling Calli's face. I had thought her an angel at first, but then again, I was half mad with grief. "I had been there for hours in the cold stall without a jacket."

Another tear escaped and he caught it before it made it to my cheek, "Go on."

I took a deep breath, exhaling slowly, thinking. "Jake was my everything. He was there when my mom died last June. He was the rock I clung to while she faded away from cancer. When I lost my rock, I…I…well I had nothing to hold on to."

He sat for a moment, silent, wiping the occasional tear from my face with his finger. Finally he asked, "When did this happen?"

"February 8th."

"This past February?" He was incredulous. "Lauren, I'm so sorry… had I known, I-I-I wouldn't have, I mean."

"He had a ring with him." I squeezed my hands together, wringing out the courage to continue. "In his pocket. He was going to propose. He had already asked my Dad."

My fingers ached, "That is why I must seem so, how did you put it? Hot and cold," I forced a smile, as another tear broke free. "You see, Craig, there is a part of me that knows I will move on one day. That I have to move on and yet there is another part of me that feels as though I am being unfaithful." I searched his eyes for a response, an understanding. "And then you came along."

He thought for a moment then cleared his throat. "I canna replace another man. That wouldn't work for you or for me." His voice was rough. "What I can do is love you, if and when you are ready."

"But no," he said, shaking his head, "I canna replace him nor weel I try. I am my own man and I want all of you. I don't aim to share you with another or fill his shoes. It needs to be you and me." Blinking hard, his auburn eyelashes brushed the top of his cheeks. "That day I saw you ridin', you remember?" I nodded. How could I forget the first time I had seen those bottomless green eyes?

"Funny, but you were mine from that moment." As he said the words, his eyes flashed with such intensity that my heart stopped.

Sweet Jesus, I was falling in love again. In spite of everything, I was falling in love. My heart beat like a tympany drum in my chest. With Jake there had been common ground, a familiarity while growing up together, a constant. With Craig there was electricity, yearning, and somewhere deep down inside, a knowing. The two were as different as the sun and moon, each of which I loved in their own way. Each felt right. And then it hit me, "Craig, I need to know."

Picking up on the change in my voice, he shifted in the seat, turning slightly so his body faced mine. "That night at the resort, before we made love, you said that 'this was between us'. What exactly did you mean by that?"

"Honestly, I had a gut feelin' that there was another man in your life, but I couldn't put my finger on why. I went out on a limb, Lauren. As far as I could tell you weren't seein' anyone, you never mentioned it, and Hamish said you were single. Now I understand, it makes sense, I just had to make sure that you were mine and only mine that night." He shrugged, "As I said, with me it is all or nothin'," there it was again, that unmistakable finality to his voice.

All or nothing.

With that, he ended the conversation, put the Jeep in gear and moved off down the road. He reached for my hand, and held onto it for the rest of the drive. After parking by the barn, he stepped out of the Jeep and slipped around to open my door. My head was spinning as I stepped out onto the gravel drive. With the flick of his wrist he shut the door behind me then stepped forward, pinning me against the side of the Jeep.

Burying his hand in my hair, he pulled my face towards him with his calloused hands as his lips sought mine with a commanding fierceness. It was as if he felt the need to possess me as his own in some ancient primeval way and I gave in to him. In a wave of passion and need I pulled him to me hard. Once again he stoked the flames of desire in me and I could feel the heat spread from somewhere deep in my belly. The butterflies never even had the chance to pick up a rhythm. His kiss was rough, possessive. When he finally pulled his mouth away, he laid his forehead against mine, breathing hard. Softly, he murmured three little words, "I am yours."

He pulled back, studying my face. My lips felt bruised. Gently I ran a finger across them, still reeling from his kiss. We were both breathing heavily.

"I'm so sorry, did I hurt you?" His voice was gentle, apologetic.

"No, I'm fine."

"Well then, I believe you have a lesson. I will be up at the house workin' on AJ's computer while you ride. When you are done, I'll drive you both home."

Pulling away, he turned on his heel and headed towards the house. As I entered the shade of the mahogany tree I saw Maria's face glaring at me from inside Mariposa's stall window. Her dark eyes flashed pure hatred before retreating into the dim interior. Brushing it off, I headed around the corner and into the barn.

**

The next two days were carbon copies of each other, well, except for my lesson. Cronos was fit and raring to go. With our departure for Wellington looming, Colleen had beefed up our lesson schedule. In order to save money, I started swapping barn work and riding other horses to help fund my riding habit.

Gold Herr had taught me to half pass, something which he did fluidly. While Cronos did know how to half pass, she had unfortunately fallen into the bad habit of leading with her haunches. It was a habit I had seen Maria struggle to fix with Mariposa. Since this was very incorrect and would lead to her 'falling' in the direction of motion, we concentrated on correcting and fine-tuning this movement.

Colleen had us start by going back to basics. We worked on the shoulder in movement down the long side of the arena, until she was tracking correctly, her ribs filled out my outside leg, and she was flexed to the inside at just the right angle. She then had us perform shoulder in down the quarter line, straighten, then return to the shoulder in. We made a point bending and straightening her front end repeatedly, while keeping her haunches behind her.

Next we moved on to just a few steps of shoulder in then a few steps of half pass at a time, making sure to ride straight out of each movement. Once again, by keeping control of her bend and limiting the number of steps in each movement, we were able to keep her moving correctly and she never really had the chance to fall in with her haunches. For the next few rides, Colleen instructed me to only half pass from the quarter line or centerline. The centerline was an option, only if she was travelling correctly and not leading with her haunches. By keeping the movement short, we could better control her haunches and build correct muscle memory for both of us.

The one superb movement that Cronos could lay claim to was her walk. Her swing at the walk was so fluid and ground covering it took my breath away. I had never in my life had trouble sitting, or much less adjusting to a horse's walk gait before. In fact, if any of my former eventing pals heard me say such a thing they would have thought me crazy. With Cronos though, it was different. If my hip joints froze up, or in any way didn't move in a manner which was absolutely free and loose, then I would find myself nearly bounced to the opposite side of the saddle. Colleen was ecstatic over her walk and bold enough to say that if a judge worth their salt didn't give us a 9 or a 10 for our walk movement, then they were blind. Two of the walk movements in the Prix St. Georges test were scored with a coefficient. This meant that our score for that movement would be multiplied by the coefficient, thereby resulting in a much greater score. It was a good way to increase your overall score.

After a few days, Craig had to fly back to the resort and Dad made Haley and me travel everywhere in one of the company cars. As it turned out, our driver, while nice enough, usually only said about five words in any given day and had a neck the size of a pro football linebacker. That and he made a face and wrinkled his nose each time I climbed into the back seat of the car after a day at the barn. Fed up, I finally asked Mr. Neck, as I had taken to calling him behind his back, if he would like to give riding a try. He merely grunted and started the engine in answer. Halfway home I heard him mumble, "Men don't wear tight pants."

Over the next couple of weeks I felt increasingly imprisoned and stifled. I had forgotten just how much freedom comes with driving yourself around since I'd had a car from the age of sixteen.

Craig and I were together whenever he was in town. After I told him about Jake our relationship seemed to move to a new level.

Dad was very surprised that his connections had not been able to trace the origins of the huaca which Craig had given him. The emeralds were most definitely Columbian, but that in itself was not a surprise, especially since they lead the world in emerald mining. All indications pointed to the huaca being made by a local artisan and not a big name jeweler, which made it all the more difficult to trace. There also was no maker's mark anywhere to be found on it. With no local answers to be had, Dad began checking with some overseas connections he had, especially those in South America.

Towards the end of June, Craig and I escaped again to Las Brisas for a few days. Colleen said we needed a break and I couldn't have agreed more. After being babysat by Mr. Neck for the last three days, I desperately needed some alone time with Craig. The problems he'd had with the local drug mules had stopped and things were back to normal. Although hesitant at first to return, Craig assured me that only a brazen fool would try to get to me with so many people around. And of course, I stayed in his bungalow under his watchful eye and his warm body.

This time the resort had almost a full complement of guests, and Craig put me to work as a hostess of sorts. I found myself truly enjoying meeting the guests and getting to know them. Craig later admitted he was using me to charm them and mumbled something about me being able to carry on a conversation with a ketchup bottle. I took this as a compliment, though I wasn't sure.

When we returned, I was somewhat shocked to find that Maria had packed up and left. She gave Colleen only twenty-four hours notice before a trailer arrived to pick up Mariposa. She hadn't even told Colleen where she was going or given any explanation for leaving. Although everybody had to admit the barn was a better place without her, I could tell that the situation surrounding her abrupt departure bothered Colleen.

I dove right back into my training and we set to work trying to create a musical freestyle. Colleen had ridden quite a few freestyles and, luckily, she had a few rides complete with music that would work for Nicola and William. Hamish and I would have to build ours from the bottom. Patina's gaits didn't match any of Colleen's freestyles. Because of the size of her stride, the transitions within the music occurred at all the wrong times. The same was true of Cronos.

**

July was gone before we knew it. Rachel was only able to make the trip from Florida to train one time. Colleen worked with her for five days straight. She rode Gold Herr every day, and Nicola every other day. I made myself available to film her every chance I could. Pablito, who I had grown to really like, filled in when I was busy. It was important for her to be able to take what she learned in her lessons home with her so she could apply them to her rides on Otter, otherwise known as Otterbein. While we had the benefit of regular, systematic lessons with Colleen, she had to make do with one or two mega sessions per month. Although once we arrived in Wellington next month, Colleen could work with her and Otter more consistently.

Deanne had given up on Hamish, but was trying to balance her time between parties at the Embassy and the barn. She was working overtime to fill the void left from not chasing after him. Even though she and Hamish had never actually been an item, she had sunk all of her energy and drive into the pursuit. If only she could apply those same tactics to dressage she would be unbeatable. Colleen was clearly not happy with her lack of focus.

William went lame in his right front leg the first week of July. Rather than take precious training time to figure out the cause, Elaine pulled his shoe and had a full set of x-rays done. He had an elongated abscess deep within his hoof. Using the films, her farrier was able reach it through the hoof wall, and released the pressure. Unfortunately, they lost nearly two weeks of training.

Hamish and Patina were very much in sync with each other. Their rides showed marked improvement with every passing week, which was amazing since they were one of the strongest pairs we had. Hamish spent his spare time at the barn watching videos in the office of some of the horse and rider teams that we would compete against. He also went everywhere with his Ipod, listening to the music of his freestyle.

His competitiveness surprised me. He had such an easy going nature about everything else in his life. While he didn't exactly avoid Deanne, his demeanor would change when she skipped into the barn late for her lesson, babbling about Joe You Know Who or Kevin Somebody Or Other whom she had met last night. Nobody else seemed to notice, but I almost thought he looked jealous at times. Just like his brother, Hamish had the ability to hide his emotions well.

AJ made all the arrangements for shipping the horses to Miami. We would use one of the four horse trailers from the racetrack to get them to the airport. Colleen decided we would leave in August rather than in September. Apparently September was a busy month for equine air transport companies and it would be tough to get us all out on the same flight if we waited. Most of the horse transport by air in September was taken up by the Thoroughbred industry. Farms in the northeast would sell off some of their excess stock before the winter season kicked in. In an effort to avoid shipping horses to tracks in Florida, or feeding them through the winter months, they would ship the lesser grade thoroughbreds to breeders and trainers in Central and South America.

Our first recognized show would be in October. Where it would be was another question. Since thousands of competitors flock to Florida during the winter months, there were at least three shows a month for us to choose from between November and April. The problem was we didn't want to cluster all of the shows too close together and put undue physical strain on the horses. On the other side of the coin however, sat a big ticking clock. We had to obtain three qualifying scores at the Prix St. Georges level, and one at the Intermediare level. An additional Intermediare freestyle was needed, although the score for the freestyle didn't count towards the final tally. The good news was that if we obtained the necessary scores, we could represent Panama. Unlike riders in larger countries, we were the only ones from Panama, so we did not have to go through an additional selection process and be chosen from a large group of riders. We were it. Colleen was also able to verify that because I was currently a resident of Panama, I could declare that I would ride for Panama. She was also instrumental in sorting out Cronos's paperwork, registrations, and obtaining her passport so we could not only travel but we could compete legally under the guidelines set for the Games. It felt as though a weight had been lifted from my shoulders once that was all done. In the process we found Cronos's previous competition record. She had indeed competed in Europe up to the Intermediare level and from what we could tell she definitely had some limited experience with Grand Prix training.

The horse trailer from the racetrack was not available until the day before we were to ship out. This made Colleen absolutely nuts and I was right there with her. We were both trying to organize all of the tack and horse paraphernalia that would be shipped with us just inside the covered arena. Unfortunately, it wouldn't all fit into Mariposa's empty stall. Tripping over it in the barn aisle was out of the question, so that left either the spot just inside the covered arena where the picnic table and Colleen's stool sat or inside the actual dressage arena. At one point I thought we might lose the picnic table under the weight of all of our stuff. But at least, this way we could gather, check, and re-check everything on our list without getting everything mixed up and still have a place to ride. To a non-horse person, the idea that horses require so much paraphernalia can be mind-boggling and I was beginning to agree.

WELLINGTON

The green and white shipping van lumbered ahead of us down a picturesque two-lane road leading to Rachel's barn. Newly planted oak and magnolia trees, stabilized by twine and wooden stakes, lined either side of the road. Peering out one of the back windows of the SUV, I gawked at the grandeur of the never ending privacy gates, stone walls, and fences as they came into view. Rachel, in the driver's seat, had clung to the bumper of the shipping van like a tick all the way from the quarantine facility at Miami International Airport.

According to her, the drive normally took just under an hour and a half; however the shipping company had arrived just thirty minutes before the Friday afternoon rush hour. By the time we had all four horses processed through a mound of paperwork and loaded into the van, it was 5:15 p.m. The neon green, digital numbers on the stereo clock read 7:38 p.m., but according to my body it was way past exhaustion time. At least we stayed within the same time zone.

I glanced surreptitiously at Deanne, sitting quietly in the front seat. The airline had lost her luggage yesterday, and she had finally stopped complaining when we exited off I-95. Colleen and Hamish had efficiently tuned her out and Elaine, ear buds in place, was milking the last remaining power from her I-Pod, listening to music in order to gain some peace. Rachel, unfortunately having just picked us up, had gotten an earful. With no one else to vent to, the SUV had finally become quiet.

The dust coated red taillights of the van made a feeble attempt to alert us as it slowed. One faint, flashing bulb blinked on the right side of the van. Rachel deftly swerved around the van and slipped in ahead of it. Clicking the remote control on her visor, a set of black wrought iron gates swung wide, revealing a paved brick driveway. The bricks and concrete walls on either side of the gate were an unusual shade of mocha. The steady hum of the tires changed abruptly as we rolled over the stones and through the gates. The last few days had been stressful and I couldn't help but feel like we weren't in Kansas anymore. *Follow the yellow brick road. Follow the yellow brick road.*

Rachel slowed half way up the drive. Glancing in her rear view mirror she made sure the van had cleared the gates before clicking the remote again. Thick, freshly mowed grass lined the drive on either side of us. Natural wood lampposts with black wrought iron accents sprouted from small, immaculately maintained, circular flowerbeds, leading the way up to the main house. Looking closely at the lampposts, I saw the initials OSF burned into the side of the wood, One Spirit Farm. Rachel pointed the SUV towards the barn, which sat just off to the right and slightly behind the house.

The house, a sprawling ranch style, had a wide wooden porch running all the way around. A combination of matching mocha bricks, a lighter shade of tan colored stucco, and wood accents comprised the exterior façade. A rather large, metal, five pointed star reminiscent of a sheriff's badge hung just above the porch and below the highest peak of the roof. Its weathered patina was set off by the stucco behind it and it only served to add charm to the house. Considering Rachel and Troy met in Texas, it was just perfect. There were even a couple of wooden rocking chairs and an old wooden barrel on the porch.

The stone drive came to an end and the tires crunched on a well maintained gravel road. We parked in front of the barn and got out as the van rolled to a stop on mocha colored gravel. The gravel road appeared to make a big circle around the barn and back towards the house. Stretching my cramped legs I thought, rather wryly, that I would make a perfect Tin Man. I just wished that a can of oil could fix my aching back. Bending over at the waist, I stretched out the long muscles of my back as everyone else poured out of the SUV. If I was cramped, I could only imagine how poor Hamish felt. He had been crammed in the middle between Colleen and me.

"Oh, wow you guys are finally here!" I looked up into a smiling face, which was framed with the wildest curls I had ever seen. She wore a navy and white bandana folded neatly into a triangle and tied at the base of her neck in an attempt to contain her curls. The voice was attached to a petite girl who I guessed to be in her early twenties, with mousy brown hair and hazel eyes that sparkled with delight. She was dressed in a pair of jeans, a navy blue polo shirt, and wore a pair of Dansko clogs. A huge smile split her face, showing off a solitary dimple on the left side. I liked her immediately. "I thought I might have a heart attack waiting. Everything is set up, the stalls all have fresh shavings, and water buckets are topped off."

Colleen cut her off with a huge hug, "Katia, I had no idea you were here, how utterly fabulous for us! Rachel, you sneak, you didn't tell me you had kidnapped her."

"Trust me, the ransom was steep," Rachel replied, raising an eyebrow. She shut her door behind her. "Come on girls, oops, sorry Hamish. Let's get the horses settled."

Between us, and the van crew, we made quick work of unloading the horses and gear. Another young girl named Ann came out of the barn to help out. I quickly learned that Katia was the barn manager and Ann was vaguely related to Rachel somehow or another. Although young for a barn manager, Katia clearly took charge with her no nonsense attitude. Her maturity belied her youthful face.

I hadn't realized that Colleen was well versed with the Wellington scene. When I stopped Elaine in the tack room and asked her, she told me that Colleen had competed here for years before moving to Panama. Katia had been a student of hers, and now she managed the barn, and had a small following of younger kids whom she taught on the side in order to support her horse habit.

Hamish, who had been unusually quiet since we left Panama, took over carrying the heavier stuff to and from the barn, until Elaine presented him with a wheelbarrow to use. The young Ann couldn't seem to take her eyes off of him. She had found the wheelbarrow, but was too shy to approach him. Elaine had adroitly stepped in and taken charge, giving Ann a knowing wink which sent her blushing back towards the barn. Neither Hamish nor Deanne seemed to notice.

All four horses had travelled amazingly well and this last leg of the trip was no different. Patina was the last to unload and Hamish stepped up to take her lead rope. Elaine tipped the van crew and Troy arrived home just in time to open the gate for them as they pulled out. The horses were settled in and our bags had disappeared from the back of the SUV, no doubt they were waiting in the guesthouse for us. Twilight was fast fading into night as a hot Florida day gave way to a hot Florida night. Not a breeze stirred as we slowly trudged up to the house for a late dinner.

The barn was attached to the back porch of the house by a covered walkway. We entered through a set of glass French doors, which were etched with a cutting horse motif. One door featured a dodging cow whilst the other showed a cowboy on a Quarter Horse with its front end lowered, legs splayed for balance, keeping the unruly cow at bay on the opposite door. As Rachel held the door for us, the smell of Italian food made several stomachs growl at once. Laughing, we stepped into the cool air conditioning. The interior of the house welcomed us with warm, overstuffed, leather furniture, and reclaimed pine plank floors.

Troy, wine bottle in hand, ushered us around a large homey wooden table with eight mismatched wooden chairs. He had stopped by and picked up dinner for everyone on his way home. Katia joined Rachel, Troy, and the five of us for a meal of salad, garlic rolls, and lasagna. As we settled around the table, Rachel grabbed two more bottles of red wine from a wine cooler in the kitchen.

"This is wonderful, guys, we can't thank you enough."

"Colleen, you know Troy and I have been trying to get you to come back to Wellington for years. We are just so excited to have everyone." Rachel had finally settled next to Troy. Troy blessed the food and then everyone dug in to a delicious meal. Conversations slowed and the wine disappeared until exhaustion began to set in. One by one we excused ourselves and drifted towards the guesthouse. Elaine's and my bags were in the last room down the hall, so that is where we ended up.

After digging through my bag for my toothbrush and something to sleep in, I shoved it into the floor of the closet and headed for the guest bathroom. I would deal with unpacking tomorrow. Exhaustion was written on everyone's faces and before long we were all settled for the night.

**

Although I slept like the proverbial log, my internal alarm clock managed to go off at six a.m., otherwise known as o'dark thirty. Knowing it was futile to try and regain some measure of sleep, I gave up and wandered down the hall towards the kitchen. The red wine and salt from the garlic bread had left me thirsty. After finding a fully stocked fridge, I grabbed a bottle of water. Twisting off the lid, I took a moment to check out the guesthouse.

Colleen had referred to it as a cabana, but bunkhouse was more apropos. Set on the opposite corner of the house as the barn, it had three rooms, two full baths, a small eat in kitchen, and a sitting room with a large flat screen TV. The interior was similar to that of the house, but with a slightly more Southwestern feel. A set of sliding glass doors in the kitchen afforded an unobstructed view of a large covered arena set directly behind the house. I could also see nearly half of the barn.

After jumping into the shower, I slipped into my riding clothes and headed out to the barn. The sun was just breaking through some low clouds on the horizon as it began its daily trek. My paddock boots left footprints in the dew covered grass of the back lawn as I headed across the grass. A shed row style, the architecture of the barn mirrored that of the rest of the property. A row of stalls lined the west side of the barn where the transport van had parked last night. The east side sat open to catch onshore breezes. A row of reclaimed tree trunks served as supports for a wide veranda that formed the barn aisle. Terracotta pots overflowing with white geraniums hung from black, wrought iron hooks on every other post. The pitch of the vaulted ceiling was such that the back veranda remained wide and inviting while at the same time keeping the rain out. It was the perfect style for the hot, humid weather of Florida.

As I stepped under the roof, the unmistakable sounds of horses enjoying their feed reached me and I smiled. I immediately felt at home in the cozy barn. Wandering around, I checked in on each horse and stopped to admire Rachel's gelding, Otter.

Lost in my own world, I heard a whistle from the far end of the veranda and turned just in time to see a brown and white blur of a small dog go racing down the barn aisle. Sliding to a sudden stop a few feet from me, he looked up. His pink tongue hung from the side of his mouth. Swiveling his tiny head, he glanced to the left, and then to the right, looking undecided. Another whistle echoed down the aisle. The mischievous look on his face made me halt in my tracks. I was curious to see what he was up to. Just then, a third whistle, this one louder than the others, sent him scurrying past my legs and out onto the grass.

I watched as he dodged frantically in every direction like a pursued rabbit, finally disappearing under the wide back porch of the house. Hearing footsteps behind me in the barn, I glanced one last time at the porch where the dog had disappeared. The brown and white face of a Jack Russell popped out. He was wearing a grin. Out of breath and panting, his tongue lolled out of one side of his mouth, nearly hitting the ground. In the blink of an eye, he disappeared abruptly into the shadows just as Katia rounded the corner.

"Did you see a dog go running through here?"

"Dog?" The playful look on the dog's face made me want to know more before I gave up his hiding place. "I didn't know you had a dog." Well, that sounded stupid, I thought, especially since I had only known her for a few hours.

"No. The last couple of days I have seen a brown and white dog around the barn. I have no idea who he belongs to, and I can't seem to get close enough to catch him or see if he is wearing a collar."

"Um, did you try under the porch?"

Her face lit up and she turned on her heel and headed across the grass.

"Sorry little guy," I muttered under my breath and headed to check on Cronos. I had not been able to ride her for the last five days, and to say I was Jonesing to ride would be the understatement of the year. Lifting the metal latch to her stall, I slipped in.

A smile split my face when I saw her lying down in the middle of the stall. Her first morning at Colleen's barn I had panicked when I saw her lying down after finishing her morning grain, but had since learned that this was her way of doing things; grain, sleep, munch on some hay, sleep some more. "Mornin'," her ears pricked at the sound of my voice. She was curled up, her legs tucked underneath her, munching away at a pile of hay. More than once over the past few months, I had caught her sprawled out in her stall sound asleep with chunks of hay sticking out of her lips in all directions. It was almost as if she fell asleep in the middle of chewing.

I knelt down and ran my hands along her neck, down her massive shoulder, and to her right front leg. Long ago I had made a habit of knowing every inch of my horses. It was a good habit to get into and one that many good horsemen shared. Skimming along, my fingers rose and fell along the familiar terrain of her legs. I checked for heat, swelling, soreness, or anything unusual. As I moved to her right hind she kept munching away ignoring me. I would check her other legs once I could get to them, but for now this would do. With a final pat I left the stall and headed for the tack room. Lazy or not, it was time for both of us to get moving. If I had to be up early, then so would she.

I rode Cronos in the indoor arena lightly, just enough to stretch her legs after being cooped up for so long. She was feeling fresh and decided to spook at everything, including her reflection in the arena mirrors. As if she had never seen herself before, I thought wryly. One by one Hamish, Elaine, and Deanne made their way to the arena to stretch their horse's legs. Still dragging from all of the excitement of the last week, everyone kept their rides short.

Today was a good day for Colleen to focus on Rachel and Otter. I enjoyed watching other riders take lessons. I found that I could learn quite a bit even though I was sitting on a chair instead of the back of a horse, so when Rachel led Otter out to the covered arena I grabbed a cold can of Coke and followed them. Otter was a blood bay gelding with one hind white sock and a snip of white on his nose. He was registered as an American Warmblood, which is more of a sport horse registry than a breed registry. He was a cross between a Clydesdale and Thoroughbred. Within minutes Deanne had joined me. Her mood had lightened quite a bit last night at dinner, when Katia suggested she could replace her riding wardrobe at one of the many tack shops or vendor tents here in Wellington. This morning she had borrowed some riding clothes from Colleen to get her through the day.

For the last month or so Deanne's behavior had been unpredictable at best, and I learned to judge her mood before saying much of anything. She had dropped her pursuit of

Hamish cold turkey one day, and from that point on she became moody and he became focused and sullen. Looking from the outside in it was obvious that although never really a couple, they couldn't seem to get along in life or be happy without their strangely symbiotic relationship, a relationship that consisted of him being oblivious to her every move and her chasing him like a puppy. I rolled my eyes just thinking about it.

"So, I guess Colleen wants us to do our first show the last week in October."

"October, I thought we were starting in November?" I was trying to form a mental picture of a calendar in my head. Craig had bought tickets to fly up for a week in November. I was hoping he would make it to at least one show.

"She wants us to aim for at least one show per month. So that is," she began ticking the months off on her fingers one by one, "October, November, December, January."

"That only gives us four shows." I knew we needed three Prix St. George scores, one Intermediare 1 score and a freestyle.

"That's a start. Remember some of the shows are two shows over the same weekend." Overhearing something Colleen had said, she turned her attention, focusing on the pair working in the arena.

"Right, I have to adjust. I am used to one show that lasts three days, not two shows over as many days. I'll say this, the show venues get the most bang for their buck by charging double for a weekend." I had lost Deanne, focused as she was on Rachel, so I turned my attention to the arena.

Towards the end of the lesson, Ann brought out another horse for Rachel to ride; actually, it was technically a pony since he stood about 14.2 hands tall. He was a dark dapple gray with inky black legs. His mane and tail were mostly black with generous streaks of gray hair mixed in. It was a good thing Rachel was petite enough to match the pony's size. Had I ridden the little guy my knees would have been up around his withers in order to keep my feet off the ground. Ann took

Otter's reins from Rachel and headed back towards the barn as Rachel mounted the pony.

Elaine pulled up a chair next to me. "German Sport Pony?" She asked trying to gauge just what breed the pony might be.

"Nah, not refined enough. He is built like a tank," Deanne chimed in.

"Connemara," I said with certainty.

"Five bucks says it's not a Connemara, there just aren't that many of them around here." Elaine studied the gelding as Rachel began to stretch him while talking to Colleen.

"I think she's got you, Elaine," Deanne mused, still studying the pony.

"You're on."

Turning our attention back to the arena, we watched Rachel ride for a while. The little guy's looks were deceiving. For a small tank, he sure could move and we watched him float across the arena. While he was not as advanced as our horses, he had all the moves of Third Level down pat. At the tail end of the lesson, Colleen got on him and started to introduce him to the concept of tempi changes. She managed to get three flying lead changes across the diagonal without too much fuss, although the grey pony appeared startled when she asked for the third change. The look on his face said, 'I just did that!' She didn't count strides between the changes, rather she asked him to swap when he was straight underneath her. A horse has to swap all four legs at the same time, and beginning such a feat while crooked or bent the wrong way won't work.

After rounding the corner in the counter canter, she did one more change across the diagonal. She brought him down to a trot, halted him squarely, then rewarded him by allowing him to stretch out his neck and walk in a large circle around Rachel. I could hear them reviewing the lesson and evaluating Rachel's strengths and weaknesses. The videos she had made while in Panama appeared to have helped her stay on track.

In the midst of Rachel's lesson, I realized we were missing someone. "Hey, where's Hamish?" I had seen him un-tacking Patina earlier.

"Not my day to watch him," came Deanne's snide remark. I couldn't see her face, but I had no doubt she was rolling her eyes.

Getting up from her chair Elaine stretched, reaching her arms for the sky. "He went for a run. He said he'd be back for lunch."

"Oh." Setting my elbows on my knees, I propped my chin in one hand and went back to watching. Without notice, a familiar white and brown furry object flew across the arena towards us. The pale pink skin on the underside of his ears was clearly visible as he raced along with his ears folded back. He zipped under the grey pony's belly and popped up over the white vinyl border of the arena, landing smack in Deanne's lap. Remarkably, the gray pony, too hot and tired to care, simply cocked an ear in our direction and shifted so as to rest a hind foot.

"Ooof," muttered Deanne in shock as she caught the little dog in mid-leap.

"What the heck?" Colleen had instinctively stepped back to allow space between her and the pony should he explode in her direction in a panic.

The usual spotless Deanne was covered in tiny orange paw prints from the clay arena footing. She quickly scooped the puppy up off her lap and was trying to pin him against her chest to still his wiggling. In no time at all he had regained control of his pink tongue and was slathering her face with sloppy kisses. Rather than pull away, Deanne let him kiss her face, all the while crooning to him like a baby as we all stood around in utter shock. It was the first genuine smile I had seen on her face in a long time.

"Ooohh, isn't he just adorable?" The little Jack Russell that I had seen earlier, hiding from Katia, had settled down in

Deanne's arms. Thoroughly enthralled with him, Deanne didn't seem to notice that she was filthy. "Well, hello there little guy." Deanne continued to coo to the dog while the rest of us stared on in shock.

"Where did he come from?" Rachel had ridden over to get a closer look.

"Katia was looking for a stray dog earlier. She said she had caught glimpses of him around the barn a couple of times but never could catch him." In response to my explanation the dog began to bark.

Deanne stood up and headed towards the guesthouse. "I better see if he is thirsty," she mumbled over her shoulder as she walked away, still cooing to the dog as if he was a baby.

As she walked away we all glanced at each other in disbelief. Never would I have imagined Deanne so overcome by a dog. It wasn't that she was a snob. Rather, each one of us in life has our own idiosyncrasies. For some it may be a shoe or purse fetish, for others maybe their food can't touch on their plate. Whatever it may be that makes us each unique, for Deanne it was her impeccable clothing.

Elaine began to giggle first. She tried desperately to squelch her giggling, but Colleen was quick to jump in. Within moments we were all laughing so hard we hurt. After a few minutes, clutching our bellies no longer seemed to help.

**

Over the next few days we rode diligently. Colleen made sure each of our rides was videotaped so we could analyze our weak spots as well as to see what movements looked like when we rode them correctly. Other than running into town to pick up a few essentials here and there, we spent most of our time at the farm.

We also worked on polishing our freestyle tests. Troy had a knack for all things electronic, which really came in handy. In fact, I would have felt sorry for him having to put up with so much estrogen and horseflesh under any other circumstances, however like a trooper, he would come home at night from his office and jump right in to help us out. As it turned out, he was a master at watching videos of our tests, analyzing each move the horses made. We made a couple tiny adjustments in each of our musical scores to better enhance our rides. Watching Troy and Hamish work together, I had no doubt that they enjoyed having a man to talk all things techno with.

Over the next few weeks we settled into a routine of training. We also had a chance to drive to a couple different show venues which were nearby so we could watch other riders. Deanne was enthralled with her new dog, which she named Javier. *Javier?*

**

Late one afternoon, Elaine and I ran out to Target in Rachel's SUV to pick up a few essentials. While we were out, Rachel called and asked if we could pick up dinner on our way home. Troy was stuck in Miami with work and poor Rachel had been riding with Colleen since just after lunch and was exhausted.

We swung by a Chinese restaurant in the strip mall next to Target and placed an order before we went shopping. We made quick work of our lists, and bags in hand, Elaine headed for the SUV to drop them off while I walked down to pick up our food. The lady behind the counter spoke little to no English and when I asked if our order was ready all I got from her was, "Ten min." I could only assume she meant to say ten minutes. Stepping back out onto the promenade I settled on a bench and waited for Elaine.

"It's not ready yet? Geesh, how long does it take?" Elaine quipped, plopping down next to me. Her stomach growled loudly and mine answered it. We both started giggling. Colleen had been pushing us hard this last week and physical exhaustion was beginning to make us silly. Even though we thought we were in shape before leaving Panama, Colleen had made each of us start working out on a regular basis. Hamish, Elaine, and I had started running. I preferred to run in the evenings, while Hamish and Elaine usually set out together in the pre-dawn hours. Deanne had joined a local gym. Thank goodness she didn't care what we ate. I would have been forced to revolt if she had challenged my diet.

Elaine snorted loudly, trying to recover her composure. To pass the time we began the fun job of people watching. Wellington was chock full of all kinds of characters and we were assured of spotting some unusual subspecies of human, especially in a strip mall. We saw plenty of old men with what was left of their hair combed over to cover their balding heads, the requisite number of overly rich women clearly overdressed for an evening of shopping at Target, and one really hot man, still wearing his polo boots who ran into the cigar store next to us.

About to get up and check on our order, Elaine spotted a woman crossing the parking lot. "Well, would you look at that?"

Turning, I followed her gaze. "That looks like Maria. No, it can't be. What are the chances she is here, too?" As I watched, the woman headed across the parking lot at an angle away from us. Dressed up in a short dress and heels, it was hard to recognize her. After all, I had only seen her in breeches. A sports car headed our way failed to stop when the woman stepped out in front of it. The driver slammed on the brakes and the cherry red car came to an abrupt stop. Waving his hand out the window, he yelled at her. In a flash the elegantly dressed woman morphed into someone I did recognize. Hurling Spanish curse words back at the driver she flung her scarf over her shoulder and stomped off.

Elaine clucked her tongue. "I think I know," her eyes never left Maria's back, "the Pan Ams."

"No way!" Even as I said the words something in me clicked. Maria was from Columbia. "Do you think she is trying to ride for Columbia?"

"Or worse, Panama?" Elaine turned towards me.

"Holy crap, wait until Colleen hears. We should go ask her," I said.

Elaine grabbed my wrist before I could walk off. "Uh, uh," she shook her head. "I don't want anything to do with that bitch ever again. Better to let a sleeping dog lie. Besides, we are only speculating."

As we watched, Maria disappeared into an upscale eatery on the other side of Target. Heading back in, we picked up our food. On the way out I heard the lady behind the counter say, "Ten min," to another customer and I rolled my eyes in sympathy. It had taken nearly forty minutes to get our food.

PRIX ST. GEORGES OR BUST

Thank goodness for Ann and Katia. They had taken the horses to the show grounds the night before with Rachel's trailer, set up the tack stall, and were up early this morning to help everyone get ready. I was a bit uncomfortable, at first, with having someone else take Cronos to the show grounds without me. I had always been a 'hands on' rider, everything from bedding down a stall and unloading equipment to braiding my horse's mane. Although I had to admit that it wouldn't take much for me to give up the braiding. Tedious, monotonous, and aching finger joints were all synonymous with braiding a horse's mane.

We had set up a tack stall in between Patina and William. This way we could store some of our stuff under lock and key overnight. The deep midnight blue and grey fabric of Rachel's farm colors adorned the walls inside the stall, creating a secluded place for us to change clothes or sit and relax. Tack trunks sat on the floor, taking up nearly every square inch along the edges of the stall and a plethora of hooks held everything from bridles and helmets to coat bags and purses. A portable carpet had been laid on the floor and several directors chairs sat open in the middle. The girls had even brought a cooler full of ice cold drinks and fresh fruit.

Deanne and Rachel had their rides early in the morning. It was unusual to split up an upper level class, but with the Pan Am Games looming, it seemed as if everyone was trying to qualify. I assumed the show grounds also wanted to hold the interest of spectators so rather than lump all the good stuff like Intermediare, Grand Prix, and of course, the Prix St. Georges classes together, they had spread them out. Maybe, I thought, it was to give the judges a mental break as well. Even though I was now considered a dressage rider, even I couldn't watch the same movements over and over by the hour and not go nuts. A part of me would always be an eventer at heart, anticipating the cross country course.

I had dragged a folding lawn chair out into the barn aisle in front of the tack stall and with my feet up on an overturned bucket was finishing a protein smoothie. Deanne had stopped and picked one up for everyone. She had rattled off the ingredients in it that would give all of us a boost. I had gotten lost after the protein powder. All I knew was that it was mango flavored, cold, and filled my belly. Out of habit, I shrugged my shoulders, trying to release the stress I had been carrying with me all week, but I met the resistance of the concave shaped lawn chair. Leaning forward, I tried again and found the relief I was looking for. It felt good. Setting down my half finished smoothie, I reached for my toes, grasping my tennis shoes firmly under the arches with my hands. Stretching slowly, I loosened my calf muscles. Moving my hands to under the front of my shoes, I stretched again, this time feeling it in my arches. *Ahh, but that felt good.* Colleen had truly clamped down hard on us in an effort to ramp up our riding right before the show, and my muscles were complaining.

Both girls had done well this morning. Once the afternoon rides were complete we could all sit down with Colleen and go over each of our scores one by one. It was a good practice and one that I thought was truly helpful. Well, as long as I didn't overanalyze each aspect of my ride. Sometimes Colleen would remind me just to ride, not dissect it, but just ride the movement and let it flow. But then again I tended to over analyze most things. What could I say… I was a work in progress.

Craig was due to arrive in just over two weeks and I could hardly wait. I had missed him more than I had expected. So much so, that my heart ached just thinking about him. I had tried not to think of his touch ever since he kissed me goodbye at the airport. If I wanted to stay focused on qualifying, I would need my head and my heart in the game. I didn't have time to become a blathering basket case.

We talked at least twice a day, before the first boat pulled away from the dock and sometime around dinner, if he was able to extricate himself from the guests. Not only did he handle the boats, but ate dinner with the guests and shared 'big fish' stores. Several times a week our conversation would be cut short due to a lost cell connection. The newly updated landline installation would be completed sometime next week. Until then, Craig insisted we keep the regular phone lines free for business calls. Thank goodness the resort had a satellite connection for their Internet, although storms made its use spotty at best. We emailed as much as possible.

August through March was a very busy time for the resort. Sport fisherman wanting to escape dreary winter weather flew south, and as it turns out, those were some of the best months for fishing in Panama. Ganso would be handling the guests while he was gone. Craig had purposefully booked the resort on the light side so he could combine both boat crews into one. I knew he was sacrificing profits to come see me, and my heart swelled when I thought of it. It solidified in my mind that he really wanted to come. He truly missed me.

AJ, ever the businessman and always thinking ahead, had suggested that he set up space in the vendor tents to advertise the resort. The show grounds were filled with men walking around, bored, while the ladies did most of the riding. It represented a target rich environment for reeling in bored husbands, bored husbands with money who like to fish. The chips were in his favor, and the opportunity to haul in some wealthy clients looked promising.

Ahead of his arrival, Craig had shipped some brochures and tee shirts to Rachel and Troy's place on one of AJ's boats that had been bound for the port of Miami. Troy had kindly brought the huge steamer trunk home with him one night and found room for it in his garage. The trunk had apparently belonged to his father and looked like a prop from a movie. It was huge, and took two very strapping men to carry it. Constructed of wood and covered in dark brown leather, it had thick black leather straps and brass buckles running across the domed lid to keep it shut. Through contacts, Troy had procured a tent, table, easel and a few other items needed to make a proper show of it. All we needed now was Craig. *All I needed now was Craig.* I just had to stick it out for a little while longer.

In the meantime, Troy had agreed to set up the tent and get the ball rolling for him. Troy had even talked his secretary's daughter into working the tent until Craig arrived. Blonde, curvaceous, and with a winning smile, Rachel and I had teased him no end when we found out she was a model. He had laughed, admitting that he'd hired her on purpose to help draw men to the tent. He said he needed something to compete with saddles, bridles, and all the stuff here for horses and women.

I smiled, thinking of Craig. He and Troy were clearly great friends and it was nice that Troy would go to such lengths to help Craig with his business. Inhaling the sometimes pungent aroma of the show grounds, I tried not to think about how much I missed him. I had a class to get ready for.

**

As we circled the dressage arena I began to grab ahold of my show jitters, stuffing them deep down inside and away from the process at hand. The judges were completing their scoring of Elaine's ride. I wanted to keep Cronos's mind focused on me instead of the spectators lining the outer show ring and in the bleachers so I kept her busy with transitions between trot, extended trot, and canter. The announcer played classical music softly in the background between each ride. No doubt the spectators thought it was for their benefit; however Colleen had explained that the music worked to the rider's benefit by muting the sounds of the shuffling crowd. The occasional clang or thump created by spectators as they shifted and moved about in the metal bleachers was magnified under the covered arena. At least it was cooler in the shade. I felt sorry for the lower level classes that were being held outside under the October sun. Thank goodness we only had one class today.

Inhaling deeply, I took notice of my tense shoulders and tried to relax them. Just then, the whistle sounded and I made my last circle around the arena and prepared to enter at A. The overhead music faded just as I picked up the right lead in a collected canter. Cronos's large brown ears flopped gently with each stride as we entered at A and cantered up the centerline to X where she stopped with all four feet perfectly square, each white leg even with the opposite black one. We saluted; a smile of relief on my face. I would much rather be competing than waiting to compete. At least now, win, lose, or draw, I was busy instead of dealing with nerves and anticipation.

Another breath as I split the reins up between both hands after my salute and asked her to move off my leg. From that point on, we were in the zone and the remainder of the test became a blur as each movement flowed flawlessly into the next. As we approached the first set of flying lead changes, the anxiety I had so carefully stowed away crept back. Counting the changes seemed such a simple task, and yet one that I still struggled to get. The first four strides went smoothly as I counted in my head, *one, two, three, four, change, two, three, four,* so far so good. We rounded the corner and cantered along the short side of the arena before heading back across the diagonal. Five sets of four, I thought as we set off again. *One, two, three, four, change, two, three, four, change, one, two, three, four…*Crap! I lost count and added a stride. Quickly running out of time before we reached the letter M, I was forced to ask for the final lead change early and leave out a stride. Her transition was choppy, tight. Still stewing about the counting flub I nearly forgot the extended canter at H, and would have blown that movement as well if not for Cronos who tugged lightly on the reins in her eagerness to stretch out. *Good girl!*

Crossing the diagonal I had time to collect my thoughts, remember where I was in the test, and prepare for the next movement. Thank God she had a better memory than me, I thought to myself ruefully. The rest of the test flowed seamlessly, one movement into the next. Her half pass at the trot was fluid and I could feel her shoulders and haunches reaching and stretching beneath my seat. Our time spent fixing her half pass had paid off. I had the chance to collect my thoughts, take another deep breath and release my tension in the walk before shortening the reins for the rest of the test.

Once again Cronos halted squarely at X. With a crisp salute and well-deserved praise for saving my butt, we turned and left the arena at a walk, the loose reins swinging gently on either side of her neck.

Colleen, identifiable by her oversized straw hat, gave me a cursory nod, letting me know she had been able to watch part of our ride and went back to warming up Hamish and Patina. Ann, who had been standing with her, stepped lightly between two horses that were crossing paths on the dirt access road and popped up beside me like a Jack in the box as I slid exhausted from the saddle. Working from either side we ran up the stirrups and loosened the girth.

"Thanks, Ann."

"How'd it go? Did you nail it? I bet she was awesome. Hamish is up next. He is last in the class. So far his warm up is spectacular."

After umpteen cups of super latte something or other with frothy stuff on top, she was stumbling over her own words with alarming speed. Something told me that the heat of the day wasn't helping the situation either. Without giving me time to answer, she bounded off again, this time towards the main show building. I rolled my eyes at her retreating back glad, she had moved on. I liked Ann, but she needed to lay off the caffeine.

She reminded me of a mockingbird, constantly flitting about, never still for long, and chatty.

Turning my attention back to Cronos, I gave her a pat on her sweaty neck and a kiss on her nose. "Thanks girl, you saved me." She blinked and I could see my face reflected in her luminous brown eye. Twisting the crest of her neck towards me she tried once again to scratch the braids out of her mane. Oh how she hated her mane braided. "Let's get these braids out girl." Slipping off my helmet, I tucked it under my left arm. Grabbing the reins with my right hand we ambled back towards the barn, moving slowly in the oppressive heat. She seemed to know that her work was done for the day.

I missed Hamish's ride as I was cooling out Cronos and hosing her off. Rachel was on the wash rack next to us, smearing on poultice and wrapping Otter's legs for the night. Both too tired and hot to chat, we worked in companionable silence. Around us riders and grooms drifted past, each on a mission of their own. Show barns were rarely static places.

We both heard Ann prattling on before we saw her coming towards us across the grass. Rachel shot me a look of annoyance and I stifled a grin just in time. Ann really was a sweetie, but someone needed to send her to Coffee Drinkers Anonymous and yank the caffeine out of her life for good.

"OMG! You gals just missed the most hilarious thing e-v-e-r."

The mockingbird was back. Her pupils even looked dilated and I had to look twice. Ann just blinked at me like I was slow. Catching up, I said, "Oh, what did we miss?" Clearly glad that I was following her she continued. I heard a snort coming from the other side of Otter.

"So, Hamish has this picture perfect test. Well at least I would have given him mostly sevens and eights, but then he comes to his final halt at X." She paused, waiting for us to engage.

"Okay, so he halts at X," I offered. Maybe more caffeine would push her over the edge I thought to myself, a bit too enthusiastically, for she caught my grin as a sign to continue.

"Okay, so he halts, salutes, and then when he goes to leave the arena, Patina moves off in a Spanish walk towards the judge at C. Like, she really did it on her own, without his help. You know, showing off or something." She grinned like a schoolgirl sharing gossip. Raising her arms out in front of her, lifting one, then the other as the first fell, she mimicked the front leg movements of the Spanish walk. "Just like a circus horse."

Yet another snort, louder this time, came from the other side of Otter. "Did Colleen crap her pants?" Rachel glanced our way from under Otter's graceful neck.

"The whole crowd, well those that stayed until the end, you know, since he was the last ride. Anyway, they just started howling." She glanced quickly over her shoulder. Most likely to see if Colleen was within earshot and then continued. "She was furious. She went on about how Spanish walk isn't a dressage thing, it's a circus thing and about how he will mess up Patina's head and she may get confused later."

Out of the corner of my eye I saw Hamish and Patina cutting across the grass towards the barn aisle. We heard the *clop, clop* of her shoes as they reached the concrete slab under the aisle roof. Hamish's eyes were downcast.

"Hey buddy, can I buy your circus pony?" Rachel's voice was dripping with sarcasm and I had to cover my mouth with a wet hand to keep from laughing out loud.

Coming to a stop, Hamish bent over, hands on his knees and started howling with laughter. We could hear him snorting between gulps of air from where we stood. Shocked by the noises, poor Patina had jerked her head up, pulling back on the reins. Her tiny grey ears flicked to and fro, searching for danger.

When he came up for air, his face was beet red and tears flowed freely down his hot cheeks. Patina planted her warm muzzle in the small of his back, gently nudging him. Rachel had joined him and was making noises of her own as she tried to control her mirth. Ann, standing stock still in the grass, was silent for the first time all day.

"Oh, I wish you guys could have seen it. The judge at B couldn't look me in the eye," he snorted, gasping for air. "She was trying so hard not to laugh. Colleen, poor Colleen, wanted to melt into a puddle right there." He wiped the tears from his face with the backside of his muscular arm. "And the crowd," he nearly choked. "The crowd went wild, clapping and hooting. It was more like a football game than a dressage test. The judge at C looked mortified."

"How in the world did you teach her to do the Spanish walk? I mean, when did you teach her? I had no idea." Cronos shifted, pulling on her lead rope, trying to get a better view of Patina. She welcomed her with a soft nicker. Pushing her hind end over with my index finger I bent to free the bright green garden hose from under her left front hoof. Horses always found a way to step on hoses.

Wiping his face one last time, the laughter faded quickly and his eyes grew distant. "I've had some extra time on my hands the past month."

As if on cue, Elaine and Deanne drifted around the corner of the barn from the direction of the vendor tents. Elaine was leading William and Deanne had a plastic shopping bag dangling from her hand. *Speak of the Devil. Oh, Deanne, don't you know he's nuts for you?*

Elaine, noticing the recent mood shift, but not sure of what had transpired glanced at each of us in turn, trying to figure out just what was up. Turning her focus on Hamish she asked, "How did your ride go?"

Hamish recovered and managed to smile. "Well, her half canter pirouette to the right wasn't so great, but we fixed the walk." Reaching up, he scratched her sweaty forehead then led her into her stall. Rachel and I tried to stifle a snicker when he mentioned the walk.

Rachel turned her attention back to Otter. "Those two just need to get over themselves and sleep together." Rachel murmured under her breath to me, before yanking the lead rope from a metal ring on the wash rack wall. "They are perfect for each other, but neither of them can see it." I merely nodded. I had to agree. Hamish and Deanne were like two peas in a pod.

The rest of the afternoon seemed to crawl by as we waited for our score sheets to be tallied. When all was said and done, we had all garnered qualifying scores on this, our first day of competition. That in its self was remarkable, borderline amazing. Buoyed by the possibility of breezing through the qualification process, I caught myself humming as I wandered down the aisle towards the arenas. The afternoon was drawing to a close, but there were still some lower level riders left to compete and I wanted to find a spot along the rail to watch them ride.

As I passed a small set of metal bleachers, full of riders, parents, friends, and trainers who obviously had the same idea, I saw Colleen standing alone along the outer rail of the arena. Bypassing the crowded bleachers I headed her way.

"Hey." Folding my arms across the top rail, I settled in to watch. Intense in her observations, Colleen gave me a cursory nod, the brim of her hat bobbing up and down. She never seemed to tire of studying horses and riders. That, I thought was a key difference between good trainers and great trainers. She had a thirst for knowledge and never tired of watching horses.

We settled into a companionable silence for the first few minutes. Allowing my eyes to rove over the kaleidoscope of horses before us, I selected two from the group that seemed to be worth watching as they warmed up for their classes, a dark brown gelding with a mealy muzzle and a bright coppery chestnut mare with four white socks. By the looks of their warm up I guessed they were probably second level horses, but without my program, I couldn't be sure.

As I followed the chestnut mare and her rider, a tall but thick-bodied man around the arena, I caught a look of utter disgust on Colleen's face from the corner of my eye. Not sure what she had been looking at, I scanned the arena looking for the cause of her evident distaste. And then I saw it on the far side of the arena, where a short, wiry rider who appeared to be in her forties was warming her horse up. The poor black mare was being ridden horribly. As we watched, the rider circled the mare then moved off into a shoulder in. It took everything the mare had to move down the arena with her nose planted on her chest. The rider, rather than pushing the horse from behind as is correct, was instead riding with her hands, which were flopping around in time to her bouncy seat. Attempting to sit the trot and follow the motion of the horse beneath her, she instead had created a vicious cycle from which there was no recovery.

With her nose on her chest, the mare could not lift her back muscles or bring her hind legs up and under her belly, so instead she did her best to accommodate the pain in her mouth and neck caused by the rider's bad hands and backward riding. The game little horse's black tail swished back, forth and all around in a textbook display of tension while the rider bounced and pinged off the mare's now stiff back. Had she been allowed to use her hind end correctly, her back would have instead naturally lifted, creating a place for the rider to sit and softened the concussion of the trot.

"This just pisses me off. Sometimes I wonder why I choose to come to horse shows anymore," the angst in Colleen's voice was unmistakable. "What I wouldn't give to wrap a nylon cord around that woman's lower jaw, tie it to her belt buckle nice and tight, then ask her to go around like everything was normal. She'd find out real fast how much it hurts!" The brim of her hat swayed from side to side as she nodded her head in disgust. "Better yet, I'd make her run around in circles all the while yanking her head to the left and right while tied down."

By this time the veins on the mare's sweaty neck were bulging and the rider was becoming more frustrated with her efforts to sit the trot on the mare's unforgiving back. Either not having the knowledge to fix the problem or not caring, the rider simply spurred the mare on down the arena.

Looking around, I saw a lifeguard style chair with an umbrella perched on the back. Seated under the shade, clipboard on her lap was the ring steward. A well-worn paperback book sat balanced in one hand. "Well, nothing is going to be done about it with her,' I jerked my head in the direction of the steward, "on duty."

Colleen grunted, "It wouldn't matter anyway. More and more people are turning their backs on correct training because it takes too long to see results." Sighing, she grabbed the brim of her hat between two fingers as a refreshing breeze skipped across the show grounds threatening to carry it away. "Sadly, we live in a drive through society."

She snorted in disgust, "Even McDonald's isn't fast enough for some people. Everyone wants instant results, thanks in part to our instant communication, texting, internet... everything must be faster nowadays. People don't live or ride for the journey, just the goal." She sighed.

I nodded, turning to follow her as she headed toward the barns.

"Do you know how *dressage* came to be?" she inquired.

Uh oh, I thought, here comes more theory. "The usual stuff, like Xenophon. Yeah," I answered hesitantly, afraid I was wrong. I still had so much to learn about the theory and intricacies of dressage, stuff that could only be garnered with time and elbow grease.

"There's much more to it than that. As an eventer you should appreciate the necessity of dressage. Imagine if you will warfare hundreds of year ago. When soldiers went to war they were often in foreign lands or in unfamiliar territory, right?"

Again I nodded, trying to picture a scantily clad Mel Gibson wearing a kilt and charging across a field. I tried not to grin, thinking of Craig's Scottish brogue and picturing him in Mel's role, kilt and all. *Yum!* I felt myself blush, grateful Colleen was looking ahead.

Letting go of her hat, she held her arm out from her hip and made a fist. "They had a shield, say in this hand, and a weapon in the other." She held her other arm out then stopped in the dirt path. Eyeing me she continued, "How the hell do you think they directed their horses?"

I knew this. "Seat and legs," I answered. I knew this from riding cross country for so many years, but I had never stopped to make the connection with classical dressage.

"Exactly, and if you really think about it, you will realize the important partnership between a warrior and his steed. A warrior's life depended on his mount. A warhorse needed to be strong, well-muscled, fit, easily guided by seat and leg, as well as stay sound and last for many years." She chuckled softly to herself, lowering her arms. "When you jumped a cross country fence you knew what was on the other side, because you had walked the course, right? Now, imagine leaping hedges and walls, not knowing what lay beyond and trusting only in the surefootedness of your mount. Trusting in the hours you spent building the correct muscles to support his frame, to keep him sound." In the end, you are totally reliant on his ability to carry you safely into battle and then home again."

She started walking again, "Now, would you rather ride Cronos into battle, or that poor black mare with a sore neck. Over time, she has had too much strain placed on her joints from carrying her body incorrectly?" Not waiting for an answer she said, "Me, I'd take the sound horse with proper training and musculature. They stay sane and sound longer. Problem is people don't see that dressage is about the journey with your horse, not the ribbons, applause, or accolades because those all fade quickly, especially when you are forced to retire a broken down horse early."

"For me, this is not dressage," she motioned around her with a wave of her hand. "Dressage horses were meant to last a lifetime; not be broken down before they reach the age of fifteen. They were also meant to be all around riding horses. They could jump, pull carriages, and could gallop cross country. When your life depended on your mount diversity was a good thing."

"Is that why you don't compete much anymore?" I asked, hoping I wasn't being too intrusive, too personal.

She sighed, "It's a large part of it. For me, well, the way I was taught, dressage is about the journey and not the competition. As humans we feel the need to quantify everything. We quantify our worth with money, our abilities with competition, and so on."

She let out another sigh then her face changed as if something new had occurred to her. "Heck, look around you. This is the ultimate example of that. This weekend of showing is costing the average rider well over $500 in expenses just for the horse. Never mind the hotels, food, and trainers they have to pay for. This is the ultimate example of man trying to quantify dressage." She stopped and turned, "Don't get me wrong, I can be very competitive and I think competitive dressage has a place, but in the interest of quantifying who they are, people tend to rush their horses. As I said, we live in a drive through society. Our phones are fast, our food is fast, and most people," she frowned.

"Americans more than Europeans want instant results with their horses, so they resort to using all kinds of gadgets like draw reins and elaborate training systems to 'put' their horses into the position they think is correct. Or, like that rider we just saw, hand riding." She began walking again, "Sorry, I must seem so negative, but as a chiropractor I see the damage done by such things."

We had reached the barn. I processed what Colleen had said, agreeing with her. I had seen many talented event horses break down because they were rushed. For years I heard people complain about how Thoroughbred racing is cruel and ruins horses because they are raced too young. Their legs can't handle the pounding of the track, especially as two and three year olds. They haven't even finished growing at that age, and yet, I saw people jumping their horses at the age of two and three. If I really thought about it, there wasn't much of a difference.

**

Before leaving the show grounds for the day, I stopped by the concession area and found the Las Brisas tent. Troy had done a fabulous job of setting up shop for Craig. Apparently the large trunk had contained a really fabulous Goliath grouper mounted on a mahogany board. The Goliath is one of the largest groupers to be found and it looked spectacular hanging against the dark ocean blue fabric of the tent. Brochures, bumper stickers, and T-shirts lined the front table while a video played non-stop on a flat screen TV. A wicker basket full of patches with the Las Brisas logo sat on one end of the table. Game fish leapt and crashed into the ocean over and over while cameras both on board the boat and underwater captured the action. The video must have been made recently, for the new Contender was in most of the shots. Troy was resting a cold beer on one knee and sporting his Las Brisas visor.

"Where's our golden girl?" I asked, referring to the model AJ had hired.

"She left for lunch. Apparently she only eats salads and all we have around here is burgers, dogs, and sandwiches," he shrugged his shoulders.

I smiled. It was no wonder she looked like a waif, a gorgeous waif, but a waif all the same. Before leaving, I swiped a patch for my saddle pad.

******

We trickled back to the farm one by one. Hamish had done his best to avoid Colleen for the rest of the afternoon. As it turned out, Colleen was upset about Hamish's circus act, sure, but in the end she too had seen just how comical the whole scene was. Hamish agreed to lay off the circus tricks. Unbeknownst to us, he had taught her to bow as well. In the end, all four of us garnered qualifying scores in our Prix St. George classes. Tomorrow, we would ride again in hopes of achieving another round of scores. After a grueling day in the hot Florida sun we headed back to One Spirit Farm. Ann would be handling the late stall checks tonight.

With about an hour of daylight left, I slipped into my bikini and wrapped a towel around my hips. Digging into my hiding place, behind some frozen broccoli in the freezer, I pulled out a pre-frozen Acai margarita and dumped it into a red Solo cup I had found in the cupboard. Out of respect for Rachel and Troy I didn't want to bring glassware poolside with me. Besides, it wasn't a matter of if I would break something, but rather when. A bottle of Patron sat on the kitchen counter. Pulling the cork I dumped a halo of clear tequila on top of my margarita, giving it a swirl with my finger. Further digging produced a half open bag of wasabi peas, not exactly gourmet, but it would have to do.

Throwing a plastic lounge raft into the crystal clear, warm water I set the cup on the pool edge and climbed aboard. Once steady, I paddled backwards to retrieve my cup from dry land. The bag of peas sat on my towel, waiting until I docked once again.

The sun sank low over the horizon, turning the sky into a watercolor palette of gold, pinks, and raspberries. The water jets of the pool kept my raft travelling in lazy circles around the pool while I nursed my icy treat. Other than the birds in a nearby oak tree, the only sounds I heard drifted up from the barn as Katia finished up for the day. After who knows how many circumnavigations and with the colors of the sky fading to light grey, Rachel wandered out.

Stepping out of her Reef flip-flops, she walked down two steps into the pool until her legs were submerged in the warm water. The tip of her nose was pink from the sun. "Mind if I join you?"

"No, come on in, the water's fine." I pushed off from the far wall and glided towards her, causing a small wake across the surface. Stretching my right leg out, I could just grip the side of the pool with my toes and prevent my raft from drifting away. The water bounced off the sides of the pool and returned a wave that was just big enough to get my belly wet. "Oooh, that feels heavenly."

We sat in companionable silence. I liked Rachel. She didn't always feel the need to gab. That was a rare thing to find in a female friend. Calli had much the same traits and they reminded me of each other. Small, white solar lights set along the landscaped edges of the pool started to glow, giving off a soft halo of light as dusk settled. Rachel's home truly was lovely, I thought, looking around.

"I know I've thanked you and Troy already, but I wanted to take a moment and thank you again. Without One Spirit Farm's hospitality, I doubt any of us would be here."

"You are welcome, again." She smiled.

"So, where did you get the name for your farm, it is unique."

She chuckled softly, "Most people would never guess, but when I met Troy in college he was attending seminary with the hopes of becoming a pastor."

My jaw dropped open. That wasn't what I had expected. Troy? She saw the surprised look on my face.

"Shocked? Yeah, I know. Most people are. He was actually an associate pastor at a small church in Texas before his father passed." She shrugged, "There was no one else to take over the business, so here we are."

Her comment made me think about the twists and turns in life that come along and completely change the direction you were headed in. "Yeah, I can relate. Life doesn't always go as planned." *Yeah, I'd had some hair pin turns and a few roll backs.*

It must have been the tone of my voice, because Rachel gave me a questioning look. Deanne suspected, but Colleen and Craig were the only ones who knew. I wanted to keep it that way. When I didn't respond, she had no choice but to let it drop and we both went back to enjoying the quiet the surroundings.

After a few minutes Rachel piped up, "Hey, did you hear the news?"

"Hmm, what?" I said.

"Deanne saw Maria at the show today."

"What in the world was she doing there?" I replied, splashing water on my legs. Then I remembered the woman Elaine and I had seen at the shopping plaza. I had forgotten all about it.

"Don't know, but if I had to bet I would say she is trying to qualify for the games. That would be just like her, you know."

I nodded. While Maria was a nasty, grumpy person, what did I care if she qualified? Frankly I didn't think she had a chance.

**

The next day everybody rode and added another qualifying score for Prix St. George, except for Elaine. We were on a roll. William had been a handful in the warm up arena and unfortunately she was never really able to get him completely relaxed. The good sport that she was, Elaine shrugged it off and went right back to work the next day.

Tuesday morning dawned overcast and breezy. A cold front had moved through the night before, bringing with it torrents of chilly rain and the increased chance for colic. Abrupt shifts in weather patterns had the ability to affect horses in unusual ways. Colic was the most common calamity. Why a sudden drop in barometric pressure affected their gastrointestinal systems was a mystery to me, but every good horseman knew to keep one eye on their stock when the weather turned.

For the first time in several months Jake had paid me a visit last night. Unlike the nightmares, this dream was draped in happiness, not pain. I couldn't recall much about the dream after waking, but I could still hear his soft Oklahoma accent as I lay in the darkness of the room. *Oh, Jake.*

The bright green numbers of the clock read 4:12 am. With the flick of a wrist I pulled back the sheets and comforter. The room was ice cold and I was grateful I had thought to put on flannel sleepwear. Quietly grabbing a pair of socks from the top drawer of the dresser and my worn out dark green, fuzzy robe from the back of the door I slipped out into the living room.

Easing onto the cold leather of the couch, I shivered. Out of habit I ran my fingers through my curls, trying to tame them. The soft hum of the refrigerator filled the room. The blinds on the sliding glass door in the kitchen were open and I could see the lights of the barn as they cast a frosty glow on the grass behind the house. Without even looking down, I slipped on my socks. It was still too early for Ann or Katia to be starting their day, I thought. Pushing each arm through my robe, I tied the sash in a quick release knot and quietly slid the glass door open. Shoving my feet into a pair of cold rubber boots on the porch I paused, listening to the crisp morning air. I wiggled my toes, searching for warmth. They were Hamish's and at least three sizes too big, but mine were in my closet and curiosity about the barn kept me from venturing back to retrieve them. Hearing nothing but silence, I tromped across the grass, careful not to trip in the oversized boots.

Entering the light I took several more steps before the rubber boots hit the rubberized brick floor of the barn aisle. Movement at the end of the barn caught my attention and I set off in that direction. Before I reached the stall I heard an engine start in the driveway. Peering in, I saw Rachel gently scratching the neck of Louie, her Connemara pony.

"Hey, is he okay?" My voice sounded rusty in the quiet air.

Glancing up, Rachel forced a smile, "Yeah, he just had a mild colic. Bull just left. He tubed him, and now we wait. He doesn't think it is an impaction, but rather, more of an upset tummy."

"Bull?" I leaned against the open stall door. Rachel had a plastic coated stall chain across the entrance.

"He's our vet."

"Oh," I replied. "Want me to sit with you or take over?"

"I would love that. I've got to get a few last minute things done before Troy takes off for Miami this morning. Do you mind?"

"Nah, as long as Louie here doesn't mind my fashion sense," I said mockingly.

Glancing at my flannel, fuzzy robe and rubber boot ensemble, Rachel's face split into a grin. "You look perfect." She reached under his maroon colored stable blanket and checked to see that he didn't feel too warm. Pulling her arm free, she slipped under the stall guard and headed for the house.

I found a clean saddle pad in the tack room and laying it on the shavings I sat down with Louie who eyed me carefully. Poor little guy looked miserable.

"I don't blame you, buddy, I would feel the same way if someone stuck their arm up my rear and a nasty tube of oil down my gullet."

Deciding he could trust me, he shuffled over and stuck his nose on my shoulder, mouthing the green fuzzy fabric of my robe. Running my nails along his jaw with one hand I slid the other hand under his cheeks and scratched. He stood quietly, enjoying the attention. Time ticked by slowly as I sat watching him, making sure he didn't roll around in his stall or take a turn for the worse. Without a watch or my cell phone I had no idea how much time had passed before I heard Katia whistling in the aisle.

"I passed Rachel up at the house," she said slipping under the stall guard, "she sent you this." A mug of hot chocolate, its steamy goodness rising in the cold air appeared in front of me.

"God bless her," I said gratefully, taking the proffered mug of warmth. She had even dropped a couple of marshmallows on top. It smelled like chocolate covered heaven.

"Let me drop feed and I'll take over so you can have a break."

I nodded, cupping my hands around the mug. "I'll be right here."

Sensing something good was going on, Louie tried to investigate my chocolate with his muzzle. Laughing, Katia shoved his whiskered face out of the way and dipped back under the stall guard.

**

The next time I saw Rachel she was hurrying towards the covered arena, looking shell-shocked. Colleen was riding Otter while I worked with Cronos who was practically bounding around the arena enjoying the cool air. Deanne came across the grass behind her with Javier gripped firmly against her chest. Ever since she first laid eyes on Javier, he and Deanne were practically inseparable. She had run out the very next day and bought him a matching collar and leash. He even shared her bed.

Sensing her panic, Colleen brought Otter to a perfect halt out of the right lead canter against the long side. "Louie?"

"No, worse," she spat.

That got everyone's attention. For us, there were few things worse than a sick horse. Pulling Cronos up I stopped to listen.

"The benefit for Troy's charity has been moved to this!" She raised her arm up in the air, swung it around in a circle then let it drop by her side. Seeing that we were clearly lost on her point she continued, "This, the arena, my house!" Her voice rose to a hysterical pitch. Exasperated, she took a deep cleansing breath before continuing, "The hotel that we normally use has broken water pipes or something so I have to turn this," her arm swung overhead again, "into a romantic night in Tuscany by Saturday."

Taking charge, Colleen spoke first. "Okay, what can we do?" Her calm, take charge tone seemed to work on Rachel and I could see her shoulders slacken. "Just tell us and we can help. We can use the outdoor arena until then so you can start setting up now."

"We don't need this now. Not with trying to qualify, but there is no where else, I called." She looked truly apologetic. "The holidays are around the corner and every place is booked."

Deanne set Javier down, "Can the rental company simply bring all of the decorations and props here?" Javier sniffed around for a second and then was gone, chasing an unseen scent into the bushes.

"Yes, but I will have to try to find a dance floor for rent that is big enough to cover the whole arena," she replied, clearly stressed.

"We'll make it work. Let's finish our rides in the outdoor arena. Why don't you make some calls about the dance floor?" She nodded at Deanne who nodded back in acknowledgement.

After Cronos and I finished up, Deanne filled me in. Troy held a benefit every year to support overseas missions. Apparently everybody else had heard about the upcoming event and somehow I had slipped through the cracks, though they swore they told me. This left me four days to buy a dress for the event. Doing my best to beg off, Deanne put her foot down and insisted I attend for Rachel's sake. We had to stick together on this. Worse yet, Deanne had announced to the world that she was on a mission to dress me for the occasion. Elaine gave me a nudge and a conspiratorial wink in the barn aisle. On her advice I decided to give in and make the best of a day out shopping with Deanne, after all, she was a fashion diva.

I truly liked Deanne, but she had tastes in clothes that were miles above my budget, and my biggest concern was bringing her expensive tastes down to earth. Hamish laughed at me when he overheard my predicament, for which I punched him hard in the shoulder. Feigning pain, he stalked away, chuckling under his breath.

The rest of the week was spent grading the arena and setting up the decorations. Hamish worked tirelessly with the crew from the rental company to set up the arena. Deanne had been unable to get enough dance floors to cover the floor of the arena so Hamish had the brilliant idea to create a garden walkway. He laid heavy-duty plastic gardening sheets on the arena floor then covered them with wood chips. Potted plants and trees were then used to line the paths. Sparkling white lights wound up the trees and votive candles were hung from the branches, creating a softly glowing canopy.

AJ was in town, so he and Colleen would be spending some time together. He had rented a room at a hotel out on the beach. Bummed as she was for missing the party, I could tell she really wanted some time with AJ.

Friday morning Deanne and I went shopping and I was pleasantly surprised. I always knew she had taste, but I had never realized that she didn't pay full price for anything she wore. Feeling as though I was in a fashion tornado with the Tazmanian Devil, she flew in and out of shop after shop without having me try on a single dress. Assuring me that she would know it when she found it, I had no choice but try to keep up.

Sometime after lunch, or so my stomach told me, she found it. The dress was a soft matte satin in warm sunflower yellow. The bodice had a v-neck with one-inch straps over the shoulders. The shoulder straps were a shiny version of the same fabric. Another one-inch strap ran around the waist then fell down the full length skirt along either side of a rather long slit. The slit began about mid-thigh and opened up just enough when I walked to show my well-toned thighs. The back of the dress was completely open with the exception of two straps of shiny satin, which crisscrossed at the small of my back.

Hesitantly, I slipped it on and stepped out in front of the full length mirror. The sunflower hued dress screamed Tuscany and the warm summery shade of yellow stood out against my red tresses. Although it made my skin appear even fairer than it already was and my freckles stand out, I had to admit it looked good.

"See, I told you I would find it," Deanne crowed.

Turning around once more in the mirror, I decided to take the plunge. Deanne had found the dress on the clearance rack since yellow was definitely not considered part of the winter stock. We picked up a pair of nude heels at a shoe outlet and headed home.

BULL

Saturday dawned bright and sunny, especially since I had the chance to talk to Craig. He was in a hurry to head out on the water with some guests, but before he hung up he let me know that he was going to have to change his flight. I had been counting the days until he arrived and the news left me feeling hollow. I would have to wait even longer.. My mood worsened the moment we hung up. In fact, it was in the gutter. I would have loved to show him the dress, but even more, I would have loved to have him here. The distance and the time between us hurt and lately I had to work harder at counting my blessings to have found him. Pulling myself up by the boot straps, I set to work keeping my mind and hands busy.

We gave the horses the day off and pitched in to help Rachel and Troy make their event spectacular. Spreading out, we directed caterers, the lighting company, the band, and the DJ. Everybody was on a mission to get the arena transformed into Tuscany. The long shadows of late afternoon sent everyone racing back to their rooms to get ready. The temperatures would be down into the mid sixties tonight so I decided to leave my hair down to keep my shoulders warm. The first to be dressed, I headed for the kitchen where I poured myself a glass of water and drank it down. Everybody had talked about letting loose tonight and I wanted to take offensive action against the dehydrating effects of the alcohol I fully intended to consume. I had seen cases of expensive champagne unloaded from the caterer's truck earlier and I had every intention of spoiling myself.

Hearing a click down the hall, I looked up. Deanne's door opened and she stepped out in a stunning floor length strapless, black evening gown. In an understated trumpet style the dress clung to every curve of her body, then widened slightly just above her knees, forming a small train of fabric behind her when she walked. Without a single embellishment on the dress, it allowed Deanne to become the center of attention under the smooth fabric. She wore her hair softly gathered to one side, reminiscent of a Flamenco dancer, although without a flower. As she strode down the hall, a slit along the left side of the dress opened, revealing her shapely leg all the way up to mid-thigh. A pair of very sexy black heels with a single strap around her angle completed the look. With her bright red lipstick and smoky eye shadow, she was dressed to kill.

Before I had the chance to tell her how incredible she looked, Elaine stepped out behind her. She wore a bright red dress that showed off her warm tan and brunette hair. The dress was simple, elegant, and made her appear taller than she was. The red fabric fell across one shoulder to a tight fitting bodice, then clung to her body until it reached mid-thigh, from there, alternating wide strips of satin and organza hung freely from the hem, just skirting the floor. As she walked, the fabric panels flowed and moved, reminding me of the petals on an overturned rose. Shocking red lipstick finished the look.

Taking stock of each other, we let out a "wow" almost in perfect unison. It was so nice to see everyone in something other than jeans or riding breeches.

Deanne, our fashion police designee, made sure we passed muster. When she reached me I heard her cluck her tongue. *Uh, oh...* "Hair needs to be up, not down," she instructed.

"It will be cold tonight," I tried not to be defensive.

Giving me a look of disgust she shot back, "How in the hell will anyone see the back of your dress with your hair down. The back simply makes this dress."

I had to admit she was right and I let her hustle me back into the bathroom so she could remedy the situation. With skilled hands, she twisted, pinned and sprayed until my hair was up, albeit loosely. She left a few long tendrils down to give the updo a slightly tousled look. It was what Calli had called the JF or just fucked look. Staring at myself in the mirror I knew she was right. Turning around, I positioned a hand held mirror so I could view her results from behind. The dress hung much lower than I had remembered, the bottom stopped just above my underwear. *Better not move around too much, Todd. You don't want to flash some old man and give him a heart attack.* I smiled wickedly at my reflection. Deanne, standing behind me, saw the look on my face and laughed smugly, proud of her finished product.

"You clean up nicely with a little help."

"I'll take that as a compliment." I shot back with a smile. Looking back, I had actually had fun shopping with her.

She rolled her eyes at my reflection in the mirror, but I saw her red lipstick turn up at the corners. "You still need help though. Someday I'll get you out of those dark, drab colored riding breeches."

Leaving the bathroom a step behind Deanne, I felt her stiffen as she quickly stifled a gasp. Hamish stood in the kitchen with his back to us in a black tuxedo. The finely tailored lines highlighted his height and broad shoulders. For the first time, I realized that he and Craig shared the same strong, square shoulders. They must come from their father, I thought to myself. He looked absolutely, charmingly, debonair and edible. He looked like James Bond. I fought the urge to slap the back of Deanne's head to bring her to her senses. Hamish was hot and I had no doubt he was hot for her. *And you think I need help sister? Hmph!.*

Making our way towards the arena, or rather, the Tuscan garden, we ran into Troy and Rachel coming from the house. In a tux as well, Troy looked like a different man altogether. Rachel was resplendent in a cream colored, strapless lace dress with a sweet heart neckline and a straight, full-length skirt. A rose colored satin sash was wrapped around her waist and the ends of it fell down the back of her dress.

Music wafted towards us as we made our way toward the party. Tiny white lights hung from the ceiling of the arena in long strips like falling stars. Hundreds of potted trees, their trunks wrapped in lights, lined the walkways and decorated the interior space. Tiny votive candles hung from the branches of the largest trees, suspended in hand blown glass globes wrapped elegantly in copper wire. We entered the arena through a large wooden Italian-style arbor hung generously with more votive candles and fresh flowers. I was utterly amazed at the transformation from riding arena to Tuscany in just one afternoon.

Tucking my elbow under his arm, Hamish tactfully guided me away from the others as we passed through the arbor. Glancing up, he met my questioning look with a reassuring smile. One quarter of the arena served as a romantic garden, thanks to his inventive use of the portable dance floors. The party planners made great use of space by having the romantic garden spill out behind the arena and onto the grass next to the stables. Large stand alone outdoor heaters were strategically placed to provide heat if it became too chilly as the night wore on.

Stepping lightly into the garden, my senses were assaulted by thousands of hand cut fresh flowers spilling from terracotta pots and oversized floral arrangements nestled along the path. I had never seen so many fresh flowers and the smell was positively heady. "I've been given orders to keep an eye on you tonight," he said in a decidedly conspiratorial tone, from one side of his mouth. He winked exaggeratedly.

Playing along, I spoke from the side of my mouth, "Did you accept the assignment?" *James Bond*…I had to stifle a giggle and hide my thoughts.

He answered with a smile, "It was my pleasure." Growing serious, he stopped, turning me to face him. "He called me as I was getting dressed and filled me in on what happened at Las

Brisas. Good God, Lauren, how come you never told any of us?"

Not sure how much Hamish really did know, I took my time framing a response. "Um, it was really no big deal, probably a question of mistaken identity or someone with a sick sense of humor," I tried to blow it off.

"Hmph." He clearly wasn't buying it.

At that moment he looked and sounded so much like Craig, and my heart squeezed in my chest like a lemon.

"He told me all about it," he was frowning down at me, his tone admonishing. "He wanted me to tell you that they traced the huaca to a shop in downtown Panama City." He paused, studying my reaction.

My palms had begun to sweat and the unmistakable sour taste of bile rose in the back of my throat. Swallowing hard I replied, "What did they find out?"

"It was ordered and picked up by a man, or rather a boy. The jeweler said he was in his late teens or early twenties."

A boy? "Is that all we have to go on? That isn't very much."

"He gave the name of Santiago. First or last name, we don't know. Either way, Craig wanted me to keep an eye on you." He paused, as if contemplating whether to continue. Glancing around to make sure we were alone, he cleared his throat. "Also, there was another break-in at the resort." The shock must have shown on my face for he placed a comforting hand on my arm. The weight felt good, reassuring, and safe. "This time they ransacked one of the boats. That makes three incidents in the last few months." He shook his head in wonder, "We never have problems like this, especially because the resort is so far removed."

"Three?" I couldn't help the tremor in my voice as I searched his brown eyes.

Hamish looked confused, then worried. His hand fell away, leaving my skin chilled in the night air. Realizing his mistake, he quickly tried to change the course of the conversation but I would have none of it. "Three? What are you not telling me?"

Swallowing hard he quickly weighed his options then gave in. "Once before you and Craig met. Someone ransacked his bungalow." Somewhere beyond the ornamentals and fresh flowers, the band struck up a new tune.

"When?" I asked, clearly recalling the day I saw Craig in the hanger before flying to San Blas. *Was it then? I remembered seeing them talking, Craig had looked tired and upset.*

"It was a week or so before you first met, about the time we flew to the islands."

I nodded, mentally putting the timeline together. "I can't believe someone would follow me all the way here. That's just crazy. Besides, I don't have any enemies. Heck, I don't have many friends." After the words left my mouth I realized how stupid they must have sounded. "Really, this is overkill." I tried to interject some modicum of confidence into my voice.

Ignoring the last statement, he went on, "Well, you have more friends than I think you realize, and now you have your own handsome body guard." His smile was warm and sincere. "And, I must say, you will be in need of my services tonight. I'll be working full time just to keep the men off of you and that dress you're wearing." He smiled, "Best not to tell him how beautiful you look."

Playfully, I smacked his shoulder with my hand, "Come on, let's go party." Offering me his arm, we followed the sounds of music back to the party.

We all managed to squeeze into the same table. Katia had joined us with her date, a rather subdued but amiable guy whose name I quickly forgot after one glass of champagne. Dinner was incredible and I found myself wishing I could simply loosen the top button of my jeans so I could enjoy everything on my plate. Frowning down at my gorgeous dress, I was beginning to view it as a prison, especially when I only had room for half of my tiramisu. Oh well, I thought, at least the champagne is fabulous.

A not so silent auction followed next. Troy had managed to procure donations from some fabulous companies. They included spa certificates, riding lessons, a fishing trip to Las Brisas, and fine artwork, among other things. The grand prize was a date with the man considered to be Wellington's most eligible bachelor. Poor sucker, whoever he was.

I felt my phone vibrating in my purse, just as the last item, or rather the date, was called to the stage. Snatching my phone up, I saw Craig's name flashing on the screen. Hastily excusing myself, and pleased to have an excuse to leave before the auction started, I headed out onto the lawn and away from the festivities so we could talk.

Craig filled me in, including everything Hamish had already told me. Dad was working things from his end and trying to track down the mysterious Santiago. I made sure he knew that his donation of a fishing trip had brought in a very large bid for Troy's charity. Unfortunately he still didn't know when he would arrive. He had almost sounded evasive when I had asked. After saying our goodbyes I hurried back to the party, not wanting to be rude. Again, my heart felt heavy. I was becoming tired of the emotional roller coaster our phone calls elicited. My emotions would swing upward in anticipation when he called, then crash and burn when we hung up, leaving me feeling hollow and empty. It wasn't because I didn't think he cared, I just needed him. *I needed to be touched, to feel him physically. I needed more than words.*

Pushing those thoughts aside, I made a beeline for the bar to get another glass of champagne. The music had shifted while I was talking to Craig, and the pulse of the party changed. Tapping my toe to the beat of the popular dance music, I placed my order. The bartender handed me a glass and I reached for my purse. The hot flush of embarrassment ran across my chest and neck when I realized my purse still sat on the table.

"Here you go."

My heart jumped in my chest in reaction to the smooth, soft, earthy drawl of an Oklahoma accent as a tuxedoed arm reached from behind me, handing the bartender a tip. Turning, I was caught off guard by the most charming of smiles. He looked me square in the eye, boldly, almost daring. His ice blue eyes met and held my gaze and my knees grew weak.

"Um, thank you. I, um, forgot my purse at the table," I glanced over his shoulder towards the table where I could see the back of Hamish's dark head. He turned, and followed my gaze.

"Boyfriend," he inquired.

Butterflies took flight in my belly. Oh Lord, he sounded like Jake. I shook my head, taking a sip of the effervescent champagne. Tiny bubbles of the sweet, cold liquid slid down my dry throat. He was my height with blonde hair, broad shoulders and a decisively athletic build. "Well, um, thank you." *Push off, Todd. Now, before...*

Leaving the bar and Mr. Oklahoma behind, I pushed off, setting course for the safety of Hamish and the girls. Halfway to the table I noticed my hand shaking. Not wanting to spill my champagne, I clutched the flute with both hands and wound my way through the tables. I could still hear the smooth dulcet tones of his Oklahoma accent in my head.

As soon as I arrived, Rachel and Elaine dragged me out onto the dance floor. Downing my champagne in two gulps I barely had time to set it down. In my hurry to not waste my drink, I had lost track of Deanne and I scanned the crowd looking for her. No luck. We stayed on the dance floor for several songs. Working up a thirst, we headed back to the table where Hamish sat alone, looking thoroughly morose. Just then Deanne came bounding up with a cute boy toy in tow. She was flushed with alcohol and excitement.

"Who's your young friend?" The ice in Hamish's voice caught me off guard.

Either choosing to ignore him or simply not noticing his barb, she pulled her dance partner forward for all of us to meet. He looked to be in his early twenties and good looking in a metro-sexual playboy sort of way. *So not my type.* A glass in each hand, he passed one to Deanne. "Here baby doll, I got you a drink. Drink up."

Baby doll? Rachel and I exchanged glances and she mouthed, "Baby doll?"

He had shocking blonde hair, a slim but muscular build, and what looked to be a very, expensive tuxedo. His roving eyes met my breasts rather than my face with a seditious leer. In fact, he met everyone other than Hamish the same way, or at least, everyone who sported breasts. When introduced to Hamish, he snaked one arm protectively around Deanne and pulled her towards him tight. He nearly succeeded in pulling her off her feet, which caused her in turn to spill nearly half of her drink. He scowled, "Hey now, you need to drink it, not wear it," he scolded. Grabbing her glass he righted it so she wouldn't spill anymore. It bothered me that Deanne didn't seem to be fazed by his possessive behavior in the least.

She introduced him as Kincaid and rather than shake his hand, Hamish simply nodded menacingly at him. I couldn't really blame him, the more I was around him, the more Kincaid, the playboy, made my skin crawl. He was cocky as hell. Apparently he was from the Hamptons and his father was a real estate tycoon, as if that was supposed to mean something to us.

In the background, the band switched to something slow and Kincaid propelled Deanne back onto the dance floor. Rachel shot me a look of concern from across the table, then walked around and stood by my side. Turning our backs to the table, we tried to keep Deanne in our sights through the throng of party goers.

"This guy gives me the creeps." Rachel crossed her arms and shifted her weight onto one leg.

Nodding, I replied, "I've never seen her act this way. She's-" I was at a loss for the right word, but Rachel nodded just the same, as if we shared the same thought.

"Would you care to dance?"

My heart jumped in my chest when I heard his voice above the music. Mr. Oklahoma had slipped in next to me. With a tilt to his head, he waited patiently for my answer. I so wanted to keep a keen eye on Deanne and the dance floor would be the perfect place to be. Before I could answer, Rachel slipped in front of me.

"Bull, I should have known it was going to be you tonight." Her eyes lit up when she saw him. Her smile was warm and sincere. "I mean, who else could be classified as the most eligible bachelor in Wellington?" She flung her arms around him and gave him a hug. Stepping back, she grabbed me by the arm, turning me until I faced him, "Lauren, this is my dear friend, Bull Callahan."

Before me stood Mr. Oklahoma. Nodding politely, I kept one eye fixed on the dance floor. Dang it, Deanne, where did you go I thought to myself, trying not to be rude to Rachel's friend.

With a shove, Rachel pushed me towards Bull. Her eyes were as big as saucers. They flashed towards the dance floor then back at Bull. Picking up her cue, I smiled sweetly at Bull, "Yes, I would love to dance." Never taking my eyes off of Deanne's blonde hair moving through the crowd, I nearly dragged Bull behind me towards the dance floor. Finding a good spot to cautiously observe Deanne and Kincaid I stopped, turned, and offered him my left hand.

For such a big man, he was surprisingly agile and light as he guided my every step. Craning my neck every time we turned, I was able to keep my targets in sight while we danced.

"Whom are we spying on?" Catching me off guard, his voice made me jump and my palms began to sweat.

Caught in the act, suddenly I felt guilty. With nothing to lose I decided to fess up and come clean, "The blonde bombshell in the black gown at three o'clock." No sooner had I gotten the words out, when he dipped me. Bending backwards towards the dance floor, I could feel his strong hand behind the small of my back, skin on skin. *Oh geez.* His focus was not on me, but straight through the crowd towards Deanne and Kincaid. Pulling me upright with ease, he smiled wickedly at me and continued to dance, holding me close. Too close. He kept his hand in the small of my back and I could feel my blood pounding.

"Kincaid, huh? Your friend sure knows how to pick 'em."

Suddenly wary, I asked, "You know him?"

"Missy, everyone in town knows *of* him, or wished to hell they'd never met him." He spun me again so I could see Deanne clearly over his massive shoulder.

"It's Lauren, not Missy," I said.

"Seth."

Confused, I turned from Deanne and looked him in the eye. His smoke blue eyes were full of laughter and sparkled with a hint of mischief.

"Bull is my nickname," he offered by way of explanation, a smile splitting his ruggedly handsome face. He was big, muscular, and built like a linebacker. I could see the hint of a long faded scar running from the corner of his left eye to his temple.

"Pain in the ass, are we?" I looked him squarely in the eye, challenging. Damn, I could feel the champagne kick in the more my pulse raced, the more we danced.

He laughed out loud and more than a few heads turned in our direction. "I like you, missy. You've got spunk." Suddenly my view changed as he dipped me one last time as the music faded. Leaving me there, suspended, held up only by his massive arm, he smiled. "Nope, job hazard."

With that, he righted me, kissed the back of my hand and stalked away, laughing to himself. I stood frozen, confused, watching him move through the crowd. He left me shaken and unsure of… I couldn't quite put my finger on it. As I watched, people went out of their way to stop and talk to him, nod their head, or pat him on the shoulder or back as he threaded his way towards the bar. Obviously, Mr. Oklahoma was well liked.

Rachel and Hamish were gone when I got back to the table and Elaine sat nursing her drink. Lost in thought, I startled her when I pulled out a chair and sat, "Where did everyone go?"

"Troy is running around making sure his guests are okay, and Rachel joined him. Hamish stormed off right after you left, and I needed to get off my feet. These heels are killing me. I'm going to have to ride without stirrups for a week just to get my calf muscles to relax enough to lower my heel again."

"Ditch the heels."

Frowning at her feet, which were propped up on the chair next to her she said, "Seriously considering it." Playing with the tablecloth between her thumb and forefinger she glanced up, "Is that leech Kincaid still hanging on Deanne? I swear that guy is up to no good. I simply can't understand why she and Hamish don't just get over themselves so we can all be one big happy dysfunctional family again." She smiled at her humor.

"Crap! I forgot to see where they went." Shoving back my chair, I grabbed my champagne glass. Elaine shot me a knowing smirk before I managed to escape from the table. "Crap, good going Todd," I mumbled under my breath. I headed for the bar to refill my drink and began a grid search for Deanne and Mr. Playboy. I couldn't get rid of the nagging feeling in my gut that he was trouble. Mr. Oklahoma, um, Bull had confirmed just that. Drink in hand I headed for the Tuscan garden to begin my search.

Nearly fifteen minutes later I had covered the garden twice, the tables, bar, dance floor and lawn, and still no Deanne. Starting to panic, I stood on the lawn with my back to the house. The temperature had dipped quite a bit during the evening, but unless you were out in the open you wouldn't have noticed. The space heaters and crush of bodies under the arena had made for a much warmer feeling. The wind picked up and I shivered hard as it raced across my exposed skin and through the thin fabric of my dress. I could feel millions of tiny goose bumps rise to the occasion along my arms and back. *Where are you, Deanne?*

The sharp crack of a horseshoe meeting a stall door drifted towards me, born on the night wind. "What have you got to lose, Todd?" I muttered, changing course. Teeth clenched against the chill, I struck out for the barn, hurrying across the grass and out of the wind.

The lights of the barn were off as I stepped under the overhang. Waiting for my eyes to adjust I slipped off my heels. I didn't want to disturb any horse that may have lain down to sleep. Stooping down, I gathered my heels by the straps, twining them in my fingers. On the way back up, I grabbed a handful of my dress in the other hand.

The rubber brick floor felt good to my tired feet as I padded down the aisle. About half way down the aisle I thought I heard a noise. "Deanne?" I whispered. Standing stock still, I waited for a response but heard nothing. Continuing down the aisle I peered into each stall, subconsciously performing a barn check on each horse. Old habits die hard, I thought, shrugging my shoulders.

Reaching the end of the barn I stared out into the night sky. There were few lights at this end of One Spirit Farm, and the flat expanse of Florida grasslands extended from the end of the pasture fence westward towards the center of the state under a cover of darkness. A horse shifted nervously in a stall down the aisle, pulling my attention back to my search.

Reluctantly I left the quiet darkness and headed back towards the party. I could feel the muscles of my cold face tight with worry. "Where in the hell did you go?" I muttered aloud.

Down the aisle, a nervous horse threw its chest against the stall door and I heard a feed bucket rattle as it hit the ground. Hitting resistance, the horse started to weave frantically back and forth. I could see the whites of its eyes as I trotted down the aisle, my shoes banging against my leg. The nervous horse was Nicola and as I neared her stall I heard noises from within.

"Bitch! I'll teach you." The male voice was raspy, the words formed with each new breath. "Ouch," the voice hissed in surprise. It was followed by a loud *smack* and a whimper, a decisively female whimper.

Fear snaked up my spine. Hurrying, I unlatched the stall and flung it open. "Deanne!" I screamed as Nicola bolted for the door, desperate to get out. Jumping aside, my shoes hit the ground, and I let her go, hoping she would be noticed and elicit a search.

The interior of the stall was dark, but I could see the stark white hair that could only belong to Kincaid practically glowing like a beacon. Stooping, I picked up Nicola's hard, plastic feed bucket in both hands. Raising it over my head, I crossed the stall as fast as I could in the restrictive dress. Using every ounce of upper body strength I aimed the bucket towards his head.

He had heard me coming and was prepared. The bucket made a glancing blow off his head and my forward momentum sent me sprawling into the shavings. As I hit the ground I could hear them scuffling around. Getting to my feet I screamed, "Get off her, you pig! Get off!" Instinct kicked in and pulling my leg back, I sent a driving blow into what I thought was his midsection. My bare foot made contact with his gut and I felt the soft tissues of his midsection give way with a sickening, squishy feeling. With a grunt, he rolled off Deanne and for the first time I could see her blonde hair against the dark backdrop of the stall as she scurried backwards in the shavings.

"We're not finished yet, bitch." He was gasping for air. One arm clutching his belly, he started towards Deanne on his knees, his white hair moved ghostlike in the dark.

I heard screaming and the sound of running feet coming down the aisle. He had reached Deanne, and letting go of his belly he grasped handfuls of her dress with both fists like a mad man. Yanking hard, she slid towards him in the shavings and the sound of tearing satin cut through the night. I could hear her struggling beneath him. "Help," I screamed, my voice sounding foreign and weak. I started back towards him.

Out of nowhere, a massive dark form hit me from the side, scooping me up and carrying me backwards towards the rear of the stall and safety. My feet left the ground and a pair of huge arms engulfed me. Behind us, the sickening, crunching noise of a fist connecting with someone's gut was followed by a sharp intake of breath and a shocked gasp. A second later the sound of a fist meeting bone reverberated through the stall and the overhead lights flicked on. My eyes, having grown accustomed to the dark ached and burned. Fighting to keep out the bright lights, I buried my face into what I guessed to be a tuxedoed covered chest. It smelled good. Clean. Manly. The huge arms wrapped around me, creating a cocoon of warmth and safety.

"Oh God, Deanne," it was Rachel's voice. Lifting my head, I tried to peer through slits in my eyelids. The painfully bright lights made it impossible to open them fully and I crammed them shut.

"Keep them closed a bit longer, your pupils need to adjust. They dilated too rapidly."

The soft Oklahoma drawl was soothing and I buried my face into the front of his tuxedo. Beneath his jacket and shirt lay a rock hard, muscular chest. The well-tailored tuxedo aptly hid just how massive his upper torso was. I felt his huge arms shielding me from the melee in the stall as the punches continued, one after another.

"Stop it, Hamish, you're gonna kill him." It was Rachel's voice. The punches continued. "Bull, do something." She was pleading now, but he just shook his head.

I heard more feet running down the aisle and felt Bull twist slightly to see who it was.

"Hamish, that's enough." It was Troy's voice. *Hamish?*

"Hamish, I said that's enough." Troy's voice grew louder, sharper. "You've made your point."

Cracking my eyelids I pulled away from Bull and scanned the stall. Hamish's tux was ripped along the shoulder seam and he stood bent over, hands upon his knees sucking in gulps of air. His jet black hair was a mess and his sweaty face was beet red with anger and exertion. Straightening, he flexed his right hand, studying his bloody knuckles intently, as if they belonged to someone else. He turned his hand over and flexed it again.

In the corner of the stall, curled up under the automatic water trough, Kincaid cowered. His face was bloodied, one eye had already begun to swell, and his nose sat at an odd angle to the rest of his once pretty face. Rachel was bent over, comforting Deanne whose eyes were glazed and unfocused.

"You crazy bastard," Kincaid grew suddenly brazen and sliding out from under the trough he tried to stand up. "How dare you hit me, do you know who I am?" With one hand on the wall, he managed to get his feet under him and stand up. "You'll be hearing from my attorney." He reached inside his coat pocket for his phone.

Letting go of me, Bull moved swiftly across the stall. Grabbing Kincaid's small wrist in a vise grip he said, "Call them, really? And tell them what exactly? That you were trying to rape someone or maybe that you drugged her and then tried to rape her?" Bull towered over him.

Kincaid's face looked pinched as he winced under Bull's grip. The cell phone slipped from his hand, dropping to the shavings below. "I didn't drug her, and besides, the bitch asked for it. She was hanging all over *me* tonight. I have plenty of witnesses that will say she was drunk and chasing after *me*," he sneered. "Besides, you can't prove a thing. Me, just look at my face, I'm the damaged party."

Hamish lunged at Kincaid, trying to claw his way past Bull. Moving swiftly, Bull planted one hand in the middle of Hamish's chest, effectively stopping his charge. The two men exchanged looks and Hamish backed down.

Turning his focus on Kincaid, Bull threw him hard up against the wall. "I've ridden bulls with balls the size of your head punk, and won. So if you think I'm scairt of you, you're dumber than you look." Kincaid's eyes grew big and his mouth opened and closed like a fish out of water.

"He can't breathe, Bull," Troy said, "set him down."

It was then that I noticed Kincaid's pricey black dress shoes wiggling just above the shavings.

Holy crap!

"What did you give her?" Bull had released his grip enough for Kincaid's feet to just barely reach the ground. "Kit Kat? Ruffies?" Kincaid simply glared at Bull defiantly. "Would you rather I punch you or let him finish the job," he said, jerking his head toward Hamish who had caught his breath and was now standing up. "Either way, we are going to mess with that pretty face of yours."

Panic flashed across his face for a split second in time then was replaced with a wary cockiness. "I'm not stupid enough to confess. Besides, she's fine. No harm, no foul," he sneered.

Deanne had managed to stand up with Rachel's help. Her gorgeous dress was torn to pieces. One tear, where her slit had been, ran all the up the left side, exposing her waist and lacy black underwear. Hamish quickly shrugged out of his torn jacket, wrapping it gently around her shoulders. Her hair was full of shavings and her mascara made her eyes look bruised. Her gaze was decidedly unfocused and she looked lost and small.

The trauma nurse kicked in full gear and I rushed to evaluate her. Reaching for her hand, I slid my fingers down her wrist. Glancing at my watch I counted each beat beneath my cold fingertips. It was a bit on the slow side, considering what just happened I would have expected it to be faster. Dropping her wrist, I pried one eyelid open. Her pupils weren't excessively dilated or contracted. Holding my index finger in front of her I said, "Deanne, honey, follow my finger." Her eye movement lagged a little behind the motion. Reaching out, she grabbed my finger, wrapping her hand around it. "Stop, I'm okay. I just want to go to bed." She looked exhausted. Without warning, she slid to the ground in a heap of black silk and shavings.

Hamish was by her side almost instantly. He stooped down in front of her, wrapping his arms around her. "Put your arms around me." Like a sleepy kid she complied, and he pulled her to her feet. Once standing, he scooped her up in his arms and headed out of the stall towards the guesthouse.

"We caught her." The sound of a man's voice pulled our attention from the stall to the barn aisle.

"Thanks man, take her down there. Someone will take care of her." Hamish was short, his consonants clipped and business-like.

Within moments Nicola stood at the stall entrance with a vaguely familiar man holding her halter. Her lips played with the shiny lapel of his tuxedo.

"Thank you, Rob. I'll take her." Rachel moved quickly to take charge. Trying to divert Rob's attention from the scene in the stall, she continued, "Why don't you come down here and give me a hand with her. Is Katia around, is that who..." her voice trailed off. After an astonished glance into the stall, Rob obediently followed her down the aisle.

Troy stepped up to take charge of the mess. "Bull, he's right. As much as we want him to pay for what he did to Deanne, he'll drag all of us into court for assault. We know who is right and who is wrong, but with his high-powered, big shot attorneys from up north, the water will get muddy very quickly.

"Stalemate, is that what you are saying, Troy." Bull still had Kincaid pinned against the wall. "Shit, you know that's not right!" Bull was still seething.

"Better listen to Troy or I will set my lawyers loose on you, on all of you." His one remaining eye, the other having swollen shut had a wild look to it as he spat the words.

Bull gave the front of Kincaid's shirt a quick, hard jerk for emphasis.

"Let him go, Bull, he'll get what is coming to him. Men like him always do, it is just a matter of time. Besides, there are two sides to every coin and unlike Vegas, what happens in Wellington, rarely stays in Wellington." He shot Bull a conspiratorial look.

Bull let go, but didn't move. Once free, Kincaid ran his hands through his hair. Surveying the damage to his tux he glared at Bull, willing him to step aside. When he didn't, Kincaid was forced to walk around him. As he passed Troy, he said, "Smart move."

"I'll follow you out and make sure you find your car okay, and Kincaid, I don't think I need to tell you that you are never welcome in my home again. For that matter, if I see you on my street or anywhere near one of these girls I will disregard what I am sure would be the sage advice of several of my attorneys, and hand you over to Bull. Are we clear?" With a smirk, Kincaid headed down the aisle. Troy was just a few steps behind.

And then there were two. The strange thought crossed my mind. Looking up, I felt Bull's eyes on me. Smoothing out my dress with both hands I was suddenly reminded of the night Craig had found Stitch and me. At least this dress wasn't ruined, I thought ruefully.

A growing unease crept through me. For a moment, I felt as though I had been cheating on Craig. While not in the biblical sense, I hadn't at all minded when Bull had his arms around me. In fact I had felt safe and comfortable, secure. I quickly squashed the feelings that were beginning to surface, along with the idea of being with another man. *Ooops, I didn't mean it like that.* I grew more desperate to squelch the thoughts that bubbled to the surface. It's just nerves, I told myself sternly. *Just nerves.*

"Missy, I mean Lauren, you sure have a penchant for trouble don't you?" He broke the ice by speaking first.

Hands shaking with nervousness, I tried in vain to tuck a few wild strands of hair behind one ear. He was a nice mix of Jake's Oklahoma charm and Craig's sensual charm. I shook my head hard, trying to round up the thoughts going around in my head. "So I'm told, listen, thank you for helping out, but I better go check on Deanne." I moved to leave, not wanting to be alone with Bull.

He chuckled softly. "I don't reckon that boy is going to want anyone around her but him."

"What do you mean?" I wanted to re-check her vitals. I still didn't know what she had been given or how much.

"Oh, right, your eyes were shut," there was a twinkle in his eye when he said it and I felt myself flush with embarrassment at the memory of his arms around me. "That guy is head over heels for her."

"What makes you say that?"

"When a guy lays into another guy like he did, well he is either defending his family or his love, and she doesn't look much like family." His grin spread from ear to ear like a kid with a secret. It made him look even more attractive and totally inconsistent with his very manly physique.

Not sure of his logic I simply nodded, my curls tumbling free from the few pins that still remained. With one hand I deftly searched for the rest, pulling them free one by one and letting my hair fall. Clutching the pins tightly in one hand, I searched for a clean goodbye. "Well, it was nice meeting you, goodnight." I turned and headed for the guesthouse.

As it turned out, Bull was right. When I got back to the guesthouse, Hamish had put Deanne in his room on the spare bed. The door was closed and Javier sat just outside his door looking mournful, his black and white face resting across one paw. Exhausted, I gratefully took a hot shower. After picking wet shavings out of the shower drain, I wrapped an oversized towel around me and sat on my bed trying to find the rest by feel. At some point my body must have given out on me as I woke with a start in the middle of the night, still somewhat wrapped in my damp towel with a blanket over me. *Thanks, Elaine.* Elaine slept soundly in the next bed. Jake had occupied my dreams, only they weren't the usual nightmares. I had no doubt that meeting Bull tonight had brought Jake to the forefront of my dreams.

Wiggling out of my damp towel, I fumbled around in the dark for something to sleep in. I pulled what felt like an old T-shirt from a drawer and climbed back into bed.

**

Deanne and Hamish spent most of the next day in his room. Elaine finally dragged Javier outside in an effort to perk him back up. Within seconds he had picked up a scent and was bolting towards the pastures on the east side of the property. Although it still disturbed me that Deanne may have been given something, I had to let it drop. She was obviously better according to Hamish's report when he surfaced in the kitchen to make her lunch.

Today we concentrated on cleaning up our freestyle routines. Rachel rode first on Otter and Troy filmed her. The refined sounds of classical music flowed through the loud speakers as she rode her test. Colleen wanted to have it filmed so we could make sure that Otter's transitions in the arena were occurring in time with the music. This way she could have Troy make any last minute changes to the musical score if necessary. Looking bored, Otter went through the motions of each movement, but Rachel struggled to get the pizzazz that he normally exhibited.

Sitting on Cronos waiting for our turn, I found myself yawning as well. The music, while a good fit for Otter, just wasn't my cup of tea. I smiled, wondering if I could pull off a freestyle routine to Lynard Skynyrd's *Sweet Home Alabama*. Now that would rock the house.

Colleen waved us over to the arena and gave us a few minutes to warm up before the staccato sounds of the *Mission Impossible* theme filled the air around us. I had laughed when Colleen had first selected our music. *Mission Impossible* couldn't have been more fitting, especially considering our journey to get here. We rode our test with just a few bobbles, but it was good enough for today's purposes. Leaving the arena, I passed Elaine and William. Still tired and a tiny bit hung over from last night I didn't stay to watch her ride, but I could hear the trumpets and trombones of her 1940's Big Band music back at the barn.

Cleaning up Cronos and wiping down my tack took only about thirty minutes. Glancing at my watch, I hurried back to the guesthouse to shower and change before running to the store. Craig would be calling around five o'clock today and I wanted to make sure I was alone so we could talk freely. He said he was still working on his schedule, but it would probably be sometime next week before he made it out. I was finding it harder and harder to concentrate on my riding rather than on the calendar where I had scrawled his name on his original arrival date. That was days ago, and the bold black marker seemed to mock me. I was beginning to wonder if Craig was having second thoughts about us. *Why was it so dang hard to come see me? Couldn't he leave the resort for me?*

We had our Intermediare ride this coming weekend and although Colleen assured us we were ready, I found myself dreading it. This and the freestyle were going to be the hardest tests for me.

As I reached for the sliding glass door to the kitchen, Javier appeared from nowhere and darted through my legs. Once inside, he made a beeline for Deanne's room. After checking both beds to assure himself that she wasn't there he ran back down the hall, his tiny nails clicking against the wooden floor until he reached Hamish's door. Wedging his little black nose under the crack between the floor and the bottom of the door he sniffed intently, until he picked up Deanne's scent. "Poor Javier," I muttered, "in less than twenty-four hours you've been bumped to the end of the line behind Hamish. I'm beginning to know how you feel. Come here." Following me with his liquid brown eyes, he ran to one side of the door as I turned the knob and let him in. Deanne's joyous laughs and Javier's whimpers were followed by Hamish's mumblings. As I let go of the handle I heard, 'Thanks, Lauren.' It was Deanne, but how she knew it was me that let him in, I had not the faintest idea.

**

Rachel and I drove over to the show grounds in the trailer. We were going to have to make two trips today, what with all of the horses and gear. Katia was already at the show grounds with Hamish and Deanne, while Ann and Elaine stayed behind at the farm. Although most of my life had involved horses, it still amazed me just how much stuff they required. Actually, I thought ruefully, they didn't require much of anything really; all of the accoutrements were solely for the use of the riders.

Rachel pulled out of the wrought iron gates and slowly onto the street in front of One Spirit Farm. Pausing in the street, she waited for the automatic gates to shut behind her before rolling forward again. Picking up speed, we headed towards the show grounds to begin our day.

Rachel waited for me to hang up with Colleen, who had made a last minute run to the tack store for a new girth. "Troy spoke to some of his business associates about Kincaid and what happened the other night." She glanced at me before turning her focus back to the road ahead. I nodded, waiting for her to go on. "All of his, shall we say, engagements that he was to attend this weekend have excluded him."

"You mean they've shut him out of Wellington society," I drew the last two words out in a mock British accent.

"Exactly," she sighed and a look of wonder crossed her face. "Sometimes Troy amazes me with just how many influential people he really knows. He doesn't ever flaunt it or use it," she cleared her throat, "well, I've never seen him flaunt it, but he definitely used his influence this week. Word is that pretty boy is heading home to the Hamptons before the season is over." Imitating me she drug out the word 'Hamptons' in a near perfect British accent, which set us both to giggling.

Catching my breath I switched subjects, hoping not to sound eager or worse, interested. Well beyond the normal curiosity. "What's the deal with Bull? I mean, with the nickname and all?" I had found myself wanting to know more about him, but hadn't had the chance before now. I felt comfortable asking Rachel, especially without the rest of the gang around.

From where I sat I could see the corner of her mouth turn up in a smile. "Seth is his real name. He was born in Oklahoma, but went to vet school in Texas. That is where I met him. Remember I told you that I used to ride western, well that is how we met." She stopped talking for a moment and concentrated on maneuvering the rig through a narrow right hand turn at the first intersection. "He was one hell of a bull rider. He competed on the intercollegiate team in college. He got a scholarship doing what he loved and that is how he paid for most of his schooling. During the summers he worked at a big ranch that specialized in prize winning bucking bulls." Glancing to see if she had my attention, she continued, "He was the guy that got to try them out for the first time, see if they were worth keeping."

"Wow," was all I could muster.

"He is the real deal, you know, what you see is what you get. Bull has never been one to play games with people. I think that is why people love him or hate him. He has a way of weeding the bad ones out." Turning on her blinker, she studied her side view mirror before changing lanes. "He's also a damned good vet, very instinctive. I think that comes from being raised on a ranch. You know, a lot of vets love animals, but only a special few really *know* animals if you get my drift." Looking to change lanes again in order to get into the entrance of the show grounds, she peered across me into the passenger side mirror.

"You're good," I offered. Pulling up in front of the barn to unload, we shifted gears and got to work with the horses.

SHOW TIME

I decided not to go with everyone to get breakfast from one of the food trucks at the show grounds. I never could eat before a show, no matter how hard I tried. It had been that way as far back as I could remember. The one time I had caved and eaten a bacon and egg biscuit the morning of cross country I had nearly lost it between a trakhener, fence number 13, and a solid stone and timber corner combination at 14 a and b. Never again would that happen. I had learned to subsist on beef jerky, a bag of sour Skittles candy, and a steady supply of Coke. This diet worked only after I had competed and the jitters associated with showing had passed.

I smiled, remembering Mom fussing at me before every show to eat. I still had the video of that fateful cross country ride in which you could see my head disappear on the far side of Mac's shoulder at a full gallop, only to pop back up about two strides before the corner combination. Mac had been my first Preliminary horse and he was aptly named Mac Truck. Like the good solid eventer he was, he just kept trucking along while I fought down the nausea and clung to his neck at a gallop.

The early morning sun felt heavenly on my face. I had pulled two folding chairs out of the tack stall, one for my butt and one for my feet. I was already dressed and ready to go for my class. I had on a pair of old scrub pants that had followed me home from work one day and underneath them, my new white, full seat breeches that Craig had bought me. I intended to stay clean while I worked around the horses. My white show shirt, black belt, and neatly pinned stock tie were all in place. My boots sat beside the chair, freshly polished. I would keep my sneakers on until the last possible moment. I had even pulled my hair back in a chignon and slipped my navy colored snood over it. Now, I could relax and envision the perfect test in my head, visualizing each movement and cue as I would ride them later.

The myriad of sounds associated with a horse show in full swing were all around me. Somewhere to my left I could make out the sounds of water buckets being dumped, cleaned, and refilled from a spigot. Overhead the announcer's voice reminded everyone of the official show time, which was 9:18. Behind our tack stall was a gelding that wasn't coping well with the disappearance of his stable mate and decided to let the whole barn know about it. His kicks rang out every few minutes, along with an angry shout from his groom. Coming down the aisle towards me I could hear the crunch of what sounded like boots on the concrete barn aisle. Wait, they didn't sound quite like boots, lighter, maybe? They were definitely not tennis shoes. Dress shoes? I played the guessing game with a lazy smile on my face.

My cell phone on my hip began playing the theme song from the Pink Panther. Groaning at the interruption, I opened my eyes and gave up on trying to ride my test in my head. Pulling it free, the screen identified Deanne's name with a picture of her from our trip to the San Blas Islands. "Hey girl," I answered.

Her voice was edgy. "Have you seen Javier? I've lost him." In my mind's eye, I could see the panic on her face.

"No, last I saw you took him with you when you went to breakfast. Was he on his leash?"

"No!" she squeaked. "I took him off for just a minute and he's gone. Maybe he headed back to the barn." She tried to sound hopeful, but I could tell she was freaking out.

"All right, I'll start looking." I clicked off her call as I swung my feet down from the chair. Sensing a pair of eyes on me, I glanced up and saw a man standing above me, with a quizzical look on his face. He was dressed in a pair of khaki slacks, a patterned Tommy Hilfiger button up shirt with short sleeves, woven belt, and matching alligator loafers. Ah, loafers, not boots. I had my answer. He was tan, my age, and had hazel eyes that leaned more toward golden.

"I am so sorry, I didn't mean to eavesdrop, but are you looking for a lost dog?" His accent was unmistakably Latin. He flashed a bright white smile that should have been in a dental commercial. The sun sparkled off of a large diamond earring in his left ear lobe, lending him a very metro-sexual look.

I stood up, pulling the chair out of the way as I did. "Um, yes, have you seen a Jack Russell about this tall?" I held apart my hands to indicate just how small Javier was.

"You do realize that all dogs must be leashed when on the show grounds."

Oh great, I thought. This guy must be a member of the show staff. I bet he'd love to throw Javier into the dog gulag. He certainly wasn't dressed to ride.

"He's not mine. Listen if you find him could you announce it overhead. I'm going to go look for him. My friend is really upset." With that, I headed off toward the trailer parking at the end of the barn row. He stood watching me go, and I could feel his eyes on my back.

After searching around the trailers I took a moment to survey my surroundings, trying to think where the little bugger might have run off. Behind me was a large retention pond, its banks lined with tall reeds and cattails. Lord, I hope he didn't go that way, I thought. The chances that there was a gator lying in the murky water was pretty likely, and Javier would have made a perfect snack, gator bait to be exact. Changing course, I headed past the blue and white temporary tent stables, calling as I went. There were two extra barn tents set up to accommodate the overflow from the permanent barns, but I knew from hand walking Cronos around the grounds that there were coarse limestone foundations for additional tents beyond those already set up. The winter crowd had still not reached its peak, at which time there would be the two permanent barns and up to eight additional tent structures. As I cleared the corner of the last tent, walking wide to avoid tripping on one of the support stakes, I heard my name.

"Lauren."

The show staffer with the super bright smile I had met in the barn aisle was heading my way, waving an arm to get my attention. *Crap! It was the dog gestapo.* That was odd, I thought. I hadn't remembered giving him my name. Shrugging it off, I decided that maybe he read the name card on the tack stall. I always made sure to write both my name and an emergency contact number on the 3 by 5 inch card attached to the stall door. I walked in his direction, the coarse limestone of the tent foundation crunching underfoot. As he stalked towards me I had the opportunity to get a better look at him. He was rather good looking. His curly black hair was cut close on the sides and slightly longer on top in a very modern style. He was a bit shorter than I recalled, but then again I had been sitting when we met. He might make a decent prospect for Elaine or Deanne I thought. If the opportunity presented itself I might have to get his number and play matchmaker. That is if he didn't end up being a complete jerk about Javier. *Oh, and he ditched that earring.*

"I am glad I caught you Lauren. Someone spotted your dog in the tractor shed over there." He pointed towards an old concrete building at the far southern end of the clearing. It sat nestled up against the edge of the woods. A couple of metal arena gates sat propped up against the outer wall. Just outside the entrance to the left, two wooden saw horses with a load of old jump poles, their dull paint hinting at better days, faded in the morning sun.

"I'm sorry," I said. "I don't think I caught your name."

For a moment I thought I saw a look of wariness cross his face. He recovered quickly, but not quite quick enough.

"I am truly sorry," his voice was oddly formal. "My name is Joe and I represent the company that owns the show grounds. I simply overheard you talking in the aisle and thought I could help out." He flashed his super bright smile again and his countenance lightened, "How about we find the little guy so no one gets in trouble?" He paused to let his words sink in, "So, what is the escapee's name?"

"Huh? Oh, the dog. Sorry. His name is Javier."

"Well, then why don't I help you find him so we can get him on a leash." He moved off toward the shed fully expecting me to follow so I fell in step beside him. As we came closer, I noticed that the tractor shed had once been a barn. It was the perfect place for a Jack to get lost chasing rodents. The doors of the barn had been left open and in the dim light of the interior I could see tire tracks on the dusty floor where the tractor normally rested. The barn was a good size, with about twelve or so stalls. The entire back half appeared to be unused for some time.

As I crossed the threshold, dust motes stirred underfoot. Stopping just behind me, Joe reached for his cell phone. Answering it, he waved me on with one hand while he carried on a conversation in Spanish.

Making my way through the barn calling for Javier I began to notice that mine were the only footprints in the dust. Had Javier come through this way, he would have most assuredly left tracks just as I had. Glancing around once more, I decided that whoever thought they saw him in here was mistaken.

Suddenly, I felt an overpowering presence behind me and without warning all of the hairs on the nape of my neck stood screaming for attention, a most primeval reaction, if there ever was one. Simultaneously tiny alarm bells went off in my head. Reacting solely to gut instinct, I started to spin around just as a solid, wooden 2 x 2 connected with my head and the world went black in the blink of an eye.

**

A complete darkness had settled all around me. A stillness like I had never known; without a single sound, not even a breath of air stirred. I could feel the hard ground beneath me, as I lay curled on my side. If it were not for that I would have floundered in the darkness without my internal compass to guide me, lost to the reality of which direction was up and which was down. As the darkness absorbed me I tried to find something, anything to focus on. It was no use, everything was black as night.

The soft yellow glow of a single candle slowly materialized several feet in front of me. The warmth of the light brought reassurance with it, a surety that I was not lost in the complete blackness around me.

Raising my head slowly, I tried desperately to focus on the light, which flickered subtly before me. The flame wavered, danced, split into two flames then melded back into one until my vision reached a point of relative equilibrium. My head felt oddly disconnected from the rest of me as it struggled to follow the simple command to lift. I felt my cheek pull away from the ground for a moment, then without a sound, the side of my head hit the ground again. At least it felt like the ground. The light dimmed and went out. I could feel my heavy eyelids open and close, but the blackness never changed. I closed them one last time and gave in to the darkness. Again, the candlelight flickered, stronger this time. I floated between the blackness and light, lost in both but never fully enveloped by either of them. The blackness threatened to swallow me again and surely would have, save for the candlelight, which grew brighter and stronger than before. This time it stayed.

As time crept by, the candle flame was the only witness to the darkness that enveloped me. After what seemed like years, I tried again. This time I managed to keep my head off of the ground for a moment longer before collapsing back silently to the ground.

"Lauren." It was a faint whisper from the direction of the light.

The cords of my neck bulged in an effort to raise my head up. Giving out, again my cheek met the ground gratefully and the glow from the candle wavered and nearly vanished.

"Lauren," pleaded the voice again.

The gears in my head slowly started to whirl; locking into place as my consciousness crept slowly through the darkness; searching. I knew that voice, or at least I thought I did. Fighting back, I lifted my head again as the flame grew brighter, stronger.

"Lauren." The voice was more insistent than before.

And then it hit me, "Jake?" Was that my voice? I closed my eyes again, tired. Suddenly, I was sure, like I had never been before. I had heard Jake's voice. There was no mistaking his soft Oklahoma drawl. I opened my eyes, trying to focus on the candle.

"Hey Baby." The voice was stronger, coming at me through the dark like a lifeline. Holy crap, I was dead. My head hit the ground with finality.

"Lauren, I need you to get up." His soft voice was pleading, begging. The glow from the light started to fade again. "Lauren!" Now he was mad.

"What!" I squeaked. I had tried to shout back at him, but my throat was too dry. It was then that I began to feel the rest of me as my body awakened. My whole right side felt as if it was no longer a part of me, cut off completely from what remained of my body. Slowly the sharp needle-like tingling of numbness found its way to my brain. That was it; my entire right side was completely numb. Numb past the feeling of tingling needles to the point that I couldn't even feel it.

"That's it. I need you to get up for me, Ladybug."

The light from the flame had grown brighter each time Jake had spoken, but I still couldn't see him. And yet, without a doubt it was Jake. It had to be Jake. Only he had called me his "Ladybug." Pushing off from what I finally realized was indeed the ground, for the first time I felt something heavy on top of me. As my senses started to return, my nose was assaulted by the fetid air around me, a sickening mixture of the sharp metallic smell of iron and the earthy, acrid notes of mold.

"That's it. I need you to fight for me. I need you to kick on." I could almost feel him smile when he said 'kick on' and my heart squeezed tight inside my aching chest.

A tarp, that's what it was, I could feel the heavy waterproof fabric as I clawed at it, trying to find a way out. Light began to creep in along the ground next to me and with a final push I freed myself from the darkness. The fresh air assaulted my starved lungs and I clung to the tarp in my lap, gasping for some modicum of fresh air, my head reeling. Along with the darkness, the candle flame had died. Frantically I searched the space around me screaming, "Jake!"

I was alone. A dark green tarp lay across my legs and I focused on one of the many silver grommets that ran along the edge until my breathing slowed. Sweat poured off of me in buckets. I could feel it run down my face and neck until it disappeared into my stock tie. Straightening my shoulders, I tried to fill my lungs with more air. The sweat continued its course, running down my back and trickling between my breasts. I glanced around and the events of the morning came rushing back. Javier, Joe, the old barn.

Slowly, I took stock of my surroundings in the dim light. I was in a stall, a stallion stall to be exact. The musty smell of old pine shavings mixed with dust filled my nostrils. Kicking the tarp off with one foot I clawed my way out of the haze and managed to right myself. Standing up, the stall around me began to spin violently and my head was engulfed in searing pain. Quickly plopping back down, I clutched my now throbbing head in my hands, trying desperately to still the ever spinning world around me. Bile rose in my throat. For a moment I thought I might be sick.

Keeping my head down, I found a dark sweat stain on my scrub pants to focus on. Taking in slow, even breaths of the musty air, my body found its equilibrium. Slowly the world stilled and my head felt less likely to explode. Cautiously, so as not to disturb my newly found equilibrium, I looked up. The sun shone through the metal bars of the window at the back of the stall revealing dust motes as they danced in and out of the shafts of sunlight around me. Once again, I got my feet under me and stood upright, slower this time, the nausea at bay.

My show breeches clung to me underneath my scrub pants and my show shirt was sopping wet with perspiration, a few shavings stuck to the damp fabric. Pulling the fabric away from me, I peered down at my grimy stained shirt and groaned. My hands, filthy as they were, only made the problem worse. Dropping the shirt, I took a hard look at my hands. One whiff and I knew they were covered in dried blood, not dirt. Instinctively I reached for my head. My snood hung on precariously by one plastic clip, the other clip was shattered. I could feel the stiff crunch of dried blood tangled in the midst of my hair as I ran my fingers through it. Almost instantly I found the source. My fingers met with a golf ball sized knot at the very back of my head.

"Holy crap!" I spoke aloud, just to hear a sound in the dead silence that was the shed. From this distance, I couldn't even hear the announcer and without a doubt, nobody could hear me.

I bolted for the stall door. Reaching it, I jerked the metal bars hard in my haste to get out. I felt the jolt clear up to my shoulders. The door wouldn't budge. Pressing my forehead against the metal bars I tried desperately to see the latch on the outside. Finding it, I shifted position to get my left arm through the bars. My arm slid through all the way up to my shoulder, then stopped. Groping blindly with my hand I found the cool metal of the latch. With a flick of my wrist I slid the bar loose, freed my arm and pulled on the door again. It was stuck. I fought to control the panic that was beginning to creep in. Checking the back of my hand, I could still read what was left of my ride times written in black ink that morning. My first Intermediare ride was at 1:18 pm.

Instinctively I reached for my cell phone. My clip was empty. He must have taken it. I wasn't wearing my watch either. Oh Lord, I had no idea what time it was. Spinning on my heel I began to circle the stall. "Think, Todd, come on," I muttered aloud. Circling the stall, I tried to put the pieces together. Who in the hell was Joe, and why would he try to kill me? Or was he really trying to kill me? Once he hit me, he could have finished the job. I stopped in my tracks, an ice cold chill running up my spine. My body shook involuntarily in the stifling heat of the stall and I had to reach out to steady myself on the wall.

I thumped my palm against the wall out of frustration. The walls of the stall were solidly built, but of course they were, as this stall was meant to keep a stallion from seeing the horses next to him. The only sections of the stall I could see out of were the back window and the sliding door. The smooth wood of the stall walls made it impossible to climb up and out. Returning to the front door I grabbed a bar in each hand and tried to pull myself up. Lifting my leg as high as I could, I tried to wedge the toe of my tennis shoe between the bars to gain a foothold. Struggling, I managed to lift myself off the dirty floor, but found that I hadn't the upper body strength to pull myself up enough to shift my weight to my foot. Giving up, I slid back down.

Pausing to rethink my options, I peered through the bars again. I had freed the latch, so what was holding the door shut? Pressing against the bars as hard as I could, I noticed an old pitchfork lying against the side of the stall. Stepping down to the other end of the door, I slipped my right arm through the bars. Groping around with my hand, my fingers brushed against the wooden handle. It was wedged between the sliding door and the outside wall of the stall.

With the tips of my fingers I tried to knock it aside. The handle popped up, then slid back down. Taking a deep breath I said a prayer then shoved my hip into the door, at the same instant that my fingers flipped the handle up and out of the way. The pitchfork clanged to the ground. Pulling my arm free, the door slid open.

I slipped through the door and ran down the cluttered aisle, ignoring my pounding head. As I reached the entrance to the barn I stopped. Turning around slowly I glanced back into the dim interior and smiled. "Thanks, Jake," I whispered. Whirling back around, I set off at a run for the main barn.

As I passed the first set of temporary stables I saw Rachel hurrying towards me. "Where in the hell have you been? We've been trying to find you. You just up and disappeared, and we couldn't get you on your cell pho…," she stopped short, her eyes taking in the ragged site before her. "Holy shit, what in the hell happened to you? You're bleeding. Craig is gonna freak."

"Craig? He's here, when?"

"He flew in to surprise you. He was waiting for us at the tack stall when we came back from lunch." Her face grew suddenly serious, "Lauren, what in the hell happened to you?"

Craig. Here? Rather than tell the story twice, I wanted to wait until I was back at the barn with everyone there to listen. Besides, I needed some more time to think and try to put the pieces together. "I'll fill you in when we get back. First, what time is it?" Deep down, I was fervently praying that I hadn't missed my class.

On cue the show announcer came over the loud speakers. *"Good afternoon, show crowd. I hope you are enjoying our lunch break. And my, my, doesn't that food from the vendors' tents smell enticing? Don't forget to grab something and help support some of our sponsors. The official show time is twelve o'clock. We have a few announcements to make. First off, would the owner of a blue Dodge truck parked near Barn B please move your vehicle. You are blocking access to the manure pile. Also, would Lauren Todd please report to Barn A; your party is searching for you."*

Frowning I said, "Let's get going." The cogs of my brain weren't connecting with each other. I was having trouble connecting the dots backward so I started talking out loud as we ran. "Rachel, I ride in just over an hour, but I need to be on to warm up forty minutes before. Crap, I can't think," I said, the tension getting the better of me.

"You need to be mounted no later than 12:40. I can tack her up for you. I think Ann was grooming her when we left to search for you."

Just then we flew around the southern corner of Barn A. Craig spotted me before I made it past the first stall and rushed to meet us. His eyes missed nothing as he surveyed the damage before him. I heard him mutter something unintelligible under his breath as he wrapped his arms around me.

"What in the hell happened to you? You're bleedin'." Most of my hair hung matted with dried blood, my snood hanging on by the one remaining clip. His fingers sought to free the remaining hairpins and snood, dropping them on the ground behind me.

By this time Colleen, Hamish, Deanne, and Ann had rushed over to where we stood. Jumping in, Deanne helped Craig free my hair.

"Ouch!" I grimaced. "That hurts," now that the overall dull throbbing had receded, the gash in my head was starting to sting like crazy.

Gently he probed my head while Deanne held back my hair. Now and again I caught glimpses of his face out of the corner of my eye. Craig fought to keep his face expressionless as he worked. I tried to gauge just how bad it was by the look on his face, but watching him cross-eyed only made my head throb even more.

"Do you want to tell me what happened?" He was clearly fighting for control of his anger.

I thought through the events of the morning once more then blurted out, "I think it was a member of the show staff." This brought everyone up short and you could have heard a pin drop.

Colleen was standing directly in front of me and I could tell she was reading the expressions on the faces around me. "Lauren, why would someone from the show staff hit you in the head? That doesn't make sense."

"Start from the beginnin'," added Craig through clenched teeth, his anger growing.

"Some guy from the show office said that someone saw Javier in some old barn at the other side of the stabling tents." Unconsciously I gestured towards the direction of the old barn with my head, which promptly made it begin to throb even harder. I grimaced, "We went over to look for him and then he hit me." Six confused faces stared back at me like I was loco.

"Ah, Lauren, why would someone want to hit you? That doesn't make sense." Deanne was trying to be tactful. Hamish and Craig stiffened at the same time, casting knowing looks between them.

"I walked into the old barn looking for Javier. He was behind me talking on his cell. When I turned to leave he hit me. That is the last thing I remember. I woke up buried under a tarp and locked in a stud stall."

"What did he look like?" It was AJ's voice off to the left, out of my sight.

"Tan, black curly hair, dressed expensively, oh, and perfect teeth."

Deanne jumped in, "That is half the guys in this place that aren't grooms. We'll never find him."

Craig finished his assessment of my head, "You are goin' to need stitches."

"Let me take a look." Colleen moved to stand next to Craig and peer at my head.

"Anything else, did he have any tattoos, maybe in an odd place?" AJ stepped in front of me, but was looking through me to where Craig stood.

"No, but he did have a gaudy earring in his left ear, a diamond. I thought it looked odd. It was almost too big or something, very retro 1980's. Very Miami Vice."

AJ's eyes flicked to mine in acknowledgement then stared past my ear at Craig for a moment. An unspoken conversation flowed between them. Dropping my hair, Craig walked off a short distance to talk to AJ, their backs turned from the group.

Ignoring them, I took charge of the situation at hand. "Look, I don't have time for stitches. I need to borrow some clothes and get mounted."

"My breeches will fit you, but I won't have time to change. Our ride times are too close together. I tell you what. The tack trailer has tons of breeches." Quick as a flash she pulled a wad of cash from the top of her bra and shoved it in my hands. Leave it to Deanne to have a bra full of cash.

"You need to get cleaned up. I have a shirt you can use in my black bag hanging in the tack stall. The stock tie is attached. I have time, so here let me go get the breeches." Rachel snatched the damp wad of money from my hand and was off in a snap towards the vendors. "Twenty-six long, right?" She hollered over her shoulder.

"Yes." Thankfully Deanne answered her, for my head hurt too bad to yell.

Colleen stood shaking her head disapprovingly, "Lauren, you are in no shape to ride."

"I'll be fine," I said with more enthusiasm than I felt. "I just need some aspirin or something." Arms crossed, she frowned at me.

"I am riding so either you help me or not," I said with finality through gritted teeth. The defiant eventer in me took shape. Like so many times in the past, I dug deep for that extra ounce of grit needed to get me around a tough cross country course. Jake had called it 'eventing mad' and he had learned first hand not to get in my way when I dug in for a determined fight.

Turning on my heel, I brushed past Craig and AJ and headed for the bathroom to rinse the blood out of my hair and try to repair the damage. Forgetting the snood and pins, I stalked back to where they lay in the sand on the concrete barn aisle and scooped them up. I slapped the snood against my thigh to free the dirt as I headed for the bathroom.

"I'll get a brush and a rag from tack room and meet you there." Colleen headed in the other direction towards the tack stall. A few minutes later, she entered the bathroom behind me, her arms full of stuff. I had slipped off my filthy shirt and stood before the mirror in my very utilitarian riding bra and breeches. My scrub pants had a tear up the back of the leg, part of which was hanging over the side of the garbage can behind me where I had thrown them away.

"Colleen, did anyone find Javier?" In all the excitement I had forgotten the little devil was missing.

"Uh huh, he was curled up asleep in Patina's stall. He seems to have a thing for that mare. Elaine found him." Elaine had arrived late to the show grounds since her freestyle class wasn't until almost 5 o'clock. Since Deanne was riding in my class, Elaine agreed to doggy sit him.

It took some work, but we managed to cram my head under the small sink in the bathroom and rinse the blood out. Riders came and went around us, some staring open mouthed, while some feigned distaste with wrinkled noses and haughty glares. Still others tried to act as if it was perfectly normal to see a filthy, half dressed rider rinsing blood out of their hair in the bathroom sink. They probably thought I had taken a nasty spill from a horse, I thought. That was fine by me. I just wanted to get my hands on…

"Joe," I glanced up at Colleen in the mirror behind me as she towel dried my hair. "That was his name, Joe." The automatic sink shut off with a *pft* noise and the bathroom fell silent.

"Here," she said handing me the towel, "I'll go tell the guys."

Gingerly I brushed my hair back into a ponytail at the nape of my neck, trying all the while not to cuss. Once twisted and pinned I slipped the snood over the makeshift chignon and pinned it in place. I had rinsed the dirty snood in the sink and thankfully it was a dark shade of navy blue, which disguised the blood and dirt stains. My make up was a mess, but that was the least of my worries. I slipped on the clean lemon yellow show shirt from Rachel's garment bag and gathered up the remainder of our mess from the bathroom counter.

Pushing the door outward with my hip, I stepped out into the sunlight and was met by Craig. He had been waiting for me. Lines of worry were etched in his face as he met me.

"I'm okay, really." Almost before the last syllable escaped from my lips he scooped me up in his arms. We clung tightly to each other, not wanting to let go. The crack in my façade suddenly split wide open and I began to shake uncontrollably in his arms. Not saying a word, he stood firm, a bastion of strength, holding me upright until my body relaxed again.

"Aye lass, ye must let it go now." His voice was gruff with emotion and his breath was warm and sweet against my ear. Pulling back, his lips sought mine in the gentlest of kisses.

"Um, excuse me," came the sound of a voice behind me. Evidently we were blocking the door to the bathroom. Pulling away from Craig, my cheeks burned red with embarrassment. His green eyes danced with laughter for a moment then his gaze shifted. He was all business again.

Oh how I had missed him.

"Colleen said his name was Joe. Is that right?" His eyes bore into mine.

"Yes, why do you know him?" We had started back towards the barn.

"Maybe, listen, from now on you don't go anywhere, and I mean anywhere, without someone with you. Got that?"

"Craig, is there something you aren't telling me?" An angry knot grew in my gut.

"I don't know, not yet. Listen, I know I can't stop you from ridin' so we'll talk later. I know that you want this qualifyin' score so focus on that and let me take care of this... this problem. Just promise me that you won't go anywhere alone."

"Okay, I found a pair. Get over here and change," Rachel was jogging towards us, plastic bag in hand.

Slipping into the tack stall, I pulled the sliding door shut behind me and changed into the new breeches. The stark white of the new fabric was offset by the fawn colored doeskin full seat. "Rachel, good Lord, what did you spend on these?" She threw me a wicked smile as the door slid open. Snatching my breeches from the ground she deftly pulled my black leather belt free of the belt loops.

"Rachel!" She had passed me the belt and was reaching for my boots.

"Oh, come on. She won't miss the money, besides there wasn't much to choose from. Naturally, they didn't have a single thing on sale," she batted her eyes at me, feigning innocence, "not that I looked mind you and, most certainly nothing under two hundred dollars."

Yanking on my boot socks, I hopped up and down trying to keep my balance. Thankfully, she grabbed a folding chair and with one hand she popped it open and shoved it beneath my butt.

"Sit. After all that you're gonna break a leg before you even mount." Testily she shoved a boot in my direction. "There is some money left over. How about I go back and buy you a pair of proper boots with zippers in the back." She frowned as she pulled the other boot free from the boot bag while I crammed my foot down into my dress boots.

Although pull on boots were quickly being replaced with boots that had zippers, which made the chore of getting into and out of them easier, these were my lucky boots and I was loathe to part with them. Besides, I didn't have a sugar daddy like Rachel's husband or a sugar Daddy like Deanne.

"She's ready." Ann stood in the grass holding Cronos's reins, the mounting block sat next to her front legs. Stomping my foot in order to cram my heel the last inch or so into my boot, I grabbed my helmet out of its bag and headed for the door. Cronos peered at me from under her long eyelashes. Her honey bay coat gleamed in the afternoon sun. Katia had done a marvelous job of braiding her mane so as to show off her powerful neck. Gingerly, I slipped on my helmet, wincing as it hit my open gash.

"Wait! Your spurs and jacket." Rachel tossed me the spurs and went back into the tack stall for my navy shadbelly while I used the mounting block to fasten on the spurs. I had to keep my head as upright as possible to avoid the nausea that came with sudden downward movements.

"Here," she handed me the shadbelly and I pulled my gloves out of the inside pocket.

The loud speaker sat on a telephone pole next to the wash racks. It crackled and came alive just as I swung my leg over the saddle. *Good afternoon. Official show time is 12:45. I hope everybody was able to take a break and enjoy the wonderful food available here today. If not, please stop by and show your support to one of our many vendors and sponsors here at the show grounds today. Ring 1 and Ring 2 will start back up with their first riders in five minutes.*

Once on her back, Cronos moved off on her own while I fastened my chinstrap and buttoned up my coat. I squinted my eyes reflexively, as we drew closer to the warm-up arena. The bright white of the footing reflected the hot rays from the sun, making my head throb once again. Shaking my head to clear my vision only made everything around me swim. Swallowing, I fought down the nausea as I grabbed hold of the pommel to steady myself. *Come on, Todd, pull it together.* I had been fine on the ground, but under the glare of the sun I found myself second guessing my stubbornness to ride.

"Hamish will be here in a moment. He offered to get you something for your head." Colleen stood ringside studying me, "Go ahead and walk her around until he comes."

"Shouldn't I get started warming up? I am going to run out of time."

"Walk her around for a minute. I still haven't decided if I will let you go into the show arena," she said pointedly, her straw hat concealing her eyes from me.

After two trips around the arena at a relaxed walk, Colleen called me over to the side. Hamish had a blue Powerade in one hand and several aspirin in the other. The cold liquid felt like heaven to my dry throat as I gratefully swallowed the aspirin. Surprisingly, the world began to steady around me as I settled into the familiar feel of Cronos beneath me.

When Colleen finally did start warming us up, she took it easy. I knew she was babying us and it made me mad. Ann gave me the ten-minute signal from the edge of the warm up arena as I rode past her in the trot. We hadn't even cantered yet!

"Extended trot across the diagonal, bring her back, then a volte into half pass," Colleen instructed as I trotted past her.

"We haven't warmed up in canter yet," I shot back at her. What was she doing? We still had our half canter pirouettes and tempis to do.

I had gained control of the pain in my head. That is until I unleashed Cronos across the diagonal. Without realizing it, I had been holding her back, bracing from the pain. As she shot across the arena her haunches sank, her front end rose and she nearly dragged my arms out of their sockets in her eagerness to free herself from my grip. Never before, not even on Gold Herr, had I felt an extended trot like this. As I sought to slow my seat, sink into her, and bring her down to a medium trot, she shook her head angrily, sending spittle in every direction.

Crap! Taking a deep breath I wiggled my toes in my boots. Another deep cleansing breath and my shoulders loosened. With a wiggle from my inside index finger I brought her smoothly into collected trot as we prepared for half pass. I had to loosen up quickly or things were going to go south from here.

There was one other Intermediare rider in the warm up and as I passed her at the center of the arena I saw her staring at me, her eyes round as saucers. With no time to think, I straightened

Cronos out and circled back around. As we drew near the fence where Colleen stood she said, "Now you can canter. Circle a few times to loosen her up then start on your half pass." I nodded so she knew I had heard her clearly.

"Now you know why I didn't have you canter? You were stiff as a board." She shook her head, making the brim of her straw-hat bounce.

Ann gave me the two-minute signal and I brought Cronos down to a walk. Hamish handed me the blue Powerade and I finished it off. Just then, Craig walked up.

"You doin' okay?" His eyes searched mine.

"I'm a nurse, remember. I know the signs to look for. I can do this."

"That's what I am afraid of," Colleen interrupted, rolling her eyes. "Come on, let's do this." Surrendering the empty bottle, I gathered up my reins.

"I want you to ride conservatively, okay? If you try to push her she is going to explode on you just like she did in the warm up. You are tense and I can tell you are riding protectively."

My head was throbbing, the inside lining of my helmet rubbed the open gash with every step Cronos took, but I nodded anyway.

The ring steward motioned me towards the entrance. As we moved off, Craig squeezed my leg then stepped back. Nodding politely to the previous rider, we started to circle the arena waiting for the signal to enter. We cantered quietly around the arena in collected canter.

After what seemed an eternity, the unmistakable sound of a cowbell chimed twice and we entered the arena at A. Halfway to X, my mind went blank and for a moment I couldn't recall the next movement. Taking as much time as I could with my salute, the test slowly came back to me. Moving off in a collected trot, we started our first Intermediare test together.

With my head pounding, I fought to concentrate. Cronos picked up on my anxiety and our test slowly unraveled.

Exhausted, we finally halted to salute the judge. As we left the arena, I couldn't begin to recall any part of the test I had just ridden, my head just hurt too damn much. I had no doubt we would not receive a qualifying score, but at least it was over. Just outside of the covered arena, Cronos came to a stop in front of Colleen and I slid into Craig's arms.

"Well that sucked," I mumbled under my breath.

A pair of hands reached out to take my jacket, while someone else walked off with Cronos. Craig reached for my helmet, but I waved him off. I wanted to take it off slowly to avoid scraping the cut in my scalp.

Without warning, my hands started to shake, my knees felt weak, and my face became clammy. "I think I'm gonna be sick."

Before I knew it, Elaine was propelling me towards the restrooms behind the show office. I made it to the sink on shaky legs and weakly turned on the cold water. It felt like heaven as it coursed through my fingers.

"You need to get that helmet off. Here let me help." Elaine popped the clasp free and grabbed the helmet with both hands. "Ready?"

"No, but go slow." I winced defensively, waiting for the pain.

"Maybe I should do it quick like a band-aid?"

"Do and I'll kill you." My eyes met hers in the mirror and she nodded. I winced again as she gently slid the helmet off of my head. My hair was sopping wet with sweat. A small, slightly crusty patch of ochre red dried blood clung to my scalp. The gash had bled some more.

"Eeew, that's gross," Elaine's face screwed up in disgust in the mirror above the sinks.

Tiny goose bumps rose on my arms and I shivered involuntarily as the cool air of the bathroom fan blew across my sweaty head. Leaning over slowly, I splashed water on my forehead and neck, trying to ease the nausea. After a few minutes it passed. Elaine slipped out of the bathroom and came back with a bottle of cold water which she shoved at me.

"Here, drink up," she ordered. Leaning against the back wall next to the paper towel dispenser she said, "It really wasn't THAT bad, you know."

Confused, I turned to face her, leaning my butt against the counter for support.

"Your ride. I don't think I would expect a qualifying score, but considering the kind of morning you've had, it really wasn't *that* bad," she smiled. "I mean, at least you didn't stray off course and get the whistle blown on you, and, you did manage to stay *in* the arena. That is always a goal of mine," she added, laughing. "I'm thinking you pulled off a," she wrinkled her nose in thought, "56."

Screwing the cap back on the half empty water I replied sarcastically, "Thanks for the moral support. Some friend you are." I pushed off the counter and we headed back out into the sunlight.

"Ah, but at least I am honest," she replied, still laughing. "I said it wasn't that bad. I actually got a 39 once!"

"You'll have to tell me about that someday when my head hurts less and I can actually laugh along with you."

OKEECHOBEE

Craig made arrangements with a fishing contact before leaving Panama to stay in his cottage near Torry Island on the southern shore of Lake Okeechobee. It was all part of his plan for a surprise getaway weekend for me. My heart sang with the realization that he had set aside time for just the two us. Besides, I could use a break from the intense rigors of training and showing.

On our way out of town, Craig insisted I go to the ER to get checked out. The ER doctor wanted to order a cat scan of my head, but I flatly refused. I had just enough knowledge in my head to be both a danger to myself as well as an asset. A young guy, probably fresh out of med school, he was insistent until I put my foot down. After learning that I had been a trauma nurse and did indeed know what signs to look for concerning head trauma he reluctantly gave in.

Clearly not convinced that I wouldn't be incapacitated or passed out and not able to self-diagnose, he gave Craig a printout of what to look for, along with a warning that had I been whacked in the head just a few inches to the right, I might not be here. A few stitches and some loud complaining later, we left the ER. A quick stop at a drive through drug store for antibiotics and darvocet and we were headed west on SR 441. As we left the bright coastal lights behind and drove into the night, the stars became brighter, their borders all the more crisp in the sky above.

"You know, you sure are a baby for someone who used to be a trauma nurse." The orange and green glow from the GPS on the dash adjusted slightly as the road curved. Troy had been kind enough to loan Craig his car for the next few days.

"Yeah, well, haven't you ever heard that doctors make the worst patients? It's true of nurses, too. We think we know it all and can do it better." I could still smell the pungent notes of iron from the betadine on my scalp. "Sometimes we actually do."

Had I been feeling more like a warrior, I would have fought harder to avoid the emergency room. The antiseptic smells brought back memories that I never wanted to revisit and I had been a ball of nerves the entire time. As it was though, by the time I dismounted there was not an ounce of fight left in me. Craig, like a circling shark, picked up on my weakness and shuffled me off to the hospital while the girls took care of Cronos. I knew that he, of all people, knew just what it took for me to go. To my relief, he never left my side. Unfortunately for the ER staff and poor Craig, my nerves had given me a loose tongue and I had babbled incessantly the entire time. Quiet and strong, he had hung with me like a champ.

Unscrewing the top from a bottle of water he passed it to me, "You need to take those meds."

Thankfully, I had managed to eat some crackers from the vending machine at the hospital and Craig had bought a second pack, which he shoved into my purse. Pulling out the cellophane bag, I ate a few of them so my stomach could tolerate the antibiotics.

"So, what did you find out? Who is this Joe?" I said, taking another swallow of water.

Craig exhaled slowly, taking his time. He had turned down the volume on the radio so we could talk, and the soft muted sounds of music filled the void. Finally he turned at last and said, "I am pretty sure it was Jose Ramos."

Jose Ramos? Jose? I rolled the name around in my head trying to place it. It rang a bell, but my brain was still a bit slow. While I searched my memory banks, Craig focused on the dark road. Suddenly it came to me, "Maria's brother?" I sputtered.

"The one and the same. He fits the description," his mouth twitched, "especially the earrin'."

It was coming back to me now. While fishing at the resort Craig had told me about Jose. "But I thought he was from Columbia. What in the world would he be doing here and why me? I don't even know him."

"I don't know exactly. The only thing Hamish and I can come up with is your connection to me." The words hung between us for brief moment. He glanced my way in the dark interior of the car, judging my response.

"So the huaca was left by him."

Craig appeared outwardly calm, but I could see his jaw tighten. Finally he spoke, "I honestly don't know. From what I can piece together, I don't think it was him who left the huaca in your room, which would mean there is someone else. Someone or somethin' we are missin'." He slammed his wrist hard onto the steering wheel in frustration.

"Okay, back up here a second. I need to get this straight before the drugs kick in and make me stupid. Why would Jose try to knock me out at a horse show that he didn't even know you would be at? I didn't even know you were coming. I mean, if it is you he's after, then why go through me?"

"It's complicated."

The texture of the road beneath us changed and the hum of the tires deepened. The green sign on the roadside read 'Twenty Mile Bend'. I sat quietly, waiting for a response.

"Remember on the boat, when I told you about the cocaine?" His eyes found mine in the dark, searching.

I started to nod, but decided better of it. My head hurt. "Yes."

"Maria and Ricardo were also involved."

"Ricardo?"

"Her husband," he replied.

"The diplomat? The old guy?" I was surprised. According to Deanne, Maria's husband was twenty years her senior and not the most gorgeous of guys. Everybody assumed it was a marriage of convenience. Just how convenient was the real question. Knowing Maria, convenient translated into whatever Maria was after, be it money or status.

"Aye, the same, only they weren't yet married." The GPS adjusted again, illuminating the dash in an orange glow before fading again. "Ricardo was deeply involved in the smugglin'. He was the contact for the cartel here in Panama. I think he may have known more than he let on, but I had no proof at the time. Anyway, when I discovered what was goin' on, Maria knew she would lose everythin'; money, status, everythin' she worshipped and wanted. She wasn't about to give all of that up for a life on the run, or worse, prison time. I was the one person who knew her dirty secret and could expose Ricardo and Jose. Ricardo… he had diplomatic immunity so he was essentially safe, untouchable, unlike Jose."

I could see one side of his frown as he drove. "So, before the Guardia arrived at her house to arrest her," he checked to see if he had my attention, "they married."

Wow, I thought, there was just no end to Maria's ambition.

Satisfied that he had my attention, he continued, "They dragged a priest out of bed in the middle of the night. Once legally married, neither of them could be touched or even be questioned about the drugs or the missin' fishermen." He focused on driving. "Not only that, but the likelihood of someone arrestin' or even accusin' Ricardo of a crime are slim to none. He is essentially untouchable because of his connections, or palanca, as it's called."

"Fishermen? I don't remember you mentioning them." Suddenly it came back to me. "Ganso's dad?" I blurted out, incredulously. At the resort, Craig had mentioned that Ganso's dad had gone missing at sea. Now it was making sense, the pieces were falling together.

"Yes, although I could never prove anythin'. My best guess is that the crew of the fishin' boat saw somethin' they weren't supposed to, and well." The words hung in the car between us, unspoken.

"But, how? What would make you think?" I stammered. This was too much for my aching head to deal with.

"I found some boat debris about twenty miles or so from where they were fishin'," he stared pointedly at me, "the edges were charred." "That doesn't just happen. There was definitely a fire of some sort. Intentional or not," he shrugged, "I don't have that answer. But I do have my suspicions."

My mind immediately flew to Ganso. He was an easy person to like, and I knew that he had a close relationship with Craig. I wondered; did he know?

As if he heard me, Craig added, "No, I don't think he has any idea."

We drove on for a few more miles, the wheels in our heads turning in time with those of the car. Before I knew it, Craig woke me up and helped me into the cabin.

**

I awoke slightly groggy. The room was dark as night and it took a moment for me to get my bearings. The back of my head was tender, but amazingly it had stopped throbbing. Blinking hard, I tried to focus my eyes in the darkness. The room looked vaguely familiar, as if I had seen it in a dream. That made sense, I thought to myself, considering how loopy I had felt last night. I lay there for a moment suspended in time, not sure if it was day or night. I could feel the pillow against the stitches and they itched. Shifting, I rolled onto my side.

The strong smell of coffee reached my nose and my stomach growled awake in response. I could hear shuffling noises coming from the kitchen, then the unmistakable *creak* and *slap* of a screen door shutting. Pulling back the worn sheets, I slowly lifted my head from the hard, unforgiving pillow. No pain, that was good. Easing onto the edge of the bed I paused, once more to make sure the pain was indeed gone. Satisfied, I stood up and pulling back the old calico curtains, I tried to peer out the window. Aluminum foil wrinkled with time stared back at me.

One or two tiny pinholes allowed bright bursts of light past the layer of foil. Well, at least I knew it was daylight. Question was, which day?

Finding my way to the shower, I passed the doorway leading to the kitchen. I could see the outline of Craig's head through the far window as he settled into a chair on the porch. The cabin was decorated in a rustic chic sort of way. Mismatched furniture and flooring, which were most likely bound for the landfill at one time, had found a final resting place in the homey interior. A mustard brown wicker couch, its armrests and feet rubbed raw with time, sat across from a worn leather easy chair in the main room. The gold-flecked Formica countertops sagged a little in the middle where the sink sat and an old refrigerator sat guarding the kitchen. It was the only appliance other than the coffee pot and TV. All in all, it was the quintessential male fishing abode.

Once in the shower, hot wispy tendrils of steam floated around me in the small shower. Breathing deeply, I let the hot steam clear my thoughts. The added information about Ricardo, Jose, and Maria only served to complicate matters in my mind. I still couldn't quite fit together all the pieces of the puzzle. Why me? I had nothing to do with Craig, cocaine, the resort, or any of it until nearly a year after it all went down. There had to be something we were missing.

Without warning, the water spewing from the showerhead turned cold. "Crap!" Dancing around in shock I dove for the faucet and turned the water off. Shivering, I reached for a clean towel. So much for shaving my legs, I thought glumly. Stopping to brush my teeth I studied my reflection in the cloudy mirror above the powder blue sink. The greenish blue tinge of a bruise graced the left side of my face from the middle of my cheekbone to just above my eye. Working the muscles of my face into several contorted expressions I tested my muscles for soreness. *Okay, not too bad.* The bruise was mostly cosmetic, which was good.

Padding back down the narrow, dimly lit hall to our room, I dressed quickly, pulling on a favorite pair of jeans and a plain white T-shirt. Colleen had been in on the surprise and had thoughtfully packed a weekend bag for me after I had left for the show grounds yesterday. Bending over slowly, I gingerly wrapped my cold, wet hair in the towel and piled it on top of my head, deftly tucking the frayed end under the edge of the towel at the nape of my neck. Feeling refreshed, I made my way out to find Craig. I still had no idea what time it was, but my best guess meant that I had probably slept the day away.

The screen door swung easily on its hinges and Craig turned the minute he heard its musical creak. There was just something about the sweet sounds of a Southern screen door swinging on its hinges that made me smile. "Here you go," he thrust an old mug at me.

Soberly, I reached for it, not quite sure what to make of his offering. Two large breasts protruded from one side of the faded camouflage patterned mug. Faint yellow lettering just below the rim was mostly illegible, but no doubt had once been a funny one liner that only a beer drinking, camo wearing, gun toting Neanderthal would have found immensely funny. "Really? I get the boob mug?"

"Honestly, I didn't notice it until after I had poured the coffee and since there is no dishwasher…" he shrugged, looking innocent. "How's the head?"

"Better." Holding the mug up again, I threw him a look which clearly said I wasn't buying it, "Really, didn't notice the C cups sticking straight out?" He tried to hide his smile. Giving up, I settled down in a porch chair next to him, warm mug between my tactfully placed hands. This time he couldn't help but smile so I shot him a disgusted look. "Perv," I accused.

"What?" He feigned innocence and went back to drinking his own coffee from a plain black mug. "Surely you didn't expect me to use it."

I took a small sip and felt the hot liquid slide down my throat and leave a reassuring trail clear down to my belly. He had added the sugar for me, just exactly how I liked it. "What time is it?"

In typical Craig style, he didn't bother to check his watch or cell phone, he just knew, "Almost noon, you hungry?"

"Famished." The towel was beginning to aggravate my head so I gently unwound it, letting it fall on the arm of the chair.

"We passed a mom and pop style diner on the way in last night. Want to check it out?"

I nodded, swallowing a mouthful of sugar-laced brew. I was starving. I had eaten nothing other than my beef jerky and cracker diet yesterday. Right now, I might be tempted to eat a horse, I thought to myself.

Craig found the diner just where he had remembered it. The food was homemade, decisively Southern in style and served up in heaping portions. Just as hungry as I was, I realized that Craig probably hadn't eaten much of anything in the last twenty-four hours. In between bites we made plans to stop on the way home and buy me another cell phone. After yesterday, Craig was even more insistent on knowing my every move and making sure someone was with me at all times. He even talked about activating the GPS feature on my cell and downloading an application that would allow my phone to be tracked. *Suck it up, Todd.* Under any other circumstances I would have felt more like a prize dog with a microchip, but I had to admit, the incident yesterday with Jose had shaken me to the core.

I called Colleen on Craig's phone to make sure she still had a copy of my freestyle music on her laptop. She did, and promised to download it to my new phone when we got home. Feeling better, I relaxed and enjoyed what was left of my meal.

Taking our time, we made it back to the cabin a few hours later. My head had begun to throb again, but I wasn't willing to admit it. We had such precious little time together lately and an ocean between us, the last thing I wanted to do was nurse my head. The pain must have shown on my face for once the screen door slammed behind us, Craig ushered me onto the couch and clicked the TV on. Handing me the remote he headed to the kitchen where I could hear him rifling through the bag we had brought home from the pharmacy. I closed my eyes and adjusted a throw pillow behind my neck, leaving the back of my head free.

The cushion beneath my back sunk with his weight and I opened my eyes. "Here," he handed me another darvocet and a glass of water. Sitting up, I took the medicine.

"Sorry, I am spoiling our weekend together."

He frowned down at me. "Not hardly," he said then his face grew serious. "Promise me that when I leave town Monday night you will not go anywhere alone."

He looked so serious and worried, I thought. Quickly I made the sign of an X across my heart, "Promise." He bent down and kissed me tenderly on the tip of my nose, then again on the lips.

I awoke several hours later, alone save for the rambling of the TV. The pain was gone, and so was Craig. Pulling myself from the depths of the old couch I wandered out onto the porch. Running my hands through my hair I tried without success to tame my unruly curls. Giving up, I twisted my hair into a knot and using a hair band from around my wrist, I managed to subdue it. The porch light was on and knowing Craig wasn't far, I scooped up my camera from the kitchen counter and headed for the swing at one end of the porch.

The wooden porch swing felt warm and solid beneath me as I rocked gently back and forth in the still night. Closing my eyes, I rested my chin on one knee, the denim fabric of my jeans smelled faintly of the couch. I sat for a few minutes, enjoying the night. After a few minutes, I picked up the sound of Craig's voice, talking amicably to the elderly gentleman from Pennsylvania who was staying in the cabin next to ours. As the wind shifted I caught the unmistakable smell of charcoal from a grill and my stomach growled rudely.

My camera sat on the swing next to me, waiting patiently. Ann had been gracious enough to film my Intermediare test, but I hadn't had the stomach to watch it yet. I knew I would be overly analytical of my rides and I didn't want the video to spoil my time with Craig this weekend. Shifting, I placed my cheek on my knee and stared at the shiny black camera. Giving in with an exaggerated sigh, I dropped my bare foot on the porch floor, picked it up and flicked the switch from red to green. Almost instantly the flat screen on the back came to life. Punching through the buttons I scrolled through my video library.

The vibrant blue waters of the Caribbean caught my attention and I paused. Avoiding the inevitable one more time I clicked the play button. My trip to San Blas came to life in my hand and I watched as the camera panned across the white sand beaches and back out to the blue waters. Picking up the familiar voices of the gang in the background, the video passed over a sleek, expensive looking boat sitting just offshore. Hmm, I don't remember this, I thought, enjoying the view.

As I watched the camera zoomed in, then the image bounced around, making the earth appear to shake. Smiling to myself, I vaguely recalled waving to the man. "You're such a dork, Todd," I said to the bouncing image on the camera. As the camera regained focus the video showed a man staring back through a pair of binoculars. The black lenses obscured his face from view. Lowering them, he gazed into the video for a split second before turning quickly away. Suddenly, my palms began to sweat and I nearly dropped the camera when I heard footsteps.

"Hey babe, watchin' your ride?" Craig started up the front steps. Seeing the look on my face he hurried over. The swing jerked abruptly on its chains as he sat down next to me.

I rewound the video and handed it to Craig wordlessly. Setting down his half finished beer, he picked it up and pushed the play button. Time seemed to slow as I watched his facial expressions change from cautious curiosity to anger then disbelief.

"It's him," he said, laying the camera in his lap. "When did you take this video? Where were you?"

Reflexively I pulled both knees to my chest and wrapped my long arms around my legs. "San Blas, before we met."

"But that doesn't make sense, why would Jose be followin' you before we even met. I thought he was tryin' to get back at me through you. That is the only thin' that makes any sense." He shook his head as if to clear it and, punching the button, watched the video again. "This changes things," he said flatly.

We didn't bring the subject up again, but rather pushed it aside so we could spend much needed time with one another. Neither of us wanted to lose what precious little time we had together.

The next morning, I woke first. Craig lay curled on his side facing away from me, his broad back exposed. He had opened the window in the room last night to allow fresh air in and there was a slight chill to the morning. I lay there for several minutes, studying the manscape that was Craig and trying to put my life in order. With a sigh, I slid out of bed and headed for the kitchen to make some coffee. I hadn't slept much at all. In fact, I was downright jumpy, off kilter. Measuring out the coffee from the can, my mind wandered. I couldn't decide if my sleepless night was because I had been out for so long yesterday and thereby had thrown my internal clock into disarray, or if it was because of my dreams. I had dreamed last night of Jake, only this time he was walking away from me. A heavy weight sat deep in my gut telling me what I didn't want to know, what I didn't want to accept. I was terrified to admit that he may be gone from me forever.

Hastily, I poured the water into the reservoir before I accidentally spilled it, and then tucked the glass pot into the coffee maker. The red light clicked on, and much like the coffee maker, my emotions started to bubble to the surface. I had no doubt Jake had saved me in the stallion stall. It was he who had pulled me from the blackness. I ran my fingers through my hair, wincing as I inadvertently hit the stitches. *Like he had saved me so many times before.* Blinking back tears, I crossed my arms and paced the small kitchen, waiting for the coffee to brew. Pausing mid-stride, I pulled out two fresh mugs and sugar for me.

Several minutes later, I padded barefoot back into the bedroom, cups in hand. The aroma of brewing coffee had penetrated Craig's sleep and he sat up when I came through the door.

"Thanks, babe." He took the cup I offered. As I turned to walk around the bed he caught my arm, stopping me. "Hey, come here, what in the world is wrong?" His green eyes studied me with concern.

Feigning surprise I brushed him off, "Allergies, you left the window open."

"Bullshit, you opened the window. Come here," he set his cup down on the bedside table and pulled mine from my hands placing it next to his. "Sit."

I settled onto the edge of the mattress. "Really, I'm fine." I plastered my best attempt at a fake smile across my face.

His eyes flicked across my face and he repeated, "Bullshit."

"Look, you'll think I'm crazy so what's the point." I tried to get up from the bed, but he effectively pulled me back. With an exasperated sigh I gave in, "I think Jake is gone for good." *Oh, yeah that was good. Now you really sound like a nut case.*

He cocked an eyebrow, his eyes never leaving my face. I could see him processing what I had said and composing a response.

Oh boy, he's definitely thinking about this one. Way to go, Todd.

Finally, after what seemed like minutes he continued, "In what way?"

That was a safe response, I thought to myself. He didn't come out and admit that I was crazy or worse, seeing ghosts. And at the same time he left the door open for me to fill in the blanks he obviously didn't have the answers to. "After Jose hit me on the head, Jake came to me." I waited for a rebuttal from Craig. Not getting one, I continued.

"He told me that I had to get up. He wouldn't let me sleep. Oh God, how tired and sleepy I had been. After the accident, I had nightmares," I shuddered involuntarily, "Nearly every night. They were always the same. They centered around his death, the trauma room." I paused, swallowing hard as my shoulders sagged with the weight of my guilt, "My helplessness." *There, it's out. Now he knows you failed. Now he'll see you for what you really are.*

"Go on," his hand rested on my forearm, warm and safe.

"After I met you, the dreams shifted, they became…" I searched for the right word, "happier." The tears broke free and slid hot and wet down my face. "Last night, he walked away from me and all I saw was his back. I'm so confused. I can't really explain it, but when I think of him and what we had, I feel as though I am cheating you. Us."

He squeezed my arm, "I don't think of it that way at all. Remember when you first told me about Jake?" I nodded, wiping my tear stained face with the sleeve of my shirt. "I told you I wouldn't replace him. That I wanted all of you, remember?" Again I nodded. "It's time to say goodbye and move on, Lauren. Even Jake knows that. I can abide you lovin' a memory; we all do that, but not a ghost." He ran his hand through my hair, pulling the ends across one shoulder.

He was right. My brain told me that I could love only one man at a time. There wasn't room for Craig and a ghost. I could still have Craig and keep my memories of Jake. There was room enough for that, as long as I let Jake become a memory. *As long as I was willing to let go.*

Pulling me down gently next to him on the bed he ran a finger along my hairline, down my cheekbone, and along the soft skin of my jaw, memorizing each angle and curve. A lonely tear escaped and he wiped it away. "Let him go," he whispered softly then pulling me to him he held me while I said goodbye to my ghost and tears wracked my body.

Afterward, I lay still in his arms, emotionally exhausted. Lifting my chin with his finger, his lips found mine, and my mouth parted, welcoming him. The salt from my tears floated between us in the gentlest of kisses. Lost in him, I reluctantly opened my eyes only to find him watching me.

"Are you mine?" Although he spoke, his voice husky, his eyes had asked the same question.

"Yes, I am," I replied then added, "all of me." And I pulled him to me.

**

We spent the next day in each other's arms, moving around the cabin only to fix something to eat, to curl up in a different spot, or to make love. Lost in time and removed from our busy lives, we tasted the pleasures of each other again and again. In letting go of Jake I was able to knock down yet another layer of the wall I had build around my heart and our lovemaking grew in more ways than I could have ever imagined. With Jake's ghost gone, Craig seemed to open up to me as well.

Eventually, as night fell and our meager food supply ran out, Craig rolled off the couch and dressed. "Our neighbor said the food shop at the gas station has a fair supply of southern fried death." He kissed me on the forehead as I lay on the beat up old couch over which he had thoughtfully spread a clean sheet.

Stretching out my legs, my bare feet hit the wicker arm and stopped. "Hmm," I purred as the faded quilt slipped downward, exposing my breasts. Pulling it back up, I tucked my legs up under its warmth as well. "That sounds like heaven. Want me to go with you?" I sincerely hoped he would say no, my limbs felt languorous and heavy with our recent lovemaking.

Snatching the keys from the countertop he chuckled softly, "No, I've got it. You best relax while you can because I'm not finished with you." He stood just this side of the kitchen, backlit by the overhead fluorescent lights. Although I couldn't see his eyes, I knew they were dancing with laughter. In one smooth motion I flung a small pillow at him. Narrowly missing him, it sailed through the tiny kitchen and bounced off the fridge. Still unmoving he laughed. Flopping back down onto the couch I heard the screen door slam behind him.

**

The knowledge that we would have to say goodbye again and not see each other for several weeks loomed above us like a dark cloud as we drove back to the farm the next morning. Craig had a flight out that evening and Troy graciously offered to drive him to the airport. Since he had to make the trip to Miami the next morning he decided to get a hotel room and sleep in so as to avoid the morning traffic.

We said our goodbyes alone in the small kitchen of the bunkhouse, neither of us wanting to be the first to step away. With my new cell phone in hand, he made me swear again to stick close to someone and not venture out alone. After the recent events, and with the stitches as a reminder, I agreed.

**

Luckily I was able to pay a late entry fee and ride my Intermediare test two weeks later. By the grace of God, we garnered yet another qualifying score, although it was definitely by the skin of our teeth. Once again, Cronos's experience shone through and she took care of me.

LOVE

A cold front was barreling across the state, bringing with it rain, wind, and temperatures in the forties. The barn sat empty and everyone was either lazing around watching TV or gone for the day. It was a perfect day for doing laundry. In the close quarters of One Spirit Farm there were few opportunities to escape and be alone so I grabbed my dirty laundry and supplies in a basket and headed for the barn. Like most big barns, Rachel had installed a washer and dryer in the tack room in order to wash her saddle pads, polo wraps, and miscellaneous towels.

Slipping through the tack room door, I pushed it closed behind me with one foot while balancing the basket. Setting it on the floor I closed my eyes and savored the silence. Before getting started, I ran the washer through one rinse cycle in order to rinse away any errant horse hair that the last load may have left behind.

I decided to do my personal laundry first then get some saddle pads washed. Once the first load was swishing along I plopped down in a chair, slipped off my rubber barn boots and stretched my feet, nestled in a pair of thick socks, out on the coffee table. Time ticked by as I delved into a pile of horse magazines, some of which were several years old. Lost in an article on four in hand driving, I nearly jumped out of my skin when the door to the tack room opened.

"Oh, I am so sorry," Colleen glanced around the room, taking in the laundry basket. She stood just inside the door with a bag of dirty laundry, "I thought I was the only one with the brilliant idea." She lifted her bag up in way of explanation.

"There's room, come on in." I folded the magazine open along the spine and laid it in the chair next to me.

"Thanks." She shut the door and set down her bag. "Anything worth reading?"

"You have to dig around a bit." She sat across from me and I handed her a magazine. We read in companionable silence until the washer stopped. Transferring the wet clothes to the dryer I threw in a dryer sheet and started another load.

"Well, would you look at this, Caroline is still very much in business." She held up the brightly colored, shiny pages of her magazine for me to see.

Pouring in the soap I turned to face her, "Who? Do you know her?"

Nodding, she lowered the magazine, setting it in her lap. "You know I used to live in Florida." It was more of a statement than a question and she didn't wait for an acknowledgement. "Ocala, to be exact. Well, eventually I ended up here in Wellington, but I started in Ocala. I moved here after I left Germany," she sighed, remembering.

"I was so young and full of myself. Thought I could conquer the world. I got a job at a big breeding and training farm on a reference from a friend in Germany."

"Racehorses?" Ocala was renowned for its Thoroughbred breeding.

"Not exactly, they had some off the track Thoroughbreds that they rehabilitated and re-trained for other disciplines, but mostly warmbloods. You have to remember, that was back when European warmbloods were a very expensive luxury item and few riders could afford to import one. No, Caroline was smart. She had two stallions, a Holsteiner and a Hanoverian. They were the old style warmblood, massive, lots of bone. You know, the kind that cross well with a really nice Thoroughbred. She carefully selected a handful of Thoroughbred mares from the Ocala area, ones who excelled in movement and temperament, but failed miserably on the track. The results were both athletic and affordable." She chuckled, "Best of all, they sold like hot cakes to anyone who wanted a warmblood. Eventually she imported European mares with really great bloodlines and began offering her clients more options. I handled the dressage training for her."

"So what brought you to Panama?" I settled back into my chair and propped my feet up.

Following suit, she slipped off her shoes and stretched her legs out on the coffee table. She wore mismatched socks, one green, and one pink with stripes. "On a buying trip to Germany for Caroline I found the horse of my dreams," she sighed, "and what I thought was the man of my dreams."

"Gold Herr?"

She nodded, a faraway look in her eye. Shrugging her shoulders she continued, "and Rehiner." We fell madly in love and hatched a grand plan to start our own import and training business. We chose the Seattle area. We wanted to open new markets and things went really well at first." Her eyes clouded with the memory. Looking away, she shifted in her chair. I waited patiently as she had when I told her about Jake.

"We had a fire in our barn." Her words hung in the air between us, magnifying the background sounds of the washer and dryer. Barn fires were every horseman's worst nightmare. "Thank God, it was early summer and we had opened the outer doors so the horses had access to their paddocks. That is where most of them were, sleeping under the stars." Her eyes drifted away, lost in what surely was a horrific memory. Coming back, she continued, "We managed to get all of the horses out but one, Sophia. She was a half-sister to Gold Herr and the backbone of our breeding program."

"She couldn't get out?"

"Rehiner had shut the door. She was close to foaling and he didn't want her to foal in the paddock." A nervous grin crossed her face, "It wouldn't have been safe to have her foal in the paddock. How ironic isn't it?"

My heart sank like a rock, causing my stomach to flip and roll nauseatingly. "Colleen, I am so sorry. How horrible that must have been." I shivered involuntarily just thinking about it.

"You know, it wasn't anyone's fault, certainly not his. I would have kept her in under the same circumstances." She shrugged, "But I was upset and angry. And then, he opened his mouth," she shook her head, trying to rid herself of the memory. "If he had just kept his mouth shut I would probably still be there." Her voice changed, grew lighter, and she shrugged her shoulders, "although, in retrospect I think it was meant to be. Me leaving," she added.

"Ah," I responded, knowing she wasn't finished.

"You see, Rehiner, although a good man in many ways had a thing for money. We had argued about money along the way, but I always made excuses for his behavior. He wanted to be filthy rich. Me, I was in it for the love of the horse. Our ideals were bound to collide."

"What happened? What did he say that was so awful?"

She snorted in evident disgust. "I had sat down on the front porch, exhausted from moving horses into pastures where they could stay until we rebuilt. I'll never forget it. He sat down next to me and said, 'at least the barn and mare were insured for a ton of money'. The money was all he cared about. I could have killed him, the selfish bastard. My heart was breaking for Sophia and her foal and all he could see was the big paycheck because she was dead."

"Jerk! I would have left him, too," I spat.

She chuckled, "So, we divided the horses, or assets as he called them, and I got a job here in Wellington. A few years later I met AJ through a friend and the rest, as they say, is history."

"I'm sorry you had to go through that."

She nodded absently, deep in thought. Not wanting to disturb her, I picked up my magazine and went back to the story about driving.

**

Our first attempt at the freestyle class was on Sunday. Saturday would be our second attempt at qualifying in the Intermediare class. Tomorrow night was Friday, and Craig was flying in from Panama. He had bought tickets at the last minute in order to watch us compete. I made arrangements to pick him up at the airport when his flight got in at 7:56 pm.

As it stood, everybody had qualified in each of their Prix St. George classes. Hamish and Patina had already received their qualifying score in Intermediare, while everyone else was still working to obtain scores in Intermediare and the freestyle classes.

I lay in bed staring into the darkness around me. Elaine flipped over in her bed and let out a sleepy sigh. Thinking back to when we arrived, I was glad Elaine and I had shared a room. Elaine was easy to get along with, kept her side of the room neat and tidy, and was a quiet sleeper, although with Deanne now sharing a room, and a bed, with Hamish, I would have had a room to myself had we been roommates.

Grabbing my phone from the nightstand, I checked my messages. He had promised to text me when he landed in Panama City from the resort, and again when he finally took off for Miami. Less than fourteen hours from now, I would get to see Craig again. Reaching over, I set my phone face down on the nightstand so the screen would not illuminate the dark room. With an impatient sigh, I rolled over, closed my eyes and tried to steal a few more minutes of sleep. Today we would be transporting the horses to the show grounds and the next time I saw a mattress it would be really late. It would be even later before I, before we, would have the benefit of sleep. Grinning wickedly to myself, I recalled Craig's sun kissed body. I imagined that I could feel the heat radiating from him. "Stop torturing yourself, Todd," I murmured into my pillow.

Readjusting the pillow, I wiped Craig from my mind and tried once again to reclaim sleep.

Katia was showing this weekend so we all pitched in to help move the horses and all their accoutrements to the show grounds. Hamish and Deanne were still glued at the hip. Troy was off today so he volunteered to drive the trucks back and forth, which freed up another set of hands to load and unload gear.

As it was, the day actually flew by and before I knew it the horses were settled in. I jumped in the shower to clean up before heading to Miami to pick up Craig. Pulling on a pair of faded jeans and a white long sleeve thermal cotton shirt, I slipped my feet into my old pair of brown cowboy boots. I had taken the time to dry my hair and it swung free as I bent to retrieve a wide brown leather belt with rhinestones along the buckle from my bottom drawer. A glance at my phone showed I was running late. Deftly shoving the belt through the belt loops of my jeans I raced out into the kitchen.

"How do I look?" Slipping the belt through the keeper, I straightened and looked Hamish in the eye. I needed a guy's opinion.

Raising his beer bottle as if to toast he replied with a smile. "Rustic and ravishing. If my brother doesn't agree then he is either blind or..." he paused to think, "or blind."

"Flattery will get you nowhere, dear Hamish," I shot back, searching for my purse.

"Can't blame a bloke for trying, now can you?"

Just then my stomach growled loudly.

"Have you eaten today?" He peered questioningly at me from under his dark lashes. Returning his gaze I merely blinked.

"I'll take that as a no. Here, reaching into the fridge he shoved a bag of fresh strawberries into my hand. "I just washed them and you can eat them on your way."

Standing on my tiptoes I kissed his cheek, took the proffered bag, grabbed my purse, and bolted out the door.

I hit rush hour traffic but thanks to the GPS I didn't get lost. Circling the terminal several times I waited for Craig to let me know he was ready. Parking fees were extravagant and he had insisted I pick him up curbside. Reaching for the last strawberry I started to make another orbit around the airport garage when my phone rang.

"Honey, I'm home!" I could feel his smile through the phone. "I'm standing under the Delta sign near baggage pickup."

"Okay, on my way." I cut through the bright yellow jungle of taxis like James Bond as I looped back around and under the neon 'Arrivals' sign. My heart leapt in my chest when I caught sight of him standing on the curb in his T-shirt, jeans, and flip-flops, duffle bag in hand.

He threw his duffle bag into the back seat and climbed into the passenger seat. Before his door had closed he reached across the center console and kissed me tenderly.

"I missed you," I said, my head spinning.

Somewhere behind us in the chaos that is an airport terminal a car honked, then another followed suit. Putting the SUV in gear we headed home to One Spirit Farm.

Once on the Interstate, I could let go of the wheel with one hand and I reached for Craig. Slipping his hand in mine we cruised home talking non-stop about the resort and my upcoming show. While driving, I sensed a distinct undercurrent of tension in Craig, even though outwardly he appeared chatty and happy. It was as if he wanted to share something, but couldn't bring himself to do it.

Halfway home, Colleen called and asked if we could stop by the show grounds to do a late night stall check and top off the water buckets in the stalls. The grounds had a rent-a-cop on duty during the show season, but we were responsible for our horse's well being.

The GPS guided us off of the Interstate one exit before Rachel's, and the traffic thinned as we grew closer to the show grounds. The rent-a-cop was sitting in his car by the entrance to the barns and with a wave we drove on past.

"Don't you feel secure," Craig muttered sarcastically. "As much as these horses cost, you would think the show grounds would have better security."

I had to agree, it made me nervous every time I left any of my horses at a show overnight. It always had. Pulling up behind the small concrete building that held the restrooms, we walked hand in hand down the quiet aisle of the barn. A set of mellow toned lights above every fourth stall lit our way. These lights remained on all night.

Craig stopped in front of Nicola's stall, "You want me to turn on the lights?"

"No, that's okay. This will just take a minute and I would rather not wake up the whole barn." Quietly, I lifted the handle on Otter's stall and slipped in to check on him. Blinking in acknowledgement, he shifted his weight from one hind leg to the other and ignored me. Working as a team, I passed Craig a water bucket to fill from a nearby faucet while I moved on to the next stall. A few horses shifted in their stalls and a lone whinny sounded from the barn behind us, but other than that all was quiet.

Thumbing through the four digit combination on the tack stall lock, I gave it a tug and with a soft *click* the tumblers sprang free. Pushing the stall door open on its rollers, I stepped over the front lip of the stall onto Deanne's doormat. After our first show she had taken it upon herself to make sure the stall stayed spotless, so she had laid down, and tried in vain to enforce, a 'barefoot' rule to keep the carpet spotless.

Craig walked up behind me, drying his hands on the front of his jeans. "What are you doin'?" He spoke just above a whisper.

"I want to make sure the feed is set up for tomorrow," I replied, slipping out of my boots before treading across the smoke grey carpet in my socks. It wouldn't do to piss her off tomorrow, especially since there would be enough tension with everyone riding their freestyle tests. Lifting the lid of a black plastic tack trunk set against the far wall, I made sure tomorrow morning's grain was mixed and ready. Satisfied, I shut the lid, placing the clean white saddle pad that had fallen behind it, on top. Lost in my own thoughts, I never heard Craig slide the stall door shut. Straightening, I felt the heat of his body as he wrapped his arms around me, pulling me tight against him. I let my body melt into his, reveling in the feel of him. *Hmmm…*

Holding me to him with one arm, he gently pulled my hair away from one side of my neck, exposing my skin to the cool night air. The tips of his fingers felt warm and familiar as they brushed lightly against my skin, sending waves of ecstasy radiating outward from my core. My body leapt in response to his every touch and the heat from his mouth felt like heaven as he kissed the sensitive skin of my neck. Oh how I had missed him, I thought. Stoking the flames, I tilted my head back against the curve of his muscular shoulder, inviting his lips to continue their lazy journey up my neck until they reached the delicate skin just behind my earlobe. I shivered involuntarily then inhaled sharply as my body responded to his tongue as it began to follow the delicate curve of my ear.

Ripples of goose bumps cascaded like falling dominos down my neck as he murmured huskily in my ear, "I want you." His lips sent soft warm puffs of air skittering across my ear lobe.

Responding to his suggestion, my nipples grew hard and fought against the lacey restraints of my bra. I groaned in pleasure as his hand cupped my breast. Slowly, his thumb climbed the peak of my breast until it reached the hardened nipple where it stopped tauntingly, a mere thin veil of lace caught between us. Another groan escaped past my lips. Letting go of me, he slid his other hand over my mouth and whispered, "Sshh lass." "Ye don't wanna be wakin' the 'orses, now do ye." His brogue was thick as syrup on a cold winter's day.

A ripple of nervous laughter burst forth from my lips, which his hand quickly stifled. Playing offense, he sought to distract me as his thumb continued to explore my hardened nipple and I felt my legs go weak. *Oh dear God.* Settling his fingers around it, he gave it a tug and I melted right there. Trying to regain my balance, I arched my back into him and felt him hard against my butt. With a grunt he let go of my breast, leaving it aching for more. Fed by the fire that only he could ignite, I fumbled, trying desperately to unbuckle my belt and lose my jeans.

Freed from his jeans, he yanked his shirt over his head and reached for mine. Pulling it above my breasts, his rough hands slid over my ripe nipples and I moaned in pleasure. "Shh," he said, with a husky chuckle. His hands deftly popped the back of my bra open and he shoved it haphazardly, up and under my shirt, exposing my breasts to the cool night air. Again they responded until I thought I might explode.

"Oh God, I need you," his breath was hot and heavy on my neck as he squeezed my nipples between his thumb and forefinger teasingly. Trying to stay quiet, I bit my lower lip hard between my teeth and let my jeans and lace thong fall until they pooled around my ankles. The sound of our breathing echoed off the fabric walls. Stepping on each leg of fabric in turn, I slipped my feet out of them as his hand found its way to the moist spot between my legs, playing, teasing. *Oh dear God!* Reeling with anticipation and need, my knees buckled and he caught me. Reaching for something to hold on to, I grasped the metal bars of the stall, pushing the dark blue curtain through the slats until I felt my fingers meet on the other side. His other hand slid over my mouth as he entered from behind and my world shattered around me like a thousand pieces of sparkling glass.

MEANWHILE, BACK AT THE BARN...

We lay curled on a clean beach towel I had pulled from one of the tack trunks. Thank God Rachel was always over-prepared for shows. I had slipped my clothes back on to keep warm in the chilly night. Possessing his own internal heater, Craig, wearing only jeans, pulled me to him and I snuggled closer.

The musical sound of horses shifting in their stalls filtered in over the top of the tack stall. My body took its time returning to normal. Every fiber of my being still vibrated with the after affects of our love making and I smiled to myself in the dark. Craig lazily played with one of my curls, twirling it between his fingers, and for the longest time, neither of us spoke. When we did it was a whisper.

Closing my eyes, I listened to the sound of his breathing behind me. After a few minutes it slowed and deepened. His hand fell gently across my shoulder, the curl still entwined in his still fingers.

Is this what love feels like? I thought to myself. Jake and I had what I would have considered a good sex life, but this, this was unlike anything I had ever dreamed of. Or, was this just lust? No, I thought pushing the idea aside. These feelings ran so much deeper than just lustful sex. As crazy as it seemed, my body, along with all of my senses, seemed to hum when he was around. The colors, the smells, his touch, they were magnified somehow, more vibrant, more alive. Taking a deep breath, I could smell the salt air and earthy scent that was Craig as he slept. Slowly, I opened my hand, flexing it to ease a cramp. My muscles still ached from clutching the bars of the stall. I smiled a slow seductive smile at the memory.

"I love you," I whispered into the chilly night air. "I love you, Craig Duncan."

I felt him stiffen then slide his arm tighter around my chest, pulling me in closer.

"Aye, and I love you my airt."

I had thought him asleep, though in retrospect I was glad he wasn't. "Airt?" I whispered.

"Aye, it's Gaelic. It's the point of a compass." He paused, letting his words sink in. "You are my compass."

Too stunned to reply I simply squeezed his hand in mine.

"And I, your needle," he added with a grin, grinding into me with his hips in a blatant show of suggestion. "But don't go askin' for more of the Gaelic for I havena got any. It is not taught much anymore and I have forgotten what I did learn as a little boy." After a few minutes he chuckled softly, "In fact, I think that is the only word I can recall."

Smiling, I wound my fingers through his and he flinched. "What?" I said, lifting his hand gently to inspect it. Not that I could have seen much in the dimness of the stall.

"You bit me," he replied bluntly.

Stifling a giggle, I gently kissed the underside of each finger in turn.

We heard the bolt slide at the same instant then a short pause before the rollers started to move, carrying the heavy door. The sound of the metal rollers shattered our quiet cocoon. Someone was opening a stall. Sitting bolt upright, he held a finger to his lips, motioning me to stay quiet. Maybe someone else was checking on his or her own horses tonight, I thought. A horse shifted nearby and my ears searched the dark night, trying to decipher which stall it was. Shifting his weight, Craig stood on the balls of his feet, ready to spring into action.

"Back up beast," came the harsh sound of a male voice through the thin fabric walls.

My eyes grew big as saucers and I leaped to my feet. The voice came from our right, from the direction of Cronos's stall.

In a panic I tried to shove Craig aside. Pulling me back, he put a hand over my mouth and shook his head, warning me. Over what seemed an eternity he slowly, quietly slid the door to the tack stall open just enough for him to slip through the opening. Moving to follow him, he put his hand up to stop me. The look on his face in the dim light of the aisle warned me not to follow.

More shuffling noises came from her stall and the unmistakable sound of a feed bucket rattling against the side of a stall, and grain being dumped. "Eat up you stinky bitch," the voice growled.

A well, timed whinny from William hid the sounds of the tack stall door as Craig hastily pushed it back further and slipped through. My head popped through the opening just in time to see him creeping down the aisle. As he reached Cronos's stall, a man stepped out into the warm yellow light of the aisle and he stood face to face with Jose.

Seeing his escape route blocked, he shoved Craig hard. Prepared for a fight, Craig's fist slammed into Jose's gut with a dull thud and I heard his breath escape in surprise. Launched back into the stall, Craig disappeared in after him and I heard Cronos snort in abject surprise. *Oh, crap!*

The barn around us began to stir as the stall partitions rattled loudly each time a body slammed against them. Grunts, thuds, and the sound of fists connecting with their target reverberated in the small space. Worried about Cronos, I bolted out of the tack stall, snatching a lead rope from a hook near the door. Cronos would eat just about anything you put in front of her and I panicked the instant I heard the grain being dumped. Nearing the stall I heard Cronos squeal, then the sound of steel shod hooves ricocheted off the wooden side of the stall. Jose burst through the stall door, panting. With one hand he shoved me backwards then, gasping for air, he sprinted down the aisle.

Recovering my balance, I heard a slew of curses fly out of Craig's mouth. Gripping the sides of the door in each hand his head popped out. Gasping for air he shouted, "Where?"

"That way," I directed my finger at Jose's retreating back. Bursting through the door Craig took off like a shot down the aisle. His bare feet a quiet contrast to the sound of Jose's retreating sneakers drumming loudly on the concrete. I caught a glimpse of his sweaty back, arms pumping in unison just before he disappeared into the dark, unlit grass beyond the barn.

Turning my focus immediately to Cronos, I stepped into the stall. Moving slowly, I let out a soft whistle so she would recognize me. It was the same whistle I used to greet her in the pasture or to get her attention. She stood facing me, her haunches pressed firmly against the far corner of the stall. Snorting loudly, steam shot from her big black nostrils into the chilly night air, then whirled around her muzzle before dissipating into thin air. Warily, her eyes followed me and I whistled again. "Whoa girl, it's just me," I offered. The soft tips of her ears locked onto me and she lowered her head. Slowly I extended my hand towards her. Reaching for me with her muzzle she began to lick her lips.

Waiting for her to come to me, I strained to see into the feed bucket. Had she eaten any of it yet, I wondered, my heart thrumming against my chest. The thought of someone trying to hurt, or even poisoning her had my blood boiling. Sensing a change in my mood, she jerked her head straight up in the air, cocking one liquid brown eye on me from above. Every muscle in her body tensed, waiting, unsure.

I slowed my breathing, and whistled softly. Changing her mind, it took less than a second for her to step up and meet me. Her stable blanket *crinkled* as she moved. Her warm muzzle searched my hand for a mint. Slipping my fingers around her leather halter I rubbed her forehead with my other hand. "Good girl." My hand was shaking uncontrollably.

Without even looking, I clipped the lead rope onto the ring beneath her halter by feel, something I had done a thousand times before. The metallic sound of metal meeting metal struck an eerie chord in the quiet stall. My eyes, glued to the feed bucket, searched for the feed I had heard. Hanging in the shadows, the bottom was hidden from view.

Cautiously I lifted the bucket from its metal hook and carried it into the dim light of the aisle. The feed skittered across the hard plastic as I tilted it, allowing the light to reach the bottom. Any doubts I had about it being feed evaporated. Reaching in, I pulled out a handful. The hard smooth pellets shifted and settled in my fist.

Nickering softly, Cronos shoved her nose into my shoulder. "No girl, this is not for you." Peering at the feed clutched in my hand, I decided I would need better light. Dropping the handful of feed back into the bucket, I flipped the end of the lead rope up and over her neck, and stepped out of the stall. The rattle of the door echoed through the barn as I shut it. The light switch for our section of the barn sat just outside Nicola's stall and I flicked it on. The soft hum of fluorescent bulbs springing to life helped to fill the quiet air around me and I blinked hard in the white light, trying to make my eyes adjust. Where in the world was Craig? Worry began to creep in and I forced it back.

Turning my attention back to the grain, I sifted through it again, this time more carefully. A fine white powder, much like baking soda, coated the hard pellets and dusted the inside of the bucket.

An eager nicker from somewhere down the aisle alerted me to Craig's return and I jerked my head up, wanting to lay my eyes on him. Striding towards me in the stark white lights, his arms and torso glistened with sweat. Dust and grime from the stall shavings clung to his lower arms, wrapping around to his elbows, and across the front of his jeans. A look of concern on his face, he asked, "Is she okay?"

"I think so, I don't think she had the chance to eat any of it." I tried desperately to recall whether I had heard her eating during the melee. No, I didn't think she had. At least I prayed to God she hadn't. "Jose?"

He shook his head, clearly annoyed. "Little bugger can run," he scowled. "What'd he do?" He said, pulling the lip of the bucket towards him so he could peer in.

I shivered involuntarily, "I'm not sure." Reaching back into the depths of the bucket I offered him a handful of grain to inspect. "They are covered with a white powder of some sort." He sorted through the pellets, studying them.

"If I didn't know what just happened, I would probably think it was electrolytes or some other supplement." I shivered again as the realization hit me. Whatever it was, had we not caught Jose in the act, we most assuredly would have never given the powdery feed much thought and Cronos would have made a meal of it.

"Knowing Jose, I have a good idea what it is," he said, a slight edge to his voice. "Cocaine."

"W-h-a-t!" I replied in astonishment. "But why? I don't even know the guy."

He cocked a sandy brow. "Aye, but he knows you're mine," he said dryly.

"But I've never heard of giving a horse cocaine, have you? I mean does it work the same way as it does with people?" A million unanswered questions flew through my mind.

"I don't know, but we need to keep this between us until we find out."

"Surely you don't expect me to not call the cops," I said in abject disbelief. "He just tried to poison or-or drug my horse!" Like a child making a point I stomped my foot, wincing as my heel made contact with the concrete through my thin socks.

Stubbornly silent, Craig straightened, squaring his broad shoulders. The rivulets of sweat had cooled in the night air and millions of tiny goose bumps paraded across his arms.

"Here," I said, shoving the bucket into his hands. Wordlessly he took the bucket from me. Turning on my heel I stomped off to get his shirt from the tack stall. I simply couldn't think straight or be mad at him when he looked that good without his shirt. When I returned he traded the bucket for his shirt, slipping it over his head.

Better, much better.

"Are you serious? You really think this is cocaine?" I rocked the bucket back and forth in the light, studying its contents.

"Aye, I think it is a logical assumption, given what I know about Jose."

Working in the trauma room, I had been exposed to all kinds of trauma patients, gunshot wounds, fondly referred to as GSW's, suicides, car accidents or MVA's, as well as drug cases. More than once a person would be brought in and classified as a trauma based on how they were discovered. I clearly remembered one such case, in which a man had been found lying face down in his front yard by a passerby. No one knew what had happened to him but the medics on the scene had been unable to rouse him. He had met the criteria for a trauma alert and was brought in on my shift. I remembered him so well because of his size. He was easily over six feet tall and was pushing two hundred and fifty pounds of pure muscle.

Out cold on the table when he arrived, he had come to suddenly, and immediately started thrashing around and wailing his arms in all directions. Unlucky enough to be closest to him, he had latched onto my wrist with one hand. The strength of a drug-induced rage is something I never wanted to be on the receiving end of ever again. His oversized hand had encircled my thin wrist in a death grip, fingers digging down to the bone. The agonizing pain had sent me to my knees on the trauma room floor, as he wrenched my arm, yanking my shoulder hard enough to pull a tendon. It had taken one doctor, a physician's assistant, who jumped on top of the man's chest, and a male nurse to free my arm. Afterwards, I had been more pissed because I had a recognized event scheduled the following week and was barely able to ride.

Licking the tip of my index finger, I ran it along the inside of the bucket. Holding it up in the light, I eyeballed the amount of powder on my finger. It would do. Without hesitating and before he could stop me, I crammed my finger up under my upper lip and rubbed the powder into the soft, moist tissue of my gums.

Too shocked to react, Craig stared at me, mouth agape. Within seconds, my gum and the inside of my lip went numb.

"Well that was dumb," he said.

"It's numb. You're right, it most definitely could be cocaine." Seeing the confused look on his face, I continued, "The ingredients in cocaine act as a local anesthetic." Running the tip of my tongue between my gum and lip, I nodded, "It went numb almost instantly. I don't know much about the illegal side of drugs, but it makes sense that if it works so quickly, it is likely very pure." I headed to where a faucet jutted out from the wall. Turning on the spigot, I rinsed my mouth out several times.

"But," he hesitated, "that doesn't mean it is definitely coke."

"No, but it narrows the field to drugs with anesthetic properties."

His brow creased in worry. "Lauren, we need to keep this between us for now, no cops."

"But..." He cut me off with a glare.

"Think it through. You have one last chance to qualify tomorrow, right?" I nodded in ascent.

"As far as we can tell, she," he pointed towards Cronos's stall, "didn't eat any of it. If someone were goin' to drug a horse in competition with the intent of disqualifyin' or causing them harm, then you would think they would be smart enough to have a back up plan. Most likely, when we got here in the mornin' there would have been a vet, conveniently ready to take a 'random' drug test. Or maybe they would cry foul after the competition, dependin' on how well you did. Think about it, we don't know how cocaine affects horses. For all we know she could have died or just went nuts when you rode her."

And then it hit me, Maria. The answer was there all the time. "Wait a minute, the person we were missing. What about Maria?" I asked incredulously. I haven't spoken to her since she left Colleen's barn, but what if she is vying for a spot to represent Panama?" *What if she is trying to get us eliminated so she can fill our spot?*

He ran a hand over his chin absently, as the wheels of thought turned in his head. "How many spots are there?"

"Four and an alternate, just enough for the five of us. We don't have to go through a selection process based on scores because we have the exact number we need." My voice rose in pitch as I talked. "Holy crap! That is what she has been up too!"

"I don't know, it sounds reasonable, but all of it, the huaca, the chicken head, and the drugs. I'm not sure she's that smart." His voice dripped with disdain. "Either way, let's get rid of whatever is in that bucket," he pointed at the blue bucket sitting innocently on the ground.

We rinsed the bucket and dumped the water directly down the drain in the wash rack; then Craig walked down to the guard shack at the entrance to the show grounds. After explaining that we had seen a man wandering around the stalls while doing our stall check, the security guard became all business. He must have been paying more attention to the barn than we originally thought, for he was adamant that ours was the only vehicle he had seen in the last several hours.

We both agreed that Jose was unlikely to return that night, however there was no way I would leave Cronos until I was sure she would be safe. Not only that, but we were not one hundred percent positive that she hadn't eaten some of the grain in her bucket. Besides, I had no idea how cocaine would affect a horse.

"I need to call the vet."

Craig frowned, his brow furrowing. "And tell them what, that your horse ate cocaine laced feed. I don't think that would go over well."

"I think I can trust him to be discreet." I said.

One eyebrow shot up in question. "Are you sure?"

I thought back to Troy's fundraiser. Bull seemed to have the respect of everyone who knew him. I felt my face flush as I remembered how he had spirited me out of harms way in the stall. I had no doubt Bull was attracted to me and maybe that could play to my advantage. Deciding to keep my history with Bull out of the picture, I responded, "Rachel trusts him." That seemed good enough for Craig and he nodded.

I didn't have his number, or I thought wryly, his last name. No doubt I had heard it at some point, but at the moment it escaped me. I would have to call and wake Rachel. Pulling out my cell, I punched her number. It was almost midnight. After only three rings she picked up. Apologizing for waking her, I kept the story simple, Cronos didn't finish her feed and I wanted to have a vet look at her before Craig and I came home. Wishing me luck, she hung up then sent me a text with Bull's phone number. Callahan was his last name.

After saving his contact information in my phone, I dialed Bull. After only two rings he answered. Everyone must be up late tonight, I thought to myself. As I heard him answer the phone, my heart fluttered in my chest and I glanced down quickly lest Craig see my reaction.

"Bull here." His voice was gravelly.

"Bull, it's Lauren, Rachel's friend." My voice sounded surprisingly calm to my ears.

After a long hesitation he responded, "What's up? Got a sick horse?" He was all business.

"Well, um, maybe. Listen, I need to ask you something and I need it to fall under the guise of doctor patient privacy." The words hadn't come out right. Pinching the bridge of my nose between my thumb and forefinger in an effort to think, I continued, "Bull, I need to ask you a vet question and I need confidentiality." There, that didn't sound quite so stupid, I thought, digging the toe of my boot into the grass in front of the barn.

The phone was quiet for a moment. "Shoot," he said finally, his voice a bit more cautious.

"What happens to a horse when given cocaine?" I blurted out. After a few moments he responded.

"Oral or injected? I am assuming you would know the method of delivery, or you wouldn't have asked such a question at midnight," he said dryly.

"Oral, in powder form, and I assume it is cocaine, but am not positive," I paused. "It is the most likely candidate though." Suddenly it hit me, shoving the phone at Craig, I pushed past him and yanked open the stall door. "Flashlight, I need a flashlight!"

"Um, hold on just a second, she is flippin' out." Craig spoke into my phone, while pulling his phone out of his pocket. In what seemed an eternity, he turned on the flashlight function on his cell. Snatching it out of his hand I raced back into the stall, trying not to spook Cronos. On hands and knees I cautiously combed through the shavings starting near where her feed bucket had been—where Jose would have been standing. I could hear Craig's voice talking to Bull, telling him to hang on again.

Finally, the beam of light reflected off the smooth plastic cylinder of a syringe sticking straight up out of a small pile of hay. The needle lay buried out of view, and the white plunger was pulled back about half way.

"Oh shit!" Craig said from behind me as I gingerly pulled the syringe free with a shaky hand. The opaque, plastic safety cap was still covering the sharp needle. Pulling the cap off, I studied the shiny metal needle in the narrow beam of the light. It appeared to be clean, free of hair, blood, or other residue. Most likely it was unused, especially since it was still full. It was doubtful Jose had recapped the syringe in the melee. Trading the syringe for the phone I swallowed hard before saying, "Bull, what about both?"

"Lauren, what the hell is going on?" His tone was sharp, cutting through my rising panic. No doubt, the same tone he used to gain control in emergencies.

"Bull, I need to know, how does cocaine affect horses? And no, I am not using or giving it to a horse." I cut him off before he could speak. "Look, I need some answers, please. You are the only person I could call."

With a huge sigh, his demeanor switched and he once again became Bull the Veterinarian. "Coke and horses is a crap shoot. Years ago crooked trainers on the track tried it with racehorses with mixed results. Some horses ran slower, while others ran like bullets. Problem was, and is, that you don't get the same result all the time. Heroin, now that is another elephant all together."

"Elephant? What do you mean?"

"Elephant juice is a slang for heroin. Opiates, like heroin are used to make horses run. Are you sure it is coke?"

"Heroin is bitter; this was tasteless and had numbing properties." I glanced at Craig then continued, "Everything points to cocaine." Craig was staring at me in amazement, no doubt wondering how I knew what these drugs tasted like.

"Ahh, well then the question is why would someone give a horse coke? Am I right?" Not waiting for an answer he continued, "Not to get too technical, but when dealing with brain receptors, norepinephrine and all that technical stuff, essentially coke increases brain stimulation. That and it would show up in drug tests, which as you know can be done randomly at rated horse shows, especially at the FEI levels."

My brain kicked into overdrive. "I had forgotten that. It blocks the enzyme that pumps adrenaline and re-directs it to norepinephrine receptors." Again there was silence on the other end of the phone. Ignoring it I continued, "Bull, how long will it stay in a horse's system?" My stomach began to flip flop around as I realized we were scheduled to ride our freestyle in seven hours.

"Missy, you sure do attract trouble don't you. But then again, I think you already know that." This time there was no humor in his voice, just pure analytical observation. "What time do you ride and how much did your horse get?" It hadn't taken much for him to figure things out. Leave it to Bull to shoot from the hip.

"The needle looks unused. There was powder in her grain, but I don't think she had much at all." Pausing to catch my breath I added, "9:14 is our ride time."

"You should be good. Six hours is what I recall, but I will look it up and get back to you if it is different. Keep an eye on her tonight for restlessness or anxiety. That, and pray you don't get tested."

"Thanks, Bull, I owe you one."

"No, but what you will do one fine day, is fill me in on what the hell is going on and how you know all this stuff about drugs." With that he hung up.

I stared at the screen as it turned black. He had sounded disappointed in me, almost accusing and I was surprised by how much it bothered me. *Someday, Bull, I'll set the record straight.*

We stood in silence in the quiet barn, absorbing everything that had just happened. Eventually Craig moved. Striding back down to the tack stall, he made a makeshift bed on the floor out of saddle pads, towels, and a cotton cooler for one of the horses. I searched Rachel's SUV for anything else I could find. Pulling on a black sweatshirt I had found in the back seat, I made my way back to the tack stall. Katia and Anne would be here bright and early to feed and do stalls, until then we were camping out. We set the alarm on Craig's phone for 5 a.m. and curled up on the makeshift bed.

**

I awoke with a start to the musical chimes of the alarm with Craig curled behind me. Slowly, I rolled off of my left arm, which was numb and tingling from being caught between my body and the hard ground. The barn was not yet alive, but horses were beginning to stir in their stalls in anticipation of their morning feed. Sitting up, the realization that my freestyle was in just a few hours hit home; the fingers of panic began to pull at me. Seeing my anxiety, Craig sent me home to shower and clean up while he stayed behind until the girls arrived.

When I pulled into One Spirit Farm Troy and Rachel were waiting. Apparently Craig, still worried about my safety, had called ahead to let them know that someone had tried to get to Cronos. I had no doubt that he also wanted to make sure I made it home safely. Keeping relatively quiet, I let them do most of the talking, answering questions here and there. Not knowing what Craig had told them, I let them lead the conversation until I could piece together what they did indeed know. Everybody already knew about the mysterious man named Joe, but other than Hamish, Craig, and me, no one knew the full extent of the story.

I had hoped to slip into the guesthouse without notice. Unfortunately, Javier foiled my plans. After greeting me at the door, he decided that I was fodder for one of his barking tirades. Within minutes, Colleen was in the kitchen. Elaine was right behind her.

Making a face, Colleen took in my disheveled appearance in one sweeping glance. "You do remember you have your freestyle today." She reminded me of a mother hen.

"Yeah, um glad you are up. We need to talk." Colleen had invested a lot of personal time, effort, and commitment into my riding. Without her, I wouldn't be here. I decided to tell her everything. My nerves were already wrecked and I desperately needed to get this insanity off my chest. Also, I just couldn't shake the feeling that I had a duty to my friends. Besides, I couldn't live with myself if one of them got hurt. They had a right to know so they, too, could be on the lookout. "Is everyone else still sleeping?"

"Hamish and Deanne don't sleep much anyway," Elaine shot me a knowing look, "so I'll go get them." She strode down the hall towards Hamish's room, Javier leaping up and down behind her. In his excitement to see Deanne, the bell on his collar jingled in time with his joy.

I could feel Colleen's eyes boring into my back. Turning, I met her gaze. "I need to talk to everyone before the day gets started. Before the show," I added. "Can you call Rachel and see if she and Troy can come down. I really want to do this only once."

Within minutes everyone was gathered in the small living room of the guesthouse. Pulling one of the wooden chairs from the kitchen table, I sank down onto the hard seat and looked into seven pairs of curious eyes. *Where to begin*, I thought. Taking a deep breath, I jumped in the deep end. "Last night someone tried to drug Cronos with cocaine."

You could have heard a pin drop in the moments before bedlam broke out. Everybody jumped in at once with questions and shocked exclamations. Summoning the strength, I told them about our encounter with Jose the night before and that yes indeed, he was the same man that had attacked me several weeks earlier. The main question was why, and for that answer I had to delve into the history of Craig, Jose, the drugs, and last but not least, Maria.

The faces before me were a mix of anger, disgust, and disbelief. Several times I found myself glancing at Hamish who would nod his head at me in encouragement. I told them about the huaca and the mysterious Santiago as well. The more I talked, the better I felt. Unfortunately, the better I felt, the more anxious they became. They hadn't had as much time to absorb this whole fiasco as I had. Out of the corner of my eye, I saw Deanne turn pale as a ghost.

As I finished my surreal tale, the weight lifted from my shoulders. "I wanted you all to know what has been happening because I want you to be on the lookout. Who knows what Jose is capable of doing, or how much of this is Maria's doing." As I said the words I realized I still had no idea just what he was responsible for other than the attack and last night. Did he leave the huaca and just who was Santiago? "It seems that being around me may be a liability."

Leaving the couch behind, Hamish stood and crossed his arms. "No, Lauren, by telling everyone, we can all keep an eye on you." I smiled gratefully at him as everyone agreed.

"He's right," Colleen, who had remained silent through most of my story, finally spoke. "Besides, we need to keep an eye on each other's horses as well. We don't know all the players in this story or exactly what their motive is. If they are willing to go after one horse and rider, what's to say they won't go after one of us as well?" Glancing at her watch then up at me she said, "You need to get cracking, it is a quarter after six."

"Crap!" Leaping up, I headed for my room, grabbed my show clothes then darted for the shower. If I hadn't been awake before, I most certainly was now. Thank goodness the show grounds were only fifteen minutes away. While in the shower, Elaine shouted through the door that Cronos was braided and Craig was up at the house taking a shower.

FREESTYLE

I could feel Cronos's back swing beneath me with each step of the extended trot. The sheer power of her muscles carried me swiftly across the arena in time to the music in my head. On the upbeat her back swelled, filling my seat as she nimbly picked up the left lead canter. We were one with the music and I felt the notes floating around me, and my mare floating beneath me. The dark side of my eyelids provided all that I needed to feel my ride unfold.

I sat alone in the tack stall dressed in my penguin outfit, riding my freestyle test in my head. Colleen had ushered everyone out so I could have a few minutes to prepare. This was it. Everyone else had already garnered qualifying scores. Well, everyone but Maria and me. Immediately I pushed her from my mind. *That* was a distraction better left outside of the arena, although I would be lying to myself if the idea of stomping Maria in today's competition hadn't entered my mind. In fact, in some ways it spurred me on. I had always been more competitive with myself than with other riders, but recent events made me want to cram that pretty little face of hers into the deep red ochre of the clay arena. Feeling my muscles tense at the thought, I tried to pick up my ride where I had left off.

A few minutes later I emerged into daylight, buckling the straps on my helmet. A short distance down the aisle, Colleen stood holding Cronos's bridle. Seeing me, she walked Cronos out into the sunlight next to the mounting block. "Ready?" Her eyes met mine, both in question and confirmation.

Nodding, I gathered the reins, slipped my foot in the stirrup and swung over. Cronos peered around to look at me as if to say she, too, was ready. With a soft cluck we moved off into the crisp, sparkling morning towards the warm up arena.

The whole gang stood along the bright white painted railings of the warm up arena, waiting expectantly. No pressure there, I thought dryly. My eyes sought and found Craig's and he smiled warmly at me. Squaring my shoulders, I pointed her nose towards the gate.

About twenty minutes later we were ready. The warm up had gone smoothly and Colleen had timed it just right. Today, Elaine served as my watch and she gave me a wave to let us know we had one rider ahead of us. Heading out of the warm up area I reached down and gave Cronos's glistening neck a reassuring pat. Whether it was really meant for me or for her I wasn't at all sure. Katia fussed about, removing Cronos's white polo wraps and brushing the sand from her legs. Anne gave my boots a quick swipe and ran a clean towel across Cronos's face.

"Thanks," I mumbled, grateful for their help.

Glancing back up, my eyes discovered Maria heading straight for us. Her ride time was about twenty minutes after ours. Smiling as sweetly as I could manage I said, "Good luck." She hissed in return, dug her heels into Mariposa's sides and trotted past us.

Colleen fell in step with us, "Well, well, I was wondering who she was training with." Colleen's voice was a mixture of disbelief and disgust. "I don't know why I am so surprised though."

I followed her gaze and saw a rather short, thin man talking to Maria. He looked to be in his mid forties with light blonde curly hair. A dark green baseball cap sat on his head, forcing the curls at the back and side of his head to stick out haphazardly. Feeling our gaze, he turned and waved at Colleen who nodded curtly in return. "Know him?" I asked, pulling Cronos up.

"Chip, and if you ever ride with him or even think about it I'll kill you," She replied curtly, shooting me her sternest look.

"That bad, huh?"

"Worse, he takes bad riding to an art form and leaves a trail of lame horses in his wake. Besides, he thinks he's God's gift to women, which makes him lower than a newt in my book. He'll sleep with anyone, and married women are a specialty of his." She shook her head. With a heavy sigh she added, "Come on, let's go."

As we moved from the sunshine to the shady interior of the indoor arena, Colleen gave me some last minute tips then stepped away. Gathering the reins, I shifted into gear and headed for the in gate. Picking up a trot I began to circle the arena and tried to find my zone, my inner calm. Halfway around the arena I passed the previous competitor as she made her way out. I nodded, smiled, and congratulated her on her ride. As I reached the other side of the arena I found my mind drifting from the task at hand. I couldn't seem to get into the zone. Inhaling deeply, I wiggled my tight shoulders under the confines of my shadbelly coat, trying to relieve the tension. Several trot strides later I asked for a collected canter and Cronos hesitated for a moment beneath me. I was going to have to loosen up before I affected her lovely movement with my stiff body. Taking another deep breath, I let my heels sink further down in the stirrups.

The sharp metallic sound of a bell cut through the air, taking my breath away. Damn, I'm not ready, I thought slightly panicked. Beneath me Cronos tensed and broke to a trot. As I started to ask for the canter again I gritted my teeth and dug down deep within me, pulling out every ounce of grit I had. The clock was ticking and I needed to get started. Coming to a sudden halt I took another breath and muttered, "Come on, Todd, you got this. Just kick on." I lifted my right hand to signal for my music to start. As the strains of the *Mission Impossible* theme sounded over the loud speakers, I picked up a really forward trot and headed for A.

We entered at an extended trot and halted squarely at X as the music faded. As I saluted to the judge I could feel my show nerves evaporate. In my minds eye I imagined a huge cross country fence where the judge at C sat. Knowing I could tackle it, I picked up the reins, kicked on in time to the music and tackled my dressage test. The music had been blended smoothly by Troy and the strains of the *Get Smart* theme song highlighted our canter work.

Without a single bobble we came to our final halt and saluted. I hadn't realized I had been smiling through most of our test, for when I went to smile at the judge, the muscles of my face ached. Standing up, the judge at C saluted back with a nod. As I reached down to pat Cronos on the neck, the spectators along the arena and in the metal bleachers erupted in claps and cheers. So much so that Cronos suddenly dropped her shoulder, ducked hard and spooked. I nearly became unseated. Desperately seeking a handhold I grabbed instinctively for her mane, completely forgetting that it was in neat little braids. Within steps of falling off I managed to right myself.

Laughing aloud, I thanked the judge and made my way out of the arena. As I passed the next rider who began circling the dressage arena, my score flashed on the electronic board at the far side of the arena. In all my exhilaration at riding a nearly flawless test and almost falling off after the halt, I had forgotten to check my score. A 70.2 flashed in bold red letters under our names.

The crowd in the stands began to clap again as I passed through the in gate and I felt my face flush with a mixture of embarrassment and pleasure. Before I could dismount, everybody met me with smiles and thumps on the legs. Katia and Ann took charge of Cronos once I swung off her back. Running up the stirrups, loosening her girth, unbuckling the noseband, and giving her a pat, they treated her like a rock star.

Shedding my coat in the cool air, I handed it to Deanne who had passed a wiggling Javier off to Hamish, and wrapped my arms around Craig. His strong arms pulled me in as he hugged me; the familiarity that was Craig made me smile. Attempting to kiss me, his eyes flitted for a moment to the brim of my helmet. Adjusting his course smoothly, he tilted his head sideways and came in under the brim with a grin. His lips felt warm on mine. With the growing crowd around us, he kept the kiss short and chaste. As he pulled free, he gave my gloved hand a gentle squeeze.

Before long we moved en masse back towards the barn, following Katia who was leading Cronos. There were still nine riders to go in the class so if I had indeed placed, I wouldn't be needed back at the ring for a while, and I most certainly had no interest in watching Maria ride. Right now, I stood in first place. *First place!* The thought was a heady one indeed.

Physically exhausted from lack of sleep, anticipation was all that kept me going. In my gut, I knew I had nailed the freestyle, but judging dressage was in many ways an inexact science. Sure they had guidelines, and judges attended seminars and classes to keep in step with current rule changes and to keep their skills honed, but first impressions meant a lot. While one judge may score you a seven for a particular movement, two other judges sitting at different angles may award a six. One point may not seem like much, but if the movement score had a coefficient number next to it, then you were in danger of losing multiple points. While I had scored very well, I knew I could be knocked off my pedestal by any one of the other riders in the line up. Well, all except for one anyway.

Colleen kept an eye on the show schedule, comparing it to the overhead announcements so we could know who was riding and if they were indeed running on time. Craig never let me out of his sight. Elaine and Deanne kept me talking and my mind occupied; before I knew it, Katia had led Cronos out. We had been called back to the arena and I had missed it. The Intermediare and Grand Prix freestyle classes had award ceremonies, with the winner usually given a prize from one of the show's sponsors. Horse blankets emblazoned with the company's logo were the most common prizes given out. Grabbing my shadbelly, helmet, and gloves from the tack stall I slipped them on.

Before mounting, I brushed my boots off with a soft cloth that lay next to the mounting block. Exhausted from lack of sleep and the stress of competition, I swung my leg over Cronos's back. Picking up the reins, we moved off toward the covered arena. On the way to the arena the impact of what was happening washed over me. I had obviously placed in the freestyle class. The score didn't count towards qualifying for the Games. We had already garnered the necessary scores. Now that I had completed an Intermediare freestyle, we were in. Getting called back to the arena for our freestyle was just icing on the cake.

As we approached the arena gate, Colleen gave Cronos a pat on the neck and smiled up at me. "You did it," she said with a smile, "now go enjoy it."

My eyes met hers. "I did it?" I had lost track of the scoring while talking to Elaine and Deanne.

She nodded a wide grin splitting her face. "Look" She pointed at the electronic sign. Sure enough, our names were on top.

The arena steward opened the gate and Cronos marched in as if she owned the place. We were shown where to stand, between the inner dressage arena and the outer arena fence. There were four other riders beside myself who entered the arena. Turning so that we faced the main set of bleachers, we lined up. Glancing around to take in the scene I caught Maria glaring at me from the far end. Maria and Mariposa had placed a surprising second.

Feeling her gaze still on me, I casually glanced her way and was met by her dark gaze. Her eyes, nearly black with hate, had narrowed and bore into me with such intense hatred. My breath caught in my throat for a moment as I recovered my composure. I swore if looks could have killed, I would have been dead. Pulling my eyes from hers, I squared my shoulders, and made every attempt to shrug her off. Instead, I turned my focus on the announcer who stood next to a whip-thin lady with butt length blonde hair and a more than ample chest. Immaculately made up from head to toe she was a dead ringer for a Barbie. Right, I thought, the show secretary, I had heard her described by the girls.

The announcer's voice cackled for a moment as the microphone came too close to the sound system and I saw poor Mariposa spin and bolt out of the corner of my eye. The poor mare was coiled as tight as a spring, her nervous eyes flashing restlessly around in the shade of the arena.

Caught as I was in watching Mariposa, I nearly missed it as they announced the winner of the fifth place ribbon. A chestnut mare with four flashy socks and a blaze stepped forward from the line, her rider leaning down to accept the yellow and white ribbon. The pink and white ribbon was attached to the bridle of a smart looking black gelding.

The speaker cackled, just as the announcer introduced the third place finisher. A white ribbon was attached to the bridle of a handy bay gelding by Barbie. Maria was next. I felt Cronos shift nervously under me. *Sorry girl.* Reaching down I gave her a reassuring pat with my gloved hand.

With the red and white ribbon in hand, Barbie stood waiting patiently for the announcer to name the second place horse and rider combination so she could attach the red ribbon to Mariposa's bridle. I heard the name Maria Santiago de Bolive ring clearly across the indoor arena. Stunned, the scene in the arena quickly faded to background noise as it hit me. *Santiago!* That wasn't her last name, was it? My mind drifted back to the show bill I had received with my competitor's packet. I knew her name was a mouthful, that sort of thing was common in Latin countries, but Santiago?

Barbie crossed in front of us, heading for Mariposa. Cronos danced nervously beneath me, forcing me back to reality. Gathering up the reins I collected her between my seat, legs, and hand, trying to keep her from erupting in all directions. *Santiago? No, it couldn't be. What had I ever done to her?* Thinking back, I honestly couldn't remember ever even knowing Maria's last name. Obviously it hadn't rung a bell with Craig or Hamish. Surely they would have known her name.

I felt Cronos stepping neatly into a nervous piaffe, she held it for several steps before settling down enough for Barbie to approach her head. Barbie carried a blue and white ribbon in one hand, and a red and black stable blanket in the other.

Still in a fog, I slipped off of Cronos. A set of helping hands appeared in the form of a young girl who helped me slip the cooler over Cronos's saddle and buckle it in place. With practiced hands, Barbie slipped the ribbon onto the side of the bridle, just below her ear. With a snort and a shake of her head Cronos showered all three of us with white foam from her mouth and started to dance in place. From my vantage point on the ground, I tried in vain to get a good look at Maria's face. I was afraid my face had given my thoughts away, and the last thing I wanted was for her to get off scott free for what she had done.

Once remounted, the announcer signaled for us to make a victory lap around the arena. Springing into a canter, Cronos took the lead as we started past the backside of the judge's booth at C. *But it was a man who picked up the huaca, not a woman.* My mind fumbled around trying to make sense of what my gut already knew and for a moment I thought I would be sick. Faces passed by us in a blur, my mind not really focusing on the arena. Sitting up in the saddle, in a light two point position, as we made our way towards the in gate I found Craig's eyes. He'd heard it, too. Glancing from face to face, I realized that we were the only ones to put the pieces together. *But why?*

My eyes still locked with Craig's, I trotted out of the in gate. Elaine grabbed Cronos's bridle as I swung off her back just in time to see Maria exit the arena on Mariposa. Without so much as a glance she rode past us towards Chip who stood waiting for her just outside the arena.

With one hand, I unbuckled my helmet, slid it off my head and nearly threw it into Deanne's surprised hands. I could feel the hot, searing heat of anger welling up from within and I began to shake. Keeping my shaky legs under me, I made a beeline for her. By the time I reached her she had slid off of Mariposa's back.

"Santiago, huh? Did you think I wouldn't figure it out?" The sound of my voice took me by surprise as I snarled at her.

Spinning on her boot heel she turned to face me, eyes flashing darkly. Without a word she daintily unbuckled her helmet and slipped it off over her perfectly groomed black hair. The gold bling sewn into her matching snood winked at me in the sunlight as she turned those dark eyes on me. "I don't have any idea what you are talking about," she purred through her bright red lipstick. "My name is Maria Ramos Santiago de Bolive." Blinking innocently through her long lashes, she spun daintily on her boot heel.

It was all I could do not to cram that hooker red lipstick down her throat. I stood firm, fists at my side, fighting to control my rage. Ignoring me, she stalked towards the barn. Too stunned to react, Chip just stood there, mouth agape, Mariposa's reins in hand. Throwing him a look of disgust, I set off after Maria's quickly retreating back.

We were almost at the barn before I caught up with her. "Hey, this isn't over, in fact I think a trip to the show office is needed. Someone needs to know just what lengths you will go through to win." Her back still to me, she picked up the pace, the canary yellow lining of her shadbelly tails flapping angrily behind her. Her boot heels clicked across the concrete barn aisle.

Matching her stride, I stalked her down the barn aisle, ignoring the stares that followed us. "Where is he, Maria?" Suddenly she rounded on me and I was forced to pull up short to avoid running into her. Her dark eyes grew darker still as they flashed at me in anger.

"I have no idea what you are talking about and if you don't leave me alone I'll..."

"You'll what?" I interrupted her. "You'll try to poison my horse. Or maybe you'll get Pablito to come after me? After all it was him who picked up the huaca wasn't it?" She raised her right hand as if to strike me.

"What did you do to get him to use your last name, or one of them to do your dirty work? Or did he not know who the huaca was for?"

"You think you know everything, gringa, but you don't. You're.." Suddenly thinking better of it, she flew into a tirade of Spanish, the words, although unknown to me, delivered a clear message. I heard a decidedly feminine gasp from somewhere behind me and out of the corner of my eye I saw a few of the grooms and those who understood Spanish stop to stare, mouths agape.

Ooooh! You bitch! I held my ground, unbendingly. Fighting the urge to hit her, I let her finish. We stood toe-to-toe and eye-to-eye, but only one of us was panting with exertion.

When she stopped running her mouth, I lit into her. "You finished?" Not giving her the chance to reply I continued. "Good. Now where is he? Where is Jose?" While she had been hurling curse words at me I had realized that Maria for all her anger and bravado wasn't much of a threat. She may have orchestrated much of what had happened, but it was Jose who had acted, Jose who was violent. It was him that worried me.

"She is mine!" She seethed. "Mine! Mine! You stole her from me, gringa!" She hissed like a cat.

"What the hell are you talking about?" Confused and agitated, I fought to lower my voice. "Speak English!"

"She was my ticket to the Games. He bought her for me. You hear me, gringa!"

By this time a crowd had gathered. Speaking from somewhere behind me I heard Colleen's voice. "She means the horse," she said tentatively.

"What horse?" Exasperated, I threw my arms into the air.

Behind me I heard Colleen's voice again. "Cronos."

The moment she said it, I knew it was true. Not only did it all make sense but Maria's face revealed the truth. Without thinking it through I sputtered, "Is there anyone you have not slept with?" The crowd, too stunned at my response, remained quiet. Right before my eyes I watched Maria explode and for a split second I was reminded of Jose the instant before he struck me on the head. As she launched herself towards me, a set of arms grabbed her, pulling her back. As Chip fought to restrain his hissing black cat she turned on him, pummeling him until his baseball cap flew off, landing in the dirt. His blonde curls exploded around his face. Recovering from the realization that Cronos had been bought for Maria, I looked up to see Craig standing next to me.

"Maria, where is Jose?"

Like a switch, she flipped, her demeanor changing from anger to haughtiness. Sensing a shift in her mood, Chip let her go. She stood for a moment, gazing down her nose at Craig before erupting in a cackling laugh. "Why should I tell you?"

"Because either we can settle this between us, or I can involve the cops. It's that simple." He stood calmly next to me, his eyes locked with hers.

What! Handle it yourself. What are you loco, Craig? Just call the cops. I could hear shuffling feet all around us as the crowd shifted and moved, waiting for an answer to this soap opera. As far as they were concerned this was juicy stuff, the kind of stuff that made the winter circuit in Wellington so intriguing.

Just then, Elaine walked up in the grass next to the barn aisle, leading Cronos. I had forgotten them both in my hurry to reach Maria. All eyes, including Maria's, ran appraisingly over the big bay mare as she nickered softly to Mariposa who was being held by a groom. Maria's eyes flicked up, meeting Craig's, then mine. The fight quickly left her and her shoulders slumped. She looked defeated, tired. "It doesn't matter, he's gone."

"Gone where?" Craig insisted.

Maria waved her hand in dismissal, "Spain. I bought him a ticket. His plane left this morning. I took him to the airport myself." She paused, "I told him you weren't worth the trouble." For a second her black eyes flashed with hatred; then it was gone.

The crowd was beginning to disburse, with the exception of the gang. Deanne stepped forward addressing Maria. "How could you even think of trying to hurt a horse? That is so sick, Maria." Javier, picking up on Deanne's mood, let out a whimper at her feet.

Chip had stepped away from Maria in an attempt to distance himself. "I never told him to do that. I had nothing to do with any of it."

"I would never have tried to hurt her," she pleaded. Her gaze shifted tenderly to Cronos and for the first time ever I felt sorry for Maria.

Turning, she walked around a stunned Chip, picked up Mariposa's reins from the groom and traipsed, head down, towards the end of the barn.

ALL IS QUIET...

I set my seasoned steak out on the counter to allow it to reach room temperature while I took a shower. The steamy warmth of the water cascading over my tired body felt like heaven and a sense of completeness washed over me. We had qualified. We had actually done it. I found myself smiling as I reached to turn the shower off. Maria had been exposed, the show season was winding down, and we had actually qualified for the Pan Am Games.

Stepping out onto the cream colored bath mat, I reached for a fresh towel to wrap my hair in. I had taken Craig to the airport early this morning. Our goodbye had felt unfinished in a way, especially since I had not decided whether to return to Panama before the Games, or stick it out here in the States. Reaching for another towel, I wrapped it around me and headed down the hall to my room.

With everyone gone I reveled in the quiet of the guesthouse, the ability to traipse down the hall in nothing but a towel. Finally I could have some much needed alone time with just me, myself, and I and I found myself smiling.

I slipped into a pair of silky pajama pants and a cotton tank top and hung up my towel to dry. Reaching for my fuzzy green robe, I slipped it over my arms and wrapped myself in its familiar warmth before padding barefoot back down the hall to the kitchen to fix dinner.

Troy and Rachel had flown back home to Texas late in the afternoon to spend some time with his parents. Apparently their silver wedding anniversary celebration was this week and Rachel had planned a lovely surprise party. Elaine had left yesterday for Ocala to visit a friend of hers who was working at a stud farm. She had kindly invited me to come along, but the pull of some quiet time to myself took precedence, at least for me anyway. Hamish and Deanne had run away for a few days as well. I guess everyone needed some time away, I mumbled to myself as I reached for the bottle of red wine I had bought. A red from Australia, the clerk at the local specialty market had recommended it.

Reaching deftly for the drawer that held the bottle opener, I pulled it out and gave the drawer a push with my hip, sending it back along its tracks until it closed with a *thump*. I had grown accustomed to the little kitchen over the last few months and moved about it with ease. Deanne had bought a set of wine glasses for the guesthouse. Pulling one down from the cabinet, I poured a generous glassful of merlot. Stepping out onto the porch with my wine, I fired up the gas grill.

The sun had set while I had been in the shower and the pale grey of dusk settled over the still farm. Not a sound drifted my way from the direction of the barn, which meant the horses were all settled in for the night. Lazily, I twirled the glass of wine by the stem, watching the dark burgundy shades of wine dance in the glass. A chilly breeze from the west swept across the grass and instinctively, I stepped closer to the hot grill. I should have put on a pair of socks I thought, glancing down at my bare feet. The bright pink polish on my toenails winked up at me and I smiled, thinking of Calli. I had come to enjoy getting pedicures. That reminds me, I need to give her a call, I thought to myself. I needed to share our good news about qualifying.

The smoky aroma of the grill caused my stomach to growl and lurch in abject anticipation. I hadn't slowed down all day, and other than a candy bar I picked up at the gas station while putting gas in the SUV, my tank was empty.

Hamish had bought some orange wood smoking chips for the grill a couple of weeks ago so I had emptied the remainder of them into a metal pan, filled it with water, soaked them, and then set it on the grill to smoke. A steak freak, I was extremely particular about how I liked my steaks. The grill had to be sizzling hot and for the best results, the meat had to be close to room temperature before cooking. Steaks cooked on a grill were a labor of love for this carnivore, I thought with a grin, and took another sip of the ruby red wine and felt it slide down my throat to my empty belly. The stars beginning to make their debut were faint pinpoints of light above me. Stretching my head back, I looked up and took in a deep cleansing breath. Once again I allowed myself to relax, realizing that with Jose out of the country my life could get back to normal.

After a few minutes I stepped back into the kitchen to pour another glass of wine. I threw a clean potato in the microwave and grabbed my steak. Back outside, I used a set of tongs to slip the thick ribeye steak onto the hot grill then shut the heavy lid. An Adirondack chair, worn to a seasoned finish by the elements, sat on the porch and I dragged it closer to the grill for warmth. Settling into it, I bent my knees and pulled my cold feet up under my robe, waiting contentedly for my steak to cook, and savoring the moment.

Ten minutes and an empty glass of wine later, I stepped inside to get a clean plate for the steak. The sliding glass door slid smoothly on its tracks as I shut it behind me. Dropping the dirty plate into the sink, I grabbed a clean one from the cupboard, filled my glass of wine and headed back towards the porch. Reaching for the door I glanced up into a set of eyes as black as night. From the other side of the glass, Jose stared back at me with a fury that made my blood run cold. Without thinking, I screamed and turned to run. The wine glass, forgotten in my panic, slipped from my grip, crashing to the ground beside me and shattered into a thousand tiny slivers.

I made it as far as the stove. Lightning fast, he had thrown open the sliding door with a bang and reached out for me. His hands, seeking some part of me had found the towel that was still wrapped tightly around my head, my hair with it. With a sickening sound, my head jerked backwards and the floor rushed up to meet me. My back and shoulders took most of the concussion as the towel finally unraveled enough for my hair to slide free. For a brief moment, my vision swam with tiny pinpoints of light and I recalled the stars in the night sky before everything went black.

I awoke with a start, confused, and nauseated. The smooth wood floor beneath my head felt solid and slowly the room stopped spinning. My head, neck, and arms ached. The constant throbbing served to keep me awake. Blinking to focus, I searched for a familiar landmark and found it. The dusty vent at the bottom of the refrigerator stared mournfully back at me from a few feet away. Sparkling, blood red shards of the wine glass littered the floor between us. *Someone really needs to take that off and clean it.* Shifting to relieve the ache in my arms I realized they wouldn't move. Confused for a moment I tried to move them one at a time. As rational thought and consciousness returned, I realized my hands were bound and then it hit me, *Jose.*

Blinking in an effort to further focus I could hear voices from somewhere behind me. The television was on. *Think, Todd, think!* I tried to push through the muddled haze that was my brain, but my head throbbed incessantly, making it hard to organize rational thoughts. He had to be somewhere in the house my gut told me. The look in those eyes also told me that he meant business this time. The question was—what was he doing here? Maria had been emphatic about him leaving the country.

Shivering uncontrollably, partly from reaction and partly from the chilly air, I fought to keep my body still so as not to attract attention. With every move, I could feel sharp pains in my feet, ankles and the side of my face. *Glass?* Glancing down at my bare feet I saw rivulets of blood and the shimmer of several tiny shards of wine glass sticking out of my skin. Horrified, I shivered again. *Ouch!* This time the pain was more intense. I tried in vain to keep from shivering, but it was no use. I was freezing. The thin pajama pants and tank top offered little in the way of warmth. My robe had slipped off my shoulders and lay pooled around my elbows. Listening intently, my ears searched for any sounds not coming from the television. He had to still be here, I thought with a sinking feeling.

Stretching my head back slowly, I nearly gasped as a searing pain shot down the back of my neck and exploded across my shoulder blades like hot pokers. The memory of Jose grabbing my towel came rushing back to me and I blinked hard, fighting off the pain. Slowly it ebbed and I tried once again to shift my head to get a better look at my surroundings. This time I was able to move my head, only much slower than before. The sliding glass door to the kitchen stood open to the cold night air. Just then the wind shifted, bringing the smoky smell of the grill mingled with the sharp acrid scent of burning meat through the wide opening. The son of a bitch had left my steak to burn, I thought, my anger boiling to the surface. With a shock I realized the hilarity of such a thought and I started to laugh uncontrollably. Quietly my body shook at first, but before long I lost control and it rose to a hysterical pitch. Burying my face in my shoulder I tried to stifle the sounds. The idea that I was going into shock occurred to me.

Out of nowhere, a hand hot as fire latched onto my upper arm and I screamed in pain as he yanked me off the floor in one smooth motion. With one arm Jose dropped me down like a rag doll into one of the kitchen chairs. My bound wrists wedged painfully behind me.

"Shut up you bitch." His face was inches from mine and his breath fowl and misty in the cold room. I watched as his eyes danced with nervous energy, their ink black pupils dilated tightly as they tried to concentrate on my face. Letting go of my arm with a vicious jerk he stood upright. "This is all *his* fault," he hissed as he began to pace restlessly around the kitchen, the glass crunching beneath his shoes. I flinched uncontrollably with each step, the sound echoing in the small kitchen.

His voice grew sinister. "But that is okay, because I know that I can hurt him through you." His head jerked around in my direction and he smiled, "Two birds with one stone," he said. "Besides, this is a gift," his smile dissolved into a wicked sneer, "from Maria. I still owe you for that." He was talking quickly, his words almost tripping over themselves while trying to leave his mouth.

The sane part of me said to keep my mouth shut, but I was getting really tired of not having my life back, tired of getting knocked around by this nut job. I had fought through so much to survive and learn to live again. I'd be damned if I was about to let him ruin things for me. Considering my options, I watched him circle the kitchen once more. His actions told me that he was clearly on some sort of drug and logic would point to cocaine. Surreptitiously I glanced towards the living room, trying to keep one eye on him as he rambled on. A small glass pipe, one side blackened from soot, sat next to a plastic bag whose contents I couldn't see. Crap, I thought, that would explain his strength. With his build there was no other explanation as to how he lifted me with one arm. He was high. High as a freaking kite.

"He took my life. I had plans," he continued, as his voice echoed in the small kitchen. "I couldn't get her to look at me without money. Money talks. She would have come around once the job was done. That would have made all the difference."

Her? His comment caught my attention. "So you trafficked coke and blew up a boat full of fishermen for a woman!" I blurted out.

He stopped suddenly and rounded on me, his hot hand clutching my throat. "You don't get it, do you bitch." I could feel his long fingers digging into the soft skin of my neck. "He had everything, the money, the resort, and my woman. I just leveled the playing field. Besides, those stupid fishermen weren't supposed to be that close to shore. They never fish that area. Serves them right for being dumb," he hissed. He smiled a sick smile and squeezed my throat, his fingers sinking deeper into my flesh until I began to see tiny bursts of light along my peripheral vision.

Oh God, he's enjoying this! Gasping for air I fought to escape his hold, jerking left then right. Just as quickly, he dropped his hand and stalked away, leaving me to suck in mouthfuls of cold air. The cold air filled the warm void left by his hand. As the blood rushed back to my head, I shivered again—this time with the realization that he could have easily and calmly killed me.

Picking up the crack pipe from the coffee table, he held it to his lips. The metallic *click* of the lighter in his hand was followed by an orange flame, which danced along the top of the pipe. I watched in shock as the wispy white smoke curled around his face as he exhaled. Repulsed, I turned back to the kitchen, taking stock of my situation. The utility drawer, with a pair of scissors in it, was on the other side of the kitchen. *Too far.* The sharp knives sat in a knife block on the counter behind me, but there was no way I could get up from the chair and grab one with my hands bound behind me. Knowing me, I would trip on my robe and stab myself, I thought ruefully. No, that wouldn't work at all. I was left with my brains. *Great, Todd, just great!*

Turning my attention back to Jose, I watched him nurse the crack pipe. As long as he kept nursing his high, any chance of escape would be risky. He was chasing the dragon, or at least that is what I knew it as. He was at the point in his addiction that he had to fight to keep his high going. Never again would he reach the same initial euphoria as he had with his first hit. Watching him, I could see that he exhibited all of the classic signs of cocaine use, the agitation, super human strength, dilated pupils, and hyper-alertness. All of which would make it hard for the average person to overpower him.

Working to ease the numbing pain that crept up my arms, I shifted in the chair. Hearing me, he threw me a warning glare and I stopped. Finished, he set down the pipe. Standing upright, he crossed the distance between us, a determined scowl on his face. I noticed the diamond was missing from his ear, in its place was a tattoo. As he drew closer, I could see a black letter C tattooed on his ear lobe. Shifting back to his face, our eyes met. I shivered again wincing as my wrists pinched against the wooden slats of the chair.

"A 'C' for Calderon. They are my family now."

A tattoo like that usually meant a drug gang or cartel. No wonder he wore the earring to cover it up at the show grounds. Swallowing hard, I resigned myself to the situation. Since he was going to be high for at least the next thirty minutes I decided to keep him talking. "Who was she?"

He moved to stand in front of me. The fabric of his black jeans brushed against that of my pajama pants and I fought the urge to pull away in revulsion. His tiny pupils reminded me of smooth, shiny black ball bearings, cold and hard. His hair stuck out in all directions around his worn and tired face. He looked a far cry from the man I had seen at the barn that day. When he spoke, the words were jerky and abrupt. "Gabriella Ignacio de Herrera. A woman of means and style, unlike you." He spat the words at me.

Surely he didn't mean the same Gabby I had seen at the luau. Gaudy Gabby? But she had dated Craig. Not wanting to anger him further I kept those thoughts to myself. "Oh," was all I could muster. I was running out of things to talk about. *What in the hell do you say to a madman high on crack and intent on...*

Without warning, he picked up the chair next to me as if it weighed next to nothing and slung it across the kitchen towards the open door. Ducking my head to avoid getting hit, I heard the chair slam into the sides of the doorway before crashing to the ground on the patio in pieces. The sliding glass door rattled loudly in its tracks. Swallowing hard I changed the subject. "Did you leave the huaca in my room?"

His mood shifted and he suddenly began to laugh, leaning on the wooden table for support. As the laughter died down, he turned and leaned against the table so as to face me. "I was going to leave it as a calling card of sorts for Craig, but after seeing you there I knew it would have a greater effect if I left it in your room." Crossing his arms he slowly shook his head from side to side. "I knew it would make him loco if I messed with you."

"I don't get it?"

"He's never brought a girl to the resort." A dark look crossed his face. "But you, you crawled under that armor of his. That perfect person who is Craig Duncan." He nearly spat the last sentence. "The one who was too good for Gabriella," he shifted restlessly. "He broke her heart, you know. Ruined her for me." His eyes found mine and I nearly gasped at the hatred which brewed behind them.

His mood shifted again along with his train of thought. "At first I was just looking to get my cash, but then after seeing you two at dinner, walking along the beach…" he pushed off from the table and stood directly in front of me. His eyes taunted me.

Oh God, he was there the whole time.

Grasping one of my curls, he bent to sniff my hair. Cringing, I tried to pull away. Knowing I was trapped, he watched me struggle, a sick grin on his face. After a moment he chuckled, his voice dark and sinister. "Tit for tat. I wonder how Craig would like it if I ruined his woman?" Forcing his knee between my legs he shoved his way between them, effectively wedging them apart. Reacting, I tried in vain to shut my legs, but he used his other leg to shove them further apart. "If I made it so he could never touch you again."

Oh God. Fighting to stay calm I kept my gaze averted and tried once again to change the subject. "What c-a-s-h?" I stuttered. Tiny black pinpoints of light began to flicker at the edge of my vision. Whether it was because of the cold, or the panic that danced at the edge of my consciousness I didn't know. My chest tightened and I fought to pull air into my lungs. *Oh dear God, I'm going to pass out. Breathe…breathe… Keep him talking, Todd, for God's sake keep him talking.*

For several moments he just stood there in front of me while I stared at his shoes. They were grey tennis shoes. I didn't want to look ahead where the zipper of his jeans loomed, or up into those dilated pupils of his so I studied his shoes. With black and silver mesh, running shoes? Taunting me, he played with my hair as I fought to stay calm. As I fought to breathe. Every fiber of my being wanted to cringe and jerk away at his touch, but I knew that would only encourage him further. My thighs began to burn and I realized that subconsciously I had been fighting back, pushing back against his intrusion into my space, afraid of what thoughts were darting around in his head.

"What cash?" I asked again. My voice sounded far away and foreign to my ears. I felt his fingers pick up a larger section of my hair and my heart stopped. When he finally spoke I nearly cried with relief.

"My money from the first two jobs. Surely Craig didn't think that was the first job I had pulled using his precious boats?" He continued to play with my hair. "I had it stashed all over the resort so it took some patience and a few well-timed trips to get it. Well, not quite all of it." I could feel the roots of my hair pulling as he twisted the hair round and round his index finger until it was tightly wound. "The rest of it is here somewhere and you are going to tell me where."

"I don't know what you are talking about. I don't have any money." My mind raced, trying to figure out what he could possibly be talking about. "Besides, I own a horse; that means I am broke." The feigned humor was lost on him.

"Oh, yes you do," dropping the coiled hair, he picked up a much larger handful. Bringing it to his nose he inhaled. "You do, and you will tell me." Twisting his whole hand in my hair he yanked my head backwards and I nearly passed out from the pain. Closing my eyes, I fought the bile that rose in my throat and the sparkling white lights that flashed on the edge of consciousness. Hot tears began to well up from the pain. Slowly I opened my eyes to find him staring at me.

"Where's the trunk he had shipped from the resort? The big antique looking one?"

Trunk? What trunk? Like a ton of bricks it hit me, the steamer trunk that Craig had sent up with all of the stuff for his vendor tent. Craig and Troy had packed up the tent before Craig left for Panama. I had no idea whether the trunk had been shipped back or was lying around somewhere. "I don't know." I managed to get the words past my lips. Seeing that I couldn't talk well with my neck stretched back, he loosened his hold slightly. Swallowing hard, I felt the strain of the muscles in my neck.

Leaning down, his face inches from mine, he said, "Oh, I think you do, Red." His eyes traveled down my neck slowly followed by the index finger of his free hand. *Oh shit!* Jerking like a fish out of water I threw everything I had into one last-ditch effort to escape, but he had me pinned and utterly helpless. I flopped back into the chair, gasping for air and shaking.

Once again he tightened his hold on my hair, pulling it back until the stars began to creep in again, illuminating the edges of my sight. A single, fat tear fell, burning a path down my cold cheek. His round eyes grew rounder still, making his pupils appear even smaller and I watched in horror as a change came over him and he smiled. All at once he grew excited. "You need a real man. One that can make you scream for it, huh bitch." Grabbing my breast with his free hand he squeezed hard. Unable to stand it, the tears flowed down my face in agony as I fought again to free myself. "Yeah, you like that baby?"

Growing even more aggressive, his mouth covered mine. Cramming my lips together I barred him entry. In an effort to out maneuver me he gave my head a quick jerk. Opening my mouth to scream in pain he invaded me. His tongue sought mine while his hand yanked down on my tank top, exposing my breasts.

NOOOO!

The soft popping sound of stitches and the tearing of fabric were lost in the deafening stillness that enveloped me. Like it had when Jake died, my mind retreated into a locked cabinet somewhere deep inside me for safety. *Oh dear God, not this,* played over and over in my mind as my body went limp and shut down. Through the fog I saw his face appear before me, floating disjointedly in a haze. The look on his face was one of frustration and I felt his hand leave my exposed breast. Seeking a reaction, he tightened his grip on my hair and jerked my head back.

"Bitch!" His words felt thick and slow to my ears, like syrup. *That's it cold syrup, so very cold,* I thought to myself.

Letting go of my hair he lifted me out of the chair. As my feet cleared the floor I heard him say, "You're going to tell me where that trunk is. I need my money. It's mine!" He shook me violently and I watched as the ceiling, then the cabinets, flashed into view and then quickly disappeared. He then dropped me back onto the chair with a thud. I could no longer feel my arms, or my body for that matter. *How very odd.* Somewhat surprised by this revelation I blinked hard trying to remember what I had been doing but nothing came to mind. A sharp, loud noise reverberated through my head.

Something is burning.

A flash of white exploded in front of me and Jose's face disappeared from view. And then there was a welcome blackness and warmth.

**

"Lauren, can you hear me?"

No. I don't want to hear anything. Leave me alone.

"Lauren, I need to see your eyes. I need you to look at me. Lauren, its okay you're safe now." The voice was urgent, pleading and yet scared.

Floating in the warm darkness I could hear voices all around. Important voices. Commanding voices, barking orders. "Sir, I need to get to her, please. Let me do my job."

Get to who?

"Lauren." The voice was pleading now. Pulling away from the blackness, pieces of reality floated back to me, like debris from a shipwreck they told a story. Of that I was sure. Problem was, what was it? Try as I might I couldn't put the pieces together. The acrid smell of burned meat reached me, and my eyes flew open. Slowly they adjusted and the faces around me quit moving. My eyes settled on a strong, kind face with blue eyes and a worried brow.

"There she is. Lauren, it's going to be alright." The smooth dulcet tones of an Oklahoma accent made me smile.

Jake? What was he doing here? Oh Jake, I have so much to tell you.

"Lauren, it's Bull, can you hear me."

I winced as the pain in my head and neck abruptly broke through the fog and yanked me back to the present. My face began to throb like the devil and Bull's anxious face came into focus. *Bull? Where's Jake?*

"Okay sir, you've got to let us take over." The voice was very commanding and Bull's face disappeared from view. Swirls of color, some black, some white, some red flashed into focus and then disappeared only to be replaced with someone else calling my name. *I'm right here!* I was beginning to get frustrated. After what seemed like forever, the voices faded. They left me alone and I slept.

******

I woke gently to familiar sounds. Soft beeps, overhead pages, and the shuffling noises of a hospital were unmistakable.

Not to mention the smell. Lifting my head to peer around the room, I let out a whimper as the familiar pain returned.

Craig had been holding my hand. Jumping to his feet he said, "No don't move if you don't have to, you are going to be sore for quite a while. Just lie still." I felt the weight of the bed shift as he sat beside me, my hand still in his. The familiar roughness of his manly hands enveloped mine.

Licking my dry lips I wiggled my nose and upper lip, oxygen canula, right, that's what I felt. "Hey." My throat was dry and the word sounded dry and crackly to my ears. The muscles of my face ached.

A smile split his face and his green eyes danced. "Hey yourself, how do you feel?" Before I could answer he jumped in, "Bad question, right?"

"Yeah, you could say that. W-w-what happened?"

He paused, clearly contemplating his answer. "The short version, Bull happened to be in the neighborhood. Because of him you are still here." Craig looked mildly uncomfortable as he spoke. "Anyway, you don't have to worry about Jose anymore and the doctor said you'll be just fine. You got a good one, too. She is a friend of Bull's and you are getting the star treatment here at the Hotel de Hospital." His familiar smile split his face and I found myself trying to smile. *Ouch.* "Hey, hey, none of that now. No smiling for a while." He was right, my face hurt.

Reaching up with my free hand, I touched my swollen cheek. It felt hot and tight to the touch. I could feel small scabs across my cheek and temple. "Glass?"

He nodded. "They'll go away soon."

"What else?"

"Well, he did a number on your neck, but the CAT scan only showed some…."

"Soft tissue damage, but you should heal just fine." The voice came from the doorway. "Hi, I'm Dr. Nichols, but you can call me Sari. Any friend of Bull's is a friend of mine."

She was tall and willowy with a warm earthenware complexion. Her short, wavy brown hair was highlighted along her face and worn in a short full style. A very modern pair of rectangular glasses sat on her button nose. She wore a crisp white physician's coat over a black pencil skirt and a black and grey blouse. A genuine smile flashed across her face. "It's a good thing you are in great shape. I'm not sure if the average person would have come away without more damage to the neck and back." Glancing courteously at Craig she continued, shifting into doctor mode, "Being physically fit is probably what saved you from serious neck injury." She smiled in a reserved business sort of way. "The cuts from the glass will heal and you shouldn't have any scarring." She flashed a reassuring smile. "We'll have you out of here tomorrow, but I want you to consider wearing a brace on your neck for a short while."

"Consider? So, it's not a problem if I skip the brace." The thought of walking around with a brace on didn't sit well with me. Neither did calling attention to myself. I wanted nothing more than to leave the hospital and all that had happened behind me.

Flashing Craig a knowing look, she turned her attention back to me. "I was told you would be…"

"Difficult?" Craig offered his ruddy eyebrow cocked upwards for effect.

"Challenging, Bull said you would be strong willed. I'll let you be the judge. If it hurts and you are fighting to support your head, then you need to wear it." She peered over her glasses at me, pulling the doctor card with the ease of someone used to getting their way.

For a second, I wondered just what her relationship with Bull entailed. "Thanks, I think." My mouth was still dry and felt like cotton.

Her laughter was genuine. "Good luck, Lauren, and I believe congratulations are in order. I promised Bull I would look up the word dressage and watch you ride at the Pan Am Games. She patted my leg gently with her hand, said goodbye, and was gone.

KICK ON

The flight back to Panama had gone smoothly. When we got to the airport in Miami, Craig left me seated with our bags while he sweet-talked the ticket agent behind the counter at the gate. I managed to piece together what he had said when we settled into seats in first class and the flight attendant ogled me. Eventually she got up the nerve to congratulate me on our impending trip to the Pan Am Games. As it turns out, she was an avid rider, eventing mostly, and her home base was in Louisville. After agreeing to look for me at the Games in Lexington she moved off to help a portly man who couldn't quite stow his bag.

Like most guys, Craig could sleep anywhere, anytime and today was no different. After making sure I was okay, he drifted off to sleep in the deep leather chair next to the aisle. Settling in, I tucked a pillow between the bulkhead of the plane and my neck for support and stared out the oval window into the blue sky.

I had left the hospital only yesterday, the day before Colleen had made the decision to ship the horses back to Panama so we could continue our training in a more affordable environment. When she factored in the cost of hay, stabling, and living arrangements it was still cheaper to fly the horses home and back again. That, and there was also the man factor. She and I both agreed that being away from our guys for the next seven months or so would be just too much for either of us to deal with. Right now the plan was to fly back to the States in August and compete in October. For now, everyone had stepped to the plate and offered to take care of Cronos for me. Knowing she was in good hands, I was able to relax just a bit.

Trying to get comfortable, I mashed on the top of the pillow, bringing it down a bit. A sharp pain, burning like a hot poker, shot up my neck and exploded along my scalp. *Crap!* Every time I felt that pain, it took me back to that night, although only three days ago, it seemed like an eternity.

I hadn't seen Bull again, but Craig and Rachel had filled me in on what happened. In fact, it was partly because of Rachel, well and Louie, that Bull stopped by the farm when he did. Louie was apparently allergic to everything under the sun that comes in contact with a normal horse and was on monthly allergy shots. Keeping him on a regular schedule of dosing was important and Bull had stopped by on his way out that night to slip his allergy medication into the tack room refrigerator for Rachel.

Apparently, the pungent smell of my ribeye steak becoming a chunk of charcoal had caught his attention. The sound of the kitchen chair flying through the sliding glass door had held his attention. Thinking there was a burglar in the guesthouse he had called 911. Hearing me scream, he realized the situation was very different, and had decided to act before the cops arrived. Funny, I thought, I had no memory of screaming. But then again, at some point in the night my memories stopped abruptly until I woke in his arms, then again a few days later, in the hospital. Without warning, my body shook involuntarily and my elbow bumped Craig.

Awake instantly he studied me with those green eyes before asking, "You okay?"

"Yeah, go back to sleep, I just couldn't get comfortable. Sorry." I could tell that he didn't quite buy what I was selling, but he closed his eyes anyway. Turning back to the window I studied the sleek silver wing of the plane and the intricate pattern of rivets that ran along it. My mind drifted as I stared out of the window. A thin, veiled mist, or was it fog, curled over the leading edge of the wing and disappeared back into the atmosphere before reaching the back of the wing. It is cold up here so it must be mist, I decided. Seconds later I considered condensation, but that was more like water droplets, fog then?

Either way, the warmth of the wing was colliding with the cold air and it looked cool. Maybe I'd look it up when I got home.

Jose was dead. Nobody had wanted to tell me, but I had found out by sheer manipulation. Actually, I had bluffed my way into getting an answer from Dr. Nichols. I had a hard time calling her by her first name. *Did Bull call her Sari?* Guess that comes with working as a nurse. I still didn't have all of the answers, but I did find out that Bull shot him and he was dead at the scene when the police arrived. Thinking about it, I could honestly say that I didn't feel sorry for Jose, but Bull, that was another story.

Killing another person in self-defense or to save a life, I was all for that, but too often people tended to forget about the aftermath. In the end, you must reconcile your conscience with the taking of another person's life. The fact that you lived, they died, and all the mental baggage that goes along with it. I had seen too much of that sort of thing in the trauma room.

Once Dr. Nichol's had realized she slipped up and gave me too much information I had pressed her for more and found out that it was Bull's gun that had fired the fatal shot. She had made a wry comment about Bull being a 'true cowboy in everyway'. I guess you can take the cowboy off the ranch, but never quite get the ranch out of the cowboy. In true American style, he had his concealed weapons permit and packed a gun wherever he went. I found myself smiling at the thought and not at all surprised by it.

Not wanting to shoot, since Jose had been so close to me, Bull had fought him, beating him until he lay unconscious on the floor. It probably would have ended there had Jose not been on coke, for he bounced back in a rage and Bull had been forced to shoot him.

I owed Bull my life. Although I hadn't had the chance to thank him before I left, my gut told me that someday I would get the chance. Someday I would learn the whole story. Someday I would be able to fill in the empty spaces.

I had asked Craig about the cash Jose had been looking for. Apparently it had already been driven to the dock and stowed aboard a new ship that AJ had just acquired. She was due in port in a few days.

**

I had drifted asleep in the oversized chaise lounge on the porch and was wakened gently with a kiss on the forehead by Craig. He was back and the fishing had been spectacular today. "Hey, babe," he said, his voice husky with emotion. Still in his swim trunks he had taken off his T-shirt and his torso still radiated the heat from the sun. His freckles, some large and some small looked darker than usual. Sun kissed was how my mom had referred to it, I thought with a smile. Slipping out of his flip-flops he lowered himself onto the lounge chair next to me. "Wow, what a view you had today and you spent it asleep." He said teasingly.

There were only a three guests at the resort this week, and Craig had left Clementine to look after me while he took them fishing. For now, they would be back at their cabanas resting before dinner.

It was gorgeous, a regular slice of paradise. The late afternoon sun skipped across the waves at an angle, causing one side of them to resemble iridescent glass, the kind you see streaming through a stained glass window and onto the stone floor of a century's old chapel. I could smile without my face hurting now, and I did so. I could see Ganso's dark head move about the boat down below as they unloaded and prepared her for tomorrow's fishing trip. Without thinking I turned to look at him and a searing hot pain shot up one side of my neck, making my vision swim for an instant, and then it was gone.

Craig's face shadowed with concern as he watched, helpless to take the pain away or fix my injuries. "It's better, really," I assured him. It was better, and would improve slowly, with time. Some days I could even move pain free. "Dr. Nichols, Sari said it would take time."

Clementine popped her head out of the glass door. "It's here," she said before disappearing back towards the kitchen. Just then I heard AJ and Colleen's voices on the path outside the porch. Avoiding my gaze, Craig jumped up to meet them. "Stay put," he shouted over his shoulder and I heard him jump down the porch steps to greet them. Unable to turn my head much, I waited anxiously, wondering just what they were up to. A grunt that sounded like AJ came from the direction of the stairs.

"Careful you guys don't kill your backs. That's all we need." It was Colleen's voice. I could no longer stand it, and I slowly turned in my chair, trying to keep my neck straight. I tried, but failed to catch a glimpse of what was going on around me.

Craig came into view, walking backwards and carrying his share of the old trunk. *Oh crap!* It was the antique steamer trunk that Jose had been looking for. The one he was willing to rape and kill for.

"Here, set it down so she can see." Craig turned so that AJ followed him and the trunk met the wooden floor with a thump. "Well, here we go." Craig thumbed through the silver padlock, which had been threaded through the old brass latch on the front of the trunk. With a metallic *pop* the lock sprung free and he slipped it through the latch.

I felt a hand, warm and gentle on my shoulder and started to turn. "No, don't." Colleen said, patting my shoulder in reassurance. "Just wanted to let you know I was here." She paused, "And your girl is doing well. She flew like a champ."

"Hey, glad you could come. Thanks for everything." My voice trembled a bit. Biting my lower lip, I steadied myself. Looking up, I saw Craig and AJ watching me and waiting patiently. "Go ahead, open the dang thing. Let's get this over with. "Besides," I added in my best imitation of a pirate, "we need to see if there is any booty in thar." The tension shattered, Craig smiled as he reached to open the trunk.

The guys painstakingly pulled out all of Craig's supplies that he had used for his Las Brisas display at Wellington. Brochures, T-shirts, embroidered visors, videotapes, and Goliath the aptly named grouper were all set on a nearby table. Completely empty, the faded gold silk fabric that lined the inside of the trunk stared back at us innocently.

Reaching into his back pocket, AJ pulled out a pocketknife. With the flick of his wrist, he slid it open and looked at Craig expectantly.

"Go ahead, be my guest," Craig offered, hands on his hips.

"Somebody just cut the darn thing!" Colleen shouted in my ear with impatience. I could feel her fingers digging into my shoulder. If I could turn I knew I would have seen steam coming out of her ears just like it did when she fussed at me when I rode. Trying to stifle a giggle, she clouted me on the shoulder. "Next one will be your head." Glaring back at the guys she added, "Or I will do it myself. The suspense is killing me."

AJ, laughing, bent down and sunk the shiny metal blade into the bottom corner closest to him. The sharp blade cut through the silk silently as he ran the knife along the width of the trunk. Turning expertly, he continued down the front side, then the side closest to Craig. Slowly, I inched forward in my chair to get a better view. Wedging the tip of the knife in between the bottom and side of the trunk he used it to pry up the bottom. As he lifted the bottom of the trunk, a thin sheet of pale yellow plywood came into view. It was clearly new.

"A false bottom?" Colleen asked in wonderment.

AJ, nodding absently, placed his hand along the edge lifting the piece of wood so it rested against the back wall of the trunk. A collective gasp echoed across the porch.

Nestled along the bottom of the trunk in neat little bundles were stacks upon stacks of cash. Too stunned to speak we stared at each other in turn, searching for confirmation in each other's eyes of what we were seeing. Locking eyes with me, Craig cocked one sandy colored eyebrow as a slow smile slid across his face.

"No way, this only happens in movies or books, not in real life." Colleen had pulled back from peering into the trunk and stood next to me shaking her head in disbelief. My stomach, which had been clenched in anticipation, did little back flips of anxiety mingled with joy. I wasn't at all sure how to react as a thousand thoughts raced through my head.

AJ reached in to pick up a bundle, "Drug money?"

"The same," Craig responded gravely, grabbing a bundle and tossing it into my lap.

Unlike scenes from Hollywood movies, this money wasn't bright, crisp and new. It had obviously been circulated, exchanged between human hands more than once; its green ink was deeper and mellower than that of new bills. Thumbing through the stack of hundred dollar bills in awe I glanced up only to meet Craig's eyes. "Now what?" I asked.

Tossing his bundle back into the trunk, AJ sighed. "How many people know about this?" His voice was cautious.

"One is dead, the other is Maria. Beyond that, I don't know. I can only assume that Jose was telling the truth, that he earned it from runnin' drugs in my boats. If that is the case, and it wasn't stolen from one of the cartels, then it would be free and clear." Craig's fingers thrummed absently on the worn leather lid of the trunk. His words hung between us.

"If we don't know for sure, then the best thing would be to keep this under wraps," offered Colleen. "I mean if you guys are instantly rich then someone is going to start wondering how and why." She shrugged her shoulders in explanation.

Craig knelt down and picked up a stack of bills. "Ours," he corrected. "This belongs to all of us. You guys are in this, too." Pausing to collect his thoughts he added, "That is if you guys want in?" AJ shot Colleen a look then nodded soberly at Craig.

"Um, but what if the cartel is looking for this money?" I asked. Quite frankly I had experienced my fair share of being hunted lately and the thought of dealing with crazy drug guys or drug-crazed guys, for that matter, wasn't at all appealing. Swallowing hard, I rubbed my hand around my wrist, remembering what it felt like to be trussed up like a piece of meat. As the memories flooded back, pinpricks of nervous sweat broke free on my forehead and I fought the desire to jump up out of the chair and run. As I pushed the memories back down where they belonged, my eyes refocused on the scene around me. A set of green eyes searched my face until he found the answer he was looking for.

I'm okay, Craig.

"I think we need to put this money away for at least the next year. We can hide it safely and then play dumb, act as if we never saw it. No one spends a dime of it now." He dropped the stack of twenties back onto the pile and walked around to stand next to me. Picking up the stack of bills in my lap he tossed it into the trunk. Scooping my clammy hand up in his he continued. "That way, things will have time to die down. After a year we can slowly distribute what's here between all five of us."

Reaching to lower the false bottom back in place, AJ shot Craig a questioning look. Clearly there were only four of us. "Ganso?" He queried as he reached for the lid. With a deep *thunk* the heavy lid of the steamer trunk slammed shut and sat there looking innocent enough.

Craig nodded, "He lost his da because of Jose. I think it's only fair." Everybody nodded in unison and with another nod of ascent between them, Craig and AJ moved off to the far side of the porch in order to discuss what to do next.

Just then Clementine slipped through the door with a tray of salt encrusted glasses and a pitcher of freshly blended margaritas with lime slices along the edge.

**

We sat in companionable silence for a few minutes watching the snow white backs of seagulls as they dipped their yellow and orange beaks into the blue waters of the Caribbean, then rose again on currents of warm air. The gulls had learned to wait for the return of the boats and the feast that came with them.

A member of the crew tossed what was left of a fish he had cleaned over the side of the dock and several gulls swooped in at once for the prize. The day was warm, but a steady onshore breeze made it feel several degrees cooler than it was. Under the shade of the porch, it was cooler still.

"What now?" He asked, his eyes still focused on the scene before us. It was a valid question and one that had hung in the air around us, unspoken, for a week now, one that I had done a lot of thinking about lately. The appearance of the trunk yesterday had brought forth feelings I had been trying hard to squash. Craig and AJ had hidden the money together, then AJ and Colleen had stayed for dinner before flying home earlier today.

Taking a deep cleansing breath I replied, "Its like when you are in the start box, just you and your horse, with a really huge and challenging cross country course before you. You can't think of the thirty gigantic fixed obstacles that are between you and the finish line. Between you and that fifty cent blue ribbon," I added sarcastically. There was never much money to be made in eventing or dressage unless you competed at the international levels. "You break from the start box at a gallop with over a thousand pounds of bounding, leaping horseflesh that is intent on jumping the moon, an animal that outweighs you ten to one.

Before each fence, you have to take a hold, half halt, get their haunches under them and prepare them for the jump." I paused, feeling the muscles of Pogo's back spring beneath me as he launched himself and left the pull of the earth behind. There was simply nothing like breaking the bonds of gravity with a horse underneath you. I squeezed his hand. "Once you land and leave that jump behind, your job is to look up and kick on, to accelerate away from the jump, leave it behind and settle into a manageable stride until the next jump. It's the same for every jump on course, you take them one at a time and as long as you do your best to set your horse up for the jump you should be okay."

He squeezed back. "Aye, but it doesna work for everra jump though does it?" His broad, thick brogue wound through his words. Without looking, I knew his one eyebrow would be cocked in question.

Smiling to myself I continued, "No, but it's all you can do. If you land wrong or the horse stops suddenly at the jump, you hang on for all you're worth, if you hit the ground you are eliminated." Videos of endless horse and rider combinations that I had seen over the years, clinging sideways on their saddles or up on their horse's necks, hands clutching for a desperate hand hold in the mane played in my mind. I had found myself in the same situation more than once and had scrabbled like a monkey clutching for the safety of the tack, the mane, anything to stay upright and be able to continue on our cross country journey. To continue the adrenaline high that had begun in the start box. "The thing about being eliminated is, well, you can always ride another day."

"And so it is with life," he added softly as the cry of a gull was carried to us on the Caribbean wind.

"Yes, it is." I felt the warmth of his lips on the back of my hand and knew they would taste warm and salty. Knew they would be there today, tomorrow and always.

THE END...

ACKNOWLEDGEMENTS

This book was meant to take the reader on a fun journey, an escape if you will. It was not meant as a 'how to' book on dressage. The characters in Kick On have their own views of dressage as both a sport and a way of life. With that in mind, the author would like to thank:

My family. My loving non-horsey husband Jeff who feeds the horses every morning for me, and who simply said "Okay" in that non-plussed way of his when I announced that I was going to write a book. Thank you for having faith in my abilities and in me. Thank you to my incredible stepchildren PJ and Logan, who inspire me everyday.

Wanda Bibens, my friend, neighbor, sounding board, sommelier, show companion, and fellow former (although she may argue that point) eventer who endured listening to me build and mold this story on trail rides, in endless emails and while trapped in the same vehicle with me heading to horse shows. Now, you can finally put it together and read it as it was meant to be.

Maureen Fahrenholz, my dressage instructor extraordinaire and friend who opened my eyes to classical dressage as taught to her by such greats as Herr Egon von Neindorff, Axel Steiner, Elizabeth McMullen, Walter Zettl, and Paula Kierkegaard. And who for the price of a lesson (or not!) has the unique ability to be a dressage instructor, personal life coach, therapist, and source of laughter. Thank you for taking the time to mold us into what we are today. You had your work cut out for you! However, for me there will always be the chance that a drop fence lies just beyond C, but at least now dressage is not simply 'that thing' I must do before they let me on the cross country course.

Missy Parkhurst my dear friend, fellow beer aficionado, and source of unending laughter, without your cheery presence, the evenings at the Double J would have been quite bland indeed. You bring smiles and sunshine with you where ever you go. You are also one heck of a helping hand at shows.

Christina 'Clean Boots' Buckner (of the Bar B Buckners), Laura Reddell, and Caroline Kent, my gumshoe friend, all of who supported and encouraged me. Thank you for being there. Everybody needs friends like you.

A special thanks to the entire Fahrenholz Formula Team for your friendship, camaraderie, laughs, and inspiration, and yes horse people are indeed crazy! May we share many more 'show' memories and play musical horses in the future.

Scott Langton, DVM, my vet, for your knowledge and wit. We are fortunate to have a vet such as yourself who never tires of learning. Thank you ever so much for being my 'go to guy' for all things veterinary.

Thank you to Deeds Publishing, and the family team of Bob, Jan, and Mark who did a phenomenal job of making my dream come true. You made publishing my book a wonderful experience.

Last, but not least, I am eternally grateful for my Faith. My talents and abilities are on loan from God and I pray I make the best of my gifts.

ABOUT THE AUTHOR

Kelly Jennings is a third generation American from what was once known as the Panama Canal Zone. Her love of horses began in Panama with the local Bush ponies and has never left her. She lives on the east coast of Florida with her husband and two stepchildren on a small piece of earth that is fondly referred to as the Double J Ranch. After competing for years in three day eventing she has recently started to tackle the world of dressage with her American Warmblood mare Lexington. Like most dressage and eventing enthusiasts she competes for the love of both the horse and the sport while balancing a full time job, kids, and life in general. Her over fifteen years in the medical field and nearly a lifetime spent around horses gives her a unique and down to earth perspective, which is reflected in her writing style. Surrounded by her family, friends, horses, and her dogs she never lacks for inspiration.